CONVERGENCE OF GODS

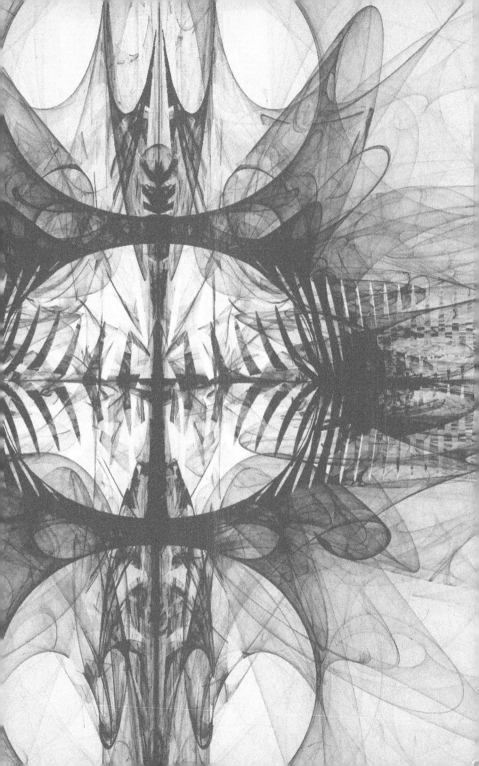

CONVERGENCE OF GODS

THE DADIRRI SAGA 04

4 Horsemen
Publications, Inc.

TY CARLSON

Convergence of Gods
The Dadirri Saga Book 4
Copyright © 2023 Ty Carlson. All rights reserved.

4 Horsemen
Publications, Inc.

4 Horsemen Publications, Inc.
1497 Main St. Suite 169
Dunedin, FL 34698
4horsemenpublications.com
info@4horsemenpublications.com

Cover by J. Kotick
Typeset by Autumn Skye
Edited by Laura Mita

Library of Congress Control Number: 2023941845

Print ISBN: 979-8-8232-0260-2
Hardcover ISBN: 979-8-8232-0262-6
Audio ISBN: 979-8-8232-0259-6
Ebook ISBN: 979-8-8232-0261-9

DEDICATION:

To my characters. I'm sorry for what I put you through. I hope in the end that the tears I, and others, shed for you help change the world.

TABLE OF CONTENTS

ACKNOWLEDGEMENTS

Always and forever, first to my wife—hashing out the plot so that everything fits together and telling me how much some of the ideas freak you out. To my editor Laura and my CareBear Beau. You're both incredible people, and I wouldn't be able to do this without you. To my writing group for listening while I processed by using the phrase "I don't know how this scene will end up" and smiling with me. Finally to the writing community on social media platforms, who overall wish the best for every writer and author they come across.

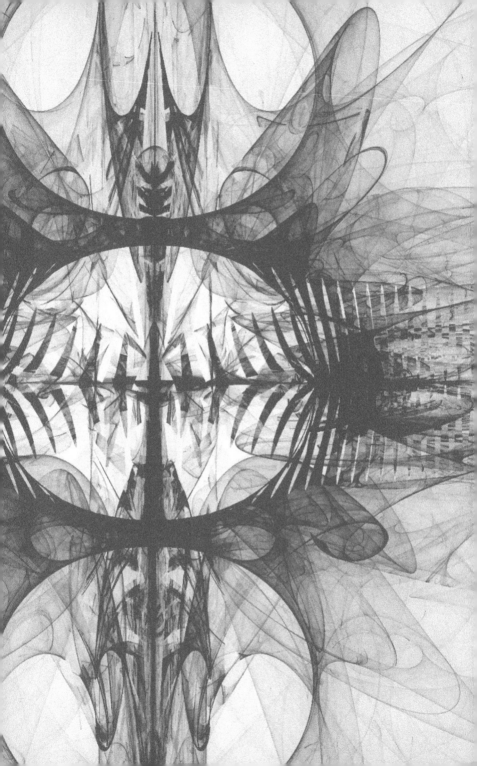

THE
GLADE

Chapter 1

Jonas couldn't open his eyes. Well, that's not true. He probably could if not for the congealing blood that oozed from a cut near his hairline. It matted his eyelashes, and when he winced from the ringing in his ears and the pounding of his head, he felt the stickiness of it covering his cheeks too. He felt covered in it.

Sound slowly began to replace the high-pitched squeal that told him something bad had happened. His mom used to say that it was an angel passing over when his ears rang. Both of his rang, and Jonas only thought of his mother's saying later. Much later.

The sounds he heard were difficult to place. There was a rhythmic dinging sound, like when a car door was open, and there was a hissing coming from above him, like water sizzling on a hot surface. Sounds came from the radio, but not music. Words. Conversation. But he couldn't quite make out all of it.

Seems we ... attack ... multiple aggressors ... no reason to ... working as a group ... Neo-...

Some words floated through the gray haze between his ears, but most of them seemed to bounce around inside the car, painfully ricocheting this way and that.

That's right. He was in a car. Had been before ... something. He'd seen something and had to swerve? Was that right? He believed it was. Was he alone?

Jonas tried to turn his head to check the passenger seat, only to find that gravity wasn't where it was supposed to be. It pulled against his back and shoulders, pulled his back against the seat instead of pulling his ass toward his feet. His neck was stiff and the natural motion of turning his head became an exhausting chore, and he gave up a moment later, panting. Tears had coursed down his cheeks and his throat hurt from the strain.

The radio was still droning on, this time he could make the words make sense, but there was a good deal of static coming in and out.

"Multiple reports... large groups... animals... vicious and aggressive..."

The cotton in his head made it difficult to process the words spewing forth from the radio. Blinking against the stickiness across his forehead, he now realized the radio was in front of and above him. He wasn't sure how that happened. With trembling fingers, he reached down—over?--toward his side to press the seatbelt release. The familiar *click* was accompanied by a tinkling between the seats. Glass.

The door, he strained to pinpoint the thought and lifted his arm to the handle as if moving in a dream. But his fingers touched nothing and he turned that direction. The door was missing. He continued reaching and felt his fingers brush against something stiff. It scratched his hand and left a thread of pain across the back of it. It hissed across his mind very much like the radio had.

It's interesting how, even in the midst of a crisis where the mind is reeling and working to decipher all manner of input, it can grab hold of something, and almost with graceless nonchalance, decode it in an instant.

That's what happened now when he scratched his hand. Jonas' mind immediately told him that a tree branch was poking him. He let his hand drop, but in his current position, gravity brought his arm down, hard, on the side panel. It should have been behind his shoulder, and he winced, which made his head hurt even worse.

He closed his eyes and they moved behind their lids as he tried to get a grip on this reality. It was beginning to make sense and would even more if he could keep his eyes open. Now that he was unbuckled, he guessed that he could roll his body out of the car, what with the missing door and all.

But what if I'm twenty feet above the ground? he thought to himself while still moving his torso toward the gaping hole on his left. He felt the crunch of broken glass beneath his feet and shoulders as he shuffled them, the sides and soles of his shoes scraping across the floor—*wall?*—of the car. His head lolled to the side as his body turned in a lazy motion. His closed eyes squinted once more against a sudden blast of static from the radio, and then were able to open briefly.

He could see nothing beyond the pale glow cast by the interior lights on splintered branches and scattered leaves.

"Please... inside... do not... outside... dangerous for... and groups alike."

He dragged his body out of the car, resisting the urge to scream and settling instead for a deep groan. The glass tinkled into the darkness beneath him and fell, sparkling briefly in the wan light. His feet left the relative comfort where they rested on the floor, dangling in the cool night air.

Through his gummed-up eyelashes, what little he could make out was veiled in a haze of crimson. It was dark, but not cold. The air moved with a restless kind of breeze and the only sounds were the intermittent radio and the incessant dinging from the car. His own labored breathing was a rhythmic rattle that he felt more than heard.

He slowly lowered himself to the ground, arms screaming in protest as he held onto the seat belt and door frame. It wasn't far, but it felt like an hour until the toes of his shoes brushed the grass. Then another hour until the soles of his shoes landed on the bare earth. His pants crawled uncomfortably up his thighs, and he tried to ignore the screaming pain in his ribs.

His knees buckled when he put weight on them, and Jonas fell into the dirt. The rough ground dug into his palms as he landed hard, causing him to gasp and slam his eyes closed. He rolled onto his side, holding it and taking frantic shallow breaths. A sob tried to work its way out of his throat, but he choked it down as tears leaked from the corners of his eyes and down his cheeks.

When breathing didn't feel like rolling in razor blades, he sat up, blinked, and rubbed away the mess that had oozed over his sockets. It took his eyes several seconds to adjust, but he tried to take stock of his surroundings.

The ground around him was torn up as if a giant toddler with claws and teeth had thrown a tantrum. A red glow suffused every surface, and he couldn't tell if it was residue from the blood or something else. Still clutching his side, he turned in a slow circle and blinked in surprise.

His car, several steps away, was standing up. Or at first glance, it was. After a moment, his mind resolved the sight into the truth. The headlights were shining into the sky, or would be if one hadn't been smashed to pieces. He had a strange urge to laugh, despite the pain that skittered through his body like tiny arcing bolts of electricity.

The taillights, which had fared better than the headlights, shone toward the ground, casting their crimson glow across everything else. They lit the surrounding brush with their eerie, angry glow. He turned from them, staring now at the brush-covered landscape. He realized he was at the bottom of a hill, one that had been cut into the landscape to make way for a highway.

He stepped toward the hill, noting that it would be a difficult climb, especially in his current condition. He'd be able to use the trees and brush around him as anchors and handholds as he climbed. The sky above was a deep violet, but the horizon—or what he could see of it—glowed with an auburn light.

Sunrise, he thought with relief.

It took much longer than he'd anticipated, and several times he needed to stop and rest to reduce the pain that roared through his exhausted body. But eventually, he reached the top. By the time he sat to rest with his back against a large stump, the sky was darker, a deep inky black now. In the distance, however, he saw a skyline. A city was a couple of miles away and most of it was dark, except for a few bands of light that polluted the night sky and eclipsed the stars. The orange glow he spied from below, however, wasn't sunrise. A steady sheet of flame lanced into the darkness above the city, climbing buildings and reaching toward the stars.

The sight was terrifying, and he hid his eyes from it, burying his face in his hands.

What happened? He thought, dismayed. He couldn't remember anything before the crash, only a vague sense of loneliness and fear.

Uncertainty clouded his mind even further and he looked around, trying desperately to find an answer. None came in the form he wanted. The darkness of night pressed in beneath the branches that stretched across the sky. In the middle of them all, where there appeared to be a small glade, the darkness lessened.

He thought about what he'd heard on the radio, trying to organize the words as best he could to make some kind of sense of them. The radio mentioned danger. But danger from what? He stared at the blazing horizon in the distance.

Animals.

That's what the broadcast had mentioned. It had said danger from some kind of animals. *Like lions?* he thought as that was the only dangerous animal that came to mind. *But why would lions be loose in the city?*

A sudden absurdity came to mind: hundreds of lions, an army of them, running through the streets, clawing and devouring anyone they came upon. It was completely ridiculous, and he smiled, began to laugh, and then stopped when his throat and ribs protested.

The eruption of sound unlike anything he'd ever heard made him tense his entire body. He turned, bracing himself for the toll it would take on his bruised and battered body and expecting to see a creature charging through the darkness toward him.

Adrenaline coursed through his body, making the pain in his ribs lessen. But he saw only the retreating form of something sleek and massive as it made its way into the darkness and—thank God—away from him.

Feeling incredibly exposed on the hilltop, he made his way into the trees and low scrub brush. The lighter part of this small wooded area was ahead, and slowly, he picked his way through the trees and branches until he emerged into a small clearing. It was an area of about one hundred square feet, empty of trees but covered in loamy moss and soft grass. The trees encircled the area, growing upward and inward, their branches closing the space above like lovers reaching after a long separation. The sky was visible only through the patchwork quilt of branches and dark forest leaves, and it comforted him.

Another growling roar came to him through the trees. This one was different, though. It was a bark that reverberated in the night but was immediately replaced by silence. Another erupted even nearer to his right. The noise barreled through the woods and sounded like it was right on top of him, but then it moved slowly away from him. The brief comfort he'd felt retreated.

There *was* something out there. Or many somethings.

Either way, he knew that the city wasn't safe anymore. Maybe it never would be again.

Jonas knew, deep down, that this glade was the only safe place. And it was now his home.

CHAPTER 2

The first night passed by in a haze of paranoia and sleep-lessness. Jonas lost track of the number of days, instead focusing on staying alive and keeping out of sight. He was lucky enough to find several wild berry plants just outside of what he was beginning to think of as "his glade." They kept his hunger and thirst at bay but did a number on his bowels. After the first three days of eating them, he cut down on the number of berries he ate and tried to ignore the near-constant grumbling in his midsection.

The first week, however, was especially miserable. On top of bruised ribs and a multitude of aching muscles and body parts, adrenaline coursed through his veins hours at a time and it took its toll. The cycle of adrenaline and exhaustion finally leveled out after a week. His body began to transition from constant flight into a rhythm of sorts. Aside from the periodic belches and growls of nearby prowling animals, it was silent for much of the day and night. Not a cricket or breath of wind stirred the leaves in the darkness. The air was hot and sticky, and his body ached, covered with bruises and scratches. He'd find his mind wandering, and then suddenly, another blast of noise would rattle through the trees. He'd have the sinking feeling that he'd been caught, that the animals had found him.

Only, whatever the hulking monstrosity was would pass, and he remained undiscovered.

He began to suspect after several restless nights that he was hidden rather well within his little glade. The creatures must have been close enough for him to hear but far enough away that he remained concealed beneath its branches. He wondered if he smelled like a human, like food, and then hesitantly sniffed his armpits. He certainly smelled, but perhaps—or maybe it was luck—they hadn't discovered him yet.

Every now and then, Jonas could see some manner of creature approaching. Its eyes glowed through the trees in the night, either with reflected light or some source of their own design. He would hide his face, curling into a ball and trying desperately to make himself as small as possible. But the creatures would turn their bulks one way or another, avoiding his sanctuary. Or rather, avoiding the trees behind which he hid.

And now, more than a week after he limped aching and bleeding into the glade, his body had flushed the exhaustion. He'd slept hard on the eighth day. Now, the mild morning of the ninth day, he was beginning to doze again. His eyelids drooped despite more of the creatures making appearances nearby when he noticed the sky was lightening in the distance. It no longer was a deep, black blanket that covered the sky from horizon to fiery horizon. Now, it was a black blanket, but gray threads were unraveling at one end.

The lighter the sky, the more of the creatures he saw. He assumed that meant they were diurnal and made a mental note to avoid much activity during the day.

He smiled in spite of his current situation. His eighth-grade teacher would be so very proud of him. Nocturnal versus diurnal. Night versus day. It all seemed so trivial now. A city on fire, giant animals stalking the world. He wondered what became of everyone else, those poor souls trapped in the city that, during the day, vomited copious amounts of black smoke into the sky, a giant roiling pillar in the distance and above the trees. And at night, it continued to burn and set the horizon aflame with a ruddy, reckless orange.

He watched the sleek outline of a distant creature as it roved slowly across the landscape, its eyes glowing malevolently in the rising light. He could only assume that these creatures were carnivores. Though, he'd only seen them distantly through the trees, glimpses of them through the night. But they *felt* predatory. Animals that size had no predators on this planet, and if they did, they would have to be colossal. It was the main reason he'd been so keen to stay out of sight.

Now, with day quickly approaching, he wondered what it would hold. He wanted little else, at this point, other than to survive. But even as he thought it, his stomach rumbled with a grim and unwelcome petulance. In order to survive, he'd need more than just a few wild berries each day. And there was plenty of food in the Burning City. But in order to get there, he'd have to cross the vast distance where the creatures roamed wild.

The Burning City—that's what he was calling it—seemed appropriate and would remind him of the danger within, should he find a place that *seemed* safe.

With this in mind, and as the sky changed from black to gray and then to a blushing rose, he built a small lean-to. Tried to, at least.

He stood, hands on his hips, and stared down at the culmination of his efforts.

In a word, it was terrible. He frowned in disapproval. The few timbers he could find and drag through the trees weren't the same length. He'd done his best, but even so, it leaned precariously to one side and reminded him of a child's playhouse.

His head hurt, and his body ached. He rubbed his side where a deep purple and yellow bruise had made its home. It turned out that his body was still recovering, and hauling small trees was more work than he was prepared to do. The branches—those he could find and separate from their trunks—were too thin and their leaves too few to make a proper roof.

Jonas limped around the perimeter of it, scoffing and sighing. There was no way his entire body would fit in it. He could crawl in, sure, but he would have to leave either the upper half or the lower half of his body exposed to the elements.

Well, *more* exposed to the elements.

Maybe, he thought, rubbing his aching ribs gently, *I can find something in the Burning City.*

Quick on the heels of that thought was another. *I'll have to go to the city for food and supplies soon, anyway.*

Dread sank heavily into his gut.

What am I doing? He thought with frustration. He was standing in his glade thinking about how frightening it might be to travel to the city. All while a host of unknown creatures stalked the area around him. He really was a moron. He wouldn't need to worry about supplies in the city because a creature could gobble him up any minute.

What's the use?

He hunkered down immediately next to his sorry excuse for shelter, wincing and taking shallow breaths between clenched teeth.

He watched the sunrise through the trees in the east. It was going to be a dreary day. The pink blush that had preceded the sunrise had faded. The clouds were high enough now that the sun would soon be behind them. Pewter clouds clustered in front of a steel-gray canvas that promised rain.

His immediate need was food. Berries weren't cutting it anymore, and he'd nearly picked the few bushes clean. He'd have to scavenge from somewhere nearby. Perhaps...

A dull throb began above his right eye, and he tried to will it away by closing his eyes and resting against his creation. The sounds of the animals, the stress of figuring out what to do, and the lack of sleep had set him on the path of a migraine.

Put it on my tab, he thought dryly.

He felt his body trying to slow down. What little nutrition the berries granted was fading and he could feel his shoulders sagging with each subsequent breath. He was uncomfortable but was comfortable *enough.*

He was tired. Dead tired. He was tired enough that just before drifting off, he thought, *If they find me, they find me.*

CHAPTER 3

Jonas was yanked from sleep by a steady growl nearby. It took him several seconds of casting about to realize where he was and what was happening. The sky had darkened considerably, but he didn't get the impression that it was nearing dusk. His back and sides ached, his position leaning against his tiny shelter not doing his injured body any favors.

Rain, he thought with a hint of despair. He was not prepared to deal with the downpour that the sullen sky promised.

As if in response, he heard a low rumble clatter across the heavens.

That steady grumble remained, and with wide, terrified eyes, he looked around his clearing, trying to catch a glimpse of whatever was making the noise. He dared not make large movements, lest he attract unwanted attention with the motion. His body was stiff and refused to cooperate with some of his demands. So he moved slowly, peering through the trees and refusing to blink.

Fifty or so yards away, where the trees thinned, he saw what he believed was making the noise. It was large, larger than him, and its hide or shell was a dull gold color, but any more than that, he couldn't tell from this distance.

Deciding it was only dangerous if he was seen, he began to creep toward it. Part of him screamed to stop, to turn tail and hide. The other part told him that the devil he knew was better than the one he didn't.

Wincing and clutching his ribs, he slowly inched himself out of the comfort of the glade and into the near-dark of the trees. He stepped over fallen logs and branches, doing his best to avoid making any noise. Aside from the crunch of moist leaves and the occasional snap of a twig, he was successful.

When only a half-dozen trunks hid him from the animal's view, he stopped and sat back on his haunches. He stared both in awe and fright. He'd never seen anything like it, and he felt like his brain was scrambling trying to fit it into the framework of what was possible.

A dozen yards away lay a hulking creature. It appeared to be sleeping and, even so, was as tall as he but twice as long. At first, his mind tried to fit it into a distant memory, something he knew from before, but he pushed it away. He'd never seen anything like this. Only, the more he looked, the more he recognized the shape, generally speaking.

It resembled a massive bug. Its chitinous armor was the gold color he'd dimly seen through the trees. It sat unmoving, humming softly to itself in a steady guttural rumble. Its legs must have been folded beneath it, as he couldn't see anything but some kind of socket or elbow at the base of the beast. It had a flat forehead and flat top, and he could tell there was strength and danger here, even without glimpsing its mouth.

He could feel the heavy rumble in his chest and despite his efforts to remain calm, he began to hyperventilate. His breath came in and out in shallow, raspy hiccups. Black dots began to flock across his vision, and the creature was fading in and out of focus.

If this is one of many, he thought, *how am I supposed to survive? How can I possibly contend with creatures this large?*

He felt himself fall back onto his elbows into the leaves and grass. His eyes never left the shape of the bug ahead of him. He could see lines where the armored plates separated, but the legs—or whatever they used for locomotion—remained hidden.

Is it sleeping? He asked himself. If so, he may be able to sneak past others like it. He filed the information away for when he needed to venture into the City.

As he watched, however, he saw movement from the corner of his eye. Another creature, this one even larger and moving incredibly fast, passed the golden bug. It *buzzed* so loudly that Jonas put his hands over his ears and closed his eyes. His sanity screamed at him to stop, to never look on these creatures again. But even as he felt the gigantic creature pass in a rush of wind, its form settled in his mind. It was a long and slender thing, two or three times as tall as the golden bug and at least that much longer. It had horns on its head, and its body was sleek and smooth and the color of egg yolk. It was segmented in the way a wasp was—large head, long body. *No wings*, his mind told his memory.

Several seconds passed until the sound of the first golden bug's rhythmic humming quivered in the air, he opened his eyes and removed his hands from his ears. He hadn't realized he'd scampered behind a larger tree to hide. He watched, transfixed, as the golden bug began to cough and splutter, and then lurch away across the ground in the same direction as the previous wasp-like thing. *Its legs must be directly beneath it*, he thought, still trying to figure it out.

A blaring scream erupted to his right, and he looked that way. Another creature—blue, this time, that reflected the light in iridescent hues—was careening toward the golden bug. The golden bug never stood a chance. The blue one landed upon it with ferocious speed.

The gold bug screamed as the blue bug latched onto it, unseen teeth tearing through its middle. Pieces of the golden bug erupted into the air and landed with unsettling *thuds* near Jonas' hiding spot. Some rattled across the ground or collided with trees. The sound was enormous, and Jonas scrambled away on his rump, transfixed. The golden bug was, as far as Jonas could tell, dead. Or dying. Its contented hum that first caught his attention had turned into a spluttering cough. A mix of ichor and other dark steaming liquids sprayed from its wounds and dripped onto the ground beneath it. By its contented sigh, Jonas could tell the blue bug was enjoying its meal. Viscera dripped from its yawning maw—a large opening between its eyes—and it ran freely into the grass just beyond Jonas' hiding spot.

The air filled with all kinds of smells—smoke from the Burning City, a sweet oily mix that clawed its way down his throat, and the smell of rotting organics from the trees behind him—and he coughed, then gagged. He bent to vomit and was thankful for his mostly empty stomach when he spit only a green string of bile into the grass.

After several more empty retches, he turned his back cautiously on the massacre to make his way back to The Glade. Back to where he knew he was hidden from view. Where he knew he was safe. Already, he saw more bugs approaching, no doubt to either feed on the mortally-wounded golden bug or to watch the blue one feed. Some were large, some were small, and some flitted this way and that around the commotion, keening loudly, but he tried to ignore them.

When he arrived back to the relative safety of his Glade, he sat on an unused log he'd wrestled from the forest and winced, but out of expectation rather than real pain. He stared dazedly in the direction of the bugs and felt the same despair that had visited him earlier begin to blossom and grow into an awful kind of dread flower. These animals were massive. They were carnivorous—*and* cannibalistic. He heard a screech and saw through the trees even more of the things congregating. A steady, reverberating growl made the air around him vibrate, and Jonas felt extremely exposed, despite being hidden behind and beneath the screen of his trees.

There was no way he would be able to survive against animals like this. It was impossible. There was no hope.

He began to cry, feeling the weight of it settle around his shoulders like Marley's chains. Tears coursed down his dirty face, catching briefly in his untrimmed beard. He sniffed, wiped his eyes, and stared up into the leaves and grumbling clouds overhead.

A fat, careless drop of water fell on his cheek, and he recoiled, blinking and wiping it away in both surprise and fright. He felt another on the top of his head and then heard *plop plop plop* around him. A steady pattering sound grew, and he watched as the leaves danced with the skipping raindrops. Without much in the way of shelter, he feared his own exposure. But enough of the leaves caught the rain so that only a drizzling mist descended upon his sagging shoulders.

After a few handfuls of the last of his berries and a drink from a small plastic bag he'd made to catch rainwater only a day or so after his arrival, he slid beneath the roof of his lean-to. Even on his back, it was only a foot or so above him. He surprised himself when he brought his knees to his battered chest without crying out in pain. It was tight, and a twinge told him any further and he'd regret it, but the ache was bearable. Any sound he made would have been drowned out by the steady rainfall, but he was all too aware of how close the feeding animals were.

He looked down at his feet and smiled weakly. Only his heels stuck out into the rain, which might be a problem later. For now, it would work. It wasn't perfect, but it helped ease the hopeless despair that had gripped him only moments before.

And right now, he needed anything that would help.

CHAPTER 4

The morning came with the pleasant coolness that usually followed a quiet rain. The sky reminded Jonas of a bucket of orange sherbet covered in bruises. The clouds hung low in sullen purple rows while the brilliant orange of dawn suffused the backdrop. It was beautiful.

Then he remembered where he was and why, and the sky lost a bit of its brilliance.

He made to sit up but pain lanced across his chest and midsection. He gasped in surprise and lay back down. Leaves and twigs gently prodded his scalp, and he felt the frustration of helplessness rising in his throat and gut. The pain had abated last night, but had returned with vengeance this morning.

"I hate this," he whispered to The Glade.

Closing his eyes, he took several deep breaths to ease the tightness in his ribs.

A breeze fumbled through the trees, and The Glade seemed to answer, "I know."

There was a steady hum nearby. Different from the golden bug of yesterday. He turned his head and through the distant trees could see the shapes moving. They droned and clicked and rattled; he hated it all, but stared anyway.

When the pain in his chest eased enough, he slowly sat up. The tightness remained. It didn't increase, but it also didn't fade. It was a steady thrum across the left side of his chest down to his right hip. He hated that pain.

When he could roll himself out from under the terribly-constructed lean-to, he leaned his back against one of its unsteady supports. It collapsed almost immediately beneath his weight, and Jonas once again felt the stab of pain in his ribs as he instinctively caught himself with a quick outstretched hand. He relaxed his body and lay awkwardly on the shelter that was now scattered unevenly across the ground at the edge of the glade. He stared up at the sky, which had now taken on the morning hues of bright blue with cotton-white clouds, and he wondered what he was going to do. He wasn't content to die in the middle of the wilderness surrounded by vicious cannibalistic bugs. That meant that he would need to go into the city. Which would mean he'd need to walk that distance. It couldn't be more than two miles. And he was perfectly healthy.

He smiled sardonically.

He was perfectly healthy except for being near starvation, probably some cracked ribs, and a case of mild dehydration.

He heaved a great sigh, taking care not to aggravate his wounded body, and sat up ever so slowly. A groan of resigned relief issued from him as he made it to fully sitting up. His body was still stiff. *Moving would probably get the blood flowing,* he thought.

He carefully made it to one knee, realizing that his chest was still in pain, but it was fading even as he moved to straighten his back. He wanted to rest in this position, to make sure his body wasn't tricking him into thinking it was fine before making the final push to a full stand.

After several minutes of wobbly one-knee balance, he decided that if his body was tricking him, it wouldn't tell him until after standing. He braced himself against the pain that was sure to come and pushed himself up from a kneeling position. His body protested briefly, and expected more pain, but none came.

Jonas stood in the clearing, panting from both the effort and worry of the toll it would take. If only he could get some aspirin or something, he knew he'd feel better.

Aspirin was in the city. Two miles back and forth at his speed would most likely take half the day, at least. It was already approaching mid-morning, and he didn't want to waste any time. Just another reason he needed to begin his trek as soon as possible.

He looked above the trees, searching for the black plume of smoke that indicated the Burning City. The steady buzz of the bugs around him grated on his nerves, but part of him was comforted by it, and he disliked that very much. He didn't ever want to get used to being surrounded by animals, but short of moving further from the city, he knew he'd need to.

A thought occurred to him. If the creatures were diurnal, then he could travel at night and stay the entire day, returning at night. It would certainly limit his exposure to them. At the same time, however, he wasn't sure what manner of animals lived in the city or prowled around at night. *Better the Devil you know*, he thought, and he stepped through the woods to where he saw the golden bug die yesterday. Its carcass was gone, no doubt devoured by any and all that needed a snack. Ichor stained the grass a sickly black color.

Nearby, the creatures traveled swiftly, paying no mind to his little domicile. He was glad for that but wondered when it would change ... when they'd realize they'd had a snack sitting right in the middle of them the whole time.

They rumbled by in a steady stream, all different colors and sizes and danger levels.

There were so many. *Too many*, he thought with despair.

The Travelers, as he thought of them in his mind and now named them, were certainly more awake during the day. He'd seen some move at night, with glowing eyes and sometimes glowing scales or shells in all colors of the rainbow. But there were less of them at night. Maybe he *should* wait until nightfall.

No, he thought with irritation. *No, I have to do this now if I'm ever going to.*

He plucked up the courage and looked around for a weapon. The only thing he came up with was a large stick. It would serve well as a walking stick. As a weapon, it was severely lacking.

He snatched it up anyway and made his way through the thicket of trees toward the branching paths the animals used. His eyes followed many of them behind the shelter of leaves. There were hundreds milling this way and that. There was barely a break in the flow of them at all, and certainly not enough for him to hobble slowly across their path.

Jonas looked both ways, up and down the path where the animals traveled. There was no shortage of them, no end in sight. They hummed and rumbled, paying him no more atten-tion than he would an ant. It seemed that they were all of one mind, actually. They were going somewhere, or coming *from* somewhere, with perhaps the same goal in mind.

He was no scientist, but he knew enough about animals to remember there was such a thing as a "hive-mind." All these creatures were tapped into the same consciousness, it

seemed, which gave them the ability to act out the same direc-
tive instantaneously.

Useful, he thought, watching the creatures skitter past his
stand of trees. *And dangerous.*

He sat back on his haunches with a grunt and laid the
walking stick across his lap, trying to think of what to do. He
wondered if they'd even pay him any mind. If, because of their
size, they might not just ignore him completely. Could he walk
all the way to the city, safely, in the middle of the day?

Flashes of color passed by him. The bugs didn't appear
aggressive ... other than the destruction he witnessed the previous day. But perhaps that was something that had more to
do with whatever hierarchy existed amongst them and less as
a random act of cannibalism.

He heard a thundering buzz from above and looked up.
The sun wasn't high in the sky since it was still mid-morning,
but he could see a shape hovering high above the skittering
creatures below. Jonas' eyes widened as he realized it was a
giant bug cutting through the air. Its wings beat a rapid rhythm
he could feel in his chest. It was sleek; its hide—armor or whatever—was black as night and its eyes took up most of its face.
Its tail tapered into what reminded him of a dragonfly, and in
that instant, it seemed that's what it used to be, or had evolved
from, or something. Long, thin body, bulbous eyes, wings that
beat faster than he could see.

He followed it across the sky, knowing full well that a gale
would kick up wherever it landed. It scared him, though he
was hesitant to admit it. Bugs on the ground, fine, he could
deal with that. But bugs that flew and could see him, even
mostly hidden within the safety of his glade was something
else entirely.

There was really only one way to find out where he stood with these creatures. He didn't really *want* to find out, but he knew his hunger wouldn't allow him any leeway in this.

He grasped the walking stick in one hand and put the other gently on his ribs, then got to his feet. He had been right, the tightness in his body had eased a bit as he moved throughout the morning, and he was glad for that.

Even though he hoped the bugs wouldn't bother him, he also wasn't a complete idiot. He knew that he'd need to wait for a lull in the passage of the hulking beasts before running across their path. That by itself would attract their attention, even if they didn't want to eat him.

The sun had nearly reached its zenith when it seemed the animals had been given another task by their hive-mind queen or whatever controlled them. Much farther along the well-worn path, the bugs began to stop. He watched cautiously as they waited. Their shells gleamed in the sunlight, and he noticed, for the first time, that most of them had antennae that wiggled idly in the breeze as if searching for something. Every now and then, one of the animals would snort or bleat at its neighbor, and the neighbor might snort or bleat in response. He wasn't sure what they were doing, and it made him wary. He hoped that if they could smell him, they would still ignore him. That would be good.

He could see that a very large beast, fourth down the line from where he stood in the shade of the trees, grumbled and snorted. While they may not be able to see him from here, he knew that as soon as he left the relative safety of the trees, he'd be detected immediately. But if he crossed in front of a very large one, there was a chance that maybe the odds of being seen and attacked would be slightly less than one hundred percent. Besides, the trees began again on the other side of this bug trail; he could hide in the shadows and make his way toward the city in relative peace.

He slunk back into the protection of the shadows and crept along the tree line, parallel to the line of shifting, snorting monstrosities. He was deep enough in the trees that the beasts were little more than flashes of color through small breaks between the dark green vertical trunks. He watched carefully and jumped when some of them made noise, sounding very much like impatient grunts and gurgles.

When he positioned himself in the tree line with the large creature he'd pinpointed previously now directly in front of him, he stopped and crouched as best his aching ribs would allow. The trees here were scraped and some were destroyed. It looked like another fight had broken out, and part of his little forest had been collateral damage. As he surveyed the damage, he looked over his shoulder in the direction of his hidden hovel. It was there, just through the trees another 70 yards deeper. He gauged that it was almost directly in the middle of this larger stand of trees, but seeing as how he hadn't walked the perimeter, he couldn't be certain.

The bugs chuffed, grunted, and snorted along the whole line of them. That feeling of dread threatened to paralyze him again. Jonas didn't *want* to venture out in the daylight, especially after seeing how brutally they attacked one of their own.

Maybe I'll be too small to care about, he thought as he tried to steady his racing heart.

The bug that he'd chosen to cross in front of was a behemoth and resembled the wasp in body structure. Its head was red and blocky with two great eyes at the front and one giant horn rising from its skull and arcing back toward the rest of its body and shell. An acrid black breath jetted from the horn as it belched and rumbled. The rest of the beast was covered in silvery skin and split into two distinct segments that vibrated with each shuddering breath of the creature. Even from the trees, he could see the air shimmer before its large mouth and nostrils beneath its eyes.

This is a bad idea. He thought fearfully.

What other choice is there? He told himself.

His stomach growled as if to curb his uncertainty.

"Shut up," he told it. "I don't need your input."

He heard a nearby bug grumble and looked down the line of bugs. He felt his world pulse as bugs in the distance began to bleat and burp at each other then move. They were slow at first, but they began crisscrossing each other, and whatever propelled them began to pick up speed. The line was moving, and he was going to miss his chance if he didn't go now.

His heart had been racing before and now it began to gallop. He swallowed hard and decided that if he was going to do it, he needed to just fucking do it.

He counted only ten bugs left ahead of his crossing point and knew that he was running out of time. Even now, the red and gray beast before him shook itself from side to side, preparing itself to lumber ahead.

He grasped a tree on both sides of him, envisioning himself as a human slingshot. He wasn't certain that his body would let him run since it was still healing, but he was going to give it a try.

Five bugs were moving, and the five ahead of his crossing point had begun to creep toward one another. His window was closing.

A loud honking sound from his right made him jump. A bug, this one significantly smaller and green, had inched closer to a blue one, and the blue one had lurched back and let loose a series of angry noises.

He turned his attention back to the red and gray monster. There was a gap growing in front of it and Jonas knew he'd missed his chance. It was lumbering ahead, the massive red head bobbing as it inched further along the path picking up speed and moving further from where Jonas intended to cross.

He found himself running through the grass toward the beast without thinking. He could see a gap between the ground and the beast's shell and in a jolt of insanity, decided his best chance could be to cross beneath it.

His ribs screamed in protest as his legs propelled him toward the animals that could very easily devour him. A deafening roar blistered the air, and he realized that the red-headed beast had seen him. Another smaller brown beetle-like animal behind it began making a loud *meep* sound that he could only assume was directed at him, its eyes boring into his skull as it watched him cross with a baleful glare.

He ducked under the moving bug, hoping it would ignore him. He dared not touch it, but it had picked up speed, and Jonas realized he was going to have to change course slightly in order to avoid running straight into the smelly undercarriage of the animal. Massive veins and other body parts hung low, and Jonas had to bend even lower despite the screams of his ribs. His breath was coming in ragged gasps and his terror had gripped him fully.

He moved to his left slightly, body bent nearly low enough for him to crawl on all fours, and he scurried along the last several feet. He could hear a chorus of noise from multiple bugs rising around him. He pushed forward, avoiding touching the beast's belly at all costs.

He didn't have time to think about it. He burst out from beneath the behemoth's shell and into the sunlight. He didn't even pause to look to either side, which probably saved his life.

A flash of white from his right was all that alerted him to a beast bearing down on him. He saw from the corner of his eye a yawning maw filled with mandibles or teeth that glittered in the sunlight. It roared at him, the sound erupting inches from his ear. He closed his eyes and forced his legs to carry him the last few steps to the tree line.

He heard the white bug snarl and clatter behind him and to his left. He heard it try to stop and imagined it turning around to hunt for him in the trees, galloping to snarl and sniff the place where he'd disappeared into them.

But he didn't stick around to find out. He raced his way through the trees, weaving between trunks and large bushes and jumping over fallen logs. Jonas forced his mind to ignore the throbbing in his ribs and the pain in his side. By the time the chorus of chirps, buzzing, and howling had faded into the distance, his sides screamed for rest, and his legs throbbed. The walking stick he'd picked up on a whim was a boon; he leaned on it more as he slowed and his aches began catching up to him.

Finally, he stopped. He could barely breathe, each breath coming in great gulping gasps. The sounds he made crashing through the trees were louder than he intended. And now that he was still, the silence was unsettling. He didn't hear anything pursuing him, which he hoped meant that nothing was. At their size, it had to be nearly impossible for them to maneuver through the trees without making any noise. And he hadn't seen anything smaller.

A spike of fear twisted his stomach with anxiety. There was so much he didn't know.

As he stood there laboring for breath, his mind wandered to the creatures. It seemed like every time he encountered them, he'd discovered something new about them. At first, it was the fact that they existed at all, then the realization that they seemed to travel together. Today, it was the flying one. He worried that he'd discover something deadly next, but his imagination was too overwhelmed to think what it might be. Too many what-ifs and not enough how-tos.

As his heart settled and his breathing calmed from razor-blades in his throat to fire in his lungs, he took stock of his surroundings. His headlong charge into the trees had carried him a great distance. He could see the top floors of several buildings peeking over the fluttering leaves of nearby trees. He gauged that he was maybe less than a mile from the city, which would mean that he'd have to be on high alert.

He took another moment to catch his breath, swallowed down the bile of fear that rose in response to the blackened skyline, then stepped toward the Burning City.

CHAPTER 5

He was farther from the city than he'd thought when he fled the line of Travelers and spied the buildings above the trees. Jonas had never been very good at determining distance; he wasn't sure why it would be different in this new apocalypse.

The sun was inching itself across the horizon by the time the trees began to thin out. He was forced to eventually jog from tree to tree, hoping nothing saw him. Luckily for him, the tree line ended only a few yards from where a high cement wall began. He wasn't exactly sure where he was in relation to the places he knew from before, but there were bound to be supplies nearby.

Jonas hesitated before continuing, pacing slowly back and forth behind the few trees that remained between him and the gray wall. It had to be at least 8 feet high. *Not impossible*, he thought, *but not easy either.*

He knew that it would expose him for several minutes if he tried to climb over the wall. He could jump and reach the top easily, but what's to say there wasn't a nest or a burrow of some kind directly opposite him inside the wall? That would be his luck.

He looked down the brown-gray cement bricks, searching for an entryway, either built or broken, but from what he could see, it stretched into the distance, intact in both directions. It was flat on top, which would mean that he could, potentially, decide on next steps once he was up there.

The light was rapidly fading, and the shadows of the trees were stretching out along the ground, appearing to run like a black river from the base of each tree. With a sigh, he sat down and began rubbing his sore muscles. Instead of risking his life in a rush, he might as well wait an hour until dark and decrease his chances of being seen.

While he waited for the velvet night to chase the embers from the sky, he sat on the grass and listened. The few nights he'd spent in the glade had made him accustomed to the familiar clicks and hums of the bugs' passing. Now, distant from their trails, he felt some discomfort from their absence. The quiet was unsettling. From the other side of the wall, he heard nothing, which was reassuring in one sense, but he still feared what he was going to find once he did cross.

He picked blades of grass and rolled them through his fingers, tearing them along their length. Small sturdy stems that ended in a bushy white flower called snowblossom rose from the grass all around him. This untouched little prairie was almost a blanket of them. And as his eyes roved around the verdant patch, he spotted wild tulips, forget-me-nots, and Indian Rose.

He wrapped a snowblossom stem around his finger and thought more about the city beyond the wall. From here, he could see several buildings that were at least twenty stories high. He was certain that more rose beyond those, hidden by the wall or tower from his perspective on the ground.

He picked another snowblossom and gazed at the tall, charred buildings. Many of the windows were missing, but shards of glass remained at the edges, making the windows appear as dark mouths with glittering teeth. The fire was still raging somewhere further into the city. Its orange glow didn't quite reach this far away, but the evidence of it was still clearly visible.

He wrapped another snowblossom around his fingers. Time had gotten away from him and the sky was almost completely dark now. He squinted and saw several gargantuan creatures rise from the ground and float over a distant hill. He could hear the buzz of their wings from here, but he couldn't make out anything beyond a dark body silhouetted against the last rays of the sun.

His fingers stopped moving, and he looked down at his hands. Shredded grass and tiny leaves littered his lap, but in his fingertips, he held a circle of woven snowblossoms. As he'd sat and pondered, his fingers had moved without thought, creating a small circlet of flowers. He smiled down at it. He couldn't remember the last time he'd done that, especially so effortlessly.

He pulled the nearly weightless circle over his head and settled it around his neck, then he looked toward the horizon.

Dark enough, he thought, standing up and stretching. The loose petals and strands of grass fell, twirling in the twilight and landing soundlessly on the ground, forgotten.

The wall was rough and cool to the touch as he placed his palms against it. The top of the wall was higher than his head, close to eight feet, he'd been right. He frowned up at it. He was almost 6 feet tall, which meant there were about 5 rows of horizontal blocks from ground to eye level. That left 3 rows of horizontal blocks to run the distance of the wall on his left and right. He stretched up, reaching for the top. His fingertips grasped the edge of the wall with a little room to spare. He guessed he would be able to jump and hold on best he could.

All of this was guesswork and he hated it.

Bracing himself, he straightened his dirty and torn jacket, wrung his hands, then bent his knees and jumped. He gripped the top of the wall easily, but the rough surface dug into his fingertips and palms. He pulled himself up, putting the soles of his feet against the wall and trying to walk his way up. They slipped several times, but he managed to get just high enough that his eyes rose above the top edge. He only had a few seconds as his fingertips started aching, a mad tingle that began to lance down his arms in uncomfortable waves. A one-story building with darkened windows dominated his view. It was nestled up close enough to the wall that he could probably touch both at the same time. It sat in a sleepy lot, from what little else he could see around it, and a single light cast a hazy glow toward the ground. He couldn't see much more before dropping to the ground with a frustrated sigh.

His ribs ached, but he ignored it. Feeling relatively confident that he would have seen bugs if there had been any, he took several steps back from the wall and then stopped perhaps twenty yards away. In his head, the plan seemed simple. He took a deep breath and lunged forward. His legs pumped harder and faster as the wall grew closer. Hoping he timed it right, he pushed and leapt with his left foot and planted his right against the wall, using his momentum to continue pushing upward. He stretched his fingers and reached for the top, only a few more inches.

This time, he was able to pull himself up on the wall with some maneuvering. He shimmied his shoulders and elbows back and forth until the top half of his torso lay across the top. The scraping and clattering of tiny stones echoed in the empty lot. He lay silently on the top of the wall and counted to twenty before lifting one leg onto it. He waited again, counted to twenty, brought his other leg up, and searched the growing darkness for movement. Surely, if something was here, he'd have seen it by now.

He rolled the rest of his body across the top of the wall to lay on his belly. Then, dreading the next step, he let his feet dangle off the side. He lowered himself as slowly as he could toward the ground. His muscles and ribs still ached, and he could feel them protesting as his body stretched more than it had in recent days. The wall suddenly dug into his midsection and he gasped. His grip on the wall failed, and he dropped like a stone to the ground several feet below.

His legs absorbed most of the shock, but the rest of his body screamed at him, and he fell to his knees, wincing. Tiny rocks that were scattered across the ground pressed themselves into his skin. The snowblossom necklace swung lightly against his chest as tears sprang from the corners of his eyes.

Jonas bit down on a knuckle to focus on something other than his protesting body. He calmed his breath and counted to thirty, clutching his side and praying for some relief as the pain faded from a scream to a hum. Eventually, he knew that he couldn't hope for any progress without food and water, and he reluctantly got to his feet.

He looked around, noting the wall that continued in each direction and trying to memorize where he crossed so that he could find his way back. The one-story building he saw on his first peek over the wall appeared to be a small garage. A tin roof reflected what little ambient light filtered through the dark, broken only by a small smokestack near the far edge. It was the kind that was topped with a cone of metal, but no smoke issued from its blackened spout. What surprised him most about this previously-familiar-now-unknown city was that, when darkness came, the eerie orange glow continued deeper in the city. Apparently, the Burning City was still burning.

There was what looked like a gatehouse farther along the wall, perhaps a hundred yards away. A naked bulb shone in the darkness to one side, and he saw movement in the nearby shadows. Ducking low to the ground, he watched the area carefully, but when nothing emerged, he relaxed.

The area around him was empty apart from the garage, and to Jonas, it looked like this area was used as a dumping lot. Wooden pallets lay scattered across the black surface, splintered and laying at haphazard angles like a child's box of Lincoln Logs.

His head began to ache.

A quiet breeze kicked up. He was so on edge that when it ruffled a nearby sheet of plastic, his mind believed it to be an apparition.

"Ghost of Christmas Past," he said quietly to the dark as it settled back to the ground.

Feeling exposed in the empty lot, he hustled across the cement toward the nearby building. He pressed himself against the cold metal siding and rubbed his throbbing ribs absently. Jonas crept along the side of the building, farther into the lot and purposely away from the gatehouse.

His nerves were shot, and this listening and waiting for some unknown surprise was wearing on him.

The corner of the garage was ahead, which meant the pool of yellow light washed across the ground but stopped with a harsh line of shadow from the edge of the building. There'd be no way he could peek around the corner without casting a shadow or moving into the light to do so. He could go around the other side, but he'd be exposing himself to whatever was moving near the gatehouse.

His head ached from trying to listen to everything at once, and he rubbed his temples, thinking.

A creak of rusty hinges echoed across the empty lot, and he froze. He could hear something moving quickly, clacking and pattering unseen in the darkness ahead. It was hard to tell, but it sounded as if it was retreating.

Excitement and fear gripped him. He risked a quick glance around the corner of the building, squinting against the light. He knew that the previously perfect angle of the shadow was now disrupted by his body, but he didn't care. He had to see.

A form moved in the distance behind a pile of broken wooden slats. Its wings—translucent but shaped like a butterfly's—lifted and fell gently against its back as it crouched close to the ground on legs and feet he couldn't see. It wasn't much bigger than him. This must be the new thing he feared. From this distance, it wasn't terrifying. It was merely a blurry form in the darkness. Up close, however, he knew it would be a different story.

Now that he'd peeked past the corner, he could see much more of the area that had been obscured by the building. There were massive piles of rocks and gravel, separated by walls of gray cinderblock. He didn't see anything else besides another large building about a hundred yards away. He realized it was a gravel quarry or something close. A hulking gray machine towered over the area, its base hidden by buildings and trees in the distance. It was a conveyor belt that funneled the gravels into their respective corrals.

His attention was drawn to the small bug-creature as it flitted once more before scurrying into the darkness. He wanted desperately to follow it, but he didn't know what he'd do when he caught up to it.

Screw it, he thought.

He clenched his fists and then bolted from the protection of the building, making a beeline for the spot where he'd last seen the creature. His footsteps crunched loudly in the dirt and grit that covered the lot. He passed the pile of broken slats where it had squatted for a moment and continued on to a stack of cinderblocks. He squinted, searching for the darkness and cursing his eyes as they adjusted to the dark.

After several seconds, he detected movement near another small structure. The creature hopped from one foot to another in what Jonas would say was unease. From the way it moved, he had the notion that it was female. Not that he cared, of course. It was the enemy after all. But if he could follow it, he might get a better clue about what was happening to his world.

He crouched behind the stack of bricks and watched. The darkness was nearly complete save for the yellow light falling gracelessly across the lot behind him, and it was easy to pick out shapes now that his eyes had adjusted.

For a moment, the creature he watched in the distance almost seemed human. Its head swiveled from left to right in a very primal way, which banished the previous thought immediately. No, this was no human. It was an animal from somewhere else.

Is it? A voice in his head questioned.

His stomach gave a low gurgle, and he was reminded of why he had even ventured forth from his glade in the first place. Giving one last look toward the creature, he quietly turned on his heel and froze.

White eyes the size of basketballs stared at him, unblinking, from only a few steps away. He'd placed one hand on the ground to help him turn, and the grit was digging into his palm. One knee was experiencing similar discomfort. He dared not move either of them. The bug's body was a dull grey, and its eyes, still staring ahead, were set low to the ground in folds of skin or armor—it was hard to tell in the darkness. The rhythmic breathing of the creature, low growling reverberations, could be felt in his chest.

Sweat began to run down his face as he stared at the bug, unmoving. His nostrils stung with the tang of its stench, and he could feel his stomach muscles begin to tremble, the precursor to an urgent gag.

He tried not to stare into its eyes. Some deep part of him began to take over, and he understood that if he met its eyes, it may take it as a challenge. Even armed with this knowledge, he couldn't help but make furtive glances at it, trying to understand what he was seeing. Something sat atop its head, reminding him of Anglerfish found in the deepest parts of the ocean. As he looked at that part of it, the cap began to glow bright red.

The ground around him turned to blood and shadow, and he instinctively dove behind the pile of bricks. His elbow caught the edge of a corral, and he had to put a hand to his mouth to prevent himself from crying out. He cowered in the small shadow as the red light swung from side to side. He heard the sound of the animal move, but it wasn't moving toward where Jonas now hid. A crackling growl filled the air, the shadows shifting as the creature stalked between the cement corrals.

Jonas followed its movements by following the shadows the bloodred light cast across the ground. It was moving away from him, but he feared it didn't just happen to be here; it was stalking prey. It was stalking *him*.

He continued to stay in the shadows as the red light washed across his hiding spot. He saw an opportunity when the shadows of his hiding place and the one ahead melded into one long black strip in a sea of red. He lunged forward, hoping against hope that the creature couldn't hear his shoes scrape the ground and his grunt of effort.

A whine echoed through the air, and the creature huffed. Red light moved slowly across where Jonas had just been. The whine sounded again from the bug, and the light moved slowly to his current hiding spot. It was searching for him, and it knew he was there.

It seemed like hours passed as he sat, holding his knees to his chest and trying to make himself as small as possible. He knew the air around him was still filled with angry red light because even with his eyes closed, he saw it washing the night. His elbow dripped blood to the ground, and he prayed desperately that it couldn't smell it.

The bug whined once more and coughed. Then it began to skitter across the ground once more. The light behind his eyelids darkened, and he let out a breath. He risked wiping the sweat from his forehead and glanced around the stack of bricks. The bug was now facing away from him, and its glowing appendage shone across the wall he'd hopped to get here.

Jonas wanted to run, but the hollowness that gnawed at his midsection made him turn his back on the stalking bug. He was facing the same way as when he'd followed the smaller creature. Perhaps it had run away now with this bigger one in the area. He knew a lot of animals were territorial, and if a larger animal wanted the territory, it was no longer a choice.

Hoping he was right, and praying for a small amount of luck, he crawled across the ground on all fours to get a better look at what he now thought of as the Stalker. It whined and stopped, shining its fishing light at the far building. It must smell his scent there.

Not one to waste an opportunity, Jonas jumped to his feet and held his breath to prevent another grunt from giving him away. He ran as fast as he could while trying to also make himself as small as possible. What resulted was a kind of hobbling roadie run that would have made him laugh had he been in a different world.

Instead of laughing, he felt tears of fear and relief sting his eyes as he rounded the corner just as red light flooded the ground behind him. He'd made it. He was safe for now. Even though he could still hear the skittering of the Stalker making its way around the lot, he knew that for now, it couldn't find him. The gravel corrals were too close together to allow its bulky body to pass between them.

His hand touched something cold, round, and metallic, and he immediately recognized it as a doorknob. Despair bubbled inside him when the knob didn't budge. He turned and grasped the knob, tugging and turning rapidly in a growing panic. Just before he could release a scream of desperate rage through the night, he realized the door had inched open inward. He grabbed it with both hands, turned, and gently pushed. The door opened soundlessly.

Knowing full well what rusty hinges sounded like in this lot, he pushed the door slowly, inch by inch, until he could squeeze his body through the gap. The hinges protested with a whispering rustle, but they didn't squeal. He slipped into the building and pushed the door closed behind him before looking around.

CHAPTER 6

The building was dark, but some ambient light allowed him to get an idea of its structure. It was a trailer with two small windows at either end. Red light glowed dimly in the closest one, illuminating a desk and a pallet stacked high, its contents hidden beneath translucent plastic. The other end of the building was completely dark, and he set off in that direction. There were cheap metal desks lining each wall. With each step, they swam out of the darkness as if by magic. Some were covered in paper, some had dusty pictures of families, and others were completely clean.

When he reached the dark end of the building, he nearly cracked his head diving beneath a desk to avoid the Stalker's light as it passed by the far window. He counted to ten as the red glow suffused the wall across from him and then faded away. When he was sure it was gone, he started to get up but paused.

He wasn't alone in this room.

He could hear something breathing, a frantic inhale and exhale. Then a pause. Then it continued. It was coming from his end of the building, but seeing as he was under the last desk against the back wall, whatever it was had to be close enough to touch.

His heart rate picked up speed, and he remembered the human-sized bug that he'd followed to this very building. It had to be that thing, unless by some miracle it was another human. Even through his rising panic, he thought, *That would be a miracle.*

With every alarm system in his body shrieking in protest, he made his way from beneath the desk, eyes darting this way and that, trying to hone in on where the breathing was coming from. In the confines of the small trailer, it shouldn't have been difficult, but it was. The sound of his heartbeat thrummed in his ears and punctuated the silence. He turned his head slowly, determining that the sound, quiet as it was, had to be coming from his right.

He saw movement in the corner across from him, and he picked out immediately the form of a human trying to squeeze itself between two shelves.

He couldn't believe it. Another human, here. What were the odds? *Miracle.*

"Hello?" he whispered, but even still it sounded too loud in his thumping ears.

At the sound of his voice, he saw the person's head move to the side, eyes squeezed tightly shut as if willing Jonas to look away.

"I'm not going to hurt you, I promise." He took a step forward. "My name is Jonas."

The person, he could see now, was a girl who risked a glance at him from the corner of her eye, and then squeezed them closed again. Her body trembled behind the shelf he now saw was stacked with bottles of water.

His mouth watered and his stomach protested when he told it, *In a minute.*

"Please come out of there. I'm not one of *them.*"

At this, her expression relaxed slightly, and she looked at him. *Actually* looked at him, not just glanced in his direction. Her shoulders sagged a little, and the slight tremor that shook her body began to subside.

"How can I be sure?" Her voice was high and scared, and he knew she had experienced something similar to what he had experienced, a front-row seat to the re-write of her life. He couldn't tell, but her accent wasn't local.

"Well," he began, wondering how he'd convince a terrified woman in a strange world that he was safe. "I'm not trying to kill you?"

Maybe not the best start. He licked his lips and tried to smile gently at her.

To his surprise, he saw her swallow hard, then she began to inch her way out from between the shelves. He waited until she pressed herself awkwardly against the wall in front of him, even after he'd taken a step back. She was near enough for him to touch, and he cleared his throat before speaking again.

"I'm Jonas," he said softly, stretching his arm toward her.

The woman hesitated, and he saw in her eyes a reflection of both fear and relief cross her features, just as he'd felt moments before.

Her hand reached out slowly, then, and she shook it once before pulling her arm back swiftly. "Alice."

"Nice to meet you, Alice."

Red light washed slowly across the far side of the room, and they both dropped to a crouch. The Stalker's roving red eye shone against the wall, but it moved on with a dry crackling skitter.

"How did you get here," Jonas whispered into the dark once they were sure the Stalker was gone.

Alice shrugged, "I was in the city when it started to burn. I'm just trying to get out."

Jonas nodded, eyes flitting to the shelves of bottled water next to Alice. They reflected the distant fiery glow just enough to appear as if an ember burned deep within them.

"I'm just gonna," he began, and he reached slowly toward the bottles. Alice followed his movement with her eyes. He stood and began to, as calmly as he could, rip open the plastic wrapping that held the bottles in place. His stomach leapt like an excitable puppy as the plastic stretched but didn't tear. Jonas could feel himself getting frustrated but didn't want to make extra noise or scare Alice. He grunted and heaved. The plastic made a loud pop. They both stared out the windows and froze, waiting for the Stalker to return.

When it didn't, Jonas lifted a single bottle of water from the decimated wrapping and unscrewed the lid. His mouth had become so dry that he didn't think he would be able to swallow. When the water touched his lips, however, he began to drink. It was all he could do to stop himself from uttering a moan of pleasure. He was more thirsty than he believed he could be, and the first water bottle crackled as he tried to suck down every last drop. It had nearly quenched his thirst, but his stomach was beginning to cramp. The second water bottle made his stomach feel heavy, and he feared he'd overdone it. He reached for a third and stopped, suddenly remembering Alice was there watching him.

"Sorry," he muttered sheepishly.

She smiled at him and placed a grimy hand on his arm. "That's okay, Jonas. There are a lot of people looking for food and water. I'm glad you found some."

He returned the smile. "Thanks. It's been a hard few days. Or week. I'm not sure how long, really."

She nodded in understanding and began looking through the shelves.

"What are you..." He trailed off when she bent down. The darkness was complete now, except for some ambient light from the city and the occasional Stalker beam. Other than those two sources, there was nothing to illuminate the room. But even in the dim light, he could see that her hair that fell across her shoulders in messy waves was a dark brown or black.

After several seconds of rustling through the bottom shelf of items, she stood and held out a large bundle of fabric. No, not fabric, he now saw. It was a duffel bag.

"There are a couple of these. It seems like they," she nodded out the window in the direction of the Stalker, "won't need them, don't you think?"

Jonas smiled, and the water in his belly sloshed uncomfortably as he bent to retrieve another.

Alice and Jonas spent the next few minutes filling the dark green duffel bags with bottled water. He knew he'd need quite a lot, but if he rationed it, maybe he wouldn't need to return for a while.

As they were stuffing the duffel bags and making sure they could carry the weight, the Stalker's beam glowed closer, briefly bathing the room in red. Alice tapped him on the arm and pointed.

Midway down the trailer, more shelves sat in the darkness. They were filled with canned and cellophane-wrapped foods. Grinning at one another, they grabbed another duffel, and after giving the Stalker enough time to move away, quietly filled another duffel bag each.

Jonas devoured several snack cakes, relishing the way the food and water sat in his belly like a lead weight. Any other time it might have made him sick, but a stuffed belly gave him enough relief that he felt like things were finally looking up. The Stalker illuminated the room again, and with the light, they both spotted a jumbled pile of sleeping bags. They each took two and stuffed them into a duffel, smiling at each other like they'd just won the lottery. She had a great smile, and Jonas could see the red light of the Stalker reflected in a young woman's face, probably mid-twenties. Not much younger than himself.

"So what are you going to do?" Jonas asked her once they'd zipped up their bags, and there was nothing left to do but leave.

Alice shrugged. "I'm not sure. I don't want to be one of those people who just wait until their executioner comes. I want to be someone who protects those who can't protect themselves. But," she lifted her arms in a helpless shrug, "I guess I fit into that category at the moment."

Jonas nodded, feeling a little like he was in the same boat.

"I know there are some people fighting back. Not very successfully, but fighting nonetheless."

Jonas hadn't heard that, but he wasn't surprised. He'd been sequestering himself in the middle of a small forest. There wasn't much in the way of news out there.

They sat in silence for a moment. Jonas squirmed a bit before speaking with uncertainty.

"I found a safe place," he said, whispering. "It's not far from here, but far enough that these Stalkers aren't around." He motioned vaguely in the direction of the red light.

Alice sat up. "Well, that's good. Is it out of the city?"

Nodding, he said, "Yes. Not too far from here. It's over the wall in ... " he looked around the dark room trying to get the direction right based on his memory of the night's events, "that direction." Jonas pointed at the far wall where the window sat like a lidded eye. "It's in a small glade in the middle of a bunch of trees. Nothing can see me, except maybe from above. And while there are usually a bunch of them traveling *around* me, they leave me alone. There's no reason to venture into the trees, so I live there now ... I guess." He wrapped a clear snack wrapper around his finger.

"You live in the trees? Like the Swiss Family Robinson?"

"The who?"

Alice put a hand over her mouth as she chuckled silently. "Nevermind. That's good. I guess you're going to just wait it out, then?"

He nodded, feeling the prickle of defensive shame.

The Stalker's light rolled through the building again, but this time they didn't shy away from it. It was outside, and its light only shone in the two windows. If it hadn't seen them yet, it wasn't going to.

"Well, that's all we can do, isn't it?"

Jonas looked at her in the dim light and felt a vague sense of familiarity. Not with Alice, though. No, with what she said. There was something in that phrase that was familiar, but he couldn't place it. It had to be from before all this happened.

He couldn't think on it too much or his head would start hurting again like it always did when he tried to remember life before the bugs. His brain was no doubt overwhelmed with the trauma of their arrival.

Hefting the bags over his shoulder and positioning their straps so that each made an "x" across his chest, he stood.

"I should probably get back to the glade," he said, aware that this girl had nowhere to go, either. He shuffled his feet, unsure now about how to leave without making the point obvious.

Thankfully, she saved him the embarrassment. "I'll be fine, you know."

Jonas nodded without meeting her eyes, then said, "Are you sure?"

She forced a smile. And despite the nearly complete darkness, what little light there was in the air caught a glisten in her eyes. "Yeah. I'll be fine." She shrugged. "I've made it this far, you know?"

Jonas helped her lift her own duffels of food and water over her head. He met her eyes, and by some ridiculous impulse, he said, "If you need a place, you can always come to the glade. It's maybe a couple miles in that direction." He pointed again in the direction of what he now called home.

"Thanks, but I'll be okay," she said nodding.

"Of course."

They both shuffled awkwardly for several seconds.

"Good luck, Alice." He made to shake her hand while she reached in for a hug. He tried to return it, but it was even more awkward thanks to the large duffels slung across both of their shoulders. She did her best to return it, taking the opportunity to sniff her runny nose while Jonas wasn't looking at her.

"Well," she said when they stepped away from each other. "You'd better get going." She placed a hand on his shoulder. "But make sure it's clear before you just charge out there like a man."

Jonas smiled and chuckled. The Stalker's light hadn't shown in a few minutes, and he wondered if maybe it had left. Of course, he hadn't heard it approach, so it may not mean anything if he couldn't see it.

He crept to the door. His heart hammered against his chest as he clasped the cold metallic knob in both hands to ease the door open. Jonas couldn't see much as he peered through the crack. But the darkness didn't give much of a chance, even with the dull yellow from the light down the lot and the distant amber fires.

Before he continued on, he turned to her.

"Here," he said, lifting the snowblossom necklace from his neck, careful to avoid ripping the delicate flower chain, and held it out to her.

"What's this?" She took it, but looked at him curiously.

"It's a necklace. I didn't know I could make it, but I did when I was waiting for it to get dark. Some muscle memory from the Before."

She smiled at him and put it over her own head. It settled across her shirt just above her breasts. She traced the line of small white flowers with her fingertips.

"Thank you, Jonas."

He shrugged. "You're welcome. I figure it might bring luck or something. And if it doesn't, it's pretty at least, right?"

They both laughed lightly, and then Jonas went back to the door and peered through. He searched for several seconds again, ensuring that he hadn't attracted any unwanted attention in the seconds it took to give Alice the necklace.

He jumped in surprise when Alice whispered from behind, "Anything?"

He looked over his shoulder at her and shook his head.

Jonas pulled the knob just enough to inch it open a bit more. He realized in the middle of this that he'd need to get both duffels and his body out at the same time, which meant the door would need to be almost completely open. The door opened slowly, inch by terrifying inch, until he was sure each of them could squeeze through with their supplies.

His eyes never stopped moving as he searched the perimeter and the shadows for any sign of the Stalker, or the smaller bug he saw flitting across the lot earlier.

After several seconds of looking and listening intently, he stepped tentatively onto the gravel outside the shelter. The crunch of it sounded like a gunshot in the silence, and he froze, waiting for a red light to wash across his face, a guttural roar to rend the air, and a massive beast to bear down on him.

Instead, he heard and saw nothing. No skittering crunch and no red light.

He took another tentative step, heart racing and legs trembling.

When he'd gone far enough as he dared, he turned back to the door. He could just make out the outline of Alice standing against the opposite wall inside the building. Jonas gripped the outside knob, smiled at her, and whispered, "Good luck, Alice."

He saw her nod and lift a hand in goodbye before the door swung shut, the soft *click* of the mechanism punctuating the words. He knew he'd never see her again, and while part of him was sad, another part of him felt relief. He wasn't responsible for her, he was responsible for himself. Saying that to himself didn't help, but maybe, at some point, it would.

He crouched and walked slowly toward the edge of the building. He knew the Stalker had prowled outside of their building for several minutes. He didn't see it now, but he knew it was silent enough to still be there. Waiting.

Part of him still tugged at his leaving Alice behind. Was it the part of him that agreed with her? That he was able to protect those who couldn't protect themselves and was just choosing not to? Didn't he *want* to protect those weaker than he was? Hadn't he before?

He sighed with irritation despite the fear he felt. He'd already fought off a potential headache by avoiding the thoughts of the Before, and now here he was, in a dangerous situation, entertaining the same thoughts. And the headache he knew had been waiting now began to pulse above his right eye.

Feeling he had to take the chance now or face hiding in the building with Alice until morning, he lunged forward toward the stacks of cinder blocks. Crouching there and holding his breath, he prayed nothing was near. His headache beat in time with his heartbeat, and he rubbed the spot above his eye as cautiously as possible.

28 ... 29 ... 30, he counted in his head.

Thirty seconds should be long enough before moving to the next gravel cubicle. He did this until he'd reached the last corral in the lot. Count to thirty, listen, move. Stop, count to thirty, listen, move. The large gap between his current stack of blocks and the wall was going to be the worst part. He counted to sixty this time and when nothing happened, he took a breath and ran across the gap, making a wide arc around the yellow light on the ground. He pulled up short and ducked behind the building, looking left and right, and listening frantically for any movement. His footsteps had echoed in the empty lot, but to his ears, they sounded like explosions.

Even still, it seemed like he was alone.

Knowing that the building protected him better than the field on the other side of the wall would, he took the opportunity to toss the duffels over. He hefted one and launched it with all his might. Surprisingly, it sailed easily over the eight-foot wall. He did the same with the other duffel and heard it land with a soft *whump* in the grass on the other side. His ribs protested, but the pain was manageable.

He peered left and right one final time. His heartbeat was almost a single, steady thump in his chest and sweat dripped down his temple and nose as he peeked around the edge of the building into the darkness. Nothing was there, but the hairs on his neck suddenly stood straight on end. The sudden urge to avoid turning around was overwhelming. It was the same feeling when he knew something he'd been avoiding was now right behind him. He was trapped, caught, and would soon be eviscerated.

He shook his head. The fear evaporated, but the headache increased from a minor annoyance to an aching throb. He stared up at the wall. There wasn't room to run and jump this time, but maybe he could use the building behind him. It was perhaps six feet from the wall, and if he timed it right, he may be able to leap from one to the other and gain a few additional feet of height.

He eyed the space and played out the jump in his mind, calculating this and that, determining which would give the best grip. Then, satisfied with his rudimentary assumptions, he leapt up on the vertical building, then pushed off toward the perimeter wall. It would have been great if the building was a foot closer. Instead, the noise of his foot pounding against the metallic wall reverberated around the lot with a deafening rattle. This threw his landing on the perimeter wall off. His foot slid down the cinderblock wall, and he uttered a terrified groan.

He knew he was in trouble the second he landed. The noise was far too focused on his position as the only other building was across the lot, a hundred yards away. A clattering in the distance confirmed his fears, and he looked toward the small gatehouse. A diminutive creature lumbered out of the opening and turned toward him, one huge yellow eye flashed chaotically in the darkness. A barking cry ripped through the night.

It was coming for him, and he knew it.

The crunch of gravel sounded from around the side of the building where he now cowered and the darkness fled, replaced with a blood-red glow.

Jonas bit down a scream of terror. He leapt at the wall, scrambling as high as he could and jumping uselessly against it. In his desperation, he clawed at the concrete edge near the top. He raked the tips of his fingers across the rough blocks, and smears of blood marked their tracks. A fingernail came loose suddenly, but it was a distant pain, overshadowed by the infinite terror that vibrated across his spine.

An inhuman scream pierced the air, and the creature from the gatehouse lurched toward him in a shambling run. Within the blink of an eye, it closed half the distance, all while emitting indiscernible gurgling cries.

Tears of frustration stung his eyes. All his efforts to remain hidden and he was going to be caught and eaten because he was too stupid to plan a way out before just throwing caution to the wind and trying a cobbled-together plan.

He ran his bloody fingers through his hair and used that single second to center himself. It was now or never, and with the creatures bearing down on him, there was only one way out. He leapt against the wall, stretching to the point where he knew his arms would come out of their sockets. His ragged fingertips gripped the top of the wall, and despite the sting that traveled down his elbow, he hung on with a death grip.

A screech issued from far too close, no doubt in his mind that it was from where the Stalker stood. He could now hear the rhythmic thump of the creature from the gatehouse, and a similar sound was crunching its way from the direction of the Stalker.

There are more, he thought.

His boots caught, slipped, then caught again before he was able to pull himself up. His elbows scraped across the jagged concrete blocks as he kicked and clawed his way toward the top of the wall.

Screams, growls, and other unintelligible sounds bounced between the wall and the building as the creature from the gatehouse reached his position, converging with others in the area, of course.

Cold appendages suddenly wrapped around his pants and shoes and, with surprising strength, began to pull him down. The eye that had roved chaotically across the dark expanse shone on his exposed skin. He screamed in protest as he felt himself begin to slip. More pawed at him, and he could hear the bugs beneath him clawing, scratching, and bellowing victoriously at him.

He kicked hard, refusing to be captured. His boot connected with something, and a scream of pain replaced the growling and spitting sound of the whatever was beneath him. With one occupied with its pain, Jonas began to pull himself up.

He kicked again and missed, but it was enough to make the creatures stop grasping at him long enough for him to lift his leg out of their reach and over the wall. He rolled himself over the wall just as he had done before, but he didn't have time to ease his way down to the field below. Instead, his momentum carried him off the wall, and then he was falling—falling into the darkness. His momentary scream blended into the angry barks and growls that bounced over the wall, but his voice cut off when he landed hard on the duffels. Pain exploded from his side while his chest constricted. He couldn't breathe. He groaned and rolled off the bags, trying to stand. He was shaky, but he stood, and the sound of crunching gravel and barking growls was fading.

He took as deep a breath as he could—which wasn't very deep at all—and winced against the pain in his chest and side. He was okay. He'd made it.

Light suddenly illuminated the ground around him while a bark echoed from across the field. With dread, he realized they had run to the opening in the wall and were still chasing him.

The gatehouse.

Not wasting any more time to catch his breath, he finished slinging the duffels over his head and lumbered toward the tree line ahead.

The creature—a Chaotic Eye, he'd decided—suddenly lit the area on and around him, then danced again into the darkness, back and forth. He looked behind him and saw at least three smaller creatures—*Flitters*—chasing him. Their transparent wings caught the light as they expanded behind them. He wasn't sure if it was his imagination or not, but it looked like their feet left the ground as they charged ahead.

He didn't care enough to watch. Peering ahead and holding tight onto the duffels around his hips, he made his way quickly into the welcoming dark of the trees. The Eye may be able to see him, but wouldn't for long.

He continued, dodging around trunks and beneath branches, doing his best to ignore both the pain in his body and the fading growls and chittering from behind.

Once he was sure the sounds had faded and he was no longer being followed, he slowed. Not much, but enough to let him catch a bit of his breath. The duffels didn't let him slide through gaps between trees as easily as he wished, but he forged ahead, intent on putting more distance between himself and the creatures that had nearly captured him.

The Eye had peered through the trees here and there, but he hadn't heard their chittering for several minutes. It was completely dark, and except for the nearing rumble of Travelers, he was safe.

Safe.

More or less.

He stopped and let the duffels slide down his back to the leaf-littered ground. His injured ribs protested, but he breathed in deep through his nose. To his surprise, he could take in almost a lungful of air before he felt that irritatingly familiar twinge in his side. The air smelled like moist earth and distant rain, and he smiled weakly thinking of Alice.

He looked over his shoulder in the direction of the gravel lot. It was impossible to see more than dark trees ten feet away, but he sent a small measure of hope in that direction before hefting the bags to his shoulders again.

He wasn't exactly sure where he was, or where he was heading, but the Glade was close enough, and he could search until morning. He knew the Travelers moved back and forth near his Glade. He'd follow their steady, rolling sounds and go from there.

For the first time in a few days, he wasn't worried, and he smiled into the darkness feeling the invisible weight of responsibility slide soundlessly from his shoulders.

CHAPTER 7

He hustled in the gray morning light through brush that acted as a kind of perimeter fence to the trees. He passed back through the wreckage of trees that he'd seen earlier that day, or was it yesterday? He couldn't remember, and in the end, it didn't matter.

He ducked underneath a limb that latched onto his stocking cap, then made to push another from his path when his eyes caught what he at first mistook as an oddly-shaped rock. When he looked closer, however, his breath stopped, one hand froze holding a supple branch away from his face.

There, on the ground, was a giant, colorful butterfly. Well, not compared to the actual giant bugs that had shown up recently. No, this one was maybe ten times the size of a "normal" butterfly, as best he could remember, but this one was a stuffed plush toy.

He dropped the duffels gently and went to a knee. He lifted it reverently from the ground and brushed small twigs and mud from its plush exterior. Its soft body felt both foreign and familiar, and he marveled at its mere existence. There was something comforting about the little bug. Something that brought to mind the old world, before the arrival of the Travelers, Eyes, Stalkers, and whatever else shredded his reality to bits. The antennae at the top of its bulbous head were two floppy black tubes of material that ended in soft pom poms. The wings of his new friend had once been a vibrant pattern of pink, blue, and green. The colors were now muted beneath a thin layer of dirt and grime.

Smiling to himself, Jonas tucked his new companion into his coat and hefted the duffels. Making his way through the trees toward his glade was tricky in the deep dark of night, but he'd always had a good sense of direction, and he knew he'd find it eventually.

His head had begun to hurt on his way back to the Glade and was now beginning to throb in a heavy rhythm. Reaching into his coat, he held the butterfly to his chest. His fingers traced over the soft fabric of the butterfly, feeling the tiny pricks of dirt but also feeling the silky body beneath. Beneath the comfort was a sense of urgency, something hinted at being out of place. He couldn't understand it. There was a burst of adrenaline at first, but it was dissipating now.

He hoped that was what caused his headache to worsen.

Thunder rumbled overhead, and he saw distant lightning illuminate a line of rolling clouds that looked unfriendly. The weather wasn't cooling down yet, but when it did he'd be in trouble. The only thing keeping him concealed were the leaves of the trees. Once they began falling to the ground, it would only be a matter of time before his little sanctuary was discovered, and he along with it. It was still several months away by his estimation, but he knew it was coming. There were some evergreens nearby he may be able to use, but there weren't enough to keep him both warm *and* concealed. His excursion into the city had certainly proven that it wasn't safe at all, but it was doable.

He was approaching the Traveler's Path now. He didn't see any making their way along it, but that didn't mean Stalkers or Flitters weren't nearby. He crouched on the edge of the trees and looked left and right, like a child crossing the street. Thunder rumbled and his headache took it as permission to pound harder.

When he was certain no Travelers were coming, he stood and secured the duffels. He took a deep breath and broke from cover, sprinting as fast as he could over the path and into the tree line on the other side. He heard an approaching Traveler rumble its way down the path he'd just crossed, kicking up dust and illuminating the area around him when it looked left and right with is ugly glowing eyes.

He patted his coat and felt the bulge where he'd concealed the butterfly, then continued making his way through the trees toward the glade. With the occasional lightning flash, he began to recognize certain trees and branches that lay across the ground in familiar angles. Peering through the gloom, he only picked out the glade a few yards away when lightning arced across the sky and showed the small clearing through an orange afterimage in his eyes.

Found it, he thought to himself with relief. Maybe he'd been a little more fearful than he let himself believe.

He knelt down to his meager lean-to and put the duffels at one end, using one as a pillow, which was only slightly more comfortable than a rock. He hoped the rain would hold off but knew it wouldn't. Jonas felt a smile pull at the corners of his mouth as he tugged the sleeping bag out of its sleeve. This was a very welcome addition, and it wasn't lost on him that it would change his outlook—and probably the outcome—once fall and winter replaced the warmth of summer.

Careful to avoid muddying up his new treasure, he gently pried his boots off and set them aside. He smiled with genuine pleasure as he pulled the thick and comfortable sleeping bag up around his body. Thunder above and thunder in his head helped him drift off to sleep that night, though it wasn't long before he was tossing and turning with bad dreams and a deep restlessness.

He was awake before the sun and decided it wouldn't do any good to lie in bed. He tidied up the area and reinforced his lean-to, then when enough light covered the glade, he looked around for a place to store the food he'd brought from the city.

Luckily, most of it was sealed in cellophane, and the water bottles were sealed, too. It didn't take long before he found a rotted stump at the edge of the glade where an old fox or badger had dug a hole beneath. He eyed the dark circle suspiciously before finding a stick to probe its depths. It wasn't very deep, and when he was certain there wasn't anything crouched within it, he cast the stick aside.

Jonas spent the morning digging out a small storeroom of sorts beneath the stump, which was about three feet across. The hole had to leave enough of a dirt foundation that the stump remained stable. The last thing he needed was for the lid of his cubbyhole to fall and crush everything he'd risked his life to find.

When he was done, he sat back and surveyed his work, wiping sweat from his head and leaving a muddy stripe in its place. The stump stood a little more than a foot off the ground, but now there was a very clear hole a foot wide and a couple of feet deep. Jonas had dug as deep as he could when reaching down the hole and now had a very convenient place to store his food and water without compromising the integrity of the stump above it.

He realized with some frustration that if it rained, his cubby hole would turn into a snack swamp since there was no way to drain it. In a stroke of something near genius, he realized he could simply put the duffel over the hole. It more than covered it, and since the canvas was waterproof—*probably,* he thought—it would serve as a perfect block. Or at least prevent water from pooling into it *too* much.

A morning full of problem-solving gave him a pleasurable sense of accomplishment.

He began the stoic work of filling his cubby with assorted food and water bottles. He counted each item as he placed it beneath the stump. At the end of it all, he was pleased with his haul, more than he'd originally thought, and if his calculations were correct, he figured that he could probably last about a month if he rationed himself. One water bottle per day and two food items—snack cakes or assorted nuts—one in the morning and one at night would last him between twenty-five and twenty-nine days.

He would be able to live with that.

# # #

Jonas returned to the Burning City every twenty days. The second time he went, he found the small building he'd previously pilfered full of what he could only describe as housing materials in addition to the food and water. There were canvas sheets—tarps—more duffel bags, but no tents, which was something he'd been hoping to find. He gathered what he could but was disappointed in the food available. It was more of the same snacks on the third trip, and after over a month of sugary cakes and assorted nuts and berries, he was more than sick of it all.

But it was surviving, and that's all he could ask for. Someday, things would change, and he would enjoy a steak or a burger again. But for now, snacks were the only thing available.

He'd begun to classify the bugs, first coming up with a general term for them by racking his brain to remember what he'd learned in his college Intro to Biology.

"It reminded me of Cyclopes," he said to the stuffed butterfly in his lap, "but I can't remember why." He chewed idly on some beef jerky that he'd found on his third trip during the summer months, and stared into the tree line. He silently thanked the trees for the shade that blocked the blistering sun.

"Cyclops... cycle... lopse... clops... ops..." He snapped his fingers. "Ops... or Opt... era? Optera? Something like that."

The butterfly's black eyes stared at him, unimpressed.

"Yeah, something like that. What do you think?" He turned to the butterfly.

It didn't answer.

"Yeah, I know you're impressed. Optera. Almost sounds like 'Operation,' that old game where you had to avoid touching the sides or it would—" he mimed electrocution. "So 'optera' is good, but it can't be the only thing, right? They're invaders, so how do we combine the two?"

He took another small bite of jerky and chewed slowly. "Invoptera? Invadoptera? No, no those are no good."

Jonas cocked his head as if hearing something. "That's not a bad idea. What are synonyms to 'invader'?" He looked at the butterfly intently, as if searching its dusty-colored hide for the answer.

"Attacker? Or... conqueror. Or trespasser?" He tossed them together in his head before blurting out, "Tressoptera! That works! That's pretty good, actually." He brushed his shoulders off as if he'd accomplished a great deed.

"So they're Tressoptera, I think that works."

The butterfly plush stared at him blankly.

From that moment on, they weren't "creatures" or "bugs" or even "monsters" anymore, they'd become "Tressoptera" which, to Jonas, meant something less alien and more *known*.

He'd had fewer run-ins with Flitters—the littlest of the Tressoptera, roughly human-sized and shaped, but with large wings and spindly arms. There was an increased presence of Tressoptera on the second trip to the building where he refilled his stores. He'd had to be especially careful sneaking over the wall and through the gravel corrals—which were now filled with jugs of water and pallets of all kinds of supplies rather than useless rocks.

The Stalker he'd run across that first time still roamed nearby but was easy enough to avoid.

The Chaotic Eyes that chased him and screamed were very rare to encounter. He was glad for that, they scared him with their chittering and squealing and flashes of light that seemed to penetrate the deepest protective gloom of the trees.

But when the leaves started turning colors, Jonas began to fear for his own well-being. The leaves would fall soon and reveal everything. He'd be risking everything to stay where he was now, but he couldn't imagine leaving the Glade. It was something he wrestled with daily. But every day that passed without a decision was one day closer to the decision being made for him.

When he'd returned from his fourth trip to the Burning City, more food and water scavenged from the same general area, he decided that he could delay no longer.

A small golden leaf left the branch above and floated through the glade to land on the notebook he'd snatched from the city, and now where he had begun cataloging the Tressoptera.

His fingerless gloves stopped writing, and he stared.

It was happening. The first leaf. *Not the first, that would be ridiculous*, he thought to himself. *But still.*

"Stop looking at me like that," he said to the butterfly that lay across the log next to him.

"I know. I know. It's happening. And sooner than I would have liked."

"You have to do something, Jonas," the butterfly said.

"I know I do. I know. But what? Go to the city?"

"Is that what you want to do?"

He hesitated. Alice was in the city, but so was everything else.

He shook his head. "No. No, I don't want to do that."

"The Tressies are all over the place, Jonas. You're not safe anywhere, anymore."

He nodded and looked to the sky where a dark cloud covered the sun briefly before moving on and letting it soak the glade with a blinding, chilly brilliance.

The butterfly sat on the log, staring ahead as it always had while Jonas weighed his options.

CHAPTER 8

He couldn't make a decision. Not that night. Or the next night.

Before long, Jonas was lying on blankets beneath branches that were very clearly more bare than they'd been the week before. The camouflage canvas he'd scavenged from the Burning City blocked most of the rain and sun, but he didn't think about that right now. For now, he stared at the dirty stuffed butterfly clutched in his gloved hands. The light from the kerosene lantern—another scavenged victory—was turned as low it as could go without the "off" switch disengaging the heat. Even beneath the canvas, the air was cool, and he was thankful for the coat he'd found too.

The butterfly's previously bulbous body had become lean with his near-constant holding, as if it hadn't eaten in months. Where once the stuffing had made the body round, it now had one end that tapered to two threadbare sheets of fabric. The other end, where the stuffing now resided permanently, was lumpy and misshapen. The wings had tiny tears here and there, making the butterfly look like it had been through the ringer and was on its last leg.

He stroked it gently, feeling the ripped and ragged fibers on his fingertips. The colors were fading, and while they were still visible beneath the dirt and grime, in the dim light from his lantern, it was a uniform gray. It had comforted him in the months after his first visit to the Burning City. It hadn't been nearly as dirty then, but after its constant use, it was a sad excuse for what once was a colorful and well-loved toy.

"I was well-loved," it said to him.

"I know," he replied sleepily, uncertain of *how* he knew.

Then in his head, a fuzzy image resolved into a young red-headed girl running through a sunlit yard and smiling, pretending to flap its oversize wings in her little hands. Sunlight shone through a nearby window, and it played off her red hair, spinning it into a raspberry glow that splashed across her back and shoulders.

Jonas smiled and thought about how this little bug must have been well loved indeed. At least before its gargantuan brethren invaded his world and destroyed it. Even now, the familiar hum of Travelers reminded him that, despite all the precautions he took, he was still in danger. Always in danger.

Jonas focused back on the butterfly and pretended to flap its wings like the little girl in his mind had. His head was starting to hurt again. The smell of kerosene was strong beneath the canvas, and without a vent, it built up and accosted his senses.

He turned the lamp off, the hiss and pop of it sounding far too loud in the relative silence of his glade. The filaments of the lamp turned from a glaring white to a burnished yellow, then to a melted gold, and finally to a dull, quiet cream. He counted to ten to make sure there were no other sounds around him, then carefully, he lifted a corner of his make-shift tent. Cooler air rushed in, and the smell of kerosene was whisked effortlessly away.

He closed the canvas and left the lamp off. The headache wasn't getting worse, but that didn't mean it was altogether gone. He rubbed his temples and took a drink of water from yet another scavenging victory—a metal canteen.

He hugged the butterfly to his chest, and the image of the girl rose in his mind again. That familiarity he'd felt from the butterfly's discovery deepened, and a second image began to form. This time, it was spinning stars.

Instinctively, he shied away from it, as if it was dangerous or shameful. But with his headache, he was trying to do too much with his mind. And it was a half-hearted attempt, anyway. It was kind of pretty, if unsettling.

"Don't," the butterfly said, but Jonas ignored it.

The image resolved itself into a picture of himself, reaching back. He didn't know what it meant, and he didn't necessarily care. His headache had definitely *not* cleared and began to thump across his brow in painful waves.

He shook his head trying to clear it, and the image disappeared, dissolving into his subconscious. He had bigger things to worry about and right now; he needed to worry about getting his headache under control.

Maybe he'd pushed himself too hard that day, and this was his body's way of telling him to get some rest. Come to think of it, he had only finished a single bottle of water. Experience told him he needed two each day to stave off dehydration at the very least. If he could drink twice that much, he'd be in a better state.

"Rations, you know," he whispered to the butterfly, and it nodded its head.

Jonas closed his eyes and fell asleep a short time later, the old and ruined stuffy clutched loosely to his chest.

Like most mornings, Jonas woke to the sound of Tressies nearby. They hadn't bothered him yet, though there had been a close call when one decided to charge headlong into a nearby stand of trees. That bug had been carried off by a bigger, angrier-looking bug that had simply yanked it onto its massive back and lumbered off, viscera oozing down its sides from its injured passenger. Shortly after it vacated the area, several smaller Tressies came in with their clicking and whirring to eat whatever was left of it.

He stretched and pushed the canvas off himself. The trees, growing more and more naked each day, still offered a good deal of protection from the elements and concealment from the outside world. Even still, his canvas crackled with a fine layer of frost that glittered in the morning sunlight. It wasn't chilly this morning; it was downright cold, and he was thankful once again for the coat, hat, and gloves he scavenged from the city.

His fingers clutched the butterfly, and he stuffed it into his coat then stood to stretch. The sun felt good on his face; he smiled up at the sky, happy that his headache had disappeared before the sunrise.

Jonas pivoted on his heel to the nearby stump where he'd hidden his food.

It was filled with what he would now call an abundance of food—canned goods, beef jerky, nuts, and dried fruit. Along with food, there were several other odds and ends such as a can opener, several lighters and boxes of matches, some plastic wrap, and trash bags. There was also another coat, gloves, and hat stuffed to one side. Perhaps his proudest item was a hunting knife and several feet of rope. He wasn't sure what those would be used for, but it wasn't every day that the apocalypse came in the form of giant bugs stalking the landscape.

He grabbed a snack cake and a can of Grandma Betty's Old Fashioned Tomato Soup ("It's good for the soul, too!")

and the can opener. He hated cold soup, but he was growing accustomed to it. He'd heated a few of the cans up on the fire over the past few weeks but didn't much feel like it now. Cold soup would do this morning.

Sitting on a log for a flat place to eat breakfast, he clamped the can opener on the top of the soup can and began to crank. It made that yawing metal sound with each turn of the handle, but he was careful to avoid letting any of the precious soup spill over the sides.

Being alone had its downsides, but one thing that he'd worked hard to cultivate was a sixth sense of his surroundings. Perhaps it was a vestige of his lizard brain, but the more time he stayed in the Glade, the more his ability to detect danger increased. Or at least his perception of it. And right now, the back of his neck was tingling in the way it did when he was being watched.

He hesitated for only a second before continuing to crank on the can opener as if he hadn't noticed. His eyes darted to the knife several feet away in his food hole. It was too far away to reach for without being obvious. He searched the trees around him without moving his head, but he saw nothing out of the ordinary, which meant that whatever was watching him was directly behind him.

As if to confirm his fears, a twig snapped behind him, breaking the silence of his glade like shattered glass.

He stopped cranking and sat up. He knew it would alert whatever it was, but he didn't care. They knew he knew they were there. Thinking quickly, he played out a dive for the knife, then a spin around before whatever it was leapt on him. He only let himself feel a small amount of sadness for the soup that would be wasted when it fell off his lap and spilled across the ground, but he had more cans of soup.

He had only one life.

Just as he coiled his muscles to launch toward the knife, a voice spoke behind him.

"Jonas?"

It was a woman's voice.

A *familiar* woman's voice.

He turned hesitantly, still keeping the knife in the back of his head as a backup plan.

There was a woman in the glade. *His* glade. A string of dried snowblossoms hung around her neck, and his memory placed her immediately. She was the same woman he'd met in the Burning City several months ago. She was wearing black pants and boots, both of which looked much warmer than his own, with a black shirt beneath a black combat vest with pockets stuffed to bulging. Her hair, also black, hung over her shoulder in a tight braid. A far cry cleaner than that scavenging woman huddled between a shelf and a wall. She looked like someone gearing up for a fight. Based on their previous conversation, he wondered if she was.

"Uh," he stuttered, "hi." He lifted his hand with the can opener in a stunned, half-hearted wave.

"Can I," she looked around with uncertainty, "come in, or approach, or whatever?"

Jonas hesitated, then smiled. "Sure."

He turned back to his soup and finished rotating the can opener. The soup can opened with a metallic squall when he pulled the top off and tossed it in a canvas bag he used for trash. Just because the world had gone to shit didn't mean he needed to add to it. Besides, trash attracted rodents, and rodents attracted predators. He didn't want any Tressies finding a buffet he happened live beside.

He felt the log he was sitting on shift with Alice's additional weight. She settled a respectful distance away, something he grudgingly appreciated.

"How are you?" she asked, facing him and dipping her head to try to make eye contact with his downcast eyes.

Jonas shrugged and brought the soup can to his lips, careful to avoid the sharp edge. *I should have gotten spoons the last time I was in the city*, he thought distractedly.

"I'm sure you remember me, but I'm Alice." Jonas met her eye then, and nodded, taking another silent sip of his soup as she continued. "It seems like you've been able to take care of yourself pretty well here." He saw her glance around his glade. Again, he gave her points for not looking around with disapproval or disgust.

"It's fine. It does the job." He nodded vaguely toward the outside world. "Keeps me safe from them."

She nodded. "Yeah, I remember our conversation from before. There was a lot of scary stuff going on then."

He sipped his soup. "Then?" he scoffed silently.

"You know," she began hesitantly, "it's gotten a lot better. Out there." She mimed her head vaguely the same way he had.

"Maybe," responded Jonas, unwrapping a sponge cake. "But I still hear them. Every day."

Alice flipped her braid onto her back and nodded. "Yes. They're still out there. But there are people fighting them."

Jonas nearly spit his soup out. *Shit.* "Fighting them?" he sputtered.

She sat up, excited. "Yes! Fighting them!"

He couldn't wrap his mind around it. How on earth could they be fought? Other than with military power.

It was then that he noticed the gun at her hip.

Something that had been bothering him came to the surface. He wiped soup from his beard as he asked, "How did you find me? And how did you avoid being seen?"

Alice shrugged but met his eye. "I was careful. And you told me where you were staying at the time, at least a general direction. It wasn't too hard to work out where." She scratched her head. "But it did take some searching. There are several groups of trees like this one, so I just went from one to the next until I found you."

"Why, though?" There really was no reason for him to be found.

Alice's shoulders heaved with a deep, hesitant breath that she released slowly before answering.

"Because I want you to join us."

He stopped, the last bite of the sponge cake forgotten in his dirty gloved fingers. "Us? Who is *us*?"

Alice took a deep breath. "Jonas," she began.

"Okay, hold on, Alice." He gestured at her with the last bite of sponge cake. "Anyone who starts answering a line of questions by addressing the person *usually* is about to do one of two things. Either sell you something or tell you something that's going to completely blow up your world. And I can tell by your lack of traveling bags, that you aren't going to sell me something."

Alice smiled as he spoke, and then she continued as if he hadn't spoken. "When we met, I was scared and running, just like you. There were crazy reports of things going on, and I didn't have the courage to listen to any of it and decide for myself. The choice was fight or flight, and I chose flight. I found myself in a similar situation as you, though not as," she looked around as if she'd find the word in the glade, "rustic as you. Someone found me. Or rather, I found him. It doesn't really matter. But we found each other, and he helped me see that there is a whole world out there that doesn't have direction. Hasn't had a goal in centuries. And now, it doesn't have any goal other than surviving. And if survival is taken care of, suddenly the goal becomes 'get as much money as possible and do whatever it takes to prevent others from getting it.'"

Alice paused, giving him the chance to process that. Jonas didn't respond, but he stared at her, trying to find the chink in her armor.

What about the bugs? He thought. *What does money have to do with it?*

It took several seconds before he made the connection in his own mind. *Those with the money can buy safety. Those without are forced to survive on their own.*

She was right, though. Maybe not in definition or execution, but the world did seem to be stuck in a cycle of gain, spend, hunger, gain, spend, etc. And those left out of the "gain" part of it were falling further and further into the "hunger" part of it.

"The group of people this man belongs to has found a better way. A higher purpose, you might say. Their purpose is to show the world that just because it's how things have *been* going, doesn't mean it has to be how things *keep* going. Does that make sense?"

Jonas, remembering the snack in his hand, brought the sponge cake to his lips and popped it into his mouth, chewing slowly as he thought it over. What she said made a lot of sense, and it sounded great. The problem with that was that if it sounded too good to be true, it probably was.

"What's the catch?" The words came out mumbled, but he knew she understood him.

"No catch, Jonas. No commitment, nothing. All I want is for you to come with me and hear what this group has to say. They can protect you. They're good."

Jonas stood up shaking his head. "No. No way. There's no way I'm going out there to become a part of some rebel group of kids who think they can change the world. I've seen how that plays out, and let me tell you, Alice, it's never pretty."

"We've taken Washington D.C."

She said it in a tone that wasn't full of bravado or condescension. It was toneless and matter-of-fact.

"You... what?" Jonas sat back down.

"Our group isn't some small band of children with stars in our eyes hoping to change the world because we believe we can. We are a global group of soldiers who believe the same thing and have the power to enact *real* change, to provide *real* protection and hope. Just last week we took over Washington D.C. and the surrounding area. Another group is poised to take London and another has already marched on Beijing."

Jonas was stunned. Three of the world's largest governments were under attack or had been already dismantled. It seemed impossible.

He reached into his coat and felt the butterfly. Its soft body helped him focus.

"Alice." It was a statement. He didn't know what to do. He couldn't go into the city, though it sounded like she knew what she was doing. But what did taking over those cities have to do with his immediate problem of giant bugs invading *his* city?

"What about the ... the other things? What about our immediate safety? There are ... bugs ... watching and listening."

She nodded sagely, then said, "We know, they're everywhere. We have to find them and destroy them, and then everyone—not just our people—will be safer."

He nodded. "What is this group? Or what do you call yourselves?"

Alice sat a little straighter. "I'm a member of a group that calls themselves the Neo-Pagans. We believe that there is something bigger than traditional religion, and there's now proof of that."

Proof? He thought, then said it. "Proof?"

"Several years ago, there was a small boy in the Midwest who was dying of an unknown disease. His father discovered a cure in a fight with a creature from another dimension, Jonas. An alternate reality. There's power, Jonas. *Real* power out there. People can now do things that were only make-believe before. There's another whisper of someone similar in Mexico or South America with ties to another belief system. Our leadership has dispatched agents to discover what it is.

"We've started a war, Jonas. A war against all the greed and corruption that's brought every society in history to its knees. A war against the belief that those who *have* should *keep*, and those without, should die. Our people are dying for this belief, the belief that everyone should have *enough*. We don't care about your status, your job, or what good you bring to the world if some of your bad keeps those without beneath your boot."

She was breathing hard, now. She believed what she was saying, every word. Her face was flushed with passion, and Jonas realized, that while she may be spouting zealotry, the truth was that the world had continued while he had stayed in his glade, safe and sound. People were fighting back the beasts and he was cowering here within these organic walls.

He dusted the sponge cake stickiness from his face and hands, then wiped them on his dusty pants. "I'll need to think about it. I can't just pack up and leave on your word that every-thing is safe."

"I understand, Jonas. But I want to stay with you until you do leave. Is that okay?"

He turned away from her, feeling a sudden sting in his throat that someone would *want* to stay with him. He hadn't felt that in a long time. He nodded and glanced back over his shoulder, hoping she couldn't see the redness of his eyes. He clutched the butterfly to his chest and took a steadying breath.

He spent that day cleaning up his glade. The recent rain-storm had been accompanied by one hell of a windstorm, and all manner of leaves and branches had fallen or been blown into his sanctuary. He figured with Alice's help, they could get it taken care of. He usually kept it fairly tidy, but with the chill of fall along with the impending dread of winter upon him, he knew time was limited. This new invitation was attractive to the survivalist in him. The prospect of spending winter some-where warm and protected rather than out in the open was more than tempting. It was intriguing, no doubt about it. And when he risked a glance at Alice as she lifted logs or branches out of his way, her responding smile seemed genuine.

By the time the city was backlit by a golden drop of sun, the glade was clear of debris and back to the way it had been.

They stopped, looked at one another and dusted their hands off. He handed her a bottle of water as she wiped the sweat from her brow and sat on the log. He took a water bottle from his cubby and drank deeply. It was hard work, and the chill of the evening on his warm skin was refreshing.

He risked a fire that night. The Tressies seemed to ignore him for the most part, it would be silly to believe a fire would attract them now. And since Alice agreed, he figured it would be fine.

They talked well into the night until the stars sparkled high above them and the sliver of a moon could be seen meandering across the infinite blackness.

They talked about how Alice found safety, how she avoided danger, and the philosophy of the Neo-Pagans. These rebels didn't consider themselves better than anyone else, but they certainly believed they were doing good. Every community they entered, they left it in a better state, according to Alice. Apparently, the NP had the funding to do that. Jonas was surprised but also warmed by the idea that this group was dismantling the reigning kings one by one and making sure that those who had been ignored were ignored no longer. They were keeping people *safe*.

When they settled in to sleep—separately, of course—Jonas drifted into it slowly. Hope, for the first time, was a glinting shimmer in the distance. Far enough away that he couldn't make it out, but perhaps close enough to believe it was real.

CHAPTER 9

Alice intended to leave with him the following morning.
"I'm not ready," he said a little sheepishly as she
gathered her things and asked if he needed help getting his
stuff together.

"What do you mean? The glade is all cleaned up, and it
won't take long to pack if we tackle it together. We can probably leave within the hour."

"No," he shifted his feet. "No, that's not what I mean."

Understanding dawned on her, and she looked at him
with a mixture of pity and empathy.

"It's hard to leave what you've become accustomed to,
isn't it?"

Jonas nodded and swallowed down the lump in his throat.

"I just don't think I'm ready."

"Well...I suppose that's okay. Though, I still intend
to go back."

"Of course," he said, swallowing hard. "Yes, I know."

She approached him and wrapped her arms around his
bony shoulders. It was such a shock to him that he stood there,
dumbfounded for several seconds before resting his hands
on her back.

"Do you need anything?"

Jonas hesitated. "I could always use biodegradable toilet paper." He tried to avoid meeting her eyes. Not only was it hard to come by, but he also didn't want to give her details of how he currently handled his bodily waste.

She nodded with a half-hearted shiver of disgust that they both laughed at, and then with a wave she turned away from him toward the Traveler's Path.

Jonas hadn't planned on asking her the question, but it was out of his mouth before he knew what he was doing. "How do your people survive out there?"

She stopped, placing one hand on a tree, and looked at him intently before answering. "I assume you mean the Neo-Pagans, or do you mean the group I live with?"

He shrugged and chuckled.

She crossed her arms and leaned against the tree, smiling. She looked so relaxed, so unafraid of the terrors that could be heard even now, their gentle passage marked only by the hum of their feet scuttling across the ground or the rattle of their shells.

"Well, Jonas, we... we stick together, you know?"

"No, I get that. But what do you do about the Stalkers, the Flitters, or the Chaotic Eyes? Or God knows what else."

She tilted her head, then snapped her fingers. "Oh, that's what you call them."

Jonas nodded and looked around as if to say, *What else would I be talking about?*

She took a step into The Glade. "They aren't as bad as you think, I'm afraid."

He stared at her, aghast. "Not as *bad*?"

She shrugged. "No, not at all. I mean, honestly, you barely even notice that they're even there at all."

This time, Jonas *did* gasp. "Not there—barely notice?" He sputtered in disbelief and gestured wildly toward the sound of the Travelers. "You can hear them right now! They're everywhere! They're dangerous! Why do you think I'm out *here* instead of in *there*?" He pointed in the direction of the Burning City.

She took a deep breath and let it out slowly. "Jonas. Honestly, they're just another thing everyone has to deal with. I mean, I'm free to walk around the city, and they don't bother us much. They just keep to themselves, and we keep to ourselves. The police, the NP, we all just ... kind of go along with it."

Jonas dropped his arms and stared at her. "But Alice," he struggled to find the right words, "they're so ... big. And what about the one that hunted us the night we met?"

"I think that may have been some kind of misunderstanding. They didn't know we were good guys."

"Good guys? What are you—"

She held up a hand to stop him. "Jonas, I'm worried about you." Her look of empathy turned to deep pity. "Honestly, that's why I came out here."

He sat up a little straighter, feeling the butterfly beneath his jacket for reassurance. "Worried. About me?"

"Well, yeah." For the first time since her arrival, she looked uncomfortable. "I mean, you're out here all alone, and there's no one who can help you if you run into trouble. In fact, just over the hill is—"

"Stop. I don't go over there. There's nothing to worry about. I know it's dangerous."

She eyed him. He would later remember those eyes as looking at him suspiciously, but at the moment, it still felt like pity. "Like I said, Jonas, I'm worried about you." Her forefinger tapped her lower lip. "Would you mind if I came back later today?"

"Why?" The hair on the nape of his neck was beginning to tingle ever so slightly in warning.

"I'd like to come back and check on you, maybe bring you some of that biodegradable toilet paper. But I'd also like to bring someone with me. Someone that *I* trust, and someone I think you may come to trust, as well."

"Who?" His hair was nearly standing on end now.

"His name is Malcolm Casey. He's kind of a local legend, but he's the one that found me in that trailer where we first met, not long after you left. Took me under his wing, showed me the ropes, and helped me really see what the NP is all about. He gave me a vision, gave me purpose in a world that was turning upside down around me.

"I know you don't trust many people at all, but I think Malcolm can at least help you see the benefits of moving into the city. It's not *all* on fire." She smiled, hoping he'd take the low-hanging fruit.

He smiled in response but let it slide from his face. Meeting another person wasn't that big of a deal, but at the same time, it could set him up for some kind of trap. What if Alice was working with some kind of bug leader, and by inviting this Malcolm fellow into The Glade, he'd allow the bugs to take over his mind? It *sounded* crazy to him, even as he thought it. But he'd seen stranger things in the Before and knew that these creatures were much worse.

"I don't know, Alice. That's... that's kind of a big ask."

"Jonas, I know it is. I wouldn't have asked if I didn't think it would help." She sat down before him, and in a surprising gesture, she grasped his folded hands in her own. "Please, Jonas. Let me help you."

He let her hold his hands for a moment longer than he was comfortable with, and then he took his hands from hers. He felt the bulge of the butterfly beneath his jacket and was reminded of the Before, when things seemed normal. Maybe it wouldn't be so bad to have more people in his life. After all, he *was* lonely. And he was actually pretty tired of a diet that consisted mostly of cold soup, beef jerky, and snack cakes.

"Okay, Alice, he can come. But not until evening, okay?"

She beamed up at him, not put off at all by his resistance to it. "Of course, Jonas. I'll bring him back around sunset. Does that work?"

He nodded, a little reluctantly, and then set to tidying up the area around him, but found little to do. Alice stood up, understanding that she was being dismissed. She put a hand on his shoulder before leaving The Glade. Jonas stilled, listening. Alice's steps faded into the trees until all he could hear were the nearby rumblings of the Travelers.

When he was sure she was gone, he stopped pretending to tidy up. It was as clean as it was going to be, and there was no reason that he'd need to do anything more to it. He knew it was a small clearing in the middle of the woods. It's not like the floor would sparkle or anything.

What could this Malcolm Casey possibly offer him that he didn't already have? Would he offer some way to defeat the creatures? *Not that I actually need it*, he thought, patting the knife hilt on his belt. Flitters wouldn't be an issue. The Eyes wouldn't be a problem. *A Traveler would certainly pose a challenge with this little pig sticker,* he thought. *A Stalker?* Truth be told, he'd probably not be able to take one, but maybe he could put up a good fight.

This Malcolm character wouldn't be able to help him kill the creatures. That meant that Alice believed he needed help with other things. Maybe she was being kind, and the "help" she thought he needed was more food, or water, or better shelter. Sure, those things would be nice.

His mind wandered back to the question of betrayal, back to the curious attraction the idea held. Perhaps he should prepare for that. He could hide his knife better and maybe a few rocks strewn about strategically should he be unable to draw his knife.

Yes, he thought with satisfaction, *I'd better prepare for the worst. At least then, when it doesn't happen, I'll be pleasantly surprised. And if it does, I'll be prepared for it.*

Jonas took the rest of the day setting up The Glade to serve his needs should an ambush of some kind occur. He hoped it wouldn't. He'd come to like Alice and was pleased that she wanted to return. This Malcolm character, however, had Jonas' hackles up, and it didn't sit well with him that a supposed *leader* of the NP wanted to come to see *him*.

He was piddling around The Glade when a noise outside of the hum and rumble of the Travelers bounced its way into earshot.

Voices.

His initial thought was to run, to hide. But on its heels, he realized that Alice and *Malcolm* were coming. He looked above the treetops. The cloudless blue had been replaced with a brilliant rose that stretched across the sky, brightening beyond the trees toward the horizon.

Jonas looked around, satisfied that The Glade was satisfactorily prepped for an ambush. The refuse pile had been sufficiently buried, and the stones he'd placed around his sanctuary didn't seem to be anything but random. He'd decided that a small fire wouldn't hurt anything tonight, and it sat crackling and popping several feet away.

"Hello, Jonas." Alice stepped out into the clearing. The shade darkened her hair, but the air was alive with the sun's dying light, and it washed everything with a pinkish hue.

"Hi, Alice." His voice was a bit gravely, and he swallowed hard, surprised at how dry his mouth had suddenly become.

"Jonas, this is Malcolm."

Jonas nearly screamed as a Flitter stepped out from behind Alice. He recoiled and stepped back, tripping over his couch-log and sprawling into the dirt, scrambling back on his rump in a panic toward the place he'd hidden the knife.

His heart hammered in his chest for only a few heartbeats before the Flitter *changed.* The man's features smoothed, and the eyes that seemed so insectile now appeared to be nothing more than polarized sunglasses. Jonas rubbed his eyes with dirty palms and felt a blush rise in his cheeks as he saw not a Flitter, but a man.

"Jonas, are you okay?" Alice had reached out and taken a step toward him when he fell but nothing more.

He stood and dusted himself off. He felt his cheeks burn with embarrassment. "I'm fine," he said a bit more harsh than he meant to.

The two men eyed each other: Jonas, uncertain of this man's intentions, and Malcolm, uncertain of the other man's sanity.

Alice took the quiet moment to reach into her coat. She pulled out a package of blue and white and offered it to Jonas.

"Here," she said.

Jonas had a difficult time taking his eyes off Malcolm, but when he saw the package, he reached for it. "Biodegradable paper." He smiled. "Thanks, Alice."

"It was all I could come up with, but it's better than nothing."

Jonas nodded his thanks and tucked it behind his couch-log without taking his eyes from Malcom's face. *Was Malcom's jacket just slightly too big for his frame?*

Malcolm stuck a hand out. "Hi, Jonas. I'm Malcolm Casey. I'm in charge of the major NP force around here."

Jonas had been raised to always give a firm handshake, and the impulse to shake the proffered hand was too much. He pumped it twice and said, "Jonas," then let his hand drop.

Malcom spoke in an English accent. Not altogether surprising, Jonas knew people from all over the world. But it was surprising to hear what he would consider an uncommon accent after so long.

"I hear you've been roughing it out here all on your own, is that right? How do you do it, mate?"

Jonas shrugged. "I don't know, I just do. It's better than being out there with *them*." He nodded toward the city.

Malcolm nodded thoughtfully in return, rubbing the gray stubble on his chin and smoothing a handlebar mustache on his upper lip. "Yeah. It's not completely safe. Not yet, at least. Can we sit down?"

Jonas hesitated but decades of polite society forced his mouth open. "Of course," and they settled on his couch-log.

Jonas offered a bottle of water and a snack cake to each of them in turn, which they took but didn't open. After a few minutes of small talk—something he'd always abhorred—he remembered what Alice had said earlier, that she barely even noticed the creatures in the city. The question was burning within him and he needed clear answers. "Malcom, what do you do about them, the Tressies. In the city, I mean."

Malcolm's sunglasses glinted in the evening light as he turned his head to glance at Alice, then back and Jonas. "I'm not sure I understand what you mean. What's a—"

Jonas rolled his eyes. "Tressies, Tressoptera. Trespassers, insect-class Optera. Combine them and you get Tressoptera.

"Now, Alice said earlier that she barely notices them in the city. Out here, though, you can hear them almost constantly. Even now, they're just through the trees. Travelers. Probably hundreds of them pass by this glade each day."

Malcolm looked toward the Traveler's Path through the trees and cocked an ear to listen. He nodded and looked at Alice briefly, then met Jonas' eyes. "Yeah, I hear them. Probably leaving the city. It's not very welcoming to their kind, if you know what I mean."

Sitting still without responding gave him a moment to process Malcolm's words. Was he saying that the creatures needed a certain kind of environment to live? How would he know? Was there some kind of Tressie expert working for the NP?

Jonas didn't necessarily want an answer to those questions, so he decided to change the subject.

"So the NP. Tell me about them. You. Tell me about you. And your people. Gang. Army." It was his turn to rub the beard on his chin.

Malcom laughed good-naturedly, but there was a rasp in his voice that was unsettling, and Jonas glanced at a nearby rock on the ground.

"Not a gang, sorry to disappoint. Army," Malcom shrugged, "maybe. Really, what we are is a group of people sick of the way the world has worked for hundreds of years. The rich get richer, the poor get poorer, and the poor get blamed by the rich when their profits shrink from a billion percent to only a few hundred million. The NP found strength in," he smiled, "well... in something new. For the first time in history, there's something *more* out there, something that makes money and profits and even work ... irrelevant. For the moment, at least."

"You're talking about the... the small boy?" Malcolm nodded and Jonas continued, "Alice mentioned him. What's so amazing about him? What makes this small boy so different?" Jonas wasn't sold on it, not by a long shot. But he was intrigued.

"That's not even what's important, Jonas. What's important is that he's grown up—the small boy, I mean—and is leading the NP in this charge against the status quo. And believe it or not, we're winning. Things are changing."

It seemed nice. *Too nice*, he thought. "That's great. I mean really, I applaud the goal. But aren't people getting hurt? I mean, Alice said your people took over D.C. And *London*? Weren't there casualties? On both sides?"

Malcom nodded and glanced toward Alice, who blushed. Malcolm looked like he was more than disappointed in her, he looked angry beneath this mask of camaraderie.

"Well, that's mostly true. There were losses." Malcolm sat up straighter, and he became very instructional in his tone. "Look at any point in history, when those taking advantage of others were finally held accountable, and you'll find death and destruction. The French Revolution, the Revolutionary War, the Civil War. Hell, both World Wars, just to name some of the big ones that you Americans may be familiar with.

"But in each of those cases, those who rose up to hold them accountable knew the risks and still took them. There was destruction and death when we took D.C. and London." He nodded over Jonas, who turned. The sky was dark now, a deep blue except for a distant orange glow that barely reached above the trees. "And Chicago." There was a note of pride in his voice.

"Jonas, we're more than just an angry mob hungering for violence. We're a group tired of being *normal*, tired of being just another set of shoulders to boost the rich higher while we scramble about for the scraps they drop. If I had to guess, you're sick of it too." Jonas looked away. "Don't you want to be something *more* than just a human?"

"What did you say?" The hairs on the back of Jonas' neck began to tingle. A sense of unease crept up his arms and settled across his shoulders. The veins in Malcolm's neck were flexing in a very unsettling manner.

Malcolm's black military jacket seemed to flex as if something underneath was trying to get out. "I said," he began, "don't you want to do something better than just this?" He held his hands out and glanced around. The nearby fire had died a little but even in its deep red glow, he knew Malcolm was pointing out the squalor in which Jonas now lived. The glow of the dying fire helped hide the blush of shame that Jonas felt so deeply that his eyes stung with tears.

"It's not my fault!" he wanted to blurt out. Or, "I can't help it!" But instead, he silently pushed his shame and guilt deeper.

"There's more out there, Jonas. More than this. More for *you*. You can leave this place and come to the City with us. We can clean you up, give you a nice place to sleep, plenty of food to eat. And you won't have to use that," he pointed at the bio-degradable toilet paper, "ever again."

Jonas avoided looking at him and leaned away when Malcolm knelt before him, his hands folded as if in prayer. "Jonas, you can walk up that short hill behind you and see for miles. You can see the city, those Travelers you mentioned, and fields and ponds and all of it. *You* can make it part of a new world where there aren't 'rich' and 'poor,' there's just all of us. Come on, I'll go up there with you."

"No." He didn't mean to answer as quickly as he did, but Jonas knew that hill and anything beyond was off limits. There was danger that way, and his head ached just thinking about it.

"It's not far, mate. It won't take long." Malcolm stood and began walking in that direction. Alice had stood too, but she hovered near the log, uncertain.

"I said no, Malcolm." Jonas stood and faced the man. Lit by the low fire as he was, Jonas could see the strange contours of the man before him, if he was a man at all.

"Jonas, *please*. Don't make me get my trousers dirty again by begging on my knees." The tone was playful, but it sounded more like a command. Malcom's good-natured smile that seemed so disarming before had taken on a different cast in the red evening light.

It seemed predatory, now.

This has gone too far, Jonas thought, steeling himself.

Jonas bent to the ground to pick up several sticks. He tossed them unceremoniously on the dying embers as he made his way genially toward the man-shaped thing at the other end of the Glade. The sticks began to burn almost immediately and their hungry flames cast dancing shadows across The Glade. *His* Glade.

He felt the knife at his waist and pasted a smile as fake as the mask this creature wore. "Lead on, Malcolm."

The moment Malcom's fake smiling face turned away, Jonas lifted his jacket and drew the knife. He closed the distance in two quick steps and heard Alice speak behind him in a panicked voice, "Malcom, look out!"

Malcom turned just as Jonas shoved the knife in his belly. The look of shock on Malcom's face was rewarding. The gasp that came from him was even better.

"No!" Alice ran to Jonas and pushed him savagely to the ground, then delivered a wicked kick to his head that made the world turn grayscale for a moment. Jonas felt as if his head had been kicked from his shoulders, and he groaned, clutching it as it pounded.

When the stars in his vision cleared, he saw Alice walking from The Glade supporting Malcom's sagging form. She glanced at Jonas but was focused on helping Malcom get out. Jonas was disappointed that the blow hadn't killed him immediately, but he'd injured the creature, and that was enough.

Jonas tried to stand, but his head was still ringing. His body wouldn't let him even grasp the stone that he found to finish the job, so he contented himself with yelling at their retreating backs.

"Don't come back!" Jonas' voice echoed through the darkness, following the two retreating forms as Alice fussed over Malcolm, helping them both disappear into the evening gloom.

It looked like Alice took a final glance back, but it was too dark to be sure.

CHAPTER 10

The sounds of the Travelers were fading. Months after his initial foray into this broken world, they'd become no more than background noise. Here and there he could hear one shuffle past his glade or rumble down the Path, it's chitinous armor clacking and rattling until it faded and left him in the relative quiet.

Jonas lay on his back in his sleeping bag, one duffel bag beneath his head and the butterfly, nearly see-through with the repeated motions of rubbing his fingers across its material, lay listlessly upon his chest. He stared at the stars, which were periodically clouded over with each exhale. It was cold.

Knowing that it might trigger a headache, he braced himself as he allowed his thoughts to wander. They began to open, and he began to muse about the time just *after* the Before. His first interaction with the creatures and how terrifying they were.

"Why bugs?" the words left his mouth in a whispered white cloud then became just another part of the night.

His calculations on how long each supply run would last had been almost perfect. The first had lasted twenty-eight days, the second twenty-six, and now this third had nearly lasted thirty-one. That was three whole months that he'd lasted in this apocalypse. He'd need to go again, soon.

But really, he thought with terse curiosity, *why bugs?*

His hands caressed the threadbare butterfly without realizing he was doing it. He tried to imagine their origin. Did they come from the ground? Are there great burrows beneath the surface where they hid for millennia, only to burst from the surface right now? And if that were the case, why now? Did they run out of food? That couldn't be, he'd seen them feed on each other. If food was their priority, they had been surrounded by it in the burrows.

If not burrows, did they come from space? Is that what crashed in the city and started it burning? Perhaps they'd been on a massive ship, and there was a queen somewhere directing them from a throne of bone, shaped and grown from fallen enemies. They'd conquered the stars, but needed Earth for its ... room?

Maybe they ran out of room on their planet and flung themselves into space, landing on the first rock they could find in order to propagate their species.

His fingers scratched his beard, then returned to the butterfly. He held it against the sky, the shape a formless starless smudge.

"Or is it your fault?" He made the butterfly shake its head in denial. "Are you sure?" The butterfly nodded, its antennae bobbing in the dim light. "You aren't the Queen that all these bugs are obeying?" It didn't answer this time.

"It *is* your fault, isn't it." His fingers tightened on the stuffed animal, pressing together through the thin fabric of its body. "It's *your* fault, isn't it, you little shit." The sudden surge of anger would have caught him by surprise had he not been steeped in it. He laced his fingers together and continued to squeeze. The butterfly's wings folded on themselves, and its head and antennae arched as if in pain. "It is your fault. I know it is." The sting of tears was distant beneath the layer of helpless rage and grief. Grief for everything he lost when the butterfly— "It's your fucking fault, you bitch. You piece of fucking shit." He clenched his teeth and could feel spit foaming between them and onto his lips. He ignored the tears that began to leak from the corners of his eyes and into his beard. "You goddamn piece of shit. I fucking hate you. You did this. You caused this." He squeezed the butterfly between his two hands, twisting it. The seams began to pop in diminutive staccato sounds, *pop pop pop*.

Jonas brought it millimeters from his face. The tears cooled quickly on his cheeks, which burned with shame and anger. Spittle hit the butterfly's form as he screamed, "It's all your fucking fault!" He cocked his arm to launch it out of the glade, into the trees where the dark would enfold it in an eternal embrace. He was certain it would land soundlessly on a pile of leaves, and there, he'd forget about it forever.

Instead, he let his arm drop to his chest. He could feel the tears leaking down the sides of his face. He hugged the butterfly to him, and his tears were absorbed by the nearly ruined form. "I'm sorry. I'm sorry. I'm so sorry," he whispered into it, over and over.

That rage was still there, the grief still throbbed in his chest, but the connection to the butterfly that had formed over the past months remained. He didn't want it to be gone, but he didn't want it close.

He kissed it gently, ignoring the smell of dirt and sweat that assaulted his nostrils, then tossed it a short distance away.

Jonas's chest heaved as he was overcome with emotion. Helpless to stop it, he wept into his dirty, calloused hands. He could still hear the echo of his outburst fading into the night, followed closely by the sounds of his breaking heart.

His mind was numb, and he couldn't understand where the sudden emotion had been hiding all this time. He couldn't understand why it chose to bubble up now, to force its way into the open, into the safety of his glade, his sanctuary.

He fell asleep with questions rustling dully in his subconscious, and his dreams were full of stars and trees tumbling across his vision. Butterflies sailed through the sky, unmoving except for their wide, accusatory black eyes.

When he woke up, he relieved himself a fair distance from the glade—but not close to the ravine, of course—then sat on the large fallen tree that served as his couch. He reached into his food hole and pulled out a bottle of water, which he'd stretch until around lunchtime.

He unwrapped a snack cake and grabbed a handful of nuts from a plastic container with a black lid. The almonds were his favorite, but the cashews and pine nuts weren't too bad, even though they left his mouth feeling dry long after the water had been finished.

He felt the front of his jacket for the butterfly, then probed a little deeper when he didn't feel its familiar form in his pocket. He set his water down after swallowing the rest of the nuts and glanced around. What had started out as unease began to bloom into a panic.

Several seconds passed when he was terrified that his friend had been taken, but his eyes found the familiar black and faded form of the butterfly a foot or so behind him. He remembered now, it lay where he'd tossed it the previous night. Able to finally breathe, he put his head in his hands and breathed a deep sigh of relief. Not lost.

He looked through the trees and saw a commotion in the distance. Nervous it might become something more, he kept his eyes on it but began reaching behind him for the butterfly.

He glanced behind to make sure his hand was close, then he looked again at the distant jumble near the city.

He glanced back once more.

His eyes widened.

He heard crying in his mind.

His heart seemed to stop with a final *thump bump*.

Pain like a molten metal wire arced through his temple and into the deepest parts of his brain.

It took several minutes of catching his breath and guzzling several more bottles of water before the headache faded from a stampede to a thunderstorm.

He laid his tired head on the sleeping bag and stared up at the gray sky. Pewter clouds that shone with reflected sunlight passed across, low enough to feel like he could reach up and touch them. They looked like space whales, shifting and gliding across his vision.

He wished his head would stop hurting.

His nose had bled a bit at the worst of it, but after washing and taking a few minutes to calm down, he decided to take a walk through the trees. He couldn't go far, but would gather some wood for his fire and explore a bit.

He tried to think of happier things.

Chapter 11

Jonas fell asleep that night wishing things could be different, that things didn't have to be so hard and fast in a world that could now *literally* chew him up and spit him out. He wouldn't remember his dreams in the morning, but he would have the fleeting sense that he was missing something. He looked about in a panic in the early dawn light for the butterfly, not quite understanding why it was separated from him, then remembering that since his painful memory the day before, he'd had little desire to touch it.

His hunger overtook his laziness, and he stood slowly, stretched, and walked dejectedly toward the stump where his food was cached. He tripped over a stone that wasn't usually there and picked it up in a hasty rage. The anger that had bubbled up so suddenly hadn't actually faded; it only lurked beneath the surface.

He turned and hastily threw the rock into the woods, where it sailed straight at Alice, who ducked just in time to avoid an involuntary lobotomy.

"Shit!" Her face was a defiant mix of unease and shame as if she'd been caught with her hand in a cookie jar.

"Alice!" Jonas realized he was pleased to see her. The other night's event had turned into something resembling a bad dream, only half-remembered, and only half-again remembered honestly. "God, I'm so sorry, I didn't know you were there."

She stood up and straightened her jacket, then tucked some stray strands of hair behind her ear.

"Jonas," she began in a serious tone, "I need to talk to you."

He nodded and gestured for her to come in and sit, but when she didn't move, he said, "Is everything okay?"

She looked away and then asked, "Jonas, are you armed?"

"Am I..." he trailed off, a memory of warm blood spilling around the knife clutched in his fist rose to the surface of his consciousness. "Oh. No, it's over in the kitchen." He gestured to a knife standing point-down in the stump.

Alice nodded in a matter-of-fact way and entered The Glade without sitting. She turned so sharply that Jonas took a step back in surprise.

"Jonas, against my better judgment, I've come to warn you."

"To—"

"Don't speak, just listen," she said with harsh finality.

When he didn't respond, she continued. "The other night you injured an officer in one of the biggest armies in the world, certainly an army that can stand toe-to-toe with the United States military. Not only did you injure him, you nearly killed him. He's in stable condition right now, but we aren't sure what the future holds."

"So he's alive?"

She raised her eyebrows, then nodded. "Yes, no thanks to you."

"Yeah, I'm—"

"Despite the fact that Malcolm still lives, thank the gods, there's a large group of NP soldiers headed this way."

"Headed..."

"Yes. While there may not be a world where I could ever forgive you for what you did, especially since Malcolm and I were only trying to help you, I don't think you should be punished when there's obviously something else going on in your ... head."

Jonas hesitated for a moment, processing. Then, "Well, yeah. I don't expect you to forgive me, but why the hell are they coming after me when there are plenty of things they could be going after?"

Alice began to pace. "See? That. Exactly that. What do you mean by that? I tried to get Malcolm to understand that you believe there is something else going on out there. Do you have some kind of ability to see things that we can't?"

"What—"

"Nevermind, there's no time." She waved it away, "It doesn't matter anymore. Even if you can see things, I doubt they'd forgive you for what you did to Malcolm." She began tapping her lip with her forefinger. "Although the stories coming up from Mexico might help convince them."

Jonas approached Alice, his arms upraised to show he was unarmed. "Alice, I don't know what you mean. See things that aren't there? Like what?"

She looked at him gape-mouthed. Then, "Seriously?"

"Yes!" He was getting exasperated. A little irritated.

"What did you see that first night we met?"

"The Stalker?"

"Sure, whatever you called it. What *was* it?"

"It was a Tressie."

"Right, a Tressoptera?"

He nodded.

"What *are* they?"

"Look around, Alice!" He was beyond frustrated, now. "You tell me!"

She crossed her arms beneath her breasts.

"You're telling me you don't see the things running around out there?"

She stopped and looked pointedly at him. "See what, Jonas?"

He didn't want to say it, it was so obvious to him. "The—" was he going to?

"The—" Surely, they knew already.

"The creatures." He felt his face heat in embarrassment.

Alice's eyes narrowed. "What creatures? What do they look like?"

Jonas shrugged and put his hands in the pockets of his coat. "I don't know. There are different kinds. Some are big giant things, others are little, the size of you and me."

"Where do you see them, Jonas?"

"Everywhere, Alice. They're *everywhere.*"

A trilling tone sounded from the walkie-talkie on Alice's waist.

"They're here."

"Where? Who?"

"Jonas, there's no time, you have to go, or they're going to kill you." She began to push him away from his glade, from his safe space, toward a small hill that rose to a hilltop a hundred yards away. But that way was dangerous, and he resisted.

Instead, Jonas sidestepped the small woman and ran through the trees, passing between them easily until he could see where the Travelers roved by every day and every night.

A large black beetle was creeping its way to a stop a few dozen yards away. Another stopped behind it, and yet another charged ahead and nearly crashed into the trees before stopping. Its carapace lifted and half a dozen Flitters jumped to the ground. They were covered in what looked like black bone armor, their heads were shaped like domes with two large eyes sticking out the front. Each had a kind of round snout that drooped toward the ground. They were holding some kind of weapon and they communicated to one another with voices like rusted hinges. The clicking rumble of such a number of Flitters filled him with fear and his feet were moving before he even knew what was happening.

He passed Alice on his way out back to the Glade, barely looking over his shoulder as he heard them crashing through the underbrush in his direction. There was nowhere to go but up the hill. Up the hill that he'd avoided since finding the Glade. It was dangerous.

"Jonas!" she yelled, but he ignored her.

He scrambled up the steady rise, his feet slipped on the leaves and rocks, and he avoided cracking his elbow only by the sheer luck of grasping for branches and trees to hold him upright.

He heard Alice behind him, talking to them, but he was unable to hear what she was saying. She was one of them. She knew what they were, and she was one of them.

Part of him questioned that thought. *Why would she warn you if her goal was to help them catch you?* He silenced the voice, unable to spare the energy to answer the question.

At the top of the rise, he looked behind him. The Flitters were gaining on him, their black armor shone in the morning light, and their stocky feet were much better suited to the terrain than his old sneakers were.

His heart beat against his ribs as he saw them swarming his Glade and closing in around him, dark shapes weaving through the trees with a single goal in mind: *him*.

Jonas swallowed hard. How was any of this possible, though? When they'd come crashing through his glade, he'd had no choice but to run. Alice acted as if he was special, as if they weren't surrounded by giant monstrous bugs from another dimension. Now she was talking to them. *Why!?* He wanted to scream it. But he was out of time. There was nothing left to do but run and no direction to run but down into the ravine. *But that place is forbidden.*

Why?

It's dangerous, he heard the butterfly whisper.

He couldn't remember. But the creatures were close, too close to hesitate, so he charged down the hill, grabbing trees and branches to stop himself from tumbling end over end.

At the bottom of the hill, his headache returned in full force. He had a flash of memory—darkness lit only by an eerie red glow. He squinted against the sunlight and looked around, feeling as if an ice pick were buried above his right eye socket. Sweat beaded on his brow despite the chill air.

He wove through several trees, scrambling when he slipped and heard the creatures behind him cry in triumph.

From his helpless position on the ground, he stared ahead. A familiar, rusted metal frame rose above him. In that moment, his memory betrayed him.

The gossamer curtain that he'd woven to obscure the truth was momentarily parted, and in that miniscule gap, he glimpsed the truth.

Is that a car? He thought without actually thinking it.

The car flashed and was replaced by the corpse of a massive Traveler, sprawled against the trees, it's eyes gazing lifelessly at the sky. Then it flashed back to the corpse of a car. Then back again.

What the fuck? His head pounded and he pressed his fingertips to his temple.

Sounds of the approaching bugs filtered through the trees behind and he knew that the beasts were closing in on him. He skirted the bulk of the wrecked hulk and sat, putting his back to it, hoping that the animals would believe he'd run away.

Rocks clattered down the hillside, and his meager hope of being passed disappeared. His heart beat a rapid rhythm in his chest. He was stuck. He turned and looked through the shattered windows of the car, the autumn sun shone through the ruined metal frame and reflected off the tiny shards of glass within.

He gasped and squeezed his eyes shut as another memory came rushing to the surface.

Tinkling glass, screams, squealing tires. Something he remembered hearing many months ago. He remembered his shoes scraping across the floor of the car as he tried to move them.

Blood began to run freely from his nose, and he let it fall to the ground in viscous crimson ribbons. This was *his* wreck.

This was what had been here the whole time.

It *was* dangerous.

He turned around and rested his back against the vehicle, closing his eyes.

Voices grew louder, heavy footfalls and shouting.

There was more. There was something he couldn't remember, but knew it was there, somewhere.

The radio.

"Multiple reports... large groups... animals... vicious and aggressive..."

He remembered that night, so long ago, when he wrecked and had to take shelter in the glade. But that wasn't all, was it? It was some of it, but not all of it. There was something else, there, beneath the surface. So close he could almost make it out.

Reach deeper, whispered the butterfly.

The sounds of the animals closing in on him threatened to overwhelm his mind, but he was focused now. He knew if he could just reach a little further, he'd be able to remember what it was that was there, hovering just out of reach. He gingerly opened the curtain in his mind that he'd built to protect himself.

His neck was stiff, and the natural motion of turning his head had turned into something of a chore, and he gave up a moment later, panting.

There it was. The night of the crash.

He stood and looked through the broken windows again and saw the creatures descending upon him. Their feet were covered in thick black scales, and they stood upright on two feet, but their bodies were a mixture of colors flashing in the light. They almost looked human except for the screeching bellows that issued forth from their mouths.

He made to turn away, to run deeper into the trees that stood yards away when a bright white object appeared in his peripheral vision.

He could feel himself resist the urge to look, could feel his mind issue the command to continue turning away from it, to ignore whatever it was.

Instead, he focused his vision on it and quieted the impulse to turn away.

The object resolved itself into a body, or part of one.

His nose began to bleed worse now, and that snatch of memory of turning in the darkness after the wreck began to replay.

That same liquid wire seemed to sear its way through his mind.

His neck was stiff and the natural motion of turning his head had turned into something of a chore, but he could turn just enough to see his passenger out of the corner of his eye if he stretched against the pain.

His wife, Linnie, a beautiful redhead, lay sprawled in her seat. Her neck was bent at an unnatural angle, and her gorgeous hair was matted with gore. Part of her face was hidden from him by the dark, but the part that he could see was pulverized beyond recognition. Her airbag hadn't deployed, and the force of the wreck had slammed her face into the dashboard. The subsequent roll and tumble of the vehicle had tossed her around like a rag doll. The shattered window beside her was most likely caused by the repeated impacts to her head.

A sob began to claw its way from his throat, and he looked away, searching for anything to erase what had just been burned into his mind's eye. He felt his mind splinter, an endless void beginning to leak through the cracks.

But to his infinite misfortune, his eyes found the rearview mirror. His daughter of three slumped in her car seat, lifeless. Belinda, whom he called "Bells" because of the constant noise she made when she was both happy and sad, sat motionless in her car seat. The same red hair as her mother matted across her lacerated and broken features. Her neck was at an odd angle, and the pink car seat which had protected her very little was speckled with blood. The splinters of his mind widened into chasms and darkness poured in.

Animals.

Dangerous.

Stay inside.

Jonas began to scream. And scream. And scream.

He gave up an eternity later, panting.

That was the true memory. That was what had been behind the curtain. And as he looked at the bleached skull in the front seat, he could see where it had been caved in from repeated blows to the passenger window. He dared not look, but couldn't help himself as his gaze was drawn to the back seat, toward the car seat, toward the daughter that he wished wasn't there, but knew would be.

A tiny body lay crumpled in the back seat. He stepped away from the car, a rusted gravestone, evidence of a life better left in the dark.

And he screamed.

Tears turned the blood dripping from his chin into pink rain. The people pursuing him surrounded the monument to his mistake, but he paid them no mind. He couldn't take his eyes from the body that lay in what once could only have been a pink car seat. Even as he was forced to the ground and the remains of his family disappeared from view, the image was seared into his mind. Dust and mud stuck to his bloody face. He was screaming incoherently, and each intake of breath burned like fire as he sucked dust into his lungs.

"Don't hurt him, he's sick. He needs help. Don't hurt him. He needs *our* help." Alice yelled. His mind told him that, but he didn't care.

His body thrashed, and his throat screamed, but his mind wandered into that chasm full of darkness.

Cars. He thought in a kind of peaceful disbelief. *They were all cars. Vehicles traveling to and from the city. Had it really been burning?* He was certain it had been, but now...

His screams didn't stop until his lungs refused to cooperate and his vision began to blacken at the edges. He was screaming himself to death.

Boots appeared in his vision—black and covered in dirt. They weren't the toes of a subterranean creature, or those of an extraterrestrial creature.

And people. They weren't 'Flitters' or 'Chaotic Eyes'; they were people. How could I have been so... so...

"Insane?" A voice *sounded* in his head, but he heard it in his ears.

His thrashing stopped, but the hands and feet holding him down didn't relent.

What? he thought.

"You were chosen, and we were given" the voice continued.

Who are you?

"All you need do is call. We will answer."

So I am insane, he thought with a kind of dry, humorless resignation.

And on the heels of that thought, the grief returned. In that pit of deepest regret, he resigned himself to hell.

Uncertain of how, he begged that voice to kill him, to take him and destroy him for what he'd done, for what he'd caused.

There was no answer, but he found the strength for one final scream. A scream of rage and despair that would release his mind from its tenuous grasp on sanity. He bellowed it into the air, expelling every bit of breath that he held, releasing it in a dusty, foggy cloud.

The scream tore through the air and filled it with an electric hum. Jonas' vision faded as he continued to scream. His eyes saw nothing more than a pinprick of light, and his head swam on the verge of unconsciousness.

A silver light appeared in the air above the men holding Jonas to the ground.

Jonas was still screaming and could feel his lungs running out of air. Could feel them collapsing little by little, tiny vessels bursting and bleeding and drowning him.

The silver light began to elongate into a vertical white light. The men holding Jonas down relented a little and watched, transfixed.

Jonas's scream began to taper off as blood vessels burst in his eyes with a sickening *flump*, like rain on the surface of a pond.

The silvery line opened, slowly at first. As Jonas' scream began to waver and fade, it opened faster. A yellow claw probed the edges of the light, then another, and another until it was lined with them.

The men around Jonas' still form backed away slowly, all of them eyeing it uneasily.

Jonas was gasping for breath on the ground while also hacking and spitting gobs of blood into the dirt beneath him. He was unaware of what was above him as two small antennae bobbed and twitched their way into the view of the Neo-Pagan soldiers.

Jonas's bloodshot eyes found Alice in the crowd. The pin-prick had grown to dinner-plate size, but his vision was still crowded with black specks at the edges. Her pale face was clear, however, and after taking several deep breaths, he really *looked* at her. Her face was indeed pale, but what he'd mistaken at first for fear was actually awe, and something more, something approaching... what was it?

Reverence? he thought with confusion.

Movement above him forced his attention skyward where he came face to face with a dark purple head the size of a kitchen table and two yellow eyes the size of basketballs staring down at him. A mouth hidden behind four clicking mandibles suddenly opened wide revealing hundreds of needle-like teeth.

The creature emerged from the lighted portal in the air in segments. Its body hovered several feet above the ground as it poured from the hole in the air like a god pouring midnight. The men and women of the Neo-Pagan Army stood back as Jonas made his way shakily to his feet. The creature eyed the people before it and Jonas breathed deeply, his shoulders heaving with each breath. Blood dripped from his chin and matted his face, beard, and hair, tattooing him with rust-colored mud.

When he was able, he stood as straight as he could. Several soldiers before him fell to their knees. One held his hands up in worship, and he could see several of them wiping tears from their eyes.

"What..." he croaked. His mouth was dry, his throat was still bleeding, and his voice sounded like thunder in his ears. He glanced toward the vehicle where his wife and daughter lay entombed. They were killed because of him. Killed because he took his eyes off the road for a second. Killed because he reached for his daughter's stuffed butterfly that she'd dropped. The butterfly that she'd had since she'd been born. The one thing that calmed her on those nights when she was teething, or the nights when Linnie was gone, or the nights when it thundered.

Or the night that the NP had attacked Chicago and lit the city on fire.

That thought struck a chord.

This was *their* fault. These zealots before him were the reason they'd had to flee the city in the first place. These *fucking neophytes* were what made them leave, made Bells cry, made him reach back to look for Mr. Flitty, and made their car weave off the road and into the trees that made up the small forest between crisscrossing interstate roads.

His face screwed up in rage and regret, in sadness and despair, and he knew immediately what he needed to do. Without thinking, he bade the creature above him destroy these warmongers before him. He didn't know how he did it, but he could *feel* the creature in his mind, as if he were speaking to it on the phone.

The creature responded instantly. It poured the rest of the way out of the portal that Jonas had made with his blood and tears. Its segmented body seemed to go on forever. Clawed legs several feet long traced the body as it circled above the worshiping idiots before him. By the time the creature's full length was revealed, it was a weaving, floating pattern in the sky above them. From his vantage here, Jonas could see the road just beyond. Cars had stopped to stare and people were taking pictures, pointing, and gesturing wildly.

He commanded it to begin, and its vibrating mandibles opened as it dove straight toward the mass gathered beneath it.

Screams erupted in the mid-morning air, and they filled Jonas with a sick pleasure, a payment of sorts, from the old world to the new. A blood sacrifice to usher in this new world order.

The soldiers scattered when they realized their immunity wasn't assured. Alice ran to Jonas and begged him to stop. He didn't listen, instead insisting that the creature feed as much as it wanted.

"Jonas! Make it stop! Please!" She yanked on his bloodied coat.

The creature began to chase down others as they made feeble attempts to run through the trees. Its segmented body absorbed the sunlight instead of reflecting it, and he enjoyed the sight of its dark armor writhing its way effortlessly through the air.

"Why should I? All of this is because of you and those idiot people you follow." He shouted back above the screams.

"Jonas, this is exactly what we were talking about. *You* are exactly what we were talking about."

That gave him pause. "Me?"

She nodded vigorously, a look of rapturous excitement replacing the reckless fear from before. "Yes," she nearly whispered.

Jonas called to the creature, and it returned, hovering just above him. He felt its hunger in his own mind as it eyed Alice and waited for its master's command. *His* command.

Alice eyed the creature as well. Tears streamed from her eyes, and she appeared to Jonas as if she were looking at the face of God.

Perhaps she was.

These people deserved death. They deserved it more than anyone, in his mind. But perhaps they could be used first.

Jonas looked at Alice, still struggling to breathe properly. His voice was raw, but it was returning, slowly. "And what would the NP want with me, Alice?"

She turned her attention from the creature to look at Jonas. "For you to help *lead us*, Jonas."

He'd never felt such power before. And it eclipsed the grief that crouched at the door to his heart. He could live with that. He could live with anything that prevented him from feeling the loss that made him want to command the creature to eat *him*.

But instead, he told the creature to return to its home and to wait. He didn't know how, but he willed it.

It acknowledged the instruction in some way that Jonas could comprehend and its segmented body disappeared into the silvery light that cast no shadow.

When it was gone, Jonas thought the portal should close, and it did. The portal snapped back into a vertical bar of silver light and then coalesced into a single liquid-metal orb. It rose to his shoulder and hovered there, a multi-octave chime accompanying its master.

"Let's go to the city, Alice." Jonas agreed, with wicked anticipation. "Show me what you need me to do."

Jonas walked around the dismembered bodies of NP soldiers and followed Alice as she led them back the way they'd come. Her stoicism was betrayed by her ghostly pale skin and the number of times she swallowed hard while avoiding looking at the grisly scene around them.

When they reached the Glade, he reached down and lifted the nearly-ruined butterfly that had once belonged to Bells.

"Mr. Flitty," he said quietly.

Alice turned when he stopped. "Coming, Jonas?"

"That's not my name. Not anymore."

She hesitated, then asked, "What should we call you, then?"

He thought about it for a moment. Names were powerful. *He* was powerful now. His old life was dead, rotting alongside the corpses of his wife and daughter. Therefore, his old name would be dead, too. But he couldn't forget. Couldn't forget who caused it all. Couldn't forget whose fault it was.

And most importantly, he couldn't forget who he was fighting for.

"From now on," he said, stuffing Mr. Flitty into his pocket as the vibrating ball orbited his head and cast a silvery glow across his haggard features, "I'll be known as The Mandible King."

THE
APOSTATE

PROLOGUE

The path that would lead to the cenote was easy to spot in the moonlight. But beneath the canopy of trees, it disappeared almost entirely. Luckily, Carlos had come this way plenty of times and had no trouble following it, even in the late darkness of night. The jungle yawned before them like a massive beast as they approached. The line that separated the dusty field and the verdant forest could have almost been drawn. The forest, if the elders were to be believed, had been retreating from the area, shrinking every year. It was impossible to tell in the dark, but in the day, even the edge of the jungle had a band of brown and dying timber and grass between vibrant green and stark brown stones.

He moved a large green leaf aside that arched into the walkway with his forearm. Like a guardian too lazy to actually stop him, it creaked in protest but moved out of the way. Drops of water splashed across his hand and feet as he ducked beneath it. Carlos and his friends were too busy laughing to admit their childlike fear of the dark. Distant sounds of animals—cawing, squeaking, monkeys chittering—followed them through the trees.

Lena was the same age that he was, and she was someone he wanted to get to know better. They'd been part of the same friend group since childhood, but beyond that, he knew her very little. Her cousin Francisco had been Carlos' childhood friend, and they'd grown up together. Francisco and his girlfriend Carmen clasped hands and giggled together as they wove their way along the path. Lena was cute, but Carlos didn't like how Carmen pretended to be shy around others. She always seemed so fake to him, and while it may have been his perception of her, it was off-putting. Besides, he'd seen her skinny dip alone, even when no one else encouraged her. Shyness was a mask she wore around her parents and the adults in the church. When they weren't around, she was the quintessential "wild child."

"How much farther?" Lena asked him in a petulant voice, sagging her shoulders and pouting. Yes, he wanted to get to know her *much* better.

"Not much. It's just ahead." He nodded his head forward and grasped her hand. It felt good in his, if a little clammy. But he couldn't tell if that was his fault or not.

She let him lead her through the trees while Carmen and Francisco pretended they hadn't just been sucking face behind a large mahogany tree.

The quartet of friends picked their way through the short bushes and exotic plants that blossomed in the dank undergrowth. They stepped across a small creek, each of the boys helping their partners tiptoe onto each mossy rock before continuing on.

The path split around a massive lichen-covered tree. Leafy vines twined about the trunk and disappeared into the black-green branches high above like snakes. The sky was mostly covered by the canopy, but here and there a pinprick of light poked through.

Carlos stopped and pulled Lena close to him with a hand on her hip. Francisco and Carmen came up behind them panting, and not from the walk.

"Are we there?" Francisco peeked around Carlos' shoulder.

"Yeah," he replied a little breathlessly.

Ha'Yaxche was a cenote nestled between the massive trunks of three towering trees. At one end stood a large stone that seemed to grow from the water like a pillar. The water was smooth and crystal clear, so much so that the moon reflected in the surface with glistening perfection. Small rocks protruded from the surface like peeping creatures too shy to show all of themselves.

Carlos sighed contentedly while his three friends started chattering about how "cool" it was.

The beauty of a cenote was never lost on him. Like many of the residents in La Ventana, he descended from the Mayans. His favorite stories when he was little were the ones about creation. Like most religions, the stories focused on Ixchel and her husband Itzamna, the creator. His abuela loved to tell him the story of how Ixchel took the form of a naked young woman to show Itzamna what he was missing, then after they slept together, she became the true form of an old crone. Itzamna hadn't cared, he loved her despite her wrinkled skin and toothless grin. Together, they had thirteen children, all of whom helped create the world. Abuela said that the cenotes were the doors to Xibalba, and the gods would help usher the souls of the dead through the doorways deep within the waters. He remembered a funeral for an old man who had been her friend. He was buried "the Christian way," but some of his things were dropped into a cenote that he frequented to help his spirit find the door to Xibalba.

It was a beautiful idea, that there could be a bridge between the living and the dead, but one that creeped him out, too.

A hand lay gently on his arm, and he looked at Lena's wide, dark eyes. She arched an eyebrow and jerked her head toward the water in a "We ever gonna do this?" kind of way. The surface of the cenote was black as night but still so inviting.

He looked at Francisco and Carmen, who had both stripped off their shirts and were tugging off their pants. *Oh,* he thought wryly, *I guess they're skinny dipping.* He caught Lena's eye, who had also glanced back at the two others' rapidly increasing nakedness, and he shrugged. A bird screeched to their right, but they all ignored it.

He took off his shirt and pants, careful to avoid looking at Lena lest she see the blush of embarrassment throbbing in his cheeks, but he left his boxers on. He wasn't quite ready to be naked in front of her. And some small part of him believed his abuela would be disappointed if she heard he'd gotten busy in what was considered a holy place.

Lena stripped down to her underwear and grasped Carlos' hand. In the moonlight, her blush was almost impossible to see, but only just. He knew he was still blushing himself, and suddenly, it didn't matter. They stood shivering shoulder to shoulder and looked at the water.

"Ready?" he asked after taking a deep breath.

She nodded. "Yeah."

They moved to the edge of the water and sat on the mossy rocks there, slipping their feet and legs in slowly. Carlos shuddered as the cool water overtook his thighs, waist, and chest. Lena's body trembled, but he squeezed her hand to reassure her.

"I'm nervous," she said, whispering.

Carlos puffed up his chest and held their arms above the water. "Don't be," he said smiling, "the water's perfect."

He pulled her hand gently until her arm was outstretched, fingers entwined. Another inch and she'd either have to release his hand or slide into the water to join him.

To his relief, she let him pull her in. The water lapped gently against him as she sucked in a breath against the shock of cool water, then rested her forearms on each of his shoulders. Their faces were the closest they had ever been and he could feel her hot breath on his lips. Each time she exhaled, the water between them rustled into miniature waves, then went still again. He wanted to inhale every bit of her and had to move his torso and waist several inches away from her body. He didn't want it to be *too* obvious that he liked it.

She followed him into the center of the cenote where the water was supposedly more than ten feet deep. Carlos had heard others say it was twice that at least, but he didn't really care.

"How deep is it?" asked Lena, paddling to keep her chin above the water.

He managed a half-hearted shrug. "I don't know. Some of the other guys said they tried to reach the bottom, and it had to be close to twenty feet down. But, you know." He shrugged again. "I'm not worried."

They treaded water together. And he wasn't worried; he'd always been a fantastic swimmer.

"As long as Franky doesn't do anything stupid like dive into the water before looking to see if it is deep enough, we'll be fine."

A raucous yell from the edge of the water jerked his head that way, and he caught the naked form of Francisco running in all his teenage glory toward the water. His friend leapt from the edge of the cenote, bringing his knees up to his chest in a cannonball.

Laughing and yelling in surprise, Carlos and Lena swam out of the way as fast as they could.

Francisco landed in the water with a colossal splash. The sounds of the jungle around them had momentarily quieted. But by the time he bobbed to the surface, sputtering and wiping water from his eyes, animal cries and caws were once again the soundtrack of the night.

"Carmen, come on!" Francisco shouted, treading water and playfully splashing the other two.

"Okay!" came her voice from somewhere nearby in the darkness. Then her naked form emerged. She leapt from the stone, brought her knees up and nearly landed on Francisco. Carlos was certain that was probably Francisco's dream scenario, anyway.

The friends talked and laughed, splashing each other and competing for "best splash" and "best form" while jumping and diving off the stone outcropping that jutted out above the cenote several feet. After a while, their nakedness was barely even noticeable, though Carlos had to school his eyes several times when Carmen would ready herself for a jump.

After they became bored with that, Carmen and Francisco began to cozy up against the stone wall at the back of the cenote. Francisco and Lena made themselves scarce; there wasn't a lot of room in the cenote and based on how close their two friends' bodies were, it didn't take a genius to know what was happening.

Carlos and Lena swam to the stone slab that had been their diving board. Lena crossed her arms on the moss there and rested her head. He joined her and their fingers laced together seductively. Carlos really did think she was beautiful.

Even as a teenager, he knew that some of that was the emotional high of sneaking out, swimming in a cenote naked, and playing with friends.

Still, he couldn't ignore the attraction he felt.

"Thanks for coming tonight," he said, looking at her fingers as they caressed one another's hands.

"I wouldn't miss it," she whispered.

Carlos laughed. "Well, I was afraid you wouldn't want to come with me."

She cocked her head as best she could. "Why?"

"Well..." he hesitated. "Well, you never really showed any interest." He felt himself blushing.

Lena put a finger under his chin to make his eyes meet hers. "You never tried."

That was true. While he was more than a little popular, he'd always tried to avoid being the type of person looking for a body count. He wanted to find someone important, and that meant keeping everyone at a distance.

"I know. Sorry," he said sheepishly.

She lifted his chin again and moved close to him. "It doesn't matter. You tried eventually."

Again, he could feel her hot breath on his lips.

"Yeah," he managed. It was hard to swallow.

Lena leaned closer and Carlos' heart raced. He was sure that the water lapping between their bodies was due to the thudding in his chest.

Their lips touched, and there could be no hiding his desire for her now. But she didn't shy away from it. She pressed her body against his, and he felt a thrill of expectation race up his spine and down the arms he'd wrapped around her.

Suddenly, Lena's eyes went wide, and she jerked away from him, terror plain on her face.

"What was that?" She nearly screeched. Her arms flailed as she splashed frantically around her, looking into the water and seeing nothing.

Carlos looked as well. During the day, the water was clear as crystal. At night, they might as well try to look through a stone. He felt a mix of anger—as well as fear if he was being honest—bubble up within his chest.

"What was it?"

"I don't know, something touched my foot." She backed against the rough stone they'd jumped from earlier.

"It was probably a fish. They're small, just little tiny things. Nothing to get worked up about." He hoped that would reassure her but it seemed to only increase her panic.

"No, it was—"

She managed to get the first sound of a scream out before she was pulled violently beneath the surface of the water.

"What—" said Carlos as he reached for the place where she'd gone under. He felt with his feet but even this close to the shore, he couldn't feel the bottom.

For several terrifying seconds, Carlos seriously considered that Lena had been dragged beneath the surface to Xibalba. He had no idea what to do. Panic began to set in, but just before it could take root and grow into a frenzy, Lena burst from the surface in a dizzying spray of water, gasping and gulping huge breaths of air.

A second later, Francisco's laughing face broke the surface, followed quickly by Carmen's.

The panic changed quickly to rage, as it often does. "Are you fucking kidding me, Francisco?" Carlos bellowed.

His own rage was nothing compared to Lena's, who looked at the naked duo treading water as if she intended to murder them on the spot. A string of Spanish expletives exploded in the night. Lena splashed the two, who at least had the decency to look ashamed, before turning and, still cursing them, nearly leapt out of the water. She turned and pointed a finger at them, and to Carlos' surprise, he was even *more* attracted to her. She was *beautiful* when she was angry, the way her forehead creased in the cutest way and the ire—thankfully not directed at him—rolled off her in passionate waves. He hoped to get the chance to tell her.

Lena began to pull her clothes on over her still-dripping underwear and bra. She continued to rage at the two, who had also stopped smiling, the joke long since departed as they began to climb out of the water.

Carlos wanted to get out as well, but he was also comfortable letting Lena focus intently upon Francisco and Carmen, who'd now begun to pull on their own clothes.

Lena marched into the darkness toward town, huffing and completely ignoring Carlos. He bobbed easily in the cool water, listening to the retreating form of his friends through the jungle undergrowth. The sounds of the jungle had quieted with Lena's outburst, but soon, it would begin waking up for the day.

"You coming?"

Carlos laughed a little and shook his head as Francisco pulled his pants up and buttoned them. The anger at his friend had melted away easily. Maybe some of it was still there, but not enough to grow into disdain. His friend shrugged in that "Sorry I screwed up your night" kind of way. Carlos waved it away and said, "Yeah, I'm coming."

Francisco nodded and faded into the darkness to catch up to Carmen.

But Carlos stayed in the cenote for a moment after his three friends had left, partly because he wanted to listen to the jungle and water—it was soothing, after all—and partly because he also wanted to give his body time to calm down—he'd never live it down if he got out of the water while still pitching a tent.

He turned to look at the stone wall at his back. The way the moonlight reflected off the water and cast shimmering lines across its face. The water's surface was like rippling black glass, and it made him both uneasy and excited. He knew there was nothing beneath him, but the thrill of its depths made him feel *alive*. As deep as it was, he almost felt like there was no bottom at all, just a pool of the clearest water that reached all the way to the center of the Earth.

Movement caught his eye, and he peered into the jungle night around the few rocky outcroppings nearby.

"Hello?" he said cautiously. "Lena?"

A face peeked from the side of a rock and his heart jumped into his throat.

"Uh..." he said shakily. "Hello?"

The fear of all the possibilities told him to turn and get out of the pool. Instead, he found himself swimming toward the person, a woman, he was sure. The rock had hidden most of her face and the water most of her body, but he would have sworn...

"Wait," he said as he saw more movement duck behind a rock, just a little further on.

His hand reached for a rock and he used it to pull himself faster through the water. The small waves broke around him, lapping against the rocks in dark ripples. What he saw in the moonlight behind the stone made it easy to ignore how it had nearly broken the skin on his palm.

She was there, only a few feet away, sitting on a rock completely nude. She was older than he was, but she was still young enough to be stunningly gorgeous. The moonlight spilled across her naked body, and he felt his breath catch in his throat. Her skin glowed a ghostly silver in the wan light while tiny beads of water sparkled like crystal on the curves of her breasts before sliding seductively between them. Her long legs were spread, and despite his best efforts, he couldn't look away from her.

She smiled as if she knew it, too.

His throat was dry as he swam toward her, transfixed, and she smiled in a way that could only be taken as an invitation. Her teeth reflected the moonlight, but her eyes seemed to absorb it. The invitation Carlos suspected was confirmed when she reached between her legs and began touching herself. She closed her eyes, clearly enjoying it.

Carlos tried to swallow but found it impossible to do anything but watch. Unblinking, he inched nearer to the specter he saw before him while, in his mind, he thought he heard the church bell ringing. Some part of him, some distant part, was telling him to turn away, to close his eyes and get as far away as possible. But each toll of the bell was a stroke of his hands through the water.

She opened her eyes and looked at him with a knowing, playful grin.

He tried to smile, but his mouth wouldn't respond. He stared at her, slack-jawed as if held by a spell. When he reached the smooth rock on which she perched, he stared up at her. She seemed tall. Much taller than himself, and large. Not in size, he thought, but in the way the moonlight seemed to bend *toward* her and how the area around him *flexed* with each of his breaths.

Can I touch? he thought, knowing it was out of character for him but unable to stop himself. Treading water with one hand, he reached up toward the woman's bare leg. Ever so slowly, the distance between his finger and her thigh closed.

Stop! he heard a voice within him say.

It's only a touch, replied a voice in his head. It could have been his own.

He expected the soft, inviting skin of her inner thigh to be warm and welcoming. He expected to be drawn in by the invitation of her smile. He watched his fingers close the distance until there was a sliver of moonlight between her thigh and his outstretched fingertips.

Instead of a sensual warmth, however, the skin his finger touched was cold and clammy. Like the skin of someone after the fever breaks.

Like someone too long in the water, he thought.

The spell momentarily broken, he looked at the woman's face.

The smile was still there, large and inviting. But instead of a dimple-cheeked grin full of moonlit teeth, a gaping, wrinkled, toothless grin spread across a weathered and ruined face. The invitation of sex was replaced with a predatory gaze.

Carlos jerked his hand back and began to scream. Only, his voice wouldn't obey him.

The woman—if it was a woman—loomed over him and seemed to expand, absorbing the air and light around them until his neck craned up at her.

Carlos couldn't look away from the terrible grin, but in his periphery, he saw her naked breasts sag toward his upturned face. She put a gnarled finger to her lips.

"Shhhh," she croaked, and with the other—the one that she'd been touching herself with—she gently caressed his cheek.

Panic exploded within him and he was helpless to stop it. Eyes wide, he told his legs to kick, his arms to plunge into the cool water, to propel him away from this nightmare. But his legs remained still, his arms floating gently at his sides.

Kick, you pinche pendejo. Kick! he screamed at himself.

The leering grin above him grew, as if he'd said it aloud.

Carlos felt a helpless tear of despair leak from his eye and dribble down his cheek. The old woman moved her finger to catch it before it could drip into the water. She smiled as she lifted the finger to her mouth and sucked the tear seductively from an old and gnarled knuckle. Her tongue moved around her finger like a flailing worm, and he felt bile rise in his throat.

Then Carlos began to sink. His gaze was trapped by those haunting, glowing eyes, and his body was heavy as stone.

Once more in desperation, he told his arms to move, his legs to kick, and his lungs to inhale. Do... do *anything*.

But slowly, he sank lower into the water.

Please, please, please, he thought, screaming it at the top of his mental lungs.

His chest and nipples sank below the surface.

Then his chin.

One final struggle was all he could manage, but he was a prisoner in his own body. As helpless as an infant in the paws of a jaguar.

Even still, he held onto an impossibly small glimmer of hope, believing that this was all a dream, or perhaps he'd hit his head and he'd wake up back in his bed or maybe even on the shore of this cursed place.

But that hope died when a snake as black as death slithered across the old woman's shoulder. Its tongue flicked in and out, and its scales absorbed the moonlight instead of reflecting it. The woman reached over her shoulder—never taking her eyes from his—and stroked the snake's head, watching intently as Carlos' staring eyes sank beneath the surface.

For a moment, he could see her disjointed and wavering form through the shimmering surface of the water. Then it grew, blotting out the moon, before breaking through the surface and becoming terribly clear.

Inches from his own face, she followed him into the depths, always maintaining the same space between them but never moving an arm or leg to kick. It was as if she were propelled by some other means, and the water had no affect on her ability to move or breathe. The snake was gone, he noted distantly, but he didn't care. He was dying, and this creature was letting it happen.

His vision began clouding at the edges, dark spots flashed in his vision, obscuring the water around him or the woman's mouth, but never her eyes. Even now, deeper and deeper where the moonlight never reached, they still glowed with a pale, milky light, an ancient malice smoldering within.

By the time his toes touched the gritty sand at the bottom of the cenote, he was already dead.

CHAPTER 1

Father Ramón Gonzalez—oftentimes called "Padre" by the small congregation of his church—sat with his sore and dusty soles soaking in the cool water of a local cenote called La Puerta Fantasma. La Puerta was a large, spring-fed pool a short walk into the jungle of Belize. In English, the cenote was called The Door of Spirits, but it was an old name, and probably fed by both Mayan culture and local legends. The tiny fish that lived in the cenote tickled his toes as they ate the dead skin from his weary feet while he kicked them lazily back and forth.

"Buenos días, my friends," he said to the fish as they darted back and forth around his ankles.

They didn't respond, but he imagined if they could, they would greet him in a similar manner. By now, they probably knew his feet very well, for all the time he spent doing the same thing he was doing now.

This was his favorite place, and not many in town knew of it. This cenote was a short hike through the deep jungle, and while it wasn't far, many were unwilling to risk snakes or worse. The real trick came when he had to climb through a large curtain of vines and leaves that otherwise looked like a wall.

Ramón had no such qualms about the flora and fauna. He'd been visiting La Puerta since he was a little boy and felt connected to it in more ways than one.

There were other cenotes. Thousands of them, actually. Some were tourist attractions like Media Luna near Cancun. Others were similar to this one, mostly undisturbed. But this was his special cenote.

Ramón skipped a rock across the glassy surface of the crystal-clear water. The rock bounced once, twice, and then three times before the skips were too close together to count. Then it bounced off the far wall of the cenote—a massive rock wall that arched back toward him thirty feet above the water. The ripples disturbed the perfect image of the bottom of the twenty-foot-deep pool, but after several seconds, the surface settled, and he could once again see the white sand and gray rocks that littered the bottom. Deep as it was, they took on a green hue that reminded him of death.

Reminded of that feeling so many years ago brought a verse immediately to mind. He quoted it effortlessly, having memorized it years ago and recited thousands of times. "It is by grace you have been saved, through faith—and this not from yourselves, it is the gift of God—not by works, so that no one can boast."

He sighed.

He'd nearly drowned here when he was six. That had to be close to thirty years ago now. He'd always been a strong swimmer; in fact, until that fateful day, he remembered loving the water. That day, though, something had happened that he couldn't understand. He remembered jumping into the cenote, just as he had a hundred times before. But when his head plunged beneath the surface, he found himself paralyzed. He couldn't move. And instead of his body bobbing to the surface, it began to sink deeper into the water despite his increasing panic.

He skipped another rock and remembered the panic as his mind reeled and demanded his legs to kick and his arms to claw their way toward the surface. But nothing happened, and he sank until his toes touched the gritty sand at the bottom of the pool. The sun shone gloriously through the surface, which at the time seemed close enough to touch. But it wasn't. It was more than fifteen feet above him. And just beyond the surface, the air that his burning lungs now cried out for in desperation. Black spots had then begun to appear at the corners of his vision, and the stark reality of truth hit him.

He knew he was drowning. He opened his mouth to scream. He still couldn't think why, but of course, when he did, he swallowed a mouthful of water, sealing his fate.

By all rights, he should have drowned. In almost every definition of the word, he actually had. He remembered thinking, *At least the last thing I'll see is beautiful.* He simply hadn't *died.*

But just before his lungs exploded and he no doubt would have died, an angel saved him. Staring up at the surface, body rigid, the heavenly creature descended from the sky and obscured the wavering liquid light. That was all he remembered. He woke up alone on the edge of the cenote, soaking wet and coughing up blood, but alive with no recollection of how he got there.

Since that time, he'd come to believe that the cenotes were a place of magic and beauty, and he'd been attracted to them since the old ones in his family had told the grandchildren stories of their ancestors. The Mayans believed cenotes to be a sacred place and a doorway to the underworld.

He picked up another stone and quoted another verse, this one Mark 16. "Whoever believes and is baptized will be saved." He threw the stone at the water where it splashed and immediately sank without skipping. "Quite the baptism," he whispered wryly.

"It was believed," he heard his abuelita croak in her old and quivering voice of his childhood, "that the Mayan Goddess Ixchel lived within the cenotes and that she could travel to any cenote by secret passages that connected them beneath the earth." She licked her lips between missing teeth. "New mothers were brought to the cenotes before and after child-birth, and the Goddess would bless them and their children. Supposedly, Ixchel and her husband Itzamna had thirteen sons, all of whom created all heavens and hells and everything in between."

Ramón, despite being a person of faith, didn't believe that part of it. But being here stirred some deep part of him that he didn't understand.

He knew deep down that angels were real. He'd been saved by one, after all. But he'd never experienced anything like that in the years since. He'd donned the collar and cas-sock of the church based on his experience. Angels were real; therefore, God was real. It was a simple understanding that he'd never truly *comprehend*, but he could serve, nonetheless.

In the decades since, however, his faith had begun to wane. Whisps of doubt had begun to eat away at what had once been a rock-solid belief in an unseen and omnipotent God. He remembered the angel, remembered it very well. But now, it seemed like merely the dream of a dream holding that belief by a thread.

He skipped a rock angrily, and it skipped once before clattering against the wall and disappearing into the greenish depths.

It didn't help that he'd just performed his sixth funeral in as many months.

That's what had brought him to La Puerta today. He wanted to feel close to where he saw the angel because the angel hadn't saved Carlos Garcia.

He picked up another rock to skip across the surface but lost the desire. He let the smooth stone fall between his fingers then watched the ripples dissipate. The tiny fish continued to nibble his toes, and he stared down at them. He was a god to them, no doubt. A massive giant with power over life and death for them. Their existence was simple: eat and perpetuate. They swam in the crystal waters without a care in the world, blind to the snake, bird, or eel that may venture this way now and again.

Carlos had been swimming nearby with friends when they found him floating in the water, facedown, minutes after diving in. They suspected that he hit his head on a rock beneath the surface, and a large gash on his skull confirmed it. He'd been fourteen, and he was one of those kids that had the looks and the personality to become something more than just another farmer in La Ventana. Nothing wrong with farmers, of course, but Carlos was kind and handsome and gentle with the village children. He would have been great.

And now he was gone.

Father Ramón kicked his feet, watching the slow ripples and waves lap gently against the rocks. "Everyone who calls on the name of the Lord will be saved," he said quietly and wondered if Carlos had called on the name of the Lord. Would he have been saved? Who can know?

Carlos' mother Elena and his father Diego, both from the same village where he now lived, were heartbroken. Carlos had been their only child after his violent birth rendered Elena barren. And now they were childless.

Ramón heaved a sorrowful sigh as deep as the cenote and leaned over the water to wash the mud from his hands. Then he brought his feet out of the water, stood, and stretched, listening to his knees and back crack in protest.

"Oh, that's good," he groaned, sliding his wet feet into his dusty sandals once more.

He never understood why God took the young, but He had a plan, and it wasn't up to Father Ramón Gonzalez to know. Ramón must simply continue pursuing the Lord and teaching others how to live their lives according to His Word.

Not an easy path, but his treasure was in heaven, after all.

Ramón stepped over rocks and through the curtain of leaves, vines, and branches, making his way slowly back toward the trail that would lead him toward town. After a moderate walk, the trees of the jungle gave way to a wide expanse of dusty earth. Some small, withered trees and scrub grass reached weakly from the cracked and jagged mile between the jungle and the walls of the town in the distance. He dusted the seat of his cassock off as he walked, and prayed that God would give him strength and wisdom. He would need both for the service this Sunday. These were always hard following a funeral, especially for one as young as Carlos.

CHAPTER 2

Ramón wound his way through the jungle to where the lush undergrowth met the harsh grasp of near desert. The dust puffed up around his feet as he strode across the dry ground toward town. The comfort and shade of the large trees was immediately missed as sweat began to drip down his temples and brow. Not too distant, the dusty path led to La Ventana, his homely little village of several hundred citizens. From the edge of the trees, he could see the low concrete wall running the perimeter of the village that had been installed many years ago by Miguel Castellano, the then-mayor of La Ventana. Its white paint had chipped and cracked, revealing the dull gray beneath, but rumor had it that he'd built it to help keep the jungle at bay. In the half-century since then, the jungle had somehow retreated almost a mile from the low wall.

The buildings beyond wavered in the heat, but even from this distance, it was easy to see that they were simple. Made mostly of brick and wood, the people of La Ventana did what they could with what they had. Some boasted more modern concrete walls while others were cobbled-together monstrosities that rose above the other dwellings' metal roofs.

He sighed contentedly in the heat, but not without a small bit of anxiety. His little village was far enough away from the touristy locations like Playa del Carmen and Cancun that no one paid much attention to them. Unfortunately, every now and then a tourist would stumble upon the town. When that happened, Padre was quick to take the lead, as the current mayor was a sniveling little mouse of a man named Luis Brago. The man reminded Padre of a dog that had been scolded as a puppy—at the first sign of conflict, he'd roll over with his paws in the air. Not literally, of course, though Padre chuckled at the thought of it. Sometimes it seemed a close thing.

His steps brought him to the wrought-iron gate of La Ventana, just like they always had, and he bent near the concrete anchors to retrieve the satchel he'd left there. It was full of old things, but he kept them because they were comfortable. Small things that he may or may not need at any given time.

He pulled it over his shoulder and continued toward his church, a whitewashed one-story building near the center of town. The bell tower, if it could be called such, rose above the rest of the area and could be seen fairly easily from most parts of town. He liked that about his little church—you always knew where to go if you needed help. And Ramón enjoyed helping.

"Buenos días, Padre," an elderly woman croaked at him from behind a fruit stand.

"Buenos días, doña," he said and stopped to gently grasp her hand and kiss her cheek. The woman was ancient, but she smiled up at him with a gap-toothed grin. Her wrinkled leathery skin twitched as she smiled at him. It was such a picture of tangible joy that it nearly brought a tear to his eye.

"¿Cómo está, Sofia?" he asked.

"Muy bien, gracias." Her tongue peeked through the gap in her teeth on the s, then she switched to English and leaned in conspiratorially. "I heard that the young woman Julia has returned. She was looking for you earlier."

Ramón tried to ignore the flush that began creeping up his neck and cheek, but the smile that Sofia gave him told him the flush was obvious.

He cleared his throat. "What did Julia say she wanted?"

Sofia shrugged her bony shoulders beneath the once-white dress. "No sé, pero. I think she simply wanted to talk." Sofia moved her hands in a "maybe yes, maybe no" motion. "She's waiting at the church for you. Praying, of course." The sly smile on her dry lips told Ramón exactly what Sofia thought of that.

"Thank you, Sofia. Have a good día."

Sofia nodded at him and leaned back in her wooden rocking chair as he continued toward the church.

He was sweating, now. Well, more than what the heat drew out of him. His calm and pensive morning at the cenote was forgotten at the prospect of speaking to the gorgeous young woman named Julia.

She'd come to the village years ago, perhaps ten. Ramón was only slightly older than she was, but to him, she hadn't aged a day in the time he'd known her. If anything, she'd grown more and more beautiful with each passing day.

He straightened his cassock after taking the church steps two at a time toward the large wooden door. He ran a hand through his graying hair and grasped the metal ring that served as a doorknob.

The old hinges squealed and echoed through the mostly empty church. Light from outside spilled in, showing a large room with many pews set in parallel rows. Only two of the rows were occupied.

A man sat in the first row, kneeling and praying silently—probably Juan Alvaro by the look of his bald head.

The only other person in the church occupied the second pew on his right. Dark hair the color of chocolate cascaded down her back and over the back of the wooden pew. She turned, and even though he was standing in the doorway, he knew that *she* knew it was him.

He let the door close behind him, which banged loudly in the silence. Julia had already stood and swept into the aisle, a smile on her face and a blush on her beautiful skin. Padre's hands felt clammy, and he nervously wiped them on his pants as she approached. The blue dress she wore swished in the silence, but to him, she glided across the ground without any effort.

She was everything to him.

"Hola, Padre," she said in a soft voice.

Her brown eyes were wide, and when she blinked, he felt that he could forever stare into their beauty .

"Padre?" she said, stepping closer and placing a hand on his arm.

That broke the spell, and he cleared his throat, blinking several times.

"Yes, I'm sorry, Julia, I was lost in thought." He coughed. "It's wonderful to see you. Did you enjoy your travels?"

She smiled, and he felt his heart explode. "I did. It was the time I needed with my sister. But it is good to be back. I missed La Ventana and the people here. How was your morning?"

Ramón didn't want to burden her with news of Carlos, even though she'd probably already heard. "It was very pleasant. I spent some time at the cenote and thought about a great many things. The cenote is a place of peace and tranquility for me, as you know."

She nodded. "There is no place like it."

"I stopped to chat with Doña Sofia. She said you needed to see me. Is everything alright?"

"Oh," she blushed and looked at her dusty black shoes. "I... I... wanted to talk to you about something. But I don't know if I should burden you with it."

Padre's face grew concerned and he gestured for her to sit on the nearest pew. "Julia, you are not a burden, and you know that I'm here for whatever you need." *Was that too forward?* He thought with mild panic.

Then he calmly said, "What is it?"

Julia sat and her fingers fumbled with each other.

"Julia. You can tell me anything."

She nodded and a tear fell into her lap.

"It's my sister."

Relief flooded through his veins, but he kept his emotions in check. "Is she well, Julia?"

"She's fine. She's just..." She swallowed hard, and when she spoke, she picked her words carefully. "My sister is ... unique. She has very ... firm beliefs in the way that people should behave."

"That's not so uncommon. There are plenty in La Ventana that meet that same description."

Julia hesitated. "Yes, but my sister believes that it is her job, or even responsibility to ... show them the error of their ways."

"Not to downplay this, Julia, since this seems of great concern to you, but that is still not so uncommon. There are a small number in the world who take it upon themselves to correct the many. Some do so gently while others..." He moved his palm face-down, back and forth.

She nodded and swallowed hard. He could see the smoothness of her throat tighten in the sunlight streaming in from the windows of the church.

"Yes, I know that. She seems to be more of the second type."

Ramón nodded sagely. "I see."

"She is a wonderful sister, and she knows what is right and wrong, and she used to have a much better way of handling things. But then... I don't know, things changed, the world changed, and she refused to change with it."

This wasn't a rarity. Ramón had experienced this difficulty plenty of times. Many of the older members of his congregation didn't understand why things had to change. When he was a little boy, a single rude response to a parent would result in a smack across the mouth. Now, he saw parents gently redirecting their children. It seemed a good change, but he also saw the scowls and scoffs of those old-timers as they looked upon the new way of things as a step backward instead of a step forward. Tradition was hard to change.

"Julia," he said, gently placing a hand over hers. "What is it that I can do for you and your sister."

She grasped his hand in hers, and he thought his heart would gallop out of his chest.

"I believe the only thing left, Padre, is to pray for her. Though I will admit, I believe that a change of heart is impossible." She squeezed his hand, and his vision blurred at the edges, but he nodded.

"Then pray for her we shall. What is her name?"

"Her name is Alejandra."

"Pray with me," he said softly.

Together, they bent their heads, and Miguel prayed for Alejandra, all the while holding hands. Miguel tried to keep his voice steady, but when it shook, he silently prayed Julia would believe it from emotion and not excitement at her touch.

When he'd finished, she squeezed his hand and released it. A small part of him sighed in regret, but he smiled. "I will pray for Alejandra every morning. I believe that our Lord and His saints will work wonders for her heart."

Julia bent and kissed Ramón on the cheek. He felt the softness of her lips and closed his eyes, savoring the nearness of her body to his own. He breathed deeply, and instead of getting the stink of human sweat and the dirt of the world, his nose was filled with the pleasant aromas of vanilla beans and exotic flowers.

"Thank you, Padre," she whispered in his ear.

He swallowed, and she leaned back to face him again. "Of course, Julia. Please, come by any time. I would love to see you and pray with you. Of course."

She nodded and stood. He remained seated but nodded as she thanked him again.

He watched her walk out the doors of the church with a longing in his chest that was almost unbearable.

"Ay, Dios mío," he whispered and sagged into the pew.

CHAPTER 3

Ramón spent that evening at the wake for Carlos. He tried to spend much of his time with Elena and Diego while others came to visit their humble home. Many from his congregation came to wish them well and pray with them. Julia stopped by briefly but didn't stay, regrettably. The group of friends that had been with him that night stopped by as well. Even as young teenagers, Ramón could tell they *wanted* to be there. They weren't forced by their parents to stay, but they left shortly after Ramón arrived. Overall, the family that filled the tiny home made his heart full.

"Thank you for coming, Padre." Elena wiped a tear away and hugged the priest.

"Yes," Diego interjected, eyes swollen and red. "Thank you for stopping by. Carlos would—" his voice broke, and his lips trembled.

"Of course, my friends. I'm honored." Ramón held one of Elena's hands and one of Diego's. He said a brief prayer with them, followed by a brief intercession on Carlos' behalf to Saint Philomena, the Wonder Worker.

By the end of his prayer—which had stretched on longer than he'd intended—Elena was honking her nose into a kerchief, and Diego had stepped outside for some air.

"I understand how hard this is for you. Please, allow me to help in any way I can. The church is open to you, and I would be honored to assist if I can."

Elena nodded, too emotional to respond, and Ramón moved along to allow more family and friends to offer condolences to Carlos' parents.

In the kitchen, he bumped into Raquel Perez and her husband Juan, two more members of his congregation.

"Hello, my friends," he said with a smile as he put several small strips of meat on a plate.

"Oh, Padre," began Raquel, who dabbed at her eyes with a green handkerchief. She was wearing a simple black dress and black shoes.

Juan held his hand out to shake Ramón's free one. "It's wonderful to see you. Thank you for coming to honor Carlos and his parents." Juan's simple white button-up showed patches of his hairy stomach in gaps between buttons that held the belly at bay with a thread.

"Of course, Juan. Of course. It's an honor to celebrate the life of such a wonderful young man of God.

"You know," he said with a chuckle. "I remember baptizing young Carlos under the watchful eye of another, more experienced priest. Do you both remember?" He took a bite of the meat on his plate.

Raquel and Juan looked at one another, prim smiles creasing their cheeks.

Ramón continued, "Once when he was of course only several weeks old, and once again when he was almost ten."

"I remember that!" exclaimed Raquel.

"Yes, do you remember why he said he wanted a *second* baptism?"

Juan laughed quietly and put a hand across his ample belly. "Sí, I do. He'd read about those Summer Camps in America and how the Christians there would baptize in the lakes."

"That's right," began Ramón, but he was cut off by Raquel.

"He came to school one day and wouldn't stop talking about it. As his teacher, I heard nothing else from him all day! I had no choice but to talk to Elena and Diego about it, or I'd never hear the end of it!"

"We all went to a cenote, Media Luna, and did the baptism there. I asked him to enter the cenote calmly, but instead of walking in—" he started again, but Juan and Raquel spoke in unison over Ramón.

"He jumped in!" They exclaimed loudly. Several of the attending mourners turned their heads and glared in disapproval, but Juan and Raquel ignored them. They schooled their laughter after a moment, and Ramón found himself shaking his head and chuckling quietly.

"Yes," he whispered fondly. "Yes, he was so happy."

"But his father and I," said Elena from Miguel's right shoulder, "had a very difficult time getting him to sleep that night."

Diego stood behind her, the ghost of a grieving smile on his lips.

Seizing the opportunity, Ramón looked at each of them in turn, and with a note of finality, spoke. "This is why, my friends, the Lord instructs us to love one another. Grief is the price we pay for love." He spread his hands. "And I know it may be hard right now, but I have no doubt that you would pay it a hundred times over just to close your eyes and remember that boy as he leapt into the cenote."

Elena hiccupped, began to cry, and nodded. Diego nodded once, but Raquel and Juan looked sympathetically between the dead boy's parents.

"God loves us, and therefore, we love one another. It is a reflection of His love of us that allows us to open our hearts. My friends, keep your hearts open. May the Lord bless you."

Ramón, feeling very good about his short sermon, turned to leave.

"But Padre." It was Diego who spoke, shakily with hesitation. "If He loved us so much, why would He cause us such pain?"

The silence that followed was absolute. If Ramón had an answer, he couldn't bring himself to speak it, not right then. Conversation in other areas of the house continued, but Ramón heard only a distant ringing in his ears.

He took a deep breath and sound began to return. The town priest adopted a sympathetic expression.

"That is one of the great mysteries of our faith, isn't it, my friend? Out of all the pain we experience in the world, perhaps this is the cruelest."

None of the others spoke, and Ramón felt his heart beating faster and faster. He was glad the lights were dim in the home because they may have seen the blush that crept up his neck and swallowed his face. The blush that followed his lie.

"Excuse me," he said and left the house out the kitchen door.

The night air was barely cooler than the day, and sweat immediately popped out across his bare lip. He blamed it on the heat, but he knew that was not what caused it. It was from Diego's question.

It was cruel. A loving god wouldn't allow his children to experience pain so deep, so precise, that it made them question their own existence.

But he does, Ramón thought coldly.

His mind was filled with disquiet as he walked back to the church in the dark. It was a mix of shame and apprehension. That a priest of his station would question his own faith, it was unconscionable. He certainly knew he wasn't the first to experience doubt or shame. After all, Saint Augustine did plenty of questioning before he came to understand his faith in all its depth.

That made Ramón feel a little better.

But Ramón didn't feel that his doubts were spurring him toward enlightenment as Saint Augustine's were. Instead, he felt that his thoughts were leading him further from what he'd always considered truth. He'd been raised in the Catholic Church. He knew its tenets, knew the rituals, knew the scripts and tasks.

And yet, all of those things were losing their value. And along with it, his purpose.

"Padre," muttered a guttural voice from the darkness.

Ramón glanced around. The streets of La Ventana weren't lit in any pattern. What little light there was came from the open windows and doors of nearby homes and buildings, and one lamp on either side of the church doors. Ramón was standing at the foot of the stairs that led up to the church doors, but there was a shadow that detached itself from the wall nearby and stumbled its way toward the priest.

"Who's there?" Ramón asked. He wasn't afraid, there was very little that he feared—other than water.

The form walked—or shambled—its way into the ambient light, and Ramón frowned.

When Ramón had been barely ten, his abuelo had pulled him aside after one particularly long mass one sunny afternoon.

"Ramón," his abuelo had said in Spanish, bending down on a knee in the dirt and looking him in the eye. "Every town has three things." He lifted three fingers and ticked them off with each word.

"A priest, a whore, and a drunk."

"Papa," said his mother in stern disapproval, but the old man continued as if she hadn't said a thing.

"Which one will you be, Ramón?"

He'd only been ten at the time. His abuelo had brought it up because Miguel had asked what it took to become a priest. Incidentally, that same day, a man had come into the church and stumbled his way to the altar at the front. Father Benecio had asked some of the men in the church to help the man to his office, all the while Ramón's abuelo had scoffed and shifted uncomfortably in his pew. He'd caught Ramón's eye and glared at him, daring the young man to even think about drinking in the future.

Ramón would never touch the stuff as a result.

But he would also, as a result, become a priest.

The man before him now was very much like the nameless drunk that had come into the church all those years ago. Only, this man wasn't nameless.

"Good evening, David. You look unwell, can I help?"

David swayed on his feet in the dim light and pointed at Ramón. When he spoke, his speech was slurred and almost incoherent. Ramón translated it as he had many times before and then nodded.

"Thank you for saying so. Would you like to come into the church and lie down? Perhaps sleep off some of your ... weariness?"

David shook his head and then turned toward the church. A string of drool sparkled in the dull light from the church's lamps.

The drunk man stared up at the steeple with its red tile roof and white plaster walls. The bell that hung there hadn't been rung regularly in ages. Though on special occasions like Christmas Eve and Easter, it would resound through the streets of La Ventana.

David stood in a wide stance, toes pointed in, and looking very unsteady. Ramón approached him and gently placed a hand on the man's back and forearm.

"Let me help you, David." Ramón spoke quietly, but with the kind of force that would convince David instead of scare him away.

The man replied with something more like a grunt than a word, but he allowed Ramón to help him up the steps and into the church.

After several trips into the pantry, Ramón was able to get David a blanket and several pillows so the drunk man could sleep in one of the pews in the back of the church. The man thanked Ramón in his drunken vernacular and was snoring before the priest had locked the doors.

Perhaps, despite the cruelty of losing a child, there was also goodness and mercy in the mundane. Losing a child couldn't be outweighed by making a pallet on a pew in his church for the town drunk, but perhaps it did tip the scales back from hopelessness. Just a little.

Ramón fell asleep easily that night. He dreamed of his angel, only this time it had Julia's face. Her hair floated weight-lessly in the water around her head as she descended toward his drowning form. He didn't black out, like he actually had in life. In his dream, Julia kissed him, and he was filled with such life and excitement, that even in his dream he felt his heart hammering in his sleeping chest.

He woke up with a smile and mild embarrassment. But he was also pleased. One of the great things about priesthood was his ability to keep secrets, even from himself.

It wasn't uncommon for David to be gone by the time Ramón opened the church doors to let in what little morning breeze there was. This morning was no different. The blankets were folded like they always were and stacked carefully at the end of a pew. David would find Ramón when he needed help again, and Ramón would give it. Always. It was his job, after all.

CHAPTER 4

He visited the cenote twice more that week, reveling in the cool water and enjoying the sounds of the jungle around him. He spoke to the water, sharing his hardships and inner thoughts, his fears and his desires. He even shared his dream with the water. His voice shook as he spoke the words, barely above a whisper, afraid that the trees would hear him. But the words tumbled out of him, and he felt as if voicing them was a sin in and of itself.

But the cenote listened without response, except for the quiet lapping of ripples against stone. The water reflected the harsh sunlight, splashing green and blue dancing designs across the stony wall above it. The forest responded with its usual mix of birdsong and monkey calls, and in this moment, he was content.

Something in the water caught his eye. It floated near a submerged rock, just a small distance from the safety of the stone shore where he stood. The water, at its deepest, was close to twenty feet. Even a few feet from where he now sat, it was at least eight or nine feet deep.

He stared at the floating item and, disgruntled at the thought of someone throwing garbage in the cenote, he searched around nearby for a stick long enough to fish it out.

Holding onto a tree with one hand and grasping the thicker end of the stick he'd found, Ramón leaned over the cenote. The stick grazed the curious object at first pass, but Ramón missed. He leaned further out, his breath coming in ragged gasps as he tried to ignore the hungry water so near. Fear gripped his chest and twisted his guts. His palms were sweating profusely. The tree to which he held was rough in his grip, but he dared not loosen his hold, not even for a second, or he'd plunge head-first into what he knew would be his watery grave.

Risking even more, he stretched a bit further and dipped the tip of the stick into the water. It bent in that strange way that objects do when submerged, but he managed to loop the object neatly around the stick. He held his breath.

When he was certain that he could pull the stick back to him without the tiny object drifting back into the water, he slowly leaned away. Then, one hand still grasping the tree, he fell to his shaking knees at the edge to pluck it out.

"Hola, Padre."

Ramón was so startled by the woman's voice that a jolt of surprise sent a spasm through his body. Had he not still been holding on to the tree, he would have fallen into the deep and cool water.

As it happened, he did slip, one bare foot splashing into the water and falling to his rump, then a scramble back from the edge of the cenote just as quickly.

"Oh, Padre, please forgive me. I didn't mean to scare you."

It was Julia. His heart, which was already galloping its way through his chest, began to beat even faster. He gasped for breath and tried to play it off as laughter. He mostly succeeded.

"No, no, Julia." He heaved and clutched his chest. "You only surprised me, that's all."

She looked at him with a wry smile. "You are white as a ghost, Padre. Are you sure you aren't a ghost, sitting here at La Puerta Fantasma?"

He swallowed hard while still smiling and held up a finger so he could catch his breath.

"If I am," he said between breaths, "it is because you scared me to death." He was beginning to breathe easier. "Unfortunately, I'm nothing more than human."

Julia took a tentative step forward, and Ramón felt very small as he sat on his rump in the muddy moss.

"What did you find?" she asked, indicating the red item still clasped in his fist.

Ramón followed her finger. "Oh, I don't actually know. Trash, I think."

He opened his fist and inspected the red item. It was indeed trash. A wrapper from what he could tell, but so faded and soggy that the images and words were illegible.

He held it up in the sunlight so Julia could get a good look at it.

"Trash, you see?"

She crouched, her green skirt rising just above her knees. Ramón forced himself to stare at her eyes.

"It sure is. Looks to me like someone likes *galletes*."

He chuckled and stared at the small soggy wrapper. Perhaps there was the vague outline of a cookie, but had Julia not said it, he never would have seen it.

"Hm. I think you are making that up," he teased.

She looked at him with mock offense. "Padre, if you know anything about me, you know that I would never lie."

"Do I?" He tried to get a foot underneath and stand, but he slipped and landed hard on his rump once again.

"Here," she said, holding out her hand with its soft fingers that he'd always longed to touch. *She's merely helping me up,* he told himself.

"Thank you," he said and grasped her hand tightly. She pulled him to his feet with more strength than he would have believed her diminutive frame held.

Instead of stepping back once he was up, however, she pulled him close, their noses nearly touching.

"You know," she began, but Ramón stepped away from her.

"Julia, your clothes are a mess! I'm so sorry!" They weren't *really* a mess, but it was as good of an excuse as any to avoid being so close to her that he could smell the kind of soap she used. *Rose and lavender,* he thought.

She looked down in surprise. "Oh, I—"

"Let's get back to town. I would hate for that to dry and stain such a pretty thing."

"Padre, it's alright—" but Ramón had already started along the path. He looked over his shoulder at her with a smile.

"Unless of course you'd rather stay at the cenote. I wouldn't fault you for that; it is a very special place."

She smiled at him, and he felt his stomach flutter at her beauty. "You would share it with me?"

He very nearly blurted out "I would share the world with you, if you'd let me."

But he didn't. He shrugged and smiled, feeling a sadness seep into his heart. "Of course," was all he could manage.

She nodded and turned back toward the water. He turned from her, and turning many of his thoughts into would-haves, he made his way out of the jungle and back to La Ventana.

Another cruelty, of course, and this one much more acute. A priest could never marry, could never be with a woman. His dreams of Julia would have to remain just that, dreams.

As he arrived back in town, he was greeted again by Doña Sofia and one of her many grandchildren, who sat at her feet and drew in the dust with a stick. He chatted amiably with her for some time, and the sadness faded away, briefly. She spoke of the jungle as it had been decades before when she'd been a young girl and the shade from the trees had sheltered much of La Ventana from the afternoon sun.

After that, he stopped by Juan and Elena's home and spoke with them until midday then made his way to the church to make himself some lunch.

While he cooked, he prayed that God would release him from his desire for Julia. That he would be free from the trap he'd willingly stepped into. But most of all, that God would give him clarity. The doubt and frustration that plagued him was grating to say the least. He felt like a hypocrite speaking of love and acceptance and duty in front of his congregation, while internally feeling weak and afraid.

God didn't answer. Of course. Not that Ramón expected Him to. But it would have been nice.

He ate in the solitude of his quarters and said his prayers, crossing himself before devouring the grilled meat, beans, and fresh tortillas.

Tomorrow was Sunday, and he'd been preparing for his sermon while sitting at the cenote too. He'd known what he wanted to say, but now it all seemed scrambled and haphazard, like a mess of notes thrown across the floor and then gathered out of order.

He retrieved a piece of paper and a pencil from his desk, and he began writing his outline, something he always tried to do Saturday nights. His thoughts on the loss of Carlos would have to be mixed into the sermon, of course. He didn't want to, necessarily, but the people expected it, and he served the people.

He'd also sprinkle in some metaphors of the jungle and their humble life.

But the point of the sermon still eluded him. What could he convey to his church that hadn't already been mentioned in sermons past?

He said another prayer asking for wisdom.

In the moments of silence that followed, the answer came. It slowly coalesced into something that resembled coherence, like a shadow resolving itself from formless blob into a man.

He wrote feverishly, stopping only to sharpen the pencil several times before he was finished. But when he sat back and looked at the papers scattered across his desk, he smiled and clapped his hands, praising God for revealing the answer to him and feeling proud of himself for the work.

CHAPTER 5

The morning Mass started out just like any normal Mass would. The young acolytes lit the candles, and they recited the Introductory Rites with the Greeting and the Collect. Within twenty minutes, he was ready to begin his sermon. Over one-hundred pairs of eyes stared back at him from the pews of his church, and despite the normal Sunday pressure, he felt a renewed sense of purpose. His notes, carefully stacked on the wooden pulpit before him, would help him deliver a message unlike any he'd preached in years.

"Good morning, my friends," he began.

Variations of "good morning" echoed through the church, and he smiled around the room.

"Do you hear that?" he said and cupped a hand behind his right ear.

Some smiled while others looked around the room questioningly. He grinned at their confused expressions, nodding.

"No? That my good friends is called 'silence,' and it is something I believe we as humans avoid at all costs."

A few chuckles withered in the space between the pews and Ramón.

"I joke, of course. But I want to speak about the silence that we feel in life. The silence of certain seasons," he made eye contact with Elena and Diego, who sat on the front row in blacker versions of their Sunday Best, "and the silence in an unanswered prayer."

Silence, of course, answered. As he knew it would.

"You see," he leaned his elbows on the wooden pulpit, "I have been struggling a great deal with that same silence in recent days, following the death of one of this town's beloved children." Again, he made eye contact with Diego and Elena. "I have struggled with what it means to follow a god that doesn't always answer us."

Again, silence. This time, there were looks of cautious disbelief thrown around the room. What he was saying did, in a very simple way, approach heresy.

The eyes of Carlos' friends—Lena, Francisco that he could see—avoided meeting his own. They sat on the back row with their heads bowed in shame rather than prayer, he believed.

"I'm not saying I've begun to lose my faith," he said swinging his gaze back to the rest of the congregation and laughing a little to lighten the mood. "I'm talking about those times in our lives when we each pray with all our heart, mind, soul, and strength, and instead of an answer, we get nothing in return. What do we do, then?"

A cough broke the silence of the stunned congregation.

"What then?" he asked once more. "You see, when we are faced with silence from our Heavenly Father, we have only one of two choices. We can either accept the silence as an answer, or..." He looked around at the silent faces staring back at him. "Or we can ask a different question.

"The book of Proverbs tells us in chapter eighteen verse fifteen that 'the heart of the discerning acquires knowledge, for the ears of the wise seek it out.' How do we acquire knowledge? Are we seeking it out? Are we listening with wise enough ears to hear it?"

The faces of simple farmers and butchers, mothers and housekeepers looked at him. Part of him began to think their expressions were curious, now, perhaps a little confused.

"How do we seek knowledge? Ask God, of course. But in His silence, where next? Scriptures, you might say. Yes, of course. But didn't God create this world? Does not the dog's companionship teach us loyalty? Does the river's current not teach us about guiding and accepting direction?"

Nods and the occasional muttered "Gloria a Dios."

"And doesn't the rain teach us of how larger things are happening," he twirled his hand in the air above him, "despite not knowing exactly how or when? We have dry seasons, of course. But don't we also have rainy seasons? José," a man on the third row of pews sat up a little straighter at the mention of his name. "Don't your chickens teach us about the circle of life?"

A middle-aged man nodded shyly, but smiled at the recognition in front of the congregation.

Ramón could feel the tempo of his sermon picking up. He could feel that familiar ebb and flow of recitation and response that most Sundays provided. When he spoke again his voice was calm but firm, alternating between full volume and a softer more pensive tone. "God's silence may not be the answer we were looking for, but when there is silence from Him, we can look at the instructions He left carved in stone and whispered on the breeze. Our Lord has given us dominion over this world, has He not?"

More "Amen" and a few claps, now.

"If we have dominion over the instructions that God has written, that is the world around us, then we need not wait for Him to answer. We have the answers already."

Father Ramón stepped out from behind the pulpit. His alb didn't move with him easily, but it provided a bit of ritual that lent his words instant authority. The cincture around his waist swayed as he stepped passionately toward the edge of the rise on which he now preached. He looked directly at the grieving couple in the front, Carlos' parents, and held his hands wide as if to embrace them. He slowed his pace until he was only two or three feet from them and addressed them specifically but spoke loud enough for everyone in the church to hear.

"You asked why a loving God would allow you to go through this terrible, *terrible* season."

A tear spilled down Elena's cheek, but she ignored it and met Ramón's gaze.

"I would say that he is giving you the opportunity to answer that yourself. You aren't alone in your grief. My heart breaks daily for you both, as well as your little boy. But I know that God exists, and his angels exist, and they walk among us."

He gazed out at the rest of the congregation and made eye contact with Julia. He felt himself flush, but he didn't turn his eyes away. Julia smiled at him, and Ramón briefly returned it.

Father Ramón bent to kiss the cheeks of both Elena and Diego and smiled benevolently before making his way back up the steps to the pulpit.

When he turned to face the congregation once more, Elena wasn't the only one crying.

"My dearest friends. Faith is not simply knowing God is in control. It's also understanding that we have been given the authority to seek out the answers ourselves. We can use God's creation to find the answers, and he guides us freely.

"Ask and it will be given to you, seek and you will find, knock and it will be opened to you. Are you asking, my friends? Are you seeking? Are you knocking?"

Father Ramón cleared his throat and turned in the cracked and worn Bible on the pulpit. He spoke for another hour on the mystery of the creator and the knowledge of the created. There were looks of mild shock, shouts of "Amen," even a few more "Gloria a Dios". By the time he'd made the main points in his notes, the congregation was smiling and nodding along with almost everything he said. He didn't feel so much like he was losing his faith. In fact, he felt more like he was sharing a realistic one and it resonated with his small town.

"A final word from scripture," he said, closing the large Bible he'd used through most of his sermon with a solid *thump*. "Daniel two, twenty-one says 'He changes times and seasons; removes and sets up kings; gives wisdom to the wise and knowledge to those who lack understanding.'

"God's silence is a season. He will set up kings and remove them. But 'if any of you lacks wisdom, ask God for it' because He will give it to you, won't He? We know that, now."

He paused for dramatic effect before tying the sermon up with a nice little ribbon.

"At the beginning of the sermon, I told you that I was struggling with following a silent god. I know now that god isn't actually silent. Instead, I follow a god that has already given me the instructions, and I must simply find them. He speaks to us through the dust, the trees, and the animals. Through each other, too.

"Gloria a Dios, my friends. Amen."

CHAPTER 6

Father Ramón stood outside in the mid-morning heat to shake the hands of the men and women of his congregation. After closing the service with a hymn, *How Great Thou Art*, he'd stood at the bottom of the steps and wished his little lambs well.

Julia waited just inside the doors so that she would be at the end of the line, then followed the final few stragglers out into the already sweat-inducing heat of Belize.

"That was quite a sermon, Padre," she said when she finally stood in front of him. Her hands were folded in front of her simple gray dress.

"Well, perhaps it was a little dramatic, but I felt led by the Spirit and believe that our little town could use the encouragement. Did you find it helpful?"

Julia nodded, "I find all of your sermons helpful, Padre."

She looked at him from under her eyelids and his heart began beating much faster.

"I'm glad," he managed, but he had to swallow the lump in his throat.

"I hope to see you in town today, Padre. I hear the Mendozas are hosting a potluck in honor of the spring.

Something on the Mayan calendar, I think, honoring their ancestors or something."

"Yes, I—" he swallowed again. "Yes."

She turned to go, and he reached for her, almost grasping her arm but pulling back at the last minute.

"Julia," he stuttered, now uncertain what exactly he meant to say. He landed on something safe and managed to get it out without sounding completely inept. "How is your sister?"

Julia blinked, then smiled, and said, "She is fine, Padre. Thank you for asking."

She walked away from him, dark hair whipping gently across her back in the breeze and glistening in the midmorning sunlight.

Ramón sighed longingly as he watched her retreating form, then yelped when he felt a hand on his elbow. He jerked away and looked at the figure beside him.

An older man in street clothes stood smiling genially at Ramón. The man's wrinkled smile turned into a chuckle, and Ramón began to chuckle himself.

"I'm sorry to have scared you, Father." His voice was kind and warm.

"It's okay, my friend," said Ramón, curious why the man stood there. The old man held himself in such a way that told Ramón he was a churchgoer, had been for some time, but something more, too. His gray and wispy hair was combed in such a way that it had a small part on the side. No beard or even stubble to see.

"I listened to your sermon. Though I have to admit, I was ... uneasy through most of it."

Ramón cocked his head. "Uneasy?"

The old man nodded. "Talking about searching for knowledge outside of God, Jesus, or the Scriptures is ... unorthodox at best. Despite your statement about avoiding heresy at the beginning of the sermon, you moved rather comfortably toward it, don't you think?"

Father Ramón put his hands in the folds of the opposite sleeves. "Doesn't God encourage us to seek Him out? If He didn't desire us to look at creation and see Him, why would He have created it for us?"

The old man shrugged noncommittally. "It's just an observation, of course."

The silence stretched between them as Ramón sized the old man up. Definitely a traditionalist in the church.

"I don't think I know your name, and I make it a point to know everyone within my congregation." He stretched out his right hand. "I'm Ramón."

The old man grasped it firmly. "Mucho gusto, Ramón. I am Santiago Xavier Hernandez Lopez. You may call me Santiago."

"Mucho gusto, Santiago. Are you passing through our little town, or have you come to stay?"

"I'll be staying for a short time. But I look forward to hearing more of your ... perspective on faith. Buenos días, Father."

Santiago smiled as he walked away and donned a straw hat to keep the sun from his face, but the suspicion in the man's eyes was unmistakable. Ramón knew there were nonbelievers in his town and certainly even in his congregation, but there was a deep current of traditionalism. Whether people believed or not, church attendance was basically mandatory; one person's opinion on the depth of its truth was immaterial— everyone goes to church.

Ramón watched the older man's retreating form until the man named Santiago turned around a low plaster wall and disappeared.

He felt unsettled. Santiago was without a doubt someone who knew the Scriptures. But he was also questioning Ramón's faith. And while Ramón felt a kind of apathetic peace about questioning his own, it seemed a little too invasive for someone else to do it.

Still bothered, Ramón returned to the church and hung up the clothes reserved for Sunday back into his dark closet. He changed into what he called "normal" clothes, closed the church doors, and walked down the main road that ran through the middle of town. Small shops and stands lined the dusty thoroughfare, becoming more numerous the closer he came to the town square. His church was situated only a few blocks from it, but even still, many considered it on "the outskirts" of town.

Dust clouds from passing vehicles, carts, and traveling feet rose from the road that cut through the middle of town and created a kind of haze over the city. Word had it that when the jungle was closer, there wasn't any haze at all. Now, the air always had a dusty glaze.

He took a deep breath and coughed. The air smelled good, but the dust beneath got caught in his lungs. He recognized the familiar whiff of homemade tortillas, fruits and vegetables, and many different kinds of meat. This was what La Ventana usually smelled like, and Sunday was no different.

He waved and smiled politely at several people he recognized. When a wayward ball rolled into his path, he kicked it playfully back toward a group of young children who laughed and clapped. His long robe made it only slightly more difficult than his lack of skill allowed.

He walked down the dusty sidewalk, small pieces of trash and piles of grime settling along the walls of abandoned shops. But when he lifted his eyes past the roofs and signs that marked streets and intersections, it was easy to ignore what swirled around his feet.

Trees towered distantly, and in the silence of morning and late evening, the sounds of the jungle drifted into the dark streets when the wind was just right. This was a beautiful place, and La Ventana was a perfect name for it. It was a window in the world that allowed onlookers to see something both ordinary and extraordinary. Sure, there was pain and the occasional crime in La Ventana, but the peace of everyday life was unparalleled, uncomplicated by the busy rush of traffic or chasing the highest floor of a skyscraper like those on the coast.

The citizens of La Ventana were content in their measly riches, what many in the rest of the world would no doubt consider poverty. Dirt floors, ramshackle roofs, and a lack of standard medicine and others such as dentistry and eye care were certainly apparent. But the smiles of seeing familiar faces or shopping at a mercado and spending an hour talking with friends encountered in the aisles were nothing short of beautiful. In his eyes, he would consider it something divine.

But it wasn't an easy life. It was a trying and exhausting life. Many of the families who attended his church had lived in La Ventana or the surrounding countryside for centuries. While the jungle had retreated from the walls of La Ventana, the city itself had remained more or less the same size. It was out of the way, but not so far from civilization as to be considered "the middle of nowhere."

His musings halted when he stopped at a small stand to buy a couple of tacos carne asada, his favorites. He paid with part of the meager salary his priesthood provided and waved hello to both owners of the little shop, Mauricio and his wife Dana. Their four-year-old daughter Maria had drowned several years ago. Ramón had conducted the funeral service for her, as well. Mauricio and Dana swore to never have another child after that.

But, as it happens, God had other plans.

Ramón played peek-a-boo with their young toddler, Angel. The name wasn't a coincidence. Mauricio and Dana regularly spoke of God's grace and his blessing.

Angel smiled and gurgled baby-speak while Mauricio smiled back at him. Dana tickled the baby's pudgy cheek, and he clapped and babbled all the more.

"He's getting big," Ramón said over the sound of the street and cooking meats.

Dana glanced at Ramón and went back to cooking. Mauricio smiled and leaned on his elbows toward Ramón.

"Too big, if you ask me." His voice was light and kind, younger than Ramón.

"Each night, Dana is both ecstatic that Angel is here and sad that another day has passed. It's as if every day is a day of celebration and a day of mourning." He ran a hand through his thick black hair and glanced back at Dana who was busy at the griddle. "Honestly, I don't know what to do, Padre," he said low enough for only Ramón to hear.

"I can imagine it's a difficult time, and it will continue to be for you both."

"Any advice for us?"

Ramón thought for only a moment and came up with a verse that might help.

"In first Timothy, chapter five verse eight, Paul tells us to provide for our relatives, '*especially members of his household*' he says. I'm certain you're doing everything you can," Ramón gestured at the vendor stall and Dana working through a haze of steam and smoke in the back. "But there are other ways to provide, as well. Provide emotional security. You said each day is a celebration and time of sorrow, provide a place for Dana to feel those both fully. Does that make sense?"

Mauricio's eyes had begun to sparkle with unshed tears, and he nodded and lowered his eyes.

"I'm sorry, my friend." Ramón didn't know what else to say, but he knew that usually made people feel better in some capacity.

Mauricio raised his head and looked at Ramón with an intense and pleading pain. "I am doing all of that already. But no one asks how *I* am doing with it all. I'm so focused on being a safe place for Dana that it's difficult for me to have a place to mourn and celebrate."

Ramón, having never been married much less a father, only nodded sagely and put a hand on the other man's shoulder. "Then do it for Angel. Proverbs says that '*the glory of children is their fathers.*' I think with a father like you, Angel— and Dana—will come to recognize that. Perhaps in time, she will be your safe place, too.

"I just want to know why. Why us? Why Dana? Why me? Are we being punished?"

Ramón affected an expression of grave disbelief and tried to balance it with gracious understanding. "My friend, God doesn't punish His children. Remember when the disciples asked what the blind man's parents did to cause this man's disability? Jesus corrected them, no? Allow me to correct you, gently, my friend.

"You are not being punished. Tested?" He wobbled his hand back and forth. "Perhaps. But Paul says to rejoice in the difficult times because they build character and through character, faith. Trust in the Lord, my friend. Even when it doesn't give us immediate hope, it builds the habit of trust."

Just look at me and see how difficulty has brought blessings, he nearly said, but felt the lie die on his lips. He prayed that his expression wouldn't betray his thoughts. And at that, a bitterness rose in his throat. He felt like a fraud, telling Mauricio to have faith when his own was in decline.

Mauricio nodded and thanked Ramón.

"Of course, my friend." Dana approached and handed Mauricio a steaming plate of tacos carne asada that made Ramón's mouth immediately water. "Gracias, friend. Goodbye Dana." She smiled and waved at him. "Goodbye Angel," the pudgy little cheeks jiggled as he turned and slapped the surface of his high chair, babbling.

Their laughter followed Ramón down the street as he munched on the delicious food.

His doubts plagued him though. As he continued his walk through town, they were rife with frustration and an overwhelming feeling of being lost in the dark. Instead of feeling encouraged from his talk with Mauricio—where he'd used plenty of convincing scripture—he felt drained and even more helpless.

Eventually, he found himself at the gate at the edge of town. His special place was only a short walk away in the dense foliage of the jungle that looked very much like a green smudge in the distance. It beckoned to him, and he longed to soak his feet in the cool water while he submerged his mind in the ambient sounds of the jungle, releasing the pressure his station forced upon him.

The morning's sermon, next week's sermon, and his conversations with Mauricio and Santiago sat in the back of his mind like an uncomfortable weight that seeped down his legs and into his feet. If he didn't move soon, he felt that he'd collapse beneath the burden of it all.

When he did move his foot, it felt as if he'd drawn it out of a deep mud. Each subsequent step was easier, and in less than a dozen, he was walking freely. He was going to the cenote, and each puff of dust disturbed by his step brought him closer. The burden he'd felt in the town eased the nearer the jungle grew. When it obscured his vision and the shade cooled the air around him, his shoulders sagged in relief. His feet set him on the path between trunks and logs, and he didn't even need to think about his steps along the narrow trail that appeared beneath the leaves and wound between brush.

He breathed deeply of the verdant, cool air when the town was finally obscured by thick leaves and branches. The air was thick and hot, but smelled like *life*. Immediately, his mind seemed to shuffle off the burden he'd gathered that day, like a locust shedding its skin. And by the time he sat at the edge of the cenote, the ghost of a smile touched his lips.

Ramón closed his eyes, gathering each sensation to him like a mother hen and her chicks.

The sun's gentle warmth as its golden light danced across his hands and knees, and the coolness of the patchy shade on his face.

The distant echo of waterfalls and the whispered lapping of swirling water at his feet.

The feel of the moist grass and moss against his palms.

The sound of nearby birds chattering with the monkeys.

If there's a heaven, this is it, he thought to himself and smiled. *Perhaps I'm already there.*

He dreaded to break the silence, but he wished to share his thoughts with the cenote.

Even the air around him gathered closer to urge him to speak, to confess.

So he did, laying out his thoughts, his fears, and his desires. The cenote listened intently, reassuring him with its gentle caress against his feet and legs. The jungle listened, affirming him with a breeze that cooled his skin and the rhythm of life that was unaffected by his presence.

He was in his own private confessional; one without walls or listening ears.

Or so he thought.

CHAPTER 7

For the next several days, Ramón worked within the town alongside some of the members of his congregation and some that weren't. One family, the Estradas, had a pig chew its way out of the pen and now needed help repairing it. Their son Francisco had been a good friend of Carlos. Francisco couldn't both tend the pigs and mend the fence, so Ramón helped him as best he could, managing to simultaneously guard the gap and hold each post in its designated hole while Francisco ran the wired fence between them and wired them to each post.

When that was done, which took several hours that morning, he walked to the other side of town to do a eulogy for one family's beloved cat. This was one of the benefits of being the only priest in town. Yes, there were hard days, very hard days sometimes. But there were also days where he could help the children understand God's love for *all* the creatures. Even if he couldn't help himself in that regard, kids were simpler. He could provide eternal security to them.

The father of the young girl whose cat had died waved when Ramón spied him around the side of their home.

"Thank you, Padre," said Enrique Saldo.

Ramón shook his hand genially and clapped Enrique on the shoulder. "Of course, of course. I'm happy to help."

Enrique motioned for Ramón to follow. The duo walked around the corner of the house and stopped several yards from where a small group gathered around a shallow hole. Sara, Enrique's wife, stood towering over two young children, with another babbling on her hip. To her right stood a young boy of six with dusty brown hair and a muddy smudge across both cheeks, their oldest son Luca. On Sara's left and beneath the baby on her hip, a young girl of four, little Iliana. No one except her parents called her "Iliana" as the rest of the town called her "Illy." A number of other children ringed the small grave, some crying, and others whispering, but all of them understanding instinctively the weight of the gathering.

Illy held a small box that looked to have been crafted by her father out of scraps of wood. Inside, no doubt, was her beloved cat Blanca. Despite the name, Blanca had been jet black save a single white sock on a front paw. Illy loved that cat so very much, and the cat had loved her, following her through the streets of La Ventana while Illy played with her friends or went to the market with Sara.

Ramón smiled at the group as he stood shoulder-to-shoulder with Enrique, watching in no small amount of awe as the children held hands or hugged one another. Sara caught her husband's eye and motioned him over. Illy must have seen it because she looked over her shoulder and waved at Ramón. He put a hand on Enrique's shoulder and said, "I guess that's our cue," and they walked forward to join the graveside ceremony.

It wasn't a long service. Compared to some of Ramón's others it was barely a blink. But it was perhaps one of his best. By the end of it all, there were only a few tears, and most of the children were smiling. Even Sara had grasped Ramón's hand at one point and gave it a friendly, grateful squeeze.

"Illy, should we lay Blanca to rest, now?"

Reluctantly, the little girl nodded. She knelt in the dirt, ignoring the dust that puffed up around her. The other children looked on stoically as Illy placed the wooden box gently in the rectangle hole.

"Bye-bye, Bianca," Illy said in a watery little voice that broke Ramón's heart.

Together, as was their own little tradition, each child grabbed a handful of dirt and let it run between their fingers. The dirt made a dry thudding as it rattled across the lid of the makeshift coffin. After their turn, most of the children ran off to play, grief forgotten at the prospect of play. Sara took those that needed a drink inside for some pink lemonade.

Luca ran off with two of his friends laughing and giggling in that awkward waddle that young children often have. Illy, however, hugged her father's leg the way all children do. Enrique placed a loving hand on the top of her head, and she looked up at him, squinting against the midday sun.

"Father Ramón and I are going to finish burying Blanca. Do you want to stay or go play with your friends?"

She rubbed her little eyes with a dirty finger, and for a moment, Ramón worried that she'd get dirt in it and begin to cry all over again. Instead, she blinked and said simply, "Stay."

Enrique nodded and knelt in the dirt. Ramón also knelt and together, they pushed the few handfuls of dirt that were left into the grave to cover it completely. With the simple task complete, the men stood and dusted off their hands.

"Thank you again, Padre. I think you made all the difference."

"I won't say I'm happy to do it, but you get the idea."

Enrique chuckled and nodded.

"Wait!" exclaimed Illy before waddling off. She returned a moment later dragging a large wooden cross.

"I made this," she said panting with the effort, "for Blanca."

Enrique took the cross from her—which seemed to shrink in his hands and become normal-sized—and read the paint across the horizontal slat.

"Iliana, this is beautiful. Did Mama help?"

She shook her head and said, "Only with the nails."

"It's perfect," her father said with pride. "Don't you think, Padre?"

Ramón made a play of inspecting its craftmanship, making Illy giggle. "Very good work. Straight lines, perfectly spelled words." He nodded as if making a decision. "Yes, Blanca would be very proud of your work, Illy."

With her father's help, Illy hammered the cross into the dirt at the head of the grave. The sound of it made a wooden *whap whap whap* that echoed through the dry air and set Ramón's teeth on edge.

"Thank you, Padre," said Illy in a little voice as Ramón turned to leave. The next thing he knew, Illy had run to him and hugged him tightly around the legs.

"You're very welcome, little one," he whispered.

Enrique shook Ramón's hand once more. Ramón glanced at the meager grave and the children playing in the dusty field beyond, then left the backyard to eat some lunch at the church.

During Ramón's brief interaction with Enrique, he'd had an idea for the next Sunday's sermon, and it might even be better than his last. But he needed to think on it. Santiago's presence complicated things. Ramón wasn't sure why, but the man made him uneasy. He tried to ignore it, though it gnawed at him like early morning hunger. The thought that spurned him onward was "all truth is God's truth." If that belief held, then what he had to say was not only important, but it was also vital to the people of La Ventana, Santiago or no.

He chewed on his lunch of roasted chicken and peas while mentally chewing on the lesson he hoped to teach, peaceful thoughts of the cenote drifted in and out of his mind like a mist wandering with the wind.

After his lunch was finished, he put thoughts of his sermon aside for the moment and made his way to the center of town where he knew a few of the children were having a bake sale. Before he left the church, he dropped a few extra coins from his stipend into his pocket, knowing that simply making an appearance would do wonders for their morale. When he arrived, however, he stopped short.

Santiago was standing at the children's small table, smiling and laughing with them. He had the countenance of a grand-father—someone who played with children well and then sent them home to their parents. That irked Ramón. Perhaps it was because it was easy for him to interact with children as well, but to see this stranger doing it with his own congregation felt invasive, as if Santiago was using Ramón's tactics against him.

Stop it, he told himself, shaking the tension from his shoulders and walking confidently toward the table of children.

The conversation became clearer as Ramón approached.

"...yes yes! I have been through the jungle. Many, many times! I saw many animals. But my favorite, of course, were los monos." The old man lifted one hand to the sky and tickled his own armpit with the other, blowing his cheeks out and crossing his eyes. The children roared with laughter, and Ramón smiled at the way they nearly fell out of their chairs.

Maybe Santiago isn't as bad as he seems, he chastised himself.

"Good morning, Manuel! Good morning, Laura!" Ramón greeted the children with a warm smile. "Good morning, Santiago," he said a little more subdued.

"Good morning, Padre," the children replied.

The old man's smile soured a little, and he dropped his monkey arms back to his sides. "Morning, Father," he replied coolly.

Then again, maybe he is as bad as he seems, Ramón thought with no small amount of satisfaction.

Ramón, in a play of exaggeration, asked what the children were selling this time.

Manuel and Laura both stumbled over their words to get them out before the other.

"Today, I have empanadas and—"

"I brought fresh tamales—"

Both children were almost unintelligible, and their words tumbled out like playthings from an overturned basket.

Just before Ramón could interject—he could feel the smile tug at his cheeks and his throat tighten in preparation for a playful retort—Santiago spoke first.

"Empanadas? Tamales?" Incredulous, the old man put his hands on his hips and glared at the children. They both quieted quickly, and their smiles soon faded.

It looks like I'm not the only one who notices, Ramón thought.

"You waited all this time to tell me you have fresh empanadas and tamales?" The man sounded genuinely skeptical.

After several awkward seconds of silence, Ramón moved to interject. But once more, Santiago interrupted his thoughts, as if the man *knew* Ramón was about to speak.

"I'll take five of each!"

Oh good God. Ramón had to stop himself from rolling his eyes.

The children glanced at each other in disbelief, then burst into peals of laughter as they hastily gathered the requested items and stuffed them into a plastic sack.

Santiago looked over at Ramón, and had they been friends or acquaintances, Ramón would have expected a conspiratorial wink. As they now stood as neither, Santiago sniffed haughtily in Ramón's direction and then returned his smile to the children.

Ramón waited patiently, quoting verses in his head that made him feel better about himself while Santiago finished up whatever play this was. When Santiago finally stepped aside, Ramón ordered two of each. He *wanted* to order more, but there wasn't a lot in the budget for extra spending. Besides, Santiago would be moving on soon enough. It felt as if it might even be his duty to spend a little extra in their town, if for no other reason than as a thank you for the hospitality.

The self-satisfied smirk that crawled across the old man's face, however, made Ramón's own face flush briefly in anger. With a small dash of shame.

Ramón thanked the kids profusely and made sure that the money would get home to their mothers. They nodded and assured Ramón that it was all there.

"Good, then this," he flipped them two silver coins, which they both caught with a shout of surprise and glee, "is just for you. ¿Me entienden?"

Ramón avoided looking at Santiago. Didn't even need to, really. He knew that the children would feel greater appreciation for his small gift to *them* instead of a larger gift to their mothers. And he was *their* priest, after all. Not Santiago's.

A small traditional part of him whispered, *Shouldn't you be everyone's priest, regardless of where they come from or where they're going?*

He ignored it by stepping up to Santiago and saying, "Thank you for purchasing some of the kids' treats. They have a small stall every day to help their families. I always think it's special when adults show interest in the children's lives."

Santiago took a bite of an empanada and chewed, ignoring Ramón for the moment and looking out at the bustling street. Ramón wondered if Santiago saw the potential in the city as he did, or if he saw a city on the verge of economic collapse. Ramón followed the path of several rusty cars as they drove slowly through the town, most of them old and cobbled together to make it one more day. Adults walked here and there in small clusters, usually with several children in tow. Some of the storefronts were boarded up, and those that weren't showed broken windows like snaggletooth smiles.

Ramón felt a defensiveness rise up in his chest as he looked about, expecting Santiago to say something offhand about the run-down look of the town.

Instead, Santiago said, "You mentioned the trees and jungle several times throughout your service the other day. Do you find solace there?"

Ramón was so taken aback that he could barely process the question.

Jungle? He thought, his mind racing to fit the defensiveness he felt with the question he'd been asked.

"Yes," he said hesitantly. Then remembering, he continued "Yes. I go there often to think and meditate." Santiago arched an eyebrow. "On God's word, of course."

"Of course," said Santiago after a moment's hesitation.

It wasn't entirely a lie. Ramón *did* meditate there. And it was mostly on God's word. But more recently, it was more like he had been expanding his understanding of the Scriptures and how it applies to *everything* he knew, instead of everything he knew through the lens of Christianity.

"And during these ... meditations. What conclusions do you find?"

Well I actually discover that everything I've ever believed is, if not an outright lie, a partial one.

Ramón grasped for an explanation that wouldn't immediately reveal his crisis of faith. In the end, he opted for a glimmer of truth.

"I find peace, Santiago."

The old man nodded, but whether sagely or as if a suspicion had been confirmed, Ramón wasn't sure.

They walked in silence for a few moments, Santiago munching on an empanada and Ramón wondering how to break the silence without further condemning himself.

"What brings you to our town, Santiago?"

The question seemed innocuous enough.

"Oh, business, actually. I'm here on behalf of another."

"Interesting. Are they looking to move to the area? If so, I wouldn't recommend it. It's not exactly a bustling metropolis."

Santiago flashed a smile. "No. Only, what's the phrase, 'scoping the place out'?"

It was Ramón's turn to smile. "Ah, I see." Even though he really didn't. "Is there anything I can help with?"

Santiago shook his head, and the loose skin along his jaw jiggled. "No. Continue on as normal. I'm merely an onlooker."

Ramón nodded, and they continued to walk down the sidewalk. They had to dodge several children as they chased a ball down the street laughing and jostling each other.

"Are you going to the jungle today? The two children mentioned you like to go to a cenote there?"

Ramón nodded. "That's right. Most of the congregation knows that I go there to think and pray. To meditate, like we said. But they don't know exactly where. I am planning to go there later today, to flesh out what this next sermon will cover. I have an idea, but I like to try and plan it all out beforehand so that by the end of the sermon, I land where I'd planned to."

Santiago stopped at a vendor stall and bought a small package of cookies, then put them in his pocket.

"I understand what you mean. I've experienced some of those more ... creative sermons where the priest wandered this way and that without ever really landing on a message. It left me confused and frustrated. I wanted to be given something tangible to think about, something to feel when I left the church that day. Instead, I was no better off than when I walked in the doors."

Ramón wondered if the man often felt confused and frustrated. He certainly had the demeanor.

"In any event, I look forward to your next sermon. I'll admit, I wasn't a huge fan of your most recent one. But perhaps I will be a fan of your next."

"I doubt it," almost came out before Ramón could stop it. Instead, he said, "Yes. I hope to, in your words, give you something tangible to think about."

Santiago nodded and took another bite of his empanada.

With a smile that threatened to crack, Ramón inclined his head and said, "Vaya con Dios, Santiago," then turned on his heel without another glance back. His heart hammered in his chest. Something about that man set his teeth on edge. It could be the old man's suspicions of him. Could be the old man's fairly adolescent behavior. Or something else entirely. Ramón also didn't want to think about it, but it might be that the old man had every right to be suspicious.

CHAPTER 8

Ramón spent the rest of the day at the cenote. He was half-concerned that Santiago would show up and ruin his afternoon, but there were several cenotes in the jungle, even nearer to La Ventana. No, he was safe here. He was alone.

His mind wandered this way and that, landing on verses that he could discuss on Sunday, then meandering once more to the surrounding jungle, to God's creation. And then, inevitably, always back to the angel that saved him as a child.

All these years and not another sighting. No god or angel descending from heaven to tell him that he was doing the right thing, that he was spreading the Good News just as he'd been destined to. No message from above that he'd been saved from drowning for a divine purpose, nor that he was fulfilling that purpose beautifully.

Instead, he felt as if he was a blind man walking through a dark room hoping to avoid the traps that lay waiting in the dark. So far he'd avoided them, but when would his luck run out?

The water swirled around his ankles as he moved them lazily through the crystal water. The ripples obscured the bottom, but he could see the white sand and green rocks that came alive with the movement.

And still, no answer from God. Still, God was silent. He was silent to Ramón. Silent to Carlos' family. Silent to Maria's parents, Enrique and Dana. Silent to many others. Yet he, Ramón, was charged with communicating that even through the silence, God was still with them.

He scoffed and threw a rock into the water. "It's stupid, really," he said to the water. "That I'm supposed to be the one telling all of them what God thinks and wants. Somehow I alone know that. But it's all based on what I *believe* He wants me to say. And if I'm wrong, I'm branded a heretic and thrown out of the priesthood."

The water lapped against the rock in response.

"And yet," he said, "what else am I supposed to do? *Not* teach the Word? Saved by an angel and refuse to believe what my own eyes have seen? Did Abraham refuse to believe that he'd seen the glory of the Lord in Genesis? No. He nearly died because of its overwhelming power."

He threw another small stone into the water. It sank beneath the surface, tumbling end over end until it disappeared from Ramón's view and became just one more at the bottom of the cenote.

"It would be a lot easier if the angel would just come down from heaven and—"

A rustling from behind made him turn sharply. Fears of Santiago invading his sacred space leapt to his conscious mind.

But instead a rabbit sprang from the underbrush and bounded away from him, then scuttled under a large bush and disappeared into the greenery completely.

Julia's calm countenance appeared where the rabbit had come from, no doubt spooked by her approach as well. Her beauty banished his fears in an instant. "Am I interrupting?" she said with a blush.

He smiled, genuinely pleased to see her. "No, Julia, of course not!"

He made to stand, but Julia stepped toward him with her hands out. "Please, stay. I'll join you."

She walked gracefully across the large rock that protruded from the edge of the cenote and next to him. She leaned over, took her sensible flats off, and pulled her dress up to her knees to put her feet in next to his. Ramón averted his eyes respectfully but longed to stare at her tanned legs without shame.

"What brings you out here today?" he asked her, more to force his mind to focus on something else than from genuine curiosity.

She lifted her rump from the stone and moved closer to him.

"I don't know. I saw you talking with that stranger today, and you looked bothered when you parted ways." She blushed. "I followed you out here to see if you needed some company."

Ramón thought she was simply beautiful when she blushed.

"I'm always happy to have company."

Julia looked at him in surprise.

"Well," he corrected, "*certain* company." She laughed. She had the most beautiful laugh.

"Do you want to talk about what that man said to you?"

He shook his head.

"Not really. I mean," he started, knowing that he was in fact going to talk about it, now. "His name is Santiago. He confronted me Sunday after my service about some of my teachings." He looked at her, then quickly away. "He said they bordered on heresy."

"Heresy?" Julia had the grace to sound shocked. "I thought the sermon was wonderful. You spoke truth. Isn't it an accepted saying that 'All truth is God's truth'? It seems strange that he would claim heresy when the sermon was pulled straight from the Scriptures."

Ramón nodded. "That's what I thought, too. But of course, I wanted to listen intently to what he said and reflect. Perhaps what I had been saying actually *did* border on heresy. It certainly wasn't my intention."

"Of course not." She sounded furious, now.

"It's always nice to get feedback on my sermons, even when it is negative."

They sat in silence for several minutes. Ramón swirled his feet through the water and Julia gazed at its depths.

"Anyway, it's not a problem. Santiago has his opinions and I welcome them. They can do nothing more than hone my lessons, verdad?"

Julia looked at Ramón dubiously. "I suppose so. But what does your lesson look like for this Sunday?"

He puffed his cheeks out and released his breath. "I have been toying with something. Building on last week's lesson. But after the confrontation with Santiago..." He trailed off.

Julia abruptly turned to face him. "No. No, Ramón," it was the first time she'd used his name that he could remember.

"Julia," he began.

"No. I cannot bear that you are *finally* approaching a truth that the Church has largely ignored for *centuries*. This Santiago," she nearly spat the name, "may have a more traditional perspective, but that does *not* invalidate your own."

Ramón thought for a moment. "Perhaps." It may have been the first time someone had confirmed his own beliefs.

"What is your lesson about? Or what verses are you going to use? You always do such a lovely job of including the Lord's Word in your sermons. You're so eloquent."

Ramón blushed, not just with the compliment but the person serving it, and coughed. "I was going to use Colossians chapter one. Verses fifteen through..." he shrugged. "The main message is that Christ is the image of the invisible God. 'By him all things were created,' and such. Then my goal was to move on to Ecclesiastes about the different times in life."

Julia put a hand over her heart and closed her eyes. "That is one of my favorites."

"It's one of the few places in Scripture where I feel it applies to everyone no matter what they're experiencing."

"I agree. 'A time to keep silent, and a time to speak.' Many would do well to heed that one."

Ramón laughed and nodded. "Or 'A time to cast away and a time to gather.' I like that one. So many times humanity..." he struggled to find the right word.

"Hoards," said Julia simply.

He snapped. "That's it. We hoard things. We hoard friends and money."

"And beliefs," she said quietly.

"Yes," he said in quiet surprise, "beliefs, too. But there are times when those things must be cast away. Otherwise, there won't be room for anything else."

"And what would you cast away, Father Ramón?"

Her question was blunt, and her eyes were both fierce and calming to him. It took him off guard, and he opened and closed his mouth several times before answering.

"Well." *Am I going to say it?*

"I think that I would probably..."

I'm going to admit it out loud. To a person.

To Julia.

"I would cast away *some* beliefs. Not all, of course. But some."

She nodded slowly as a smile spread across her lips. "I understand. It is important to, what is the verse, 'Trim the vine'? Even within our own beliefs."

"Yes. I agree." His heart was hammering against his ribs, and he was having trouble taking a deep enough breath.

Julia placed a hand on his knee and looked intently into his face.

"Would you like to share any of those beliefs with me?" She chuckled to cut the tension. "Perhaps a kind of reverse confession?"

He smiled, and with that, the fear melted away. She wasn't judging him, she didn't hate him, and she wasn't going to tell his secret to everyone in the church.

"No, not really. I've already confessed it to the water, anyway." He tossed another stone into the water.

"Well, I hope the water was kind enough to answer." She was staring at him, now, inches from his face.

"It's kind enough to listen," he said, swallowing hard and staring back. Her lips were so inviting, he could barely believe that he'd found himself in this position.

"I've learned that it's a rather good listener," she said in a whisper, leaning toward him.

"Yes."

She was so close now that he could feel her breath on his own lips.

"It knows all my secrets." His own voice was barely audible, but he didn't think it mattered.

"I know," she said and leaned in to close the distance.

"You ... what?" he questioned, leaning away from her puckered lips.

"What?" she said, opening her eyes in surprise and blinking.

"You said 'I know' when I said that the water knows my secrets. What do you mean 'I know'?"

Julia blushed again. "I don't know. I was distracted, I guess."

Ramón didn't know what to say, didn't know if she was being serious or hedging. How could she know, anyway? She'd never been here when he'd been whispering his secrets. She'd surprised him once before when he had been here, but not when he was pouring out his heart. No one had, as far as he knew.

"Sure" was all he could manage. "I should probably be getting back. Need to write out my sermon. Sunday will be here before you know it."

"Yes, of course." She pulled her feet from the water and let the hem of her dress drop back to the ground.

Ramón stood as well and gathered his shoes and socks. He knew he'd made it awkward. Knew that he'd ruined what would have otherwise been a very beautiful moment. But he wasn't *supposed* to kiss anyone. He was celibate! *That includes being celibate when a beautiful woman tried to kiss you!* He chided himself.

"Would you like to walk back with me?" he said, hoping to lighten the mood and reassure her.

"No, that's alright." She tucked a wisp of hair behind her ear. "If it's alright with you, I'd like to borrow your thinking spot for a little while."

"Of course, you can. I hope it brings you as much peace as it does me."

She nodded, and he nodded in return.

His walked back to town was once again troubled and he was irritated with himself for reasons he couldn't quite pinpoint.

CHAPTER 9

The rest of the week came and went. Ramón spent most of his time in the rectory jotting down sermon notes and reviewing them each evening. He was anxious, especially understanding that Santiago would no doubt make an appearance then afterward make snide remarks about it.

His hesitations about the topic of his sermon had been lessened to a certain extent by Julia's acceptance of his deepest secret, but some slight reservation remained. He was concerned that his teachings actually *were* bordering on heresy. But he couldn't continue to fake it. Not any more. The time had come when he needed to commit to speaking the truth, regardless of whom it may offend. He knew the Scriptures, he knew that God wanted His children to understand the love He had for them. Ramón was saved as a child—by an angel of God, no less—in order to tell them.

He sat on his bed—a simple wooden frame and an old mattress—reading his notes one final time.

The middle part needs one more verse, I think.

He opened his Bible. It creaked the way a well-loved and often-used book does, and he smiled. This Bible had been given to him as a child. The same abuelo that questioned him about the priest, the whore, and the drunk had given it to him after Ramón had become a priest.

"Use this as your guide, then. Read it. Memorize it. Live it."

"I will, Abuelo." Ramón had said.

The priest Ramón smiled at the memory. His abuelo had been a harsh man, but had taught him plenty of lessons. Ramón now flipped through the pages of the gift looking for one final and perfect verse to add to his sermon.

When he came to the book of Ecclesiastes, he paused. His index finger pointed at the first few verses in chapter four. He read silently and stopped, then went back and reread verse thirteen.

"Better was a poor and wise youth than an old and foolish king who no longer knew how to take advice." He read it aloud, if for no other reason than to hear it in his ears and not his head. "For he went from prison to the throne, though in his own kingdom he had been born poor. I saw all the living who move about under the sun, along with that youth who was to stand in the king's place. There was no end of all the people, all of whom he led. Yet those who come later will not rejoice in him."

Ramón sat back in his chair and thought for a moment. It certainly resonated with him, but if he used this verse, he might accidentally point it directly at Santiago. Surely, the older man would know it was for him. Was that appropriate? That Ramón use his pulpit to call out a member—well, visitor—in his congregation?

He immediately thought of the verse in Matthew, "If your brother or sister sins, go and point out their fault, just between the two of you. If they listen to you, you have won them over. But if they will not listen, take one or two others along, so that every matter may be established by the testimony of two or three witnesses." He'd already tried to talk with the man one on one. Perhaps it was time to do it with "two to three witnesses." Though, a filled church qualified as significantly more than "two or three."

It didn't matter. It was an important verse. His church needed to know that adjusting perceptions, views, and beliefs is valuable, even Scriptural. If people never changed their views, they'd grow into adults and still believe in *el Coco*.

My Church deserves the truth, he thought, *and the truth includes knowing that no single person holds the truth; the truth can be found in creation all around them.*

His previous struggles with a waning faith in God had begun to turn into an understanding that perhaps it isn't so bad, this not understanding. Perhaps it was a strength that he questioned his faith. Perhaps, through this process, he'd come to understand his faith, God, and the world around him better.

He sat up and made a note to include the verses in Matthew, then picked up the stack and tapped them on the desk to line them up.

Ramón walked through the church once more, ensuring that the rarely-used back door was closed up. But when he walked through the Sanctuary, the hair on the nape of his neck stood up. He tried to ignore it, but something about the empty pews and the echo of his footsteps made him nervous.

When he noticed a man standing in the back, he nearly yelped. He recognized the swaying form of David, however, and schooled his fears.

"David?" Ramón hadn't heard the heavy wooden door of the church open or close.

The swaying man blinked slowly in the dim light, his unfocused gaze drifting between the four corners of the compass.

His eyes were bloodshot, and he seemed in danger of falling asleep at any second.

"David," he stepped closer to the man, "can I help you, my friend?"

David nodded and teetered toward Ramón. Seeing the man so uncertain on his feet, Ramón grasped David's forearms to prevent him from falling.

"Let's get you a place to sleep." Ramón gently took the man and helped him to a pew. "Are you hungry? Thirsty?"

David's head lolled back and forth as if he had no control of it. Perhaps he didn't, but Ramón took that as a nod.

"Okay. Wait here. I'll be back shortly."

Ramón stood, intending to search the pantry for some food that might help soak up the alcohol and sober him quickly. He believed there were some crackers and a loaf of bread that he could give the man.

But David's hand sprang up and grasped Ramón's so quickly that for a moment, Ramón couldn't believe the drunk man had moved at all.

"I saw you," the man said, mixing his words into a slurry that barely resembled language at all.

"You ... what?"

"Saw you. Today."

"Well, yes, David. You probably did. I bought some food from the children and walked through town with ... a friend."

David's head shook slowly and a grin that turned Ramón's stomach to ice slid across the drunk man's face. "No friend of yours."

Ramón shrugged, one arm still grasped firmly in the drunk man's hand. "Friend or not, God wants me to love everyone."

"Does He? You believe that still?"

A chill crept up his spine and he tried to pull his hand free. But David's fingers were locked painfully onto Ramón's wrist.

"Of course I do," Ramón said shakily.

"That's not what you said earlier."

Again, Ramón tried to gently pull his hand away. David scowled and yanked down on it so severely that Ramón steadied himself by putting his other hand on the back of the pew. It was a near thing; he nearly crashed into David's face.

But the action had placed them inches from one another. "I see through you, *Priest*."

The words struck Ramón like a punch in the gut and the chill that had been creeping up his spine suddenly splintered down his arms and legs. Ramón yanked his arm back at the same time that David released it.

His momentum threw him across the aisle and his hip bounced painfully against the opposite row of pews. Their wooden feet scraped against the stone floor with a haunting hollow sound. David stared at Ramón and Ramón's breath came in fearful, ragged gasps.

"David, I... I..." he stammered.

"You're a liar."

"No, I—"

"Fake."

"I—"

"Mentiroso."

The blood drained from Ramón's face as the final word echoed through the church. Not caring anymore, he turned from David and fled. His footsteps pattered through the nearly empty church, but he paid them no mind. His one thought was on reaching his quarters and locking the door behind him.

Liar.

Am I? he thought. Everything he tried to avoid... was it all for nothing? Was David right?

He didn't have answers to the questions, but he feared them nonetheless.

He reached the heavy wooden door to his room and yanked it open. The hinges squealed, but he felt a small comfort from the dim light of several lanterns within. He slipped into his room and pulled the door shut behind him. It slammed against the doorjamb, but Ramón was already throwing the locks in place.

He breathed and leaned against the door, the barrier between him and the man on the other side of it. The lump in his throat grew until Ramón was overwhelmed with emotion. He began to sob quietly.

He was so tired. Tired of trying to work out his purpose. Trying to work out why he was saved if no other instruction would follow. He was tired of reading the Scriptures and believing he knew what they meant, but making it clear for his congregation and not himself.

And the most disgraceful of all, the thought that made the tears on his cheeks warm with the flush of shame—he was tired of caring for his congregation.

He was tired.

So, so tired.

The sound of footsteps outside the door forced him to swallow the remaining tears and listen intently.

"Ramón?"

It was a man's voice, but not David's.

"Yes?" he answered hesitantly.

"It's Santiago. I saw David leaving the church and wanted to come make sure everything was okay. I understand usually he stays when he's in his ... state."

Ramón wiped the tears from his eyes and pasted a fake smile on his lips, then unlocked the door.

When it opened, Santiago stood there, haughty and sure of himself. Ramón was immediately suspicious.

"Yes, he decided he didn't want to stay the night. I offered him food and something to drink, but he said he'd rather not."

"Did he?" Santiago did nothing to hide his doubt.

"Yes."

"You look ... drawn. Are you well?"

Ramón shrugged and decided some of the truth was better than trying to lie outright.

Liar, the echo in the church whispered.

"Late night studying the Word and preparing for my sermon. A little overwhelmed with emotion about God's grace. That's all."

"It is amazing, isn't it?" he said after a short pause.

"Anything else, Santiago?" So tired.

"No. Nothing else."

"Good night, then. Thank you for your concern."

The old man grunted in response then turned and left.

Ramón followed Santiago wordlessly to the church doors and locked them after the man left.

The sobs returned when he'd closed and locked his own room. He didn't expect to sleep. Not after that terrible encounter with David. But once the adrenaline left his body, he was asleep in moments. His dreams were rife with terror, and he woke before sunrise with a sore back and headache.

He dressed, ate, and drank a cup of coffee while reviewing his notes. The disturbing interaction he had with David the previous night had lost some of its strength with the light of dawn. What remained was a colorless echo of it. *Would the drunk man remember?* Ramón hoped and prayed he would not.

When his congregation began filing into the church later that morning, Ramón became The Priest once more. He put aside the fear he felt and put a smile on his face, greeting all of them at the door and welcoming them one by one.

Julia was one of the first through, and her reassuring smile eased much of his misgivings.

"My sister is here, as well," she said after Ramón greeted her. Alejandra stepped up beside her. Ramón hadn't seen her—or anyone else—when Julia had walked through the door, but he greeted her warmly.

"Alejandra! It's wonderful to see you!" She was tall, taller than Julia, and had a very stern expression. Her dark eyes were weighing him and he felt *seen* in a very uncomfortable way. She wore a black dress with crosses across the hem of the dress. It may have been a trick of the light, or perhaps only being able to see it from his periphery, but the sewn crosses looked to resemble bones.

Alejandra smiled. Only, it was more of a pursing of her lips rather than a response.

"Hello. I'm happy to be here with my sister. She's told me a great deal about you. I'm looking forward to hear what you have to say today."

Ramón swallowed hard. "I hope you feel blessed by the sermon, then."

They walked through the center aisle and sat, and Ramón was pleased that Julia not only came but brought her sister, who no doubt needed to hear his message today.

But when Santiago came through a few moments later with a nearly-sober David at his side, anxiety sprang into life like a molten eruption in his gut.

"Good morning, Santiago." Ramón cut his eyes to David. "Good morning, David. How are you?"

The town drunk smiled kindly at him and said, "Better this morning. I don't remember much, but I think I said something mean. I don't know exactly what, but I woke up this morning feeling regret, which is not something I'm used to." David looked at his shoes, a blush that for once was unassociated with liquor crept up his cheeks. "Santiago was kind enough to give me a place to sleep last night."

The molten anxiety burst into panic in his chest, but Ramón simply nodded, hoping nothing else showed. "That's wonderful." He graciously thanked Santiago before the duo continued on to their seat.

After the line of churchgoers began to slow to a trickle, Ramón made his way to the front of the church. As with every Sunday Mass, the acolytes lit the candles, everyone recited the Introductory Rites, and Ramón said the Greeting and then the Collect.

When he was done, he looked out upon the upturned faces of his congregation and breathed deep. He smelled the sweat of the town. The dust on their shoes, too. But he also smelled the old wooden pews, the open Bible before him, and the sweetness of the sacraments they'd just taken.

This was a good day.

"Good morning, my friends." He gazed around the room. Was it his imagination or was there less space between families? Were the pews more crowded than usual?

"Last week, I spoke to you about how we should respond when God chooses to remain silent. Despite prayers, fasting, pleading—our only answer is silence. I concluded last week that God's message can be found all around us. In the dirt at our feet. In the bark of the dog," he looked at Julia. "In the waters, too.

"It was brought to my attention that perhaps the message may be construed as blasphemy. That the Scriptures I quoted from this book," he tapped the large tome that lay open on the pulpit like a frog in the middle of a dissection, "was bastardized to fit my own agenda."

Gasps and nervous glances around the sanctuary punctuated the absurdity of it.

"Let me be the first to say that if encouraging you to explore God's creation is blasphemy," he took a deep breath and jumped, "then let us blaspheme all the louder."

He had expected silent stares, perhaps some gasps. What he hadn't expected were the shouts of "Amen" that rang through the church in what could only be described as thunderous applause.

He smiled in both relief and encouragement. Then his eyes found Santiago, seated between those standing, his face visible only briefly between hands clapping and being raised to the sky. The scowl had deepened, and the old man's eyes burned with nothing short of hatred.

David, meanwhile, glanced nervously between Santiago and Ramón.

Even the drunk can sense conflict, he thought.

When the noise in the church began to die down and his congregation took their seats once more, Ramón raised his hands to quicken the silence.

"This week's sermon will follow up on the lesson from last week.

"While last week we explored a silent God, this week we'll explore what the Scriptures say about *action*. If God is silent, it falls to us to seek him out.

"Chapter eleven in the book of Hebrews starts by defining faith. At first glance, it seems that it is simply a belief a person can have. That verse by itself can give us permission to believe and nothing else. But the rest of the chapter, perhaps the more *important* part of the chapter, details the great heroes of faith and how they *acted* on that belief.

"Many of us accept a belief and do nothing else. Our responsibility ends at our ears." A few chuckles. Good. "My friends, I'm here to tell you that your faith has saved you, but your actions *redeem* you."

Once again, his words were followed by multiple "Amen" and "Gloria a Dios."

With a gracious nod of his head, he dove into his sermon.

Ramón preached for over an hour using verses from the Bible to outline faith and action. His fears of being discovered as a blooming apostate were set aside for the confidence he had in speaking truth. His faith in God—or the God he believed in all his life—was changing. That didn't mean that his faith had disappeared. Instead, his faith was becoming something bigger than simply "one god and one truth" handed down by the old men who learned it from their old men who learned it from their old men and on and on.

Nearing the end of the sermon, he placed a hand over his heart and tried to meet every person's gaze. "Let me finish by quoting the book of Matthew. 'But seek first his kingdom and his righteousness and all things will be given to you as well.' This verse tells us what to do *first*. But what next? Live life like normal? No, my friends. We cannot live life like normal anymore. Seek His kingdom, yes, and then seek the *other* kingdoms that He created. The kingdom of creation, the kingdom of family, the kingdom of actionable faith.

"Too many times we're told what to believe." He looked directly at Santiago. "I'm here to tell you that *your* faith is something that only *you* can discover. If that faith brings you to a different understanding of God than mine, then we should be all the better for it. 'If any man think that he knows anything, he knows nothing.' That's what the Bible tells us.

"Keep learning. Keep seeking. And never settle for what you've been told to believe. Chances are that it's not exactly right."

The heavy *clomp* of the Bible closing rang through the church. Several church members began to stand and then the rest followed. Ramón made his way to the church exit and, just like every Sunday before, he wished his congregation well, or encouraged them with a soft word here and a hug or hand-shake there.

Santiago approached Ramón. The old man stared down at the younger like a hawk eyeing a mouse. Ramón was riding the high of a successful sermon and confidently stared back. Santiago looked down at his own shoes and shook the dust from them. Ramón laughed at the biblical practice of "taking nothing of the town with you" when leaving. It was absurd; it was an old-fashioned tactic meant to humiliate, but surprising even himself, Ramón didn't feel it.

Santiago's eyes continued to burn with disdain, his mouth downturned in a scowl.

"You laugh now, Ramón, but that laughter will turn to gnashing of teeth. Mark my words, you've just sealed your fate."

"I'm just sorry that you're so stuck in your ways that you can't see the very real truth when it's presented to you."

Santiago shook his head scornfully, turned on his heel, and walked away from the priest.

After several more handshakes with friends in his congre-gation, Julia approached and put a gentle hand on his arm.

"Julia! And Alejandra, too. I'm so glad you were able to make it. What did you think?"

"I'll let my sister speak for herself, but I'm very proud of you. That must have been difficult to voice out loud, especially after hearing the way Santiago spoke to you."

Alejandra stared down at him just as Santiago had, she was a head taller than Ramón. But the ghost of a smile creased a corner of her lips. "I must say that I'm surprised." Her voice was deep for a woman, the words and meter sure and practiced. "A priest of the Christian Church preaching to a congregation where perhaps everything they've been taught their entire lives is little more than the oral tales dictated by the male elders.

"You know, in many ancient cultures, it was the *women* who told the stories to the children and passed on the beliefs. Mayan and Aztec culture prided themselves on the oral traditions, as you probably know."

"Yes, I do know. It's true that my abuelo told me plenty of old stories, but it was my abuela who gave me a system of belief, sharing more of the religious stories rather than the legends."

"Your abuela sounds like a very smart woman." Alejandra smiled and while it didn't make her prettier, it certainly helped ease the fierceness of her features. "What was your favorite?"

Ramón blinked. "My favorite story from my abuela?" He hadn't thought about them seriously in some time. But the first that came to mind was the creation story, and he said so.

"It was always my favorite because I imagined Ixchel, the beautiful goddess marrying Itzamna and then having all those children. Then they worked together to create everything. I always thought it was a beautiful depiction of family working together, creating everything, each to their own desire."

Alejandra was nodding but glanced behind herself. "I can see we're holding up the line. I look forward to talking with you more, Padre. Very much so."

"Yes, I do as well."

The two sisters walked away. The tall, elder sister wearing a dress patterned with small bone crosses while Julia wore a simple green dress with yellow flowers along the hem. A strange pair, to be sure.

CHAPTER 10

Ramón napped after the church had been cleared and, in the afternoon, stopped by Julia's small home. In the past, he hadn't dared to stop. But after their conversation earlier, he felt it may be a good time.

He raised the knocker—a small round piece of metal beneath a rabbit's head—and let it fall several times.

The door opened a few moments later and Julia stood there, with Alejandra standing just behind her.

"Ramón! What a surprise. Please, come in!"

She stepped aside and gestured for him to enter, but he remained on the doorstep.

"Actually, I was wondering if you and Alejandra would like to join me on a walk. I'm planning on going to the cenote."

Julia hesitated after Alejandra shook her head *almost imperceptibly*, then said, "I'd love to join."

Alejandra's disappointment was etched plainly across her features. "Fine" was all she said before turning on her heel and stomping loudly away. Ramón was apologetic, but Julia waved it away and covered the smile that broke across her own face.

"It's fine. She'll be fine."

"If you say so," he replied, leading the way out of town through the western wrought-iron gate.

"I enjoyed your sermon today, Ramón." Julia broke the silence several minutes after they'd left the low white concrete wall of town behind. Their feet scuffed through the dirt and grit beneath their shoes. Birds wheeled overhead and every now and then, Ramón would hear the distant sounds of animal cries in the trees, growing louder as they approached the dense jungle.

"That makes me happy. And Alejandra seemed to enjoy it, too. I was surprised to see her, especially after hearing that she was struggling with her place in the world."

Julia nodded silently.

"Does she still feel the need to convince others of their wrongdoing?"

She didn't immediately answer, squinting ahead at the trees instead. Then, she answered, "She does. I'm not sure she'll ever change. It's in her nature, you know. She was created with this insatiable need to correct or ... I don't know, convince others of the error of their ways. She can be cruel."

"In what way?"

"Honestly, I'd rather not talk about it."

He shrugged and continued walking. "That's alright, too."

Julia changed the subject. "Santiago was noticeably upset after today's sermon."

Ramón made a sound that was half-laugh and half-disbelief. "Yes, he was. He wanted to ensure that I knew it, too."

"I only caught snatches of the conversation, even though he spoke loud enough for anyone to hear. He threatened to, what, strip you of your collar?"

"That's certainly what it sounded like. His displeasure seems to stem from something that plagues your sister, actually: traditionalism. He believes that he is right simply because it's the most widely accepted, or the longest-standing belief. I disagree. Now I do, I suppose. And something that I've come to understand—as I told you previously—is that perhaps beliefs should be slightly more flexible than stone. To borrow from Scripture, iron should sharpen iron, but that means that *both* pieces of iron change. Santiago wishes to be the sharpener but is unwilling to be sharpened in turn. That's the way leaders of the Church have always been. Traditionally, at least."

Julia nodded. A wisp of dark hair was lifted by the breeze and became trapped in her eyelashes. She made to move it several times and missed.

"Here," he said, stopping. He gently took the strand of hair and tucked it tenderly behind her ear. He let his hand cup her cheek for a moment longer than necessary before letting it drop to his side.

"Thank you," she said, blushing.

They continued walking in silence. Ramón had the almost unstoppable desire to reach for her hand. But he simply couldn't. His life as a priest prevented it.

Are you still a priest, though? Bound by canon law? The question was still buzzing in his head as they stepped beneath the shade of the trees. The air cooled instantly, and he heard Julia take a deep breath at the same time as he. Sweat had matted her hair to her head and began to drip down the sides of her face. She wiped it away self-consciously, and he smiled as he wiped the sweat from his own brow.

"I love it here," he said quietly, gazing up at the towering trees and the massive leafy fronds that seemed to wave at him from their branches high above. Birds of a million different colors flitted from tree to tree as splashes of color seen from the corner of his eyes.

"I do, too. It feels very much like home to me."

He looked at her. She'd never mentioned her home before, but he knew it wasn't La Ventana.

"Where is home?"

She sighed and looked at her hands. "Very far away."

Taking that as a cue to go no further, he said, "Come on, let's go to the cenote."

She nodded and followed.

Surprising himself, he held a hand out to her, intending mostly to help guide her through the trees—despite also knowing she knew the way without him.

Julia grinned and clasped the offered hand. She didn't let go after climbing over a large branch that had fallen, and Ramón didn't either. Together, they made their way through the undergrowth.

Ramón placed his palm on a moss-covered trunk that lay across the path and climbed over it. Still holding her hand, he helped Julia across it. She hiked her dress up above her knee to do it, but he carefully watched where she placed her feet to ensure she didn't slip coming down the other side. They talked quietly about the jungle, the animals, and their joys within it.

The path continued through the trees, and as Ramón ducked beneath a low branch of hanging moss, the cenote seemed to bloom before him. The crystal clear water's surface was as smooth as glass. Several ripples expanded across the surface where small drops of water fell from the rocks above. They were striated sandstone and slate, covered here and there with leafy green mosses. He could see the submerged portion of the stone as it ran all the way to the bottom of the pool, some twenty or so feet below. The depth of the water always made him nervous immediately, but he felt Julia's hand in his own and relaxed.

"I love this place more," he said.

Julia stepped up beside him. "I know you do. You're here just as often as you are in the church. I would argue that this place is more of a church than the actual building in town."

He smiled and indicated that they should sit. When they settled onto the mossy grass with their feet once again in the water with their shoes beside them, he said, "I hadn't thought of it like that, but it is. In a way, this is where I come to find clarity. I've certainly found a kind of understanding out here. I'm not sure who the priest is," they chuckled together, "but I would imagine that the same peace that churchgoers feel when they enter through the doors of the church is the same peace I feel with my feet in the water and my hands in the moss."

Julia swirled her feet through the water. Then she lifted their entwined fingers and met his eye. "It seems that the beliefs you spoke of are beginning to change in more ways than one."

It was Ramón's turn to blush, and he made to release her hand. She gripped it tighter.

"That's not a bad thing, Ramón."

He sighed. "It's like there is a war raging in my heart. On one side, everything I've ever believed, everything I've committed myself to. On the other, everything else that I see within the world. And some of those things can't both be true at the same time."

"Like what, Ramón?"

"How can God want a relationship with me, but I can't build a relationship for myself? It doesn't make sense to me, that my faith in God can be experienced better by those who are able to see an earthly representation of it. Even the Apostle Paul talked about it."

"That's true. What else?"

He knew what he wanted to say. What he wanted to say was that he was saved by an angel when he was young and, because of that, dedicated his life to the Lord. But since that day, he's never experienced anything supernatural. He's never seen any more evidence that God saved him for the purpose of preaching in La Ventana.

"I don't know if I can say it out loud." He felt his eyes sting with the threat of tears, but he forced them back down.

"Ramón. It can't be any 'worse' of a secret than the one you shared with me about your faith. I have no right to judge you."

He nodded. "Still, the war in my heart rages." He laughed without humor, then decided to share it anyway.

"I think you know that I drowned when I was young. Or nearly drowned. I was saved by... by an angel. At least, that's what I've thought all these years. Up until several months ago, I hadn't even considered that I was wrong. But recently, that particular subject—the basis for my belief—has come into question. What if it wasn't an angel? What if it wasn't supernatural at all? What if it was a dream? What if it was the final images my dying brain could muster? Or the way I remember that day is something contrived by a young and ignorant mind?"

"I need you to listen, Ramón, and I need you to listen well." She became very still and very serious. "Are you listening?"

"Yes," he said a little taken aback.

"What you experienced couldn't have been false. Deep down, deep down in your guts, in your soul, what do you think about that day?"

He swallowed. "I think it really happened."

"Do you also think that sometime in the last, I don't know, thirty years, you'd have come to the realization that it *wasn't* real?"

"Isn't that what I'm doing now, though? Maybe I'm just a late bloomer?" His attempt at levity failed.

"What's happening now isn't the same as coming to the conclusion that your near-death experience was a lie."

"How?" he questioned a little harsher than intended. "How is it different? Sure *I* believe it happened, but there's no one else to corroborate the story! Well, the angel, but she certainly hasn't shown up to say 'Hi, Ramón, I'm the one who saved you.' There's been *nothing* but my own heart telling me it's true. Only my life's telling me it's not."

"How can you be sure that the angel *hasn't* ever visited you?"

"I think I'd remember if an angel came down from heaven and admitted to saving me."

"What if the angel isn't from heaven?"

He barked a laugh. "Then it isn't an angel, is it?"

"No, it's not." The words were less comment and more of an answer.

"What?"

"Maybe it wasn't an angel."

"It couldn't have been a demon. At least, I don't think..." he trailed off.

"Ramón." She looked at him as if he'd missed the point entirely. Had he? "In your reevaluation of your faith, you've discovered that what you've been taught isn't necessarily the only truth. Make the logical assumption, here."

He thought for a moment. "We've been told everything is dualistic only. It falls into one of two categories, right or wrong. Right now, those categories are angels and demons. But that probably isn't true."

"It's not." She replied.

"How do you...?"

"Think back to your favorite story that your abuela told you. Ixchel and Itzamna. Could that one be true?"

"Creation couldn't have happened by both God and Ixchel."

She arched an eyebrow.

"But," he said studiously, "maybe they're just two sides of the same story. But that still doesn't explain the angel thing. Okay, Ixchel and Itzamna helped God create the world. That doesn't tell me *who saved me*."

The steady background sound of water changed, then. It went from *drip drip drip* to a sudden splash, and then silence. Ramón wouldn't have noticed it at all. Except Julia tilted her head and turned toward the sound. He followed her gaze, and he recoiled. A black snake, thick as his arm, was gliding through the water. Its body undulated through the glassy surface in a way that made his stomach roll.

Julia pulled her feet out slowly, and Ramón followed. The snake swam toward them, ripples spreading away from it as it swam through the space where their feet had been moments before. It's crimson tongue flicked in and out beneath obsidian black eyes that gleamed in the afternoon sun.

Julia whispered something under her breath that Ramón didn't catch. This wasn't a snake he was familiar with, and he'd been to the cenote—through the jungle, too—enough to have seen almost every species of creature that lived here.

The couple backed several steps from the water's edge where the snake's pointed nose peeked and bobbed several times before disappearing altogether. They saw the ripples of its movement, however, as it swam toward the distant side of the cenote and slithered between two huge ferns.

A yelp of surprise from that same direction made them jump and grasp each other's hand. A man bolted from the cover of the underbrush, leaping and spinning as if he'd walked through a spider's web. Clutched in the man's hand was a red wrapper.

It wasn't just any man, however.

"David?" Ramón asked, squinting at the man. Surely not. There were few who knew exactly which cenote Ramón favored, and no one aside from Julia had ever followed him.

The man stopped jumping and looked at Ramón, eyes wide and face flushed with shame. "I told you he'd be here," the drunk said, but not to Ramón.

Then it was clear and Ramón's heart sank. "Judas," he whispered.

A second man sauntered out from behind a large trunk and stood in front of David, holding a thick black walking stick that came to his waist.

"Yes. Yes, you did. Well done, my son." Santiago placed a hand on David's shoulder.

Julia hissed the old man's name with such poison that Ramón expected the man to turn tail and run.

"Well, well, well," said Santiago as he approached the two. He moved leaves and branches aside without breaking eye contact or stride. "It looks like I finally caught you in the act, *Father* Ramón."

"The act? Of what? Talking with a friend?"

He barked a laugh that rang out in the eerily silent jungle. "Oh yes, *talking* with a friend. Were you trading recipes of your favorite desserts?"

Ramón's heart began to beat faster. How much had he heard? "What do you want, Santiago? Why are you here?"

"I'm here for you, actually," said the man with a malicious grin.

"Me? What do you mean?"

"I've finally caught you in a trap you laid for yourself. Heresy is just the tip of the iceberg. Rumors of your heresy have spread like, well, like ripples in water." He pointed the large stick toward the stilling cenote's surface. "And that's not even the least of it. Blasphemy. Consorting with *whores*." The last word was directed at Julia.

"Oh? My teachings have reached so far and wide that you've come to town to hear them?" He chuckled a little at the absurdity of it, but his head was throbbing.

"It's no laughing matter, Ramón." Santiago stopped and became very serious. "In a way, your teachings *have* reached far and wide. I wouldn't take that as a compliment, though. Whispers of heresy have reached the ears of the archdiocese and I've been dispatched to determine if these rumors are to be believed. And I'm beginning to believe they aren't rumors."

Ramón crossed his arms and felt sweat bead across his forehead and temples. "The Catholic Church is so concerned with a tiny town and its one priest's teaching, that they send a Cardinal to see if it's true?"

David shifted behind Santiago, the drunkard's eyes ticked back and forth like a clock between the two men.

"Heresy is like an illness, Ramón." He began to pace along the edge of the water. "At first, perhaps nothing more than a cough or runny nose. Left untreated, however, the illness can spread into a high fever. Left untreated still..." he shrugged and continued "who knows how far it would go."

"You're equating my teachings—the teachings that for years have rallied this town to the Lord's banner, I might add— to a disease? A road that leads to death?"

"What did you say this morning, Ramón? What was last week's entire sermon on? Hm? Wasn't it on a silent God that refuses to answer? Wasn't the solution that *you* preached from the pulpit where God stationed you, to seek out your own answers?

"And this morning's? The whole lesson was pointing people *away* from the Church, *away* from His teachings."

Santiago's face was turning red, and his voice was quivering with rage.

Ramón felt flustered, and he looked away and shrugged. "Santiago—"

"You will address me as Father!" The other priest shouted.

Ramón felt the back of his teeth with his tongue to prevent himself from replying in kind. Julia, still holding onto his arm, gave it a squeeze.

When Ramón spoke, he did his best to remove all sarcasm from his voice. "Did I not also back up that solution with the Scriptures? Did I not point to the Word of God as the solution, as well?"

"Oh very conveniently, you did, using verses that supported your own agenda and ignored the agenda of the Most High God and His servants in the Church!"

And there it was. Perhaps called out more blatantly than he would have believed, but there it was. The "Agenda of the Most High God" was, historically, not a good one. Well, perhaps the agenda of the people who follow the Most High God. God's agenda was relatively unknown, as he hadn't descended from heaven in a couple thousand years to give an update.

Ramón didn't dare state *that*, as it *was* outright heresy of the highest degree.

This was going nowhere, and now Ramón was anxious that under this new priest's scrutiny, he'd be removed from his post. No doubt they'd install Santiago himself to "right the wrongs" that Ramón had supposedly inflicted upon the people of La Ventana. He didn't want that. He didn't want that at all. He wanted to continue to lead the people. He wanted to help them navigate the difficulties of losing children or loved ones, how to handle the stresses of marriage and life, how to search for divine answers in the mundane.

"Father Santiago," not *entirely* the respectful title he'd demanded, "what does the Church require of me?"

Ramón felt Julia's fingers tighten on his arm, but he patted her hand reassuringly.

Surprisingly, Santiago's features softened. His fierce eyes cooled, and the furrowed brow smoothed. "To hear you ask this is the first step. At the very least, I can report that you recognize the need for change."

Not exactly what Ramón had intended to communicate, but maybe it would make Santiago leave.

"Second, you'll need to apologize to the congregation; to confess to them your sins and the misuse of your station in leading them astray—however unintentional."

Ramón felt himself bristle at that, but only asked, "Anything else?"

Santiago walked slowly to the younger priest. He held the walking stick off the ground and put the other hand on Ramón's shoulder, looking down at him as a grandfather would look at a contrite grandchild. "You'll need to come with me to Mexico City and confess before the Archdiocese himself. This is justice."

Ramón took a moment to formulate an answer, to collect himself and weigh all the things he'd heard. His childhood belief rang through his mind. His adult faith rang in opposition to it. But so, too, did the recent words from Julia, the slight adjustments and pivots that his perspective had taken.

"I won't be doing that." He spoke plainly.

Santiago's smile faltered then deepened into a familiar scowl.

"If you want to go back to the Archdiocese and tell him that my teachings are heretical, then be my guest. But you'll be lying. It's not heresy to teach truth, especially truth based in Scripture. Is it the truth that the Church wants people to believe? Is it the truth that *you* want them to know? No. Only, last I checked, the Catholic Church doesn't hold the license for truth. In fact, if you teach that the Church knows the truth instead of God's own truth through Scripture, doesn't that border on heresy?"

Santiago's eyes darkened as his scowl deepened, casting shadowed lines across his face.

"Perhaps I should go to the Archdiocese and tell him how *Father* Santiago believes the truth is something that can only be distributed, not something that can be discovered. Perhaps all the saints in Mexico City need to hear that Santiago is giving truth as if it's sweets for children, saying 'This is what truth is, only I can enlighten you.'"

Santiago lifted a finger and Ramón was more than satisfied when it trembled with every syllable the man spoke.

"You are a heretic." Santiago's voice was soft but filled with false authority. "You are the devil's pawn. You have been bewitched by the devil himself and filled with his evil. You must be cast out of the Church. They must be notified of this wolf in sheep's clothing. They must know at once!"

Ramón, surprising even himself, said, "I'm sorry, Santiago, but you'll be sorely disappointed with their response. When you do go speak to the Archdiocese, tell him that Father Ramón in La Ventana is—in a twist he won't see coming—teaching from the Scriptures. Not only that, he's encouraging his congregation to experience God's glory through His creation. I doubt they'll even stay in their seats, clamoring over one another to dethrone this supposed heretic. If only I could be there to hear what he has to say about that."

Santiago's face had grown purple with rage.

"If there's nothing else, I think you both should leave this place."

Ramón gestured back toward town, where the trail disappeared beneath the greens and browns of jungle life.

"No," said the old priest. "No, Ramón, you're coming with me."

"I hate to disappoint you, but I'm actually not."

"You *will* come with me, or I'll drag you unconscious from this jungle!" he bellowed.

"You will do no such thing," Julia said, widening her stance and facing Santiago beside Ramón.

"Tell your whore to be quiet or I'll shut her up myself."

"Bastardo!" said someone to Ramón's right. A flash of dark material and Santiago was suddenly reeling backward as if he'd been pushed. Alejandra stood at Ramón's side. Either he'd been too slow to follow her with his eyes or she'd been too fast.

"This man is an abomination," she said. "Even for a human, he deserves to die."

"To die?" Ramón nearly squealed the same time that Julia shouted, "Ali, no!"

Santiago, who had regained his feet thanks to David's helping hand, hefted his walking stick like a club. "Ah, the *other* sister. Are you a whore, too?"

"I'm something you Christians have forgotten to fear," she said with a calm that sent chills down Ramón's spine.

Ramón tensed his muscles to spring forward. He saw himself leap through the space between them, arm cocked and fist clenched. The blow to the old man's nose would break it, and blood would spray through the air. Ramón would stand over the frail old man, victorious, as David fled through the trees like a scolded dog.

Instead, Julia stepped forward. Before anyone could stop him, Santiago swung his club in a downward arc that connected with Julia's head with a meaty *thwack*. It echoed across the surface of the cenote and rebounded off the arched rock formation.

Alejandra lunged at the man while his attention was on Julia, but Ramón pivoted, using his coiled muscles to propel him forward to catch Julia. He was a moment too late. Her body crumpled and, as close as she was to the water, her listless form broke through the surface of the liquid crystal. The blood from her wound mixed with the cenote in purple clouds that unfurled as she sank deeper and deeper.

CHAPTER 11

"No!" he screamed with desperation. The water was there, Julia was *right there*, but he couldn't reach her. He heard scuffling behind him and knew that Alejandra and Santiago were having it out, but he didn't care. Julia's form was sinking deeper into the bloody water. The green dress she'd worn trailed above her like mossy arms requesting aid.

He had a choice to make, now.

Jump into the same water he'd nearly drowned in all those years ago and try to save the woman he loved.

Or watch her finish what he'd been saved from decades before.

He hesitated for only a second, and that second may have meant the difference between life and death.

He inhaled deeper than he'd ever inhaled before and leapt into the water. The long robe he wore would get tangled in his flailing arms and legs, but he had to get in the water, he had to reach Julia. He stared through the millions of tiny bubbles for the sinking body, kicking and swimming as best he could. The waters of the cenote had always been clear from the surface. Now that he was beneath them, he was in awe. It was like looking through a single pane of glass. *Everything* was visible, from the tiny fish that swam lazily at the bottom of the deep pool to the mossy grass that waved in tiny currents near the rocks.

He couldn't focus on that now, however. Instead, he followed the purple cloud of blood down to where Julia's body sank ever deeper. She had to be nearly ten feet deep. The rest of the distance yawned beneath her, still.

He pushed off the rock face nearby and moved his arms and legs, trying to remember how to coordinate his body to swim.

Kick.

Reach.

Kick.

Reach.

He was getting closer, but his ears had an alien pressure in them that made it difficult to focus.

Julia's hair floated weightlessly around her, like a corona of wispy darkness. It looked very much like—

An angel, he thought to himself.

He pumped his legs and arms faster and faster, but all the while, the image of the angel from his childhood floated beneath him, just as in the vision it had been above him. It was impossible, perhaps a trick of the mind. But no, what had Julia said? *"Deep down in your guts, in your soul, what do you think about that day?"*

As he swam through the trail of her blood, his guts told him what he saw now was true.

He grasped a curl of her dress's green material. Julia's descent slowed but didn't stop, and he could see the floor of the pool maybe six feet below her. Her face was pale, and she looked already like a corpse. He prayed she wasn't dead. To whom he prayed, he wasn't sure.

His mind was reeling with all too many implications, but he swatted them away. He had one focus—save Julia.

Pulling with all his might, he managed to tilt Julia's floating form toward him. Her hair trailed behind her and the blood, still puffing like crimson smoke from an open wound on her scalp, did the same. He had a brief moment where he expected her eyes to fly open, but instead of the beautiful brown he was used to, he'd see the milky white of death within them.

An air bubble gurgled past his lips and wobbled its way above his head toward the surface. The pressure in his ears was painful, now, and his lungs were beginning to ache. Soon, he'd be out of breath and he still had more than twelve feet to swim *up,* but with a body in tow.

Ramón hooked an arm under one of Julia's and grasped her ribs on the other side, not caring how close it was to her breast. With his other hand, he reached toward the rising bubbles and kicked like a madman.

His lungs were burning now, and he could feel them beginning to spasm, to beg for air. He kicked frantically, desperately, reaching and kicking, swimming through blood-clouded water, feeling both of their bodies moving through the water.

Only, when he looked down, he saw that they'd barely moved. Their descent had halted, but there was barely any progress toward the surface. There would be no way to make it to the surface before his already desperate lungs collapsed.

He stopped kicking. It was useless, after all. He would drown. But perhaps she didn't have to. Maybe he could save her, somehow.

He pulled Julia's pale blue face to his, cupped her cheeks in his hands, and pressed his lips to hers. He exhaled, forcing every molecule of breath from his body and into hers. He didn't know if it would help, but she needed it more than he did.

When his lungs were empty and spasmed in response, he pulled her body up and pushed with all his might, kicking with his feet to give as much momentum to the body of his love as he could. The edges of his vision clouded over once, twice, and then settled.

The momentum it took to push her up had the reverse effect on him—he'd been pushed straight to the bottom where his feet crunched into the gritty sand and rock nearly twenty feet beneath the surface of La Puerta.

He looked around one last time at his final resting place. Black spots danced across his entire vision now. With resignation, he knew he had only seconds left.

How very fitting, the priest said to himself.

The pressure in his ears increased, and he winced, cupping his hands over his ears and blinking through the pain stabbing behind his eyes. His lips were still clamped closed, but his throat was spasming too. The water, once clear, had turned a murky violet from Julia's blood.

When he could resist no longer, he opened his mouth and took a deep breath of the deep water. It gushed down his throat and filled his lungs almost instantly. He barely registered the coppery sweetness of Julia's blood on his tongue.

He was dying, and this would be his grave.

His body convulsed, arms flailing and back arching spasmodically. He thought gruesomely, *I didn't think I'd be alive to experience the throes of death.*

The muscles in his throat flexed and clenched repeatedly in a single second. His chest, now full of water, felt heavy. He had the urge to cough, but twenty feet down, he didn't see the point and let the urge die in his mind.

His body stopped spasming, and he thought with relief, *it's finished.* He expected his consciousness to fade somehow, the same way the light does as the sun sinks behind the horizon. His life force had left him, certainly. Perhaps his soul remained and when he opened his eyes, he'd be staring at his cooling body at the bottom of the cenote as he drifted up to heaven.

He hoped. Or a part of him did, at least.

This is taking longer than I thought it would, he contemplated. And it was his thought, something he formed in his mind, not some random string of words his dying brain shuffled together.

He opened his eyes and looked around. He wasn't staring at his own body. At first, he could see nothing but a hazy blue-gray haze. He blinked several times and inhaled. He couldn't smell anything. *That was to be expected when you die,* he thought. It took several seconds for him to realize that he was staring at the bottom of the cenote. His body had drifted, and he was lying prone several inches from the floor of the pool. He turned his head the side, seeing the purple cloud of Julia's blood settling around him like a fog.

What is this? he wondered.

Then, *Julia!*

He lunged, pushing the rocky pool bottom from beneath him and spiraling upward through the water impossibly fast. Julia's body bobbed face-up at the surface of the cenote above him. He barely kicked, and then he was beside her, gliding easily through the water. Blood still leaked slowly from the wound on her head, spreading and clouding the water around her.

He gathered her in his arms. He wasn't sure how he'd get her onto dry land over the lip of rock that jutted out above the water. He kicked his feet to get as much momentum as he could and suddenly burst from the cenote in a spray of blood-clouded water.

He didn't know what was happening. Distantly, he wondered if this was the divine work of God, finally showing up in the last few seconds of his life.

He couldn't believe his eyes, and his mind told him he was crazy, but as he stared, he confirmed that he was floating several feet above the cenote. Water ran down Julia's lifeless form, and his own arms and legs to drip back into the pool in a heavy pattering rain.

He moved forward as if he were still in water. He floated toward the ground and landed gently on the mossy surface of stone.

He laid Julia at his feet. Her dark hair was plastered across her pale face, but he thought she was still breathing. Barely.

He stood and stared around the small clearing. Santiago stood over the body of an ancient woman. The priest clutched a large black snake—dead—in his fist. He stared down at the old woman, chest heaving and a victorious, a bloody grin on his face. Ramón had no idea who the old woman was or where Alejandra went, but justice for Julia burned in his chest, stoked by the man's false words.

"Santiago," Ramón began but stopped. His voice no longer sounded human. Now it sounded like clear running water, smooth and as sure as a summer spring.

The old priest turned around quickly. The limp snake in his hand swung feebly with the movement until Santiago released it from his grip, and it dropped lifelessly to the jungle floor.

"Ramón, you're alive," he said, though his voice had changed, as well. Before, it was the voice of a man who had traveled much and seen even more. Now, it seemed to sound like a dusty road, a gravelly grate with an underlying tone of menace.

"What have you done?"

Santiago smiled and glanced back at the body of the old woman.

"I've finally exacted revenge, millennia in the making."

"Revenge?"

He smiled wickedly at Ramón. "You still don't see it, do you?"

The old man stepped aside and gestured to the bloody and beaten old woman behind him. She looked vaguely familiar, and after a moment, it dawned on him why. "Alejandra?"

Santiago laughed. "That's her name now, yes, but I know her by a different name."

Ramón waited.

"Ixik Kab."

The name held power. It was strong and struck a chord of fear and respect deep within his heart. It was well known to him, he had reason to respect it. Ixik Kab was the Goddess of Death, ushering souls to Xibalba after they passed—or dragging them to Xibalba if death hadn't reached them, yet.

"The Goddess of Death," Ramón said aloud, still unused to the sound of his new voice. Santiago nodded. "How could you know that? How could you seek revenge for millennia?"

The grisly priest, still grinning, stood over the woman—or goddess—like a coliseum victor. "The church will be victorious, Ramón. I've pored over countless texts, searched innumerable towns and villages, followed clues and tips for decades. There is only one truth, and that is the truth of the Christian God. I've been tasked with removing these pagan gods from the Earth. And now," he indicated Ixik Kab, motionless and bleeding, at his feet. "there's one less in the world. Soon," he pointed the blood-spattered end of his cane at Julia, "there will be two less."

Ramón looked at Julia and back at Santiago and, nearly shouting, said, "Julia isn't a goddess. Why would you think something so insane? How would you even come to the conclusion that these legends exist? You're insane!"

Ramón's throat hurt; his whole body thrummed with an unfamiliar buzzing pain.

"You are the king of fools, Ramón, if you haven't learned Julia's true identity by now. The Mayan pantheon was led by multiple gods and goddesses. You know this. The records we have are uncertain, of course." The old man began to pace, effecting the tone of a teacher. "Tell me, Ramón, what do you know of Ixik Kab and her counterpart?"

Ramón wasn't sure what this would accomplish. "Julia needs medical assistance, Santiago. I will not stand here and debate legends."

He made to scoop her up but Santiago screamed in rage. "Answer me!"

When Ramón looked up, the calm grandfatherly priest had been replaced with a crazed zealot, eyes wide with rage and teeth bared in a grisly snarl. The man would no doubt hurt Julia if Ramón didn't comply, so he answered from where he knelt beside her form.

"Some stories said Ixik Kab was one of two deities. Either she was a beautiful young woman, goddess of fertility and love, sometimes called "the rainbow goddess," or Ixchel. Other scripts talk of the old crone, goddess of death and destruction. Perhaps two sides of the same coin, a shapeshifter of sorts. Still others report that Ixchel is one goddess, who helped create the world, while Ixik Kab is another, a separate goddess."

Santiago nodded and smiled as Ramón recited what he'd been taught as a child and never believed. "And now we know, don't we," growled the old man. "I came to La Ventana for one goddess, but to find two ... the Lord is truly with me."

Ramón stood in front of Julia, protecting her as best he could from the other, clearly deranged man. "God isn't with you, Santiago." Ramón's fists clenched and unclenched. "God has abandoned you. God has abandoned *all* of us."

Santiago's crazed grin didn't fade, but it turned predatory. "Finally bloomed into your true form, then. Heretic and blasphemer, devil's thrall. 'Take all the leaders and slay them in broad daylight, those who serve the other gods.' Numbers 25. It seems that God has given me authority to deliver life and death."

"Authority isn't given to you. God claims that for himself. We humans are meant to simply wait for an answer, yet no answer is ever given. 'Jesus said to them "authority on heaven and earth has been given to me alone."' It would seem you are mistaken."

Santiago scoffed. "The book of Luke says 'I have given you authority to trample on snakes...'" he said, kicking the dead black ribbon at his feet, and continued, "'and scorpions, nothing will harm you.' It would seem he has. As for waiting, Psalms says 'to wait patiently for him to act.' In your youthful impulsivity, Ramón, you have forgotten that God will answer. Sometimes silence *is* the answer."

"'I saw under the sun no justice in that place, wickedness replaced righteousness.' Santiago, I believe that verse is for you." Ramón glanced at Julia, his throat tightening and knowing that he could do little to protect her. "The thief comes to kill and destroy, I've come to have life and to have it full."

Santiago's face hardened. "How dare you accuse *me* of wickedness and claim the words of Christ! I have witnessed your wickedness myself." He held the bloody cane above his head. Beads of blood drooled down the haft and over his hands. "I have witnessed it in *you!* God has given me the right to exact vengeance upon you and these demons. 'What does the Lord require of you but to do justice.' And Justice I will have, Ramón. First you, and then the devil whore."

Santiago stepped toward Ramón, brandishing his bloody club. Ramón didn't how he'd fare against the old man, but the buzzing pain was gathering and circulating through his chest and arms. In two steps, Santiago was within range to swing his club toward Ramón's head. It whistled through the air, and Ramón reacted.

The club connected with his upraised palm. Instead of being diverted as Ramón intended, its momentum stopped completely, then the staff shattered. A blue light erupted from his palm and an electric *crack* resounded through the jungle.

Santiago was thrown back several steps, arms flailing and feet sliding in the dust and mud. He regained his composure after stumbling and stared wide-eyed at the cracked and splintered stick in his hand. His eyes found Ramón, and they searched. "What have you done?"

Ramón's mind was reeling, but through it all, a verse came to mind like sunlight through parting clouds. "Those He called He also justified, those He justified, He glorified."

"What?" Santiago bent closer, stunned disbelief clear on his face.

"'The Law of the spirit has set you free from the burden of death.'" It was Ramón's turn to draw himself up, and as he did so, his feet left the ground. "Santiago, I have been freed from the shackles of faith. No longer does my belief rely on what weaker men have relayed as inerrant truth. Now, my truth is found in the entirety of the world."

"*Blasphemy!*" the old priest cried. "'Just as Eve was deceived by the serpent, so too have you been led astray by its cunning.' You are condemned to Hell, Ramón. God has abandoned you, 'You have made yourself a god!'" Santiago covered his face and began to weep. "You spout the fires of Hell the book of James warns us of! I damn you to the eternal burning lake of Sulphur!"

With Ramón's attention focused on Santiago and Santiago preoccupied with his own disbelief, neither of them saw Julia struggle to her feet. Shaky but standing, she placed a hand on Ramón's leg. He turned in surprise, landed back on the ground, and immediately put his arms around her to both support and hold her.

"Julia!" he cried, checking her head and gently cupping her face in his hands.

"How many of my brothers and sisters have you killed, Santiago?" Her voice trembled, and she had to stop several times to steady her own breathing, but her eyes burned.

Santiago looked at her, lips pursed. "Enough of them that I'm surprised you and your sister didn't know about me."

"You will die today, Santiago. God-Hunter and Wound of Xibalba."

Ramón was surprised by the titles she threw. *She knew,* he thought. *She knew there was something out there killing her family.*

And with that, it settled into his mind that she was, in fact, more than human.

Julia's eyes darted to meet Ramón's, and she smiled weakly at him, some of the fire fading from her eyes as she did so. "It's true," she said. "I'm sorry to have deceived you. But it was nice for a time to pretend to be a human."

Ramón nodded and heard Santiago scream. "Fools! You insolent, wicked, blaspheming... I curse you, and Justice will find you both. I curse you to the depths of the earth and the heights of heaven. May you *never* find peace. May you always seek and never find!"

Julia tried to take a step, but weak as she was, she stumbled to the ground. She would have fallen had Ramón not reached out and eased her to the moss at their feet.

"The curse is on you, Santiago," Ramón said calmly. "And lucky for us all, Justice is here."

Ramón felt power churning within him, and just as when he'd willed himself to the ground, he willed himself above it. He floated and closed the distance between him and Santiago in the blink of an eye. He willed himself to be just before the old man, and then he was, looming over him with the surety of a god.

Santiago stumbled back when Ramón suddenly appeared before him, but Ramón grasped the man's shirt with one hand and his throat with the other. Ramón lifted the man easily. "The mystery that has been kept hidden from you has now been disclosed," he quoted quietly from Scripture. "I was worried, Santiago, that all my time chasing God would have been wasted. Instead, it brought me here, and it brought me you." The old man's eyes widened. "Doesn't the Bible also say 'He will repay you for all the years the locusts have stolen'?

"I am done waiting for God to answer. I'm done waiting for Justice to be done. Santiago, you and the church that you serve belong in Hell. Justice is now mine, and I condemn you to death."

He hadn't known it at the bottom of the cenote, it was all too much for his mind to take in. But he took only a moment to ponder the punishment for Santiago and was assaulted with thousands of memories of eons past. Knowledge to which he lay no claim flooded his mind. The creation, experiences of wars and battles with conquistadores, maps and travels through impossibly vibrant worlds and just as impossibly dark ones. Xibalba, Metnal, all of it was his to claim.

And so he did.

Holding Santiago by the throat, Ramón launched himself through the air. Santiago's scream of defiance was cut off abruptly as they crashed through the surface of the cenote. He dove deep, propelling himself forward with the same divine power that coursed through his bones. He didn't understand it—not yet, at least.

One thing that he did understand was that all this time, a door to Xibalba sat at the deepest point of this cenote—of *every* cenote.

Bubbles from the struggling man's mouth and nose rushed past their bodies as they sped through the water toward the deepest and furthest points of the cenote, where even the sunlight dared not tread. Here, it was nearly pitch black, and yet Ramón continued to dive, able to see everything through a kind of aqua-blue haze. Santiago's struggles became more feeble. It didn't matter. Not anymore. Justice would be served.

A vibrating hum crept through Ramón's mind, and he knew they'd arrived. Deep in the depths of the cenote's cave system stood a large round door. On it was carved a Mayan depiction of Cizin, or Ah Puch. The deity's head was covered with an undulating black eel, and his body was skinless bone.

Ramón brought Santiago's mostly lifeless form before the door. The old man's eyes fluttered open, and when he saw the door and the carving, his feeble struggles became slightly less feeble; little life remained in him.

The statue on the door turned toward them and, at that instant, became a living being. Ah Puch stood between Ramón and the door to Xibalba, the god's skeletal grin wide. Ramón offered the visiting priest. Ah Puch took Santiago, the eel above him writhed through the Death God's empty sockets as they gazed into Santiago's paling face. For a brief moment, Ramón feared he wouldn't accept the offering. From whatever memories Ramón now possessed, he knew this deity would accept, he must.

Just to be certain, Ramón inclined his head slightly, putting a hand to his chest and then forehead in a sign of submission.

Ah Puch returned the minor bow and, taking Santiago's body with him, turned away. The door rolled open, a stone circle rotating and grating against thousands of years of rock. Beyond the door was an infinite darkness more complete than any sunless depth that could be reached on this plane. Ah Puch tossed Santiago's body through the open door where it twisted lifelessly. Ramón cautiously approached to watch. There were no ancient memories of this.

Santiago's body floated in the darkness, no doubt Ramón's human eyes would have seen nothing at all. But empowered as he was with whatever godlike powers he now possessed, Ramón saw the pale body as it sailed weightlessly through the darkness. Only, it wasn't *all* dark. Pinpricks of light began to suddenly appear. First one, then two, then more. The lights were moving in what at first were random directions.

No, he thought as he watched. *No, they're converging on Santiago's body.*

And they were. He now saw the nightmarish black forms to which the pinpricks of light belonged. They were lanky, disproportionate things with mouthfuls of obsidian teeth. More shadow creatures and ephemeral beings than actual solid creatures that lived on Earth.

Santiago's body jerked suddenly one way then another. The creatures were feeding.

The body spasmed for several seconds before becoming completely occluded by the shadow creatures.

The door slid closed, then, and Ramón sidled away from Ah Puch, whose power could be felt even from several feet away. The God turned toward him, nodded again, and then returned once more to the door as a simple carving. The sound of stone grating on stone subsided and Ramón was left alone in the sunless depths of the cenote.

CHAPTER 12

Ramón waited for several seconds before pushing off the smooth stone floor of the cave and propelling himself back to the surface.

When his face broke through the water, his first instinct was to inhale as deeply as possible. But his lungs weren't burning, his limbs weren't heavy. In fact, there was no indication that he needed to breathe at all.

He pushed that mystery aside for later. There would be time enough for him to investigate after he checked on Julia.

He jumped easily from the water to the stone. Droplets of water scattered through the air, sparkled like gently arcing gemstones, and pattered on the jungle floor around the cenote. Julia was bent low over her sister, keening quietly as her shoulders hitched up and down with emotion. Alejandra— Ixik Kab—was motionless. From what Ramón could tell, she was truly dead.

"Julia," he said quietly and approaching slowly. She didn't turn, but she sat up a little straighter and cocked an ear. "Julia," he repeated.

Then she did turn. Her face was wet with tears, eyes swollen and cheeks red with the blush of grief. Her hair had dried almost completely, except for a swollen cut across her scalp that continued to slowly ooze blood. He wondered distantly how long it had taken to deliver Santiago to Xibalba.

She stood, then. Ramón blinked as a look of suspicious concern crossed her face. "Ramón?"

He nodded. "Yes, it's me."

She didn't approach him as she stood over her sister's body, as if protecting it from him. Ramón gestured toward the old crone on the ground. "Is that Alejandra?"

Julia glanced where he'd gestured. "Um, yes. Well..." she trailed off.

"Santiago was spouting theories that sounded more than a little crazy. Were they true?"

Julia hesitated and then knelt again beside her sister. Ramón knelt as well, watching quietly.

The dead woman didn't resemble Alejandra, if he was honest with himself. Had this woman approached him on the streets of La Ventana, he wouldn't have recognized her as Julia's sister at all. Her nose was much longer, like a childish depiction of an old witch in the woods. The skin of her face was a mass of wrinkles. Even the slackness in death didn't completely remove the crisscrossing labyrinth of wrinkles across her forehead and cheeks. Her mouth was a gaping bloody maw, nearly toothless. Her gums were clearly visible, and Ramón imagined what a terrible, vicious smile it would have been. Her thin hair was gray and stringy, barely enough to cover her scalp, and not nearly enough to cover the gaping wounds that split the scalp in several angry oozing cuts.

"That's not your sister," he said plainly.

Julia sighed with what Ramón thought was resignation. "Not in the traditional sense, no."

"Then is she..." he couldn't believe it enough to say it.

"She is."

"Then that makes you..." Again, still not enough evidence to believe it.

"I am. I am Ixchel."

Ramón sat back on his haunches, stunned. The water trickled from his clothes—which were heavy in their wetness—and ran into the grass and dirt in tiny rivers between his feet and under his palms. He stared at those tiny rivers trying to understand the magnitude of these truths.

"All this time—" he began, but she held a hand up to forestall him.

"Who I am—who I *really* am—is no different than the person you know as 'Julia,' I have and always will be true to myself. It became ... inconvenient several hundred years ago to go by my true name. Since then, I've been called by different names, but I've never changed who I am." She stared down at the old dead crone on the ground. "My sister didn't have that luxury."

It was silent for several minutes. Ramón, still processing, had no response. When Julia spoke again, it was thick with emotion. "We spoke about her nature and how she had a hard time adjusting to the new order." Julia wiped her nose and sniffed. "She was the Ferrier of souls, and she took her role very seriously. When our people began to turn away from the faith of their ancestors, Ixik Kab took it upon herself to continue. She judged many and ferried them to Ah Puch, to Xibalba."

"Yes, I've seen it."

Julia nodded as if this wasn't a surprise. "She believed that eventually, everyone would realize the truth. When I told her about you and your faith, and your subsequent crisis of it, she was intrigued. She saw you not as someone to judge but rather as someone to convince. Or at least, someone who could *help* convince the masses.

"I tried to dissuade her, but she would have none of it. She was certain that a man of the Christian faith was already set up to fail—too many contradictions and rules to be considered 'righteous.' So when you inevitably gave up on your faith, perhaps you could settle in the comfort of the old faiths, two friends of yours being gods."

Ramón nodded. That was, after all, what happened. At least to a certain extent, he supposed. His crisis of faith had opened him up to the possibilities that *everything* he believed couldn't be *exactly* right. When he began exploring it through that lens, he saw the holes clearly. And what better way to see that than through the view that the entire world was the church, and the lessons were on the leaves of trees, the chatter of monkeys, and the songs of birds.

"And Santiago?"

Julia's breath hitched, and she began to cry again, tenderly moving some of Ixik Kab's hair away from the vacant eyes. "We'd heard rumors about some of the others, that yet another madman was hunting gods. There have been many who hunted us. We've avoided or killed them easily. Many of my brothers enjoyed the latter, but I was much more content to live the simple life.

"We didn't think anything of it, Ixik and I. You see we've always been together, or at least in the same area. That's why so many stories can't keep us straight." She chuckled, but it was filled with whimsical sorrow. "No one could pin us down. Either we were the same being with different personalities, or we were two people, or something in between."

She squeezed her dead sister's shoulder then turned to Ramón, her eyes red. "I've never lived in a world without her. What am I supposed to do?"

Ramón had no response, but he knew that he needed to do *something*.

"Do you want me to take her to Xibalba?" He wasn't sure if he'd remember the way. Whatever power had come upon him in the water had dissipated somewhat. The memories were there but seen as if in a dream.

Julia shook her head. "No. Unlike you humans, when one of the Holy die, the earth takes us into itself so that we're reunited with the world we once governed. It should happen soon."

"Can I sit with you until it does?"

"I'd like that," she said and sat back on her rump, resting her arms on her knees and holding her hands together between them.

Ramón sat quietly while Julia sat and whispered something. Prayers, he assumed. There had to be some ritual that the Mayan Pantheon used to send off its own. Even in that thought, his mind felt a pressure from another plane of existence.

For nearly half an hour, they sat in silence while the body of Ixik Kab cooled before them. Several times, Ramón wondered if perhaps Julia's description was a metaphor for the physical act of burial. He intended to say so after so many quiet minutes had passed. But then the ground began to tremble before them and then the moss and rocks *rippled*. It was impossible, but at this point, Ramón's sense of possible and impossible had become something fluid.

The body of Ixik Kab, Goddess of the Underworld and co-creator of the Earth and everything in it, sister to Ixchel, daughter of Itzamna, began to sink. The ground rolled gently over her arms and legs then torso and face until she was completely buried in the ground. The earth closed over the body and resealed itself just as it had been. No blemish disturbed or stone marked the place where Ixik Kab had been taken by the earth.

Julia hiccupped and sniffed several times, then grasped Ramón's hand. "Now that she is gone and safe within the arms of the Mother, what are we to do with you?"

"What do you mean?" he asked a little defensively.

"You've changed."

"How?"

Julia pointed to the water. "Look."

He released her hand and cautiously peered over the water's edge. He expected to see himself—the drawn face he'd seen in the mirror for thirty-odd years, ragged exhaustion clear across his features below a mop of light disheveled hair. What he saw instead was completely foreign.

His hair was disheveled, yes, but the similarities ended there. His light hair had darkened to black. His skin was smoother than it had been, and while he couldn't be sure in the gently shifting reflection, he was certain that his jaw seemed ... stronger, somehow, more pronounced. But that wasn't even the biggest change. His eyes, previously a dull caramel, had changed to a vibrant aquatic blue. And not just in color. The color within resembled the ever-shifting colors of sunlit waters. They flashed as if the sun were actually shining through them, a reflective shimmer captured the essence of both his fear and the beauty of it. Wonderfully deep and dangerous in its own way.

"What is this?" he asked, still staring at his reflection and touching his face.

"Can you tell me what happened? One of the last things I remember is trying to attack Santiago. The next thing I was waking up on the stone here for only a moment before passing out again. Then when I came to, you and Santiago were gone."

Ramón decided to lay it all out, just as he'd experienced it. Too much strangeness had occurred for him to balk at a little more.

Julia sat quietly while he told his story, just as it had happened to him. Her expressions changed with the rise and fall of it, but she listened intently when he began describing his experience at the bottom of the cenote.

"You inhaled the water?"

"I had no choice, I was dying. I simply took a deep dying breath as if it were air. I felt it fill my lungs and felt the pressure on my body as it was filled with it."

"But you said my blood also colored the water."

Ramón nodded. "Yes, a good deal of it. I inhaled your blood as well. There was no way around it."

Julia sighed and ran a hand through her hair.

"What?" he asked, getting anxious.

After some sidelong glances and outright staring, she nodded. "In Mayan culture, as you probably know, water—and the cenotes by extension—are considered sacred places."

"Yes, I—"

She held up a hand to forestall him, then continued.

"There were also ancient bloodletting rituals in Mayan culture. They eventually were interpreted as nothing more than barbaric human sacrifice, but that's not true. Not entirely. The bloodletting ceremonies were done to transfer power. Many times, the ritual would take place on a holy site by a holy man, in the presence of one or many of us gods."

"What I believe happened is the transference of my own blood into your body through the sacred medium of our cenote. With the presence of a god—myself or Ixik Kab—and the presence of a holy man—yourself, I'd assume here, the ritual requirements were met."

"I don't know what that means," he said evenly.

Julia reached over and held his hands. "It means that you have been imbued with some power of the Mayan gods. What power? I can't say. I can guess, however, with what I've seen. But, even then..."

"Wait. Julia, are you saying that I'm a god?"

Julia nodded, then winced and put a hand to her scalp. "More or less. A lesser god, certainly. Do I think you could hold your own against the likes of Kulkulkan or Itzamna? Probably not. But compared to your everyday human," she gestured to the pool where he'd taken Santiago, "I think you're more than a match."

She looked into his eyes. "I need to tell you something. I believe you were not saved by an angel, but by something else. Someone else."

"It was you, wasn't it?" Ramón was calm and certain.

A little surprised, she nodded. "It was me. I couldn't let you die, couldn't let my sister take you, too. There was something special about you, and I intervened."

"I saw it, when I was swimming down to you. It was you, I'm sorry for being so blind."

"And now," she said quietly, "we move forward. Together?"

They were silent for a moment. Ramón weighed his options. Again, this new information wasn't entirely a surprise. This new and improved worldview had opened him up to infinite possibilities, and it felt right. It felt orchestrated that Julia would be the 'angel' he'd been waiting for.

For decades, he'd pursued the Christian God, believed he was saved by a holy angel and set upon a path to teach those about the truth of His Word. Instead, he found out that he was saved by an actual god of the Mayans and had now become one himself.

"Justice," he whispered.

"What does that mean?" Julia asked, cocking her head.

"For years, I've waited for God's justice. I've waited for him to make things right, or explain why things are the way they are. Or stop the needless deaths of children and loved ones before their time.

"Now, it seems that I can determine that."

Ramón reached out and snapped his fingers. A form that he'd detected hiding in the bushes a dozen yards away was yanked forcibly through the underbrush. The man squealed and thrashed as he was drawn rapidly toward Ramón's out-stretched hand.

"My Judas." Ramón adopted the tone of a disappointed father. He supposed that in a way he was. Or had been. "After all I did for you, after everything I gave you ... after all the nights I let you sleep in the church and share my own food." David's eyes were wide with terror and his mouth worked soundlessly. "We broke bread together, David."

"Don't—" was all he could get out before it ended in a squeak.

Ramón didn't know what to do with the man. "You certainly deserve death. Perhaps not the death given to Santiago. But it's your fault that Julia was attacked and injured. It was your actions that caused Julia's sister—a goddess no less—to be *murdered*.

"But it was because of those actions that I've transcended. I've become something more than I was. I have become a god."

The trembling man before him began to weep and beg, his words running intelligibly together. Ramón shushed him gently and stroked the side of David's head. "The old me would tell someone in my position that it is the Almighty's decision to deliver justice. It is for us to wait patiently for it. We humans can only wait for divine judgement and try to be better to one another."

David was nodding vehemently and pleading with Ramón to spare his life.

Ramón simply smiled. "But that's just not relevant anymore. I no longer have to wait for some silent god to answer. I am now the one you have to answer to. I am the god of this place, now and forever."

Julia stood—shakily at first, but she grew more steady with every step—then stood at Ramón's side. Her features didn't change, but the way in which she held herself changed, and Ramón saw for the first time that she was, in fact, Ixchel, the Rainbow Goddess.

He turned back to David. "What is that saying Christians always use? Eye for an eye?"

David shuddered, and the weeping began again.

Ramón reached for the humming power within himself. It surged through his outstretched hand and into David. The terrified man's eyes bulged and blood began running out of both corners. His teeth clenched, and then his jaw relaxed, mouth slack. Bloody spit drooled down his chin to the ground.

Ramón let the dead man drop to the stone beneath their feet. Then he turned to Ixchel and lifted a head to her scalp. He willed the power within him to close the wound on her head, to knit the body together. A memory—very distant and very deep—showed him how. The blood slowed and then stopped. Flesh mended itself together beneath his hand, and when he removed it, a small pink scar was the only evidence that Santiago's club had split open her scalp.

Smiling at his love, he said, "When we return to town, I'll tell everyone what's happened. Strangely enough, I have faith that they'll understand. I intend on making La Ventana beautiful once more. I think with your help, we can."

Julia's eyes burned with a power he'd never seen before but could now comprehend. "Together," she said and grasped his hand.

As they made their way out of the jungle, flowers sprang up and the dust retreated before them. The jungle began to stretch out its emerald arms in tiny clumps of clover and lianas toward La Ventana.

Ramón thought, *No longer would this town be separate from creation. From now on, it would be one with it.*

CHAPTER 13

Weeks later, Ramón knelt beside the church and fused the natural stone to the trunk of a tree that had sprouted from the dirt earlier that morning. With that addition—as well as a few others—in a few days, the church would appear to be grown from the earth instead of settled upon it.

He gazed around the town. Where once stood a failing, dusty village, there now stood a vibrant bustling town. The people had been suspicious at first, especially when the plants began to grow around the feet of Julia—now known publicly as Ixchel. Many were amazed, and they believed immediately, the stories from their ancestors now standing before them in the flesh. The few who doubted or called out heresy either left town or were eventually convinced by their peers to stay. No one was made to stay, no one was forced to leave. The new law in La Ventana was acceptance.

Ramón took a deep breath. The air that filled his lungs no longer threatened to choke him with dust but instead was clear and sweet. It was filled with the limitless combinations of nearby flowers and the deep earthy smell of the jungle. He walked calmly around the fountain in the middle of town and ran his hands across the surface of its water. It was now fed by a natural spring within a complicated growth of vines and branches. Almost two weeks had passed since Ramón and Ixchel returned to La Ventana, and life returned with them.

A young man approached Ramón and bowed deeply before addressing him. Ramón had asked them to stop with the honorifics, but it had only seemed to reinforce it. "Hosanek, there are men at the Eastern Gates to see you."

That was another thing they'd started doing, calling him "Hosanek" instead of "Padre" or "Ramón." Hosanek had been one of the gods of water and earth in Mayan culture. He thought it a little clever that it played on the word "hosanna" as well. Ramón feared that if the real Hosanek still lived, that the *real* Hosanek might have a problem with it. But Julia assured him that the Pawhatuun slept on a four-hundred-year cycle. If, when Hosanek woke up on his hundred-year rotation, there was a problem, it would take nearly a hundred years for him to do something about it. By then, he'd have to go back to sleep for another four-hundred.

That worked well enough for Ramón.

Ixchel, who had been splashing with several laughing children in a nearby pool of water, saw the interaction between the young man and Ramón. She quickly disentangled herself from their tiny clasping hands and came to stand at Ramón's side.

"What do they look like?" he asked the messenger.

"Four men, guns and armor. One large truck with a symbol on its side."

"Did they say what they want?"

"They said they represent something called The Neo-Pagans and want to speak with the leader."

He didn't know what any of that meant, but he nodded and turned to Ixchel. "Would you come with me, my love?"

She smiled and grasped his hand. "Of course."

They made their way through the town, hand in hand. Groups of people bowed as they passed and raised their hands in worship when Ramón and Ixchel talked to them or touched the tops of their heads.

The town was thriving, and the people knew they had two ancient gods to thank. Ramón, still new to the whole god-thing, was stunned by it all. Ixchel, who had been worshipped for centuries before, placed a reassuring hand on his arm when she heard her husband stutter through a blessing.

When they reached the gate, Ramón nodded in appreciation. The young man who had brought the message had been spot on. A tan armored truck sat idling at the Eastern Gate. Four men stood at each of the four doors, an assault rifle held across their chests at an angle. Their sunglasses reflected the afternoon sun in multi-colored hues as their heads swung back and forth, clearly used to standing sentry.

Two massive green trunks stood as sentries to either side of the gate. The branches overhead grew together and formed a natural arch a dozen feet above the two gods' heads. Branches and vines twined around the trunks and created an elaborate gate that separated those inside La Ventana from those outside of it.

Hosanek and Ixchel approached but stopped before the impressive arch. One man got out of the truck with both hands raised and a few extra items in his utility belt.

"Hello, there," he said in a gruff American accent. "I'm looking for the leaders of this community."

Hosanek nodded and raised his hand in greeting. "My name is Hosanek, and this is my wife Ixchel. We're the leaders here. What do you want?"

The man put his hands on his hips, and Hosanek noticed a toothpick clenched between the man's teeth. He moved it to the opposite side of his mouth and Hosanek grimaced.

"Well, we're actually looking for you."

"Who is we?"

"Well, like I told that boy. We're the Neo-Pagan army. Our leader wants to talk with you."

"For what purpose?"

"Just to talk for now. I'd be happy to leave my men here in the truck if you'd be willing to speak with me alone first." He chuckled a little. "Honestly, if the rumors are true, I doubt I could do anything to the likes of you two."

"What do you want to talk about?"

"Well," the man shifted his weight from left to right, then gazed around at the towering trees and the vibrant living city before him. "Rumors said that a month ago, this town sat in the middle of what some would call a desert, with the jungle about a mile thataway." He pointed vaguely at the horizon behind them. "Rumors can stretch the truth quite a bit. But they aren't ever *that* wrong."

"You haven't answered my husband's question," said Ixchel with a hint of impatience. The trees flexed and moved toward the men as if blown by wind, but no wind had passed through their branches.

The man held up his hands a little higher. "No ma'am, I apologize.

"Y'see, I'm part of a group of people who are, well, we're trying to change the world."

Hosanek scoffed. "Another group trying to do what others failed to finish because the world doesn't want to change."

"That's where you're wrong, Hosanek. We've found out that the world actually does want change, wants it real bad.

Up 'til now, nobody's had the power to do it. See the men and women at the top have done everything they can to stay there. I'm guessing you've experienced a little of that before."

Hosanek smiled at him and nodded. "Maybe a little," he said.

"Well now, and I think you'll begin to see where I'm going with this any time now. We've found people that can help with that. People like you, who can finally do something about the balance of power in the world. We want to put the power back in the hands of the laymen instead of letting the elite keep it to themselves." He motioned to the trees that had moved in response to Ixchel's prompt. "The people who sent me heard rumors that something like this was happenin', sent me down here to check it out."

The God Duo was silent. They couldn't speak telepathically, but there were small bits of emotion that they could pass between themselves, as long as they were touching. Right now, both of them were feeling something between excitement and fear.

After a moment longer, the American man broke the silence. "That sound like something you'd like to help with? Bring down the people who care only for the almighty dollar and keeping the power they stole?"

Hosanek met Ixchel's eyes, and she nodded. Hosanek smiled at his bride, then nodded at the man. With a wave of Ixchel's hand, the limbs that created the gate disentangled themselves with a whispering shuffle. A space the width of two men opened beneath the arch. The American had taken a cautious step back when the limbs began to move, but his astonished gaze and those of his companions told Ixchel and Hosanek all they needed to know.

"Yeah," he said with satisfaction, "yeah I think you both will fit in nicely with the others."

"Others?" Ixchel and Hosanek echoed one another as the American passed through the gate, and the branches closed together behind him.

"Yes, sir. Yes, ma'am. What you can do is unique, 'sfar as I can tell. But there are other people that can do … things… that are gathering together for a single purpose."

"And that purpose is…" Hosanek prompted.

"Well like I told you—to change the world."

The God Duo led the American to a place where they could speak over lunch. What they heard stunned them, but in the end, it was convincing enough for them both to agree to a meeting in America. Ixchel would stay behind and continue their work in La Ventana while Hosanek met someone Davis, the American, referred to only as "The Leader."

"I'll be back soon," Hosanek told his wife as they stood at the Eastern Gate.

Davis had returned to the vehicle, and his four cronies were waiting patiently while Hosanek said his goodbyes.

"I know you will. Be safe."

They kissed, and though that same longing he'd felt in the church months ago had finally been satisfied, he couldn't help but feel the thrill of each new kiss. The road toward the airport was rocky and rough, but Ixchel occupied his mind completely.

Ramón Gonzalez—once called "Padre" by his small congregation and now called Hosanek by his thriving community—sat on a plane with his full and satisfied soul soaking in the cool waters of affection and certainty that he was finally doing something important. Not because he'd been ordained to do it but because he'd chosen to do it.

And he smiled.

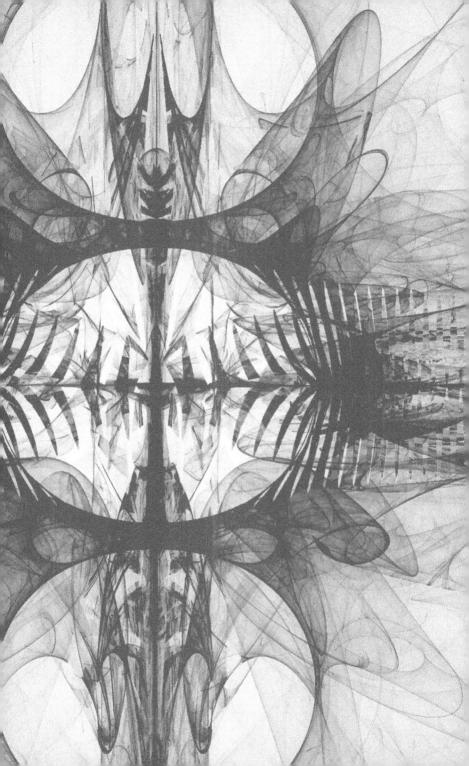

THE
CHARLATAN

CHAPTER 1

Miles Chester Jameson, often called "Mick" by close friends and the occasional eavesdropping stranger, tapped his fingers impatiently on the glass top of the front counter of his shop. The windows that faced the street were blacked out, but the entrance had a maroon curtain that obscured all of the street except a two-inch gap so he could see who was coming before he unlocked the door and let them in.

He'd opened his shop on a whim. His then-girlfriend had told him he had the uncanny ability to "lie well," something that no doubt attributed to their break-up less than a year later.

Now, eight years later the shop "Miles of Mystery and Curios" stood on the corner of West 56th and 11th in Lower Manhattan. He'd managed to snag the small store at a fraction of the price because the previous owners had been gunned down in one of the four rooms. No one liked to buy a crime scene, but it seemed the perfect place to Mick. There had been plenty of rumors as to who was responsible, but lack of evidence made the case die before it went to trial.

All signs pointed to a local crime boss, but nothing was ever officially filed against him. Small fish, but bigger than Mick.

None of that really mattered, though. Mick's little curio shop gained popularity from the simple fact that he was able to sell anything to anyone. While much of the demographic that visited his shop were widows over sixty, the occasional teen dabbling in the occult or the middle-aged woman looking for ways to exact long-distance revenge weren't uncommon. And they ate it up. All he had to do was pretend, and that was something he was *very* good at.

He drummed his fingers rhythmically again. His eleven o'clock was late, which meant that lunch would have to wait even longer. His stomach growled a little in defeat, but he patted it affectionately.

"Don't worry. Ms. Favereau is a favorite of mine, you know that."

Ms. Favereau was what he considered "a regular." Every week she'd visit and ask for another tarot card or palm reading. On one occasion she'd asked him to contact her dead husband's spirit. That had been a challenge, but one he'd been up for. She'd left very pleased and gave him "a little tip" before leaving with a salacious wink.

Movement caught his eye through the maroon curtain, and he perked up. He'd been twirling the small medallion that hung around his neck in time with the drumming of his fingers against the counter. The former a habit from his childhood that he couldn't break and the latter simply his impatience.

He resumed drumming his fingers when he saw it was just Arjesh Patel, the man who owned the deli on the other half of the first floor. Arjesh was a good man, and if Mick was being honest, Arjesh probably saw right through Mick's lies. Arjesh seemed to have a "Live and let live" mentality, and while he may joke with Mick about it, he didn't treat him differently. He'd eaten at Arjesh's deli several times a week since it opened around the time his own shop opened. The man had a way with sandwiches in the same way Mick had a way with lies.

More movement through the gap in the curtain. A white-haired bun bobbed atop a woman nearing eighty as she shuffled her way to the door in red felt slippers, a handbag swung over one white-gloved wrist.

She rang the buzzer once and stared at the door, beady eyes flicking this way and that beneath half-moon glasses. Mick had put two-way shading on it so those outside couldn't see directly in, but it allowed a clear view out.

He made sure to tidy his long hair by tucking it behind an ear on each side and giving it a sexy swoop at the front. He turned the three deadbolts and a single sliding key, then swung open the sturdy wooden door for her.

"Good morning, Ms. Favereau, welcome back!" he exclaimed joyfully.

"Good morning. Mick, right?"

He smiled warmly and took her hand in both of his. "That's right. What can I do for you today?"

Ms. Favereau, "Eleanor to my pool boy," she'd said once, gazed around at the cluttered shelves full of arcane-looking objects and the glass cases of items that appeared more valuable than they'd ever actually be.

"Well," she said in a smoker's voice that sounded like a rusty hand crank, "I was wondering if you could do a tarot card reading for me?"

"Ah! Of course! Of course. Would you like the standard reading or would you like the deluxe reading that includes an attempt to contact a spirit?"

She looked at him quizzically, then, "Just the standard reading, I think."

"Very good," he replied with a wide smile, patting her hand affectionately.

He led her through the narrow, cluttered aisles to a room at the back of the shop. They ducked beneath a macabre cluster of dangling bones that could have been Death's baby mobile, then stepped around a large pile of books that had toppled over at some point in the last three years and had never been righted.

When they reached an open doorway with black beads hanging from the doorframe, he moved a swath of them aside so she could enter to sit in a velvety red chair. The beads clattered together as he ducked beneath them to follow her into the dim room. A single lamp cast a meager light across the small square table. Had four adults sat one on each side, there'd barely be elbow room for everyone. But it worked well for card readings between two people.

Mick sat opposite Ms. Favereau, who placed her periwinkle-colored clutch on her lap and crossed her arms atop it. She wore a large coat a deeper shade of purple than her clutch that, despite the summer heat, seemed to suit her well.

She smiled at him, and Mick met her gaze with a wink.

He shifted in his seat, and when he did, a small nail in the table snagged on his black and white pinstripe vest. He heard a seam pop and looked down in surprise. The vest he wore over his white button-down shirt now had a tiny hole along the edge. A red thread was looped around the nail. Instinctively, he tried to simply move away from it, but the thread was wound tight and the tiny hole yawned wider.

"Shit," he said and used his thumb and forefinger to pop the thread off the nail, careful to avoid its surprisingly sharp point. *Need to fix that when she leaves,* he thought.

"What, dear?" Ms. Favereau croaked.

He smiled up at her. "Nothing at all, just preparing myself. That's all.

They chatted amiably for several minutes as Mick shuffled his tarot deck and set the small lamp to the side. Had this been someone younger, he may have been nervous. His training in the arcane arts boiled down to a quick internet search and maybe ten hours of YouTube videos. After that, his natural ability to spin a tale took over.

Ms. Favereau watched intently as he shuffled the cards. When he'd finished and placed the deck between them, she looked at him expectantly.

"What would you like to ask the spirits, Ms. Favereau?"

Mick knew the answer to this question but asked it anyway. She asked the same question every time she did a tarot reading.

She licked her lips and glanced at the cards.

"I would like to know what's going to happen to me."

Mick nodded sagely and picked up the deck. He shuffled it skillfully—thanks to a few more YouTube videos—in long whispering arcs between the palm holding the cards and his palm where they landed.

Mick placed the deck face-down and breathed deeply. He heard Ms. Favereau do the same.

"Spirits," he said quietly, pouring the gravity of eons into his voice. "Impart to us your wisdom. Answer this kind woman's plea for knowledge."

With another shaky sigh from Ms. Favereau, Mick flipped the first card and laid it between himself and the old woman.

"What does that mean?" she asked breathlessly.

Mick stared down at the card, a tall white-robed figure with a lantern. The Hermit.

"The Hermit signifies a pursuit of knowledge. But this one is reversed, which means there's a hesitation in you, a fear of loneliness, perhaps."

Ms. Favereau nodded a little and licked her lips again.

Mick flipped the next one and laid it beside The Hermit. The Eight of Cups.

"And this one?" she whispered fervently.

"This one is the Eight of Cups. Also reversed."

"Is that bad?" her gravelly voice had taken on a hint of panic.

Mick shook his head. "No, not necessarily. The Eight of Cups in reverse simply means you've experienced a terrible event, perhaps one that altered your worldview enough that it's difficult to move forward."

Once again, Ms. Favereau nodded.

Mick took the third card on the deck and flipped it over, placing it face-up next to the Eight of Cups. It made a soft snapping sound as he did so.

When Mick saw it, he inhaled quickly.

"What? What is it?" Panic had fully set in now for dear old Ms. Favereau.

God, this is fun, he thought with an inward smile.

"The Ten of Swords."

He waited to a count of five before continuing.

"This one is *not* reversed and signifies the end of something. The end of something *major* in your life."

"The end of..." she trailed off and put a trembling finger to her lips.

Seeing her panic at something so mundane as a picture on a card was almost enough to make him smile, but he didn't.

"You know what?" he said, gathering the cards and preparing to shuffle them again, "Let's try it again."

"What?" she said in disbelief. "But the spirits!" As if that explained everything.

Mick waved a hand vaguely. "They'll understand. Besides," he shuffled the deck again and knocked on it twice. "Sometimes, there's a bad energy that can affect the reading.

This way, we can try it again fresh." He smiled reassuringly at her, and she returned it with slightly less enthusiasm.

Once more he inhaled, invoked the spirits, and drew the first card.

"Ace of Coins. Wealth or potential, perhaps."

Ms. Favereau smiled, much more agreeable, now.

Mick drew the second card.

"The Star. Very interesting. The Star signifies the reconnection of one's soul with the divine. It can also mean potentially letting go of earthly connections."

Ms. Favereau nodded but her eyes looked vaguely concerned.

The final card turned face-up.

"The Knight of Cups. This signifies a homecoming of sorts, a reconciliation perhaps."

Mick gathered the cards and placed them face-down in the deck and slid it next to the lamp.

"What are your thoughts on the spirit's answer?"

Ms. Favereau slumped slightly, thinking. "Well, I'm confused."

Mick nodded sagely again. "Yes, sometimes they communicate in ways that we mere mortals simply cannot comprehend."

"They do? Yes, of course they do."

They sat in silence, which was always part of this little ritual. Most of his clients could easily name the events or people in their lives that the cards represented. It was easy to make a connection when someone says it exists. People don't question it. The ghost of a memory swirled in his mind, but he pushed it away.

Ms. Favereau always took a little longer. That was fine with him; she always paid for the whole hour whether it took that long or not.

"But," she began, "my sister, Ruth, who is a very rich woman, married a man named Tom. Or Tim. I can't remember which. She invested all of her husband's money in computers years ago, some fruit company, when he died. I forget the name of it. Well, I recently got a call from her son Aaron. He said that Ruth had fallen quite ill and that there was talk of a will. That coin card got me thinking that perhaps I'm in the will somehow." She shrugged with a sly smile.

"Well that's wonderful," said Mick encouragingly. "There, you see? Already the spirits are answering."

She nodded, her smile becoming more sure of itself. "And you know that Star card could simply mean that she's going to pass away, we'll have a—what did you call it—an earthly connection I have to let go of?"

Mick put a finger to his chin and made a play of thinking very hard. "That does seem to fit. Very astute of you, Ms. Favereau."

"That last one, though. A homecoming? I can't imagine..." She trailed off.

Mick tried not to roll his eyes, choosing instead to prompt her. "Do you and Ruth have a good relationship?"

Ms. Favereau's face twisted. "Not since she started shacking up with that other man. I told her not to! I told her it was a bad idea. But did she listen to me? No. No, of course not. Why listen to Eleanor, I'm only older and wiser and better at those sorts of things."

Mick didn't know what "those sorts of things" would mean, but he nodded with understanding. "Ah. Well, perhaps the reconciliation will come through that? Perhaps she's seen the error of her ways and as part of the reconciliation, may leave some money to you?"

Her face lit up and she clapped her gloved hands together. "Oh, yes. Yes! That must be it! There's no other explanation!"

"That does seem the most likely, based on what the spirits have related, of course."

"Oh yes, of course, of course."

With the reading finished, and in less than half the time it sometimes took, he led her back through the shop to the front counter.

"And how would you like to pay, today?"

She opened her clutch and pulled out a crisp hundred-dollar bill. His usual fee was fifty dollars per hour, and he hoped she didn't need change.

"Cash, please. And after that reading, I think you can keep the change. It seems I'll be coming into a good bit of money soon." She scrunched her face up in such an excited pleasure that Mick genuinely laughed with her.

"That will no doubt be wonderful for you. Thank you, Ms. Favereau, thank you so very much."

"Not at all, young man. Thank *you!*" She leaned over and gave Mick a peck on the cheek.

He blushed appropriately and waved goodbye as she left, sliding the locks back in place and breathing a sigh of relief.

The truth was, Mick had discovered with a quick internet search, was that Ms. Favereau's sister had died two years ago, leaving her nothing in the will she spoke of. The relative she mentioned—Aaron—had called to tell Eleanor to never come around again. Ruth's lawyer had actually written Eleanor completely out of the will. It wouldn't matter, anyway. Eleanor Favereau had been diagnosed with late-stage Alzheimer's the Christmas before. In the months since, her memory had declined rapidly.

Never one to miss out on a chance, he'd given her his card and written "Wednesday, 11:00" on the back. Every time she looked at it, she would think—memory working or not—that she had an appointment at the address on the card every Wednesday at 11:00. She showed up most Wednesdays and probably would until she passed away. "Strike while the iron is hot" he'd heard plenty.

Mick put his new hundred in the safe beneath another stack of books, spun the dial after closing it, and left the shop. He'd flipped the "open" sign to show "out to lunch" before locking up.

Arjesh's Reuben sounded particularly good on this sunny Summer afternoon.

With a coke, he thought grinning, tossing the keys into the air and catching them deftly behind his back.

CHAPTER 2

Arjesh was standing behind the counter wearing a stained apron and helping another patron of the deli when the bell tinkled above Mick's head. He stepped through and waved at Arjesh, who acknowledged him with a smile and an offhand "Welcome!"

Mick waited in line behind someone speaking quickly into his cell phone. Mick tried not to eavesdrop.

Well, that wasn't true, Mick loved to eavesdrop.

The guy was arguing with someone on the other end of the call about what cheese *they* liked. Arjesh waited patiently for the cell-phone man to realize it was his turn. When the cell-phone man wasn't looking, Arjesh rolled his eyes, and Mick snorted a laugh.

After what seemed like forever, cell-phone man hung up and ordered a Swiss cheese turkey on white.

Wow, daring today, Mick thought ruefully. *A white man's boring-ass sandwich order if ever there was one.*

The man paid and left, hustling out of the deli with the brown sandwich bag clutched in one fist and a fresh coffee in the other.

Mick stepped up to order but Arjesh cut him off.

"I saw Ms. Favereau leaving your shop today. You're still tapping that keg, eh?"

Arjesh didn't have a thick Indian accent, but it had an echo of his childhood in there somewhere.

Mick scoffed and shrugged helplessly. "I mean ... what else am I supposed to do? The poor woman needs some kind of direction, some kind of purpose and meaning. I'm providing that for her. In fact, I'm *helping* her."

Arjesh laughed and shook his head. "Helping empty her bank account, that's what you're doing. You're a real bastard, you know that?"

Mick shrugged again.

"The usual?" Arjesh asked, wiping down the counter to prepare the next order.

"Yep."

"I'll get it ready for you."

"I'll wait until you do." Mick grinned at him, and Arjesh flipped him the bird.

After a few minutes, Mick was rubbing his thumb across the surface of the pendant around his neck and sitting at one of the seven tables in the deli. Hundreds of people in business attire passed by the windows outside. The deli wasn't big. In fact, it was almost the same layout as his shop on the other side of the wall, just in reverse. Arjesh had added a few walls here and knocked out another in order to add a walk-in fridge for his deli, but they were roughly the same square footage.

Arjesh brought Mick's order and then went back behind the counter to help another customer.

The Reuben crunched between his teeth as he chewed it. Mick had eaten plenty of Reubens in his time, but Arjesh's was the best. He'd told the man that one day, and Arjesh had nodded as if he was telling him the difference in their skin color.

"What do you do to make it so delicious?"

"If I told you, I'd have to kill you." Arjesh answered while making the only other patron's food.

Mick rolled his eyes but left it alone. "Fine, but *don't change it.*" He could keep the secret as long as he kept the recipe the same.

He slurped on his coke and checked his watch. Half-past noon. He had a two o'clock with a new customer, a referral, which wasn't uncommon but always a surprise.

Arjesh walked over after the other man left and flipped a towel over his shoulder. "Mind if I sit?"

Mick shrugged and Arjesh sat. "The deli is slow today. Probably all the sunny weather. People are playing at the park and don't feel the need to come have a sandwich."

"Aren't you usually busy right now?"

The deli owner nodded. "Yes. Usually, I'm slammed. It's strange; I don't know why I'm not." When he saw Mick's raised eyebrows he smacked his lips together. "No, I didn't change any recipes, either."

"I'm just saying," said Mick, not really saying anything at all.

"It doesn't matter. It's just a day." Arjesh reached over and took a potato chip from Mick's basket and crunched it slowly before speaking again.

"You have anything else today?"

Arjesh spun the basket around and chomped more greedily at the chips.

Mick, now done with his sandwich, slouched in his seat and crossed his arms over his belly. His fingers brushed the new hole in his vest, and he clicked his tongue at it.

"Yeah, I have an appointment at two. New customer."

"That's a nice change. How are you going to fleece this one?"

Mick rolled his eyes but ignored the jab. "This guy wants to talk to his dead grandmother who apparently buried her life savings somewhere on her property in Oklahoma."

Arjesh's brows climbed up his forehead.

"Yeah, I know. Ridiculous."

"This guy wants you to ask Grammy where her money is?" He began rapping the chorus of *Bitch Better Have My Money*.

"Yeah, that about sums it up."

"And you're going to?"

"I'm going to make it *look* like I do."

"How?"

"I've got an idea. I did a little research on how to do it. Not easy, and I'll actually have to do a small bit of prep, but it shouldn't take any longer than an hour or two."

Arjesh nodded and crunched the last chip between his teeth.

"Then you'd better get going. I'd hate for you to be late. Time is money, after all." Arjesh stood and took the basket, emptying it in a trash can and tossing the basket in a sink behind the counter.

Mick pulled the wallet from his front pocket and paid for lunch.

"Thanks for lunch, RJ."

Arjesh sighed and glared at Mick. "You know I fucking hate that nickname, right?"

Mick laughed and shrugged again. "That's why I love it. See you tomorrow?" He tucked the wallet in his back pocket.

"God, I hope not."

Mick cackled and headed for the door, tipping his hat and holding it open for a middle-aged woman as she waltzed through.

He whistled as he walked the few steps down to his shop and unlocked the door. He was already planning out his preparations for his appointment and realized he needed to actually create a new Arcane Grace. That's what he called it, at least. It was a piece of leather that had all kinds of designs and Latin words on it. Most of them were gibberish which translated into nothing when put together. The circles and triangles that took up most of the real-estate all focused on a central point. The Grace he had right now was fine but was the first one he'd made years ago. It was a little *too* perfect. While that helped it look more authentic to his customers, he'd rather it look like some ancient relic he'd purchased from a Latvian peddler. A tear here, a frayed edge along this side, a smudged word or cross-section here.

He may be a fake, but he wanted to at least be *convincing*.

He made his way to the back of the shop, to a dark corner where he'd put in a supply closet. It was far enough back that most customers never saw it. Those that were nosy—and he'd had a few—would see it locked and assume it was a water heater closet or bathroom. He didn't have either of those, actually, and had to use Arjesh's shop to take a piss.

He opened the door and kicked a box of knick-knacks out of the way to get it fully open. He reached up and pulled a gold chain for light. Shelves lined the walls, and there was just enough room for Mick to squeeze sideways between them.

He lifted odds and ends until he found the roll of leather he'd need to create this Arcane Grace. The tools he needed were scattered haphazardly on the shelf nearby, and he scooped them up before turning off the light and locking the door behind him.

The next half hour was spent measuring and cutting the leather and drawing the designs to mirror the ones on his existing sheet. By the time he was done with the design itself, it looked great. The rest of the time before his appointment was spent fraying the edges by rubbing sandpaper across it. He also sprayed rubbing alcohol in places to age it. He avoided smudges by placing a hand over the dye he'd used and spraying around it—*Thanks, Internet*, he thought.

In the end, he had an extra ten minutes before his two o'clock should be there. He used that time to clean up any evidence that he'd been working and as added insurance, he did a quick internet search for Latin phrases. He may not need to impress this person, but if he sensed a doubter, a phrase in Latin usually did the trick.

When two o'clock showed on the rusty clock hanging on the wall opposite the front counter, Mick took a deep breath. He was nervous, which was funny to him since all he had to do was pretend. The amazing thing about his job was that most people already believed when they came in. There were few instances where he had to convince someone. But most of the time, he simply *confirmed* what they already believed. In the end, it was easy.

He gazed at the shelves that lined the entire front room, then followed the straight lines of them down the narrow hallway toward the séance room. A foot from the ceiling was a wooden shelf that simply kept junk out of the way. It was stacked full of boxes and knick-knacks, and it sagged from the weight between some of the brackets. Some of the objects were old bones—animal mostly, which were easy to come by on the internet but gave the shop a sense of gravitas. Other objects were angular wire or metal pieces meant to spark curiosity and banish the mundane.

In reality, most of those were some budding artist's attempt at capturing the abstract. He could find plenty of those on the cheap. A few objects he'd actually found himself while visiting smaller towns around the country and bought for a fraction of what he could charge.

Most of the books in a bookcase by the door he'd found that way. He had several bookshelves stuffed to the brim with old dusty tomes. Some were in other languages. If translated, the bulk of them would be revealed as school textbooks. He was no longer surprised at how frequently an old German text-book on anatomy looked like an ancient Visigoth spellbook.

Lamps that looked like skulls and melted candles were all part of the schtick. To him, it all looked like a prosaic attempt at mysticism. To his customers, however, it immediately lent him an expertise in the arcane, and they ate it up.

The buzzer at the front door rang, and he jumped.

He walked to the door, heart pounding, and pulled back the curtain a little. Suspicion made his customers feel like they were doing something wrong. A tactic he used to further rein-force their belief in his little farce.

He unlocked the door and pulled it open. A middle-aged man stepped through in a tidy blue business suit.

"Hello, there," said Mick as he locked the door once again.

"Yes, hello." The man glanced around nervously before reaching out and shaking Mick's hand. "We spoke on the phone, I'm Phillip Kilmichael. Or Phil. Whatever works for you."

"I'm Mick. It's nice to meet you, Phillip."

The man's hands were almost a blur as he rung them repeatedly. Mick took the opportunity. "Phillip," he said and placed a gentle hand on the man's shoulder, "take a deep breath. You're doing nothing wrong here."

Phillip nodded and exhaled forcefully. "You know I've never done anything like this."

Mick nodded, "You mean went into a shop to buy some-thing?" Mick stepped behind the counter to gather a few extra "spiritual" tools.

Phillip cocked his head, brow furrowed.

"That's all you're doing, isn't it? Simply an exchange. Paying for a service. Nothing more."

Phillip swallowed. "I... I guess you're right."

"I am," Mick stated absently.

"It's just that I don't know what she'll say."

"Your grandmother?" Phillip nodded. He looked like he was going to be sick.

If you blow chunks in my shop, I'm going to make you clean it up, he thought acidly.

"She may not say anything, Phillip. She may not say a word. We don't command the spirits; we simply ask them to join us. The rest is up to them."

"Right," he said, licking his lips. To Mick, the man looked like a chubby squirrel, nervous and ready to run at the first crack of a branch.

"Okay, Phillip, if you'll follow me."

Mick stepped around that same pile of books on the floor and box of rusty machine parts he'd been meaning to move for months.

"Right in here," he said, pulling aside the beads Ms. Favereau had walked beneath earlier in the day. Phillip ducked in.

Mick followed him and pulled out the Arcane Grace as Phillip sat. The Grace he'd rolled up and tied with a hempen cord only moments before Phillip's arrival. Now, he unfurled it and coughed. A small cloud puffed up from the leather sheet. "Sorry," said Mick, waving away the dusting of flour he'd applied twenty minutes ago.

Phillip tried to hold in a cough and failed, then waved the "dust" away with frantic flaps of his hands.

"Been a while since I've opened up this relic," he told Phillip.

"Do I need to do anything?" Phillip's eyes were wide with excitement.

"I don't think so, not at the moment anyway. You'll need to ask your question, but I'll tell you when. If the spirits require anything else of you, they'll ask through me."

Phillip nodded and placed his hands on the edge of the Grace. His fingertips followed some of the fading marks and designs.

"What does all this mean?"

Mick, who had closed his eyes after lighting a stick of incense, opened them to see what he meant. "Those are ancient phrases meant to build the bridge between the living and the dead," he intoned a little more distantly than he intended.

The leather satchel at his feet housed a dozen or so stones. Quartz, a moonstone, amethyst, and agates were placed around the edge of the Grace to both keep it from rolling back up and lend the ritual some spiritual weight.

The satchel also held a Ouija board, which he placed on the table with a flourish. He positioned the planchet so that it pointed at himself, allowing a larger hand space for Phillip.

When all the stones were in all the right places—mostly on the points of the drawn angles that reached out to the edges—he smoothed the Grace and placed his hands palm-down upon the planchette. He met Phillip's wide-eyed gaze and nodded once.

"Ready to begin?"

Chapter 3

Mick turned the lamp on the table low. It was one of those electric lamps with a dial for brightness, meant to mimic the oil lamps of the old world. He could hear Phillip breathing hard across the table from him. The pendant around Mick's neck fell out of his shirt as he leaned over, but he tucked it back in.

He closed his eyes and realized that he'd left his wallet in his back pocket. Annoyed and trying to focus, he took a deep breath and spoke.

"Spirits," Mick uttered with a great deal of breathiness. "We humbly ask for your guidance. We wish to perceive a glimpse of your wisdom and have but one humble request." All of this sounded ridiculous in his own head, but he knew it was all very real to the man across the table from him.

Mick released the planchette and grasped the table edges to either side of him. Another deep breath. There was a small switch hidden beneath the table that, once flipped, sent a cool breeze wafting through the room. It worked wonders for sending a chill up an unsuspecting spine and to convince someone that a spirit may indeed be visiting.

He didn't press it. Not yet.

"Wise spirits of our past, we seek a single number of you, a single question we ask and request only a single answer." He should have taken his wallet out before the session.

Mick opened his eyes and leveled his gaze at Phillip who swallowed hard. "It's your turn, now, to submit your question to any who have gathered to listen."

Phillip gazed around as if the room were full of invisible watchers, then gulped audibly. The smell of the incense was strong and the smoke created a lazy haze above their heads.

"I..." his voice was so shaky it was barely a whisper. "I ... wish ... to... to ask..."

"With certainty, Phillip. Only your belief will convince the spirits that you're worthy of an answer."

His voice got louder, but no more certain. "I wish ... to ... ask ... Esther ... Morgan ... a... a question."

Phillip glanced back at Mick, who nodded approvingly and winked.

"Esther Morgan, your grandson Phillip Kilmichael, wishes to ask you a question. Will you come? Will you sit at this table with us? Will you treat us with your presence and answer?"

Mick flipped the switch now. In the room adjacent, a small air conditioning unit kicked on. Its vent was piped directly into the wall adjacent to the room where an even smaller pipe was installed. The vents of the unit were no more than two feet long and perhaps six inches tall. But that much air forced into a tube less than two inches in diameter made for a much more forceful expulsion of cold air. The pipe was hidden very cleverly in a corner of the room and directed toward the entrance. Conveniently, it would wash across the beads that hung across the room entry and, because of the corner, rebound from it to wash across the table in the middle of the room, guest first and then Mick.

He had tested it a hundred times and, after a few tweaks, had it down to an art.

Mick flipped the switch off after counting to ten.

Goddamn this stupid wallet, he thought and leaned a little to avoid the ache in his right hip.

The beads suddenly rattled with the compressed air, swaying back and forth across the room entrance. A split second later, he saw Phillip's eyes widen and then a burst of cool air fell across his bare arms.

"Someone's joined us, Phillip."

Phillip licked his lips and looked around the room without moving his head. Mick didn't laugh, but God, he wanted to.

"Esther," Mick said conversationally, "are you here with us?"

No audible answer, but another, briefer, flip of the switch made the beads rattle.

"Ask your grandmother, Phillip."

The man, pale as a ghost, licked his purple lips and stared at the ceiling.

"Grandma... I... I'd like to know where..."

He trailed off and then stared at Mick. "I can't do it," he hissed a whisper at Mick.

Mick stared at the man and drew himself up, relieving some of the pressure of the wallet. "You've invoked the spiritual realm, Phillip Kilmichael. You cannot go back on your word. You must press forward or those who came to answer your call will have no choice but to remain here, torn between worlds, until their purpose has been fulfilled."

Phillip blanched, turning even whiter than before and nodded.

"Where... Where did you bury your money, Grandma?"

Still, there was no answer, but it was time to use the Ouija board. Before laying his fingertips on the planchette, he gripped the side of the table and rotated his hips slightly because of his god-forsaken wallet. The nail that had snagged a thread in his vest earlier hadn't been fixed. Mick had been too focused on preparing for this session. The forgotten nail sank into his thumb so deeply that he could feel it poke the underside of his fingernail and pain exploded through his hand.

Tears immediately sprang from his eyes, and he had to stifle a moan of agony.

Trying desperately to school his reactions, he gently pulled his finger free with his other hand, closed his eyes, and took a deep breath. It was shaky, and for a moment, Mick was afraid that Phillip would begin to suspect something.

Instead, Phillip asked, "Is she answering? I don't hear anything but you look…"

He had to release some of the anguish he felt as his thumb throbbed painfully and warm blood seeped out between the fingers that grasped it. The pain from his wallet was forgotten.

"Yessss," he said through a deep and pain-filled exhalation. He bowed his head, and the tears dripped from his eyes onto the back of his hands beneath the edge of the table. If he didn't grasp the planchette soon, there'd be no way to ensure Phillip "felt" like he got an answer.

"Yes," Mick said again, "she's trying to reach out to us. It's painful, I can barely make sense of it." He was breathing heavily, both from the exertion to contain the pain and rapidly thinking of a solution. He couldn't stand up, excuse himself, and go get a band-aid.

So he did what any normal fake would do, he doubled down on it.

"*Sicut erat in principio, et nunc, et semper, et in saecula saeculorum.*" It was a Latin prayer. Part of one, but he liked how creepy it sounded. Translated, it simply meant "As it was in the beginning, is now, and ever shall be, world without end." To Phillip, it certainly sounded like an incantation of sorts.

"What was that? What's that mean? Was that Grandma? Was that her?" The words came tumbling out of Phillip's pale face, and Mick could barely make eye contact. When he did, the man was nothing more than a watery shape on the other side of the table.

Mick wiped his hands on his pants and groaned as the ache pounded through his hand. But he placed them on the planchette anyway.

Phillip didn't see the blood at first, but once the small triangle started to move, it left a narrow crimson trail in its wake. Phillip gasped when the gaudy red line appeared behind the planchette. *It does look pretty great, actually,* Mick thought distantly, but he dismissed it to make sure he was focused on *this* event.

Mick knew that most of the time, a Ouija board moved because one of the idiots using it was applying pressure subconsciously. He knew that *he* wasn't, but figured that Phillip was.

The Planchette moved down first, toward the row of numbers. At 5, it stopped then angled back up the left, settling on "E." Mick gazed at the small wooden item, pretending to be transfixed and mildly intrigued by what Phillip's subconscious would tell him.

It moved then over to the M, made a reverse maneuver back to the P, and then things got interesting. Phillip made a squeaking gasp and released the planchette. It continued to move, to Mick's surprise, toward the K. Once it was there, Mick released it, and it continued to move down toward the row of numbers again, and settled on the 6.

The air in the room seemed to be heating up, or Mick was sweating for no reason at all. The pendant on a leather string around his neck had fallen out of his shirt once more and felt heavy. Mick could feel it bending his head lower toward the table.

Phillip had put a hand over his mouth while the other clutched a handful of his hair. The man's eyes were wide with terror. Or was it surprise? Mick wasn't sure, but he knew his own heart was beating faster than it ever had in one of his little plays.

Mick smiled and chuckled a little. He couldn't help it. He blamed it on blood loss.

Then the planchette started to move again.

H.

A.

H.

A.

H.

A.

It was Mick's turn to blanch. The wooden toy began moving so fast between the H and the A that it became a blur. Mick sat back in his chair, an uneasy feeling of being watched and *known* settled between his shoulders. Never before had this happened, the Ouija board was a toy for chrissakes. It was made by Hasbro. In a factory!

The planchette suddenly flew off the table and clattered against the wall.

Mick's pendant fell soundlessly back against his chest, the strange pull gone.

Mick locked eyes with Phillip. Together, they looked down at the gameboard in terrified awe.

The letters that were touched hadn't spelled anything, and it was nothing that Mick could immediately make sense of. But there, on the gameboard, was a slightly smudged upside-down star made in his own blood.

Phillip crossed himself.

A Catholic, Mick thought shrewdly but couldn't do much else.

The silence between them stretched. Phillip stared down at the drying blood on the toy.

"Do those letters mean anything to you, Phillip?" His finger felt ten times its normal size with each throbbing heartbeat.

Phillip shuddered. "E.M.P.K? They're initials, obviously. E.M. is Esther Morgan, Grandma. P.K. is Phillip Kilmichael. She was here. She was talking to *me.*"

That was … what, unlikely? Mick thought. But after what just happened, maybe it wasn't so unlikely after all.

"And the numbers?"

"Five and Six? They don't mean anything off the top of my head. Fifty-six? Sixty-five?"

To Phillip they didn't really mean anything. To Mick, they made him a little nervous. The address of his little shop was on West 56th Street. Ironically enough, it was technically "56 West 56th Street" and Arjesh's deli was "57 West 56th Street."

Mick, feeling like he should add something, quoted a Latin phrase he'd seen on a record in a music store. He'd written it down because it sounded good and figured he could use it sometime to add a little panache.

That time was now, it seemed. *"Libera nos quidam malo,"* then, not thinking, he used his bloody hand to wipe across the pentagram. *It's not a pentagram,* he thought to himself a little shakily, making two quick swipes across the board.

Because he'd used his bloody hand, and because the blood wasn't completely dry, instead of cleaning the board, two fresh crimson stripes went through the drying pentagram, which remained mostly intact.

The two lines of blood went from the letter M to the letter C to the letter J.

Mick's blood ran cold.

Miles.

Chester.

Jameson.

What the hell? he thought. The hairs on the back of his neck stood on end.

A breeze blew through the little room. The switch was on the other side of the table or Mick could have chalked it up to an accidental bump. But when the beads rattled back and forth and his hair began to move in the warm wind, he knew it couldn't be.

The blood on the gameboard began to darken then boil in little black bubbles.

"Uh..." Phillip said, pushing away from the table and standing. "What is that?"

Mick had completely forgotten the man was there. He tried to laugh, but it came out as more of a throaty burp. "I can't tell you. This has... this has never happened."

He heard a distant whine. It sounded like it came from far away, like the end of a school hallway that was all angles and brick without anything to absorb the sound.

"What is *that!*" shouted Phillip in what Mick would call full-out panic.

The wind was growing stronger, billowing through the room in heady gusts.

"I don't know!" he shouted at the man. "Follow me!"

Together, they made their way to the front of the shop. He wasn't sure what was happening, but knew he wasn't going to let Phillip leave without paying.

The wind whistled through the cramped space, knocking over teetering boxes of junk and flipping the pages of his dusty old textbooks.

Mick tried to affect nonchalance, but he was starting to panic, too.

Was there some malfunction with the air conditioning unit?

He hurriedly unlatched the locks on the door and hopped over the counter to open the cash drawer. "Hundred and fifty."

"What?" Phillip said, turning around at the door.

Mick raised his voice to shout over the howl of the wind. "Hundred and fifty!" The whine he'd heard had turned into what sounded like a voice, like wind whistling over a hole or something.

Phillip dug into his pocket and pulled out a handful of cash and, staring around the room as if it was haunted, threw the bills at Mick before running out the door. Mick reached for the bills as they were caught up in the wind and began whipping around the room.

The whining sound had changed into a recognizable syllable. Was it saying something? Something almost recognizable? *That would be impossible*, thought Mick ignoring the wind that rattled the *inside* of his shop.

But yes, he thought gathering the last of the bills Phillip had tossed at him. *It was saying something. It was* screaming *something. Or some* thing *was screaming.*

Mick strained his ears to separate it from the howl of the wind, the thump in his bleeding finger forgotten.

It was a toneless, screeching "uh" sound, growing louder and louder with the wind.

When it grew so loud that Mick had to cover his ears, he heard the keening word stop suddenly with "UCK", followed by a massive crash in one of the rooms down the hall.

At the same time, the wind died. Mick froze, listening to the very loud silence. His heart thumped loudly in his ears and the sound of his breath came in short, terrified gasps.

"What the *fuck?!*" came from the room down the hall in a screech of rage. It was followed by innumerable expletives. Mick reached for the door to leave, to follow Phillip down the sidewalk and run for his life, but a clattering behind him sent a shiver down his spine. Mick heard something enter the hallway behind him.

"YOU STUPID FUCK!" it yelled. Mick turned, stared unbelieving for half a second, and then fainted.

CHAPTER 4

Mick tried to move his face, but gravity was in the wrong place. And something was smashing his face against a rough, what, fur? He tried to rub his eyes, to rub the fuzziness in his mind away, but his arm felt like it weighed a hundred pounds and was trapped beneath his stomach. He rolled to his side, realizing he was on the floor and his arm flopped listlessly on his torso.

A string of curses came from a back room, sounding a little like a child's but the language was clearly mature.

It took several tries before Mick could open his eyes. The light from the ceiling fluorescents was bright, and he blinked rapidly before finally staring up at the ceiling of his curiosities shop.

What happened? he thought to himself.

First, there nothing beyond Ms. Favereau, then...

In a rush, it all came back. Phillip, the séance, the wind, and the—

He sat up, and his head immediately screamed in protest.

He turned slowly. His head throbbed, and his arm buzzed as if he'd cracked it on something in the fall. Papers and pieces of his shop were thrown around the room in disarray. *The wind*, he hoped.

A crash from the back of the shop drew his attention.

And then he remembered what he'd seen just before passing out.

Standing slowly and steadying himself on the counter near the front of his shop, he swallowed hard.

"Hello?" he said, hoping nothing would answer.

The rattling rummaging sound stopped briefly then continued again.

Mick grabbed a shade-less lamp from a pile of odds and ends. Brandishing it like a club, he made his way slowly toward the back of the shop where it sounded like something was tearing apart the few things he called his own.

The sound was coming from the next room. When he reached it, he peered around the doorframe, hoping against hope that whatever was in there wouldn't see him.

In the room, which was a storeroom of sorts with boxes stacked neatly against the wall at the back, was now a mess. Every box was overturned, its contents strewn across the floor in unruly piles. What looked like a small green child had his back to Mick—thank God—and was bent over one of the piles of rubble. It was taking items, inspecting them, and tossing them carelessly aside.

Mick whipped back around the corner to hide, breathing heavily and mind reeling with his limited options. He tried to take a steadying breath, then gripped the lamp in his sweaty palms. His plan to charge into the room and beat the thing senseless fell to shambles when the thing came tottering out of the room and nearly bumped right into him.

"Gah!" was all he could manage, backpedaling and stumbling over that goddamn pile of books, landing squarely on his ass with a *thud*.

At the same time, the child-thing that was definitely not a child recoiled, clutching something large to his chest. But when Mick stumbled and fell, the creature tossed the item away, drew itself up to its full height of three feet, and ran at Mick, screeching.

Mick wasn't used to being charged, by anything really, so he did the only thing he knew how to do—he curled into a ball. He'd read somewhere that this was the safest response to a bear attack. And while the thing currently running at him wasn't a bear, it was the best option he could think of.

The pattering of the thing's long-toed feet grew louder but stopped next to Mick's head. After several seconds of nothing happening, he peered out between his arms. Two four-toed feet were mere inches away. Each toe ended in...

Are those claws? he thought.

They were attached to two stick-thin legs that connected to a skinny, naked body. Mick was glad there weren't any obvious sex organs. He wasn't sure how he'd handle that.

As Mick's eyes moved up the creature's body, noting how it stood with its clawed hands on hips, nausea began to curdle his lunch. The creature's belly protruded beneath a nipple-less chest.

The face turned his stomach topsy-turvy. It wasn't ugly; it was just something he'd never seen before, and his mind reeled with trying to fit it into a known narrative. It had a long nose, much longer than any human's, with slanted cat-like eyes beneath large bushy black brows. The mouth scowled at him, but between thin lips, he could see teeth that were more or less human, perhaps a little more pointed. Its ears swept back behind its silver-colored hair by several inches. Two twisting ram-like horns protruded from the creature's head and looped once back on themselves.

It was hideous.

"Jesus Christ!" Mick shouted, scrambling back and putting as much distance between himself and it as the cramped space allowed.

The creature shook its head as if hearing an annoying sound. Then, it put a hand over its chubby stomach and turned away from Mick.

"Don't—" it began, then made a gagging sound. "Don't do that."

"What?"

It licked its lips with a purple forked tongue. "Say *that*."

"Say what, 'Jesus Christ'?"

It turned away from him and retched loudly. "For fuck's sake," it cursed breathlessly after several seconds.

Mick, in spite of himself, smiled. It was strange, but an idea began forming in his head, something that was uncomfortable but familiar.

"Wait... are you... are you a *demon*?"

The creature before him wiped a hand across his mouth, panting. Then nodded. "What took you so long, genius?"

That was impossible. Mick didn't believe in any of that crap. God, Jesus, demons, devil, all of it was just a fairy tale. Or... had been. He'd heard that demons couldn't stand the name of God's Son. Apparently that was true.

"How... how did you get here? Wait, why are you here? Oh shit, am I dead? I'm dead, aren't I?"

The "demon" shook its head, now recovered from the sickness the Christian savior's name had inflicted upon it.

"No, no you're not dead. Calm the fuck down, you fleshy sack of guts."

Mick had begun to hyperventilate, and although the demon had contradicted him, he didn't believe it. Not yet.

"How do I know that? There's no other explanation!"

The creature walked up to Mick who had clutched a handful of hair in each fist and kicked him in the shin.

"There, see? Still alive."

"Goddammit! Jesus Christ, you little shit!"

The creature—demon—bent double and retched on the carpet. It was mostly a slimy green bile with a few yellow chunks scattered throughout, and it splashed across the floor. Mick's stomach rolled, and he swallowed hard.

"Cut that out!" it screamed wetly, swaying on its feet.

"Oh, God, it's true. You're a demon."

"I already told you that!"

"So it's true! You can't hear the name of—"

The demon's hands balled into fists, and it shouted over Mick. "MOIST!"

Mick stopped, his head spinning a little bit. "Ew. Don't... don't say that. I hate that word."

The demon grew a wicked grin. "Moist. Moist. Moist moist moist."

Mick put out a hand as if he could stop the words, but his stomach gurgled loudly. "Ugh, God. That word makes me sick. Stop, please."

And even though the demon had stopped saying "moist," Mick's belly had had enough. He bent double at the waist and vomited, trying to avoid his shoes and instead ralphing right into a half-filled box of metallic objects.

"Not too fun, is it?"

"No. No, it's not." He wiped a sleeve across his mouth after spitting the nasty bile from his mouth. "I'm sorry."

It shrugged and bent to riffle through a box near its feet. Several small trinkets it took and stuffed into pockets that Mick couldn't see.

"A demon," Mick said. "In my shop. How?"

"Yeah." It stopped pilfering things and stared up at him. "About that." It pointed a black-clawed finger up at him. "You did it."

"I... what? No I didn't."

It nodded emphatically, white hair bobbing as if in water. "Yeah. You did. I don't know how, and I don't know why, but I need you to send me back."

"I don't even know how I did it in the first place! I'm not a... a... What, demonologist?"

The demon rolled its eyes. "Sure, if that's what you say. The problem is that you drew me from my world into yours. It shouldn't have been possible, but we don't have time to figure that out right now. I need you to put me back. And hurry up. Being on this Plane makes me sick."

Mick was speechless, and he stared dumbly.

"What?" it said.

"I don't know what I did. I'm... I'm a fake. I pretend to do these things for people. I've never actually..."

"Oh wow, you've never actually summoned a demon? Color me surprised. It doesn't matter. Come on, show me where you were. Maybe I'll know what you did so you can send me back."

Mick nodded, still dumbfounded, and led the demon through the cluttered hallway, carefully stepping around both piles of vomit.

"This place is a mess," it said behind him.

When they turned the corner into the séance room, the demon sniffed the air.

"Oh yeah, definitely have some residual magic in here."

"Some ... what?"

"Residual magic. You know, stuff left over after a spell."

"Buddy, I don't know what that means."

"That's not my name. And I'm not surprised. If I had a dollar for every time some novice witch or 'demonologist' accidentally summoned a demon, I'd be fuckin' rich."

"Novice? There are actually people who summon demons? On purpose?"

"Well yeah," the demon scoffed at Mick. "Of course there are. I mean ... you summoned me. Not that that's happened before. But that's not even the weirdest thing, anyway."

"What is?" Mick wasn't sure he wanted to know.

The demon sat at the table where Phillip had been and began picking up the crystals along the periphery of the table and inspecting each one before scoffing and putting them back.

"When someone wants to summon a demon, they usually want a really powerful one. They want to harm someone or curse someone or trade their soul for power or fame, that kind of thing."

"And you aren't a powerful one?"

The demon picked up an agate and licked it then put it back down.

"Nope. Not even close."

It then stood on the chair and climbed onto the table where the Grace was still spread. The Ouija board had been nearly blown off the table and lay cock-eyed to the demon.

"Now this..." it said and bent over it. After several moments of inspection, it looked at Mick scornfully. "You did this, and you didn't know what you were doing?"

Mick felt a flush creep up his cheeks. "Well," he began, but didn't really have anything else to say.

"Oh, right. You're a fake."

Mick shifted his feet uncomfortably while the demon continued inspecting the board.

"Interesting that you knew to draw a pentagram."

"Yeah, that actually wasn't me. That was probably my ... customer."

"You let your customer draw a pentagram? In blood?"

The flush deepened. "Well, it was *my* blood. And he didn't know what he was doing. I don't think so, at least."

The demon bent low and sniffed the Ouija board. "Wow. Yeah. Definitely where the magic originated." It chuckled without humor. "Not the first human that let a stranger use their own blood to draw a summoning circle."

"Listen, pal, I don't need you to judge me. I didn't know this..." he gestured wildly toward the creature, "would happen."

The demon put a finger up. "That's not my name either."

"Oh Jes—" Mick stopped and licked his lips while the demon stared him down. "I mean, what *is* your name, then?"

"Rashik. My full name is Rashik the Lesser, but I don't think there's a Rashik the Greater; it's just meant to make me feel especially stupid."

Mick nodded but didn't understand. "I'm Mick." He nodded as if that were enough, then continued. "You said you've never been summoned before but others have. More powerful demons. Do you know who they are?"

Rashik hopped off the table by way of the chair and began slowly making his way around the room, answering Mick's questions absently. "I've never been summoned *like* this, I should say. Being yanked through the Nether and tossed onto this Plane is enough to make my head spin. But because of the circumstances in which it happened, I can't stay long. I'll get more and more sick until... Well I don't know. But I need to go back."

"You'll die?"

"Like I said, I don't know. It's a curse of some sorts, to prevent demons from invading other Planes willy-nilly."

"Oh, that... That actually makes sense. What about the other demons?"

Rashik sighed. "I know a few of them, yeah. Probably the most popular is one that you humans always talk about. A guy named 'Legion.'"

Mick thought for a moment, not realizing he'd pulled the pendant from under his shirt and begun to rub his thumb over its surface. "The one from the Bible?"

Rashik nodded. "Yup. That guy's a complete asshole. He thinks because they wrote a story about him—a story, mind, where he just ends up in a bunch of *pigs*—that he's royalty or something."

Rashik put a hand against the wall across from Mick and looked at the cleverly hidden pipe where cool air would blow through the room. "Clever" was all it said.

Mick ignored him. "And others?"

"There was one that came to Earth a few hundred years ago. Made a whole mess of things before finally being banished back to its Plane."

"What was that one named?"

"Felsinar. He added a bunch of titles to it. Felsinar the Devourer. The Seventh Vein. Felsinar the All-Consuming." Rashik stopped and looked pointedly at Mick. "Also an asshole."

Mick nodded.

"Then there were others, too. Tev'nal the Cursed. Urmek. Chaaz'mar. Geldrokov. Barzumel. All of them—"

"Let me guess," he interrupted. "Assholes."

Rashik snapped and pointed a finger gun at Mick. "That's a bingo. Every last one."

The demon went back to inspecting the room but shook his head. "If you don't know how you summoned me, then we have no hope of finding out how to send me back."

"I'm ... sorry?" Mick wasn't sure what to say.

"It's fine." Rashik walked through the tangled beads and toward the front door.

"What? Fine?"

"Yeah. It's fine. We'll have to just go to someone who *does* know how to send me back."

"You ... know someone?"

Rashik turned around and stared at Mick. "It's been a few decades since I've been here, and back then I was just here as an assistant. But there was someone who knew most of us demons by name. She's kind of crazy, but she's fine."

"And where is this 'kind of crazy but fine' woman?"

"She's a doctor."

"A ... doctor? Like a regular doctor?"

"During the day. At night she's a witch. She'll know what to do."

"Well, how far away is she?"

"Just a few blocks, I think."

"Wait, there's a witch doctor nearby?"

Rashik looked at Mick as if he were stupid. "It's New York." As if that explained everything.

CHAPTER 5

R ashik led the way through bustling New York streets while Mick followed closely on his heels. Remarkably, the little demon never bumped into anyone, and no one bumped into him. Mick asked him what that was all about when they were standing on a corner waiting for the walk sign to turn green.

Rashik shrugged. "No, other people can't see me. At least, I don't think they can. And I have a large measure of control over who does and doesn't see me. I don't know exactly how it works, but if I want someone to see me, I let them. If not," he slapped the backside of a passing man, who turned and threatened Mick with all kinds of harm, oblivious to the demon who'd smacked his ass. Rashik laughed and finished by saying, "It just happens like that."

"So they can't see you, but they know you're there or something?"

"Yeah, something like that. It's like when you're in a room and you feel a cold pocket, you can edge your way around it. It's like that, only it's not cold, it's just a feeling humans have to step aside. It's subconscious for most people. There might be a few out of every thousand sensitive enough to understand the *why*, like something needs to be avoided, but they still don't *completely* get it."

Mick nodded and the walk signal turned. Just in time, too, because the man next to Mick was staring at him like he was insane. Mick nodded hello and then avoided further eye contact as he and the demon hustled across the street.

After four blocks of walking, Rashik stopped in front of a modest two-story home on a modest street lined with modest trees and modest cars out front.

"Is this it?" Mick asked.

"This is where she lived when I was here last. I don't know if she still does. But it's all I have to go on."

The demon walked up the half-dozen brick steps and made to knock on the door.

"Wait, it's almost five in the evening, she's probably still at work, right?"

Rashik eyed Mick and then shrugged. "You humans are always so concerned about time." Then he knocked.

They waited a moment or two before Mick heard footsteps on the other side of the door. The curtain moved aside and Mick smiled.

"Can I help you?" said a female voice. *That's promising,* Mick thought.

Mick waved and said a little self-consciously, "Hi. Yes. We're here to ask you a few questions, actually. If you have the time."

"Questions about what?"

Mick puffed out his cheeks and clasped his hands nervously, glancing down at Rashik.

Luckily the little demon spoke up, then. "About your night job, Mags."

"Who said that?" the woman—Mags, apparently—said in surprise.

"That was my friend, here," said Mick pointing next to him.

"I don't see him. And there are very few people who know that name."

"Lift me up," said Rashik, "so she can see me."

"I'm absolutely *not* doing that."

"Do it you little shit, or I'll melt your eyes in their sockets."

Mick wasn't sure if the demon could do it, but he wasn't going to take his chances.

With a sigh, he bent and, holding Rashik beneath the arms like a toddler, held him up.

"Heya, sweetcheeks," said Rashik with a bored wave.

Mick heard Mags gasp and then, "Rashik? Good God!"

Mick put the demon back on the brick as locks clicked and the door swung open suddenly to reveal a stunning woman just coming into her gray hair. If Mick had to guess, she was mid-fifties max. Her eyes were bright, and her smile made tiny little dimples on each cheek.

"Been a while, that's for sure."

Mags knelt and hugged the demon to her. When she stood and stared at Mick, he took that as his cue.

"Hi, Mags. My name is Mick. I'm just along for the ride, apparently."

Rashik scoffed. "Don't let this idiot fool you. If any of us are along for the ride it's me."

"Hi, Mick," she replied. Then to Rashik, she asked, "What do you mean?"

"Can we come inside? I'm dying for a glass of your peach tea."

"Yes! Yes, of course." She ushered them inside and closed the door behind them.

When they were all seated comfortably in a spacious living room, Mags brought out a pitcher of tea and several glasses of ice. The room was large enough to hold two sofas in the center around a low table. An upright grand piano stood pretentiously in the corner while large windows let the evening sun shine brilliantly across the room, Mick surprised himself by drinking greedily and was even more surprised as Rashik finished three consecutive glasses with barely a breath in between.

"Now tell me what's going on," she said.

Mags sat in a green velvet wingback chair, her back ramrod straight. Her graying hair was pulled back into a neat ponytail. She wore a simple blouse with a colorful scarf draped across her shoulders. Her pants were what Mick would have called "normal pants," which meant they were everyday slacks—not too nice and not too drab, and she was barefoot.

"This idiot human runs a curio shop. He also pretends to read fortunes, talk to spirits, et cetera. He accidentally summoned me."

Mags gasped and put a red-nailed hand to her chest. "How in the name of the Gilded Sigil did he do that?"

"Yeah, that's what I thought. Unfortunately, he doesn't know. A mix of accidental magic and incantations."

She looked askance at Mick, and he felt very stupid.

"I had no idea what I was doing," he said in his own meager defense.

"Obviously," said the demon and the witch simultaneously.

"You must be that shop owner over on West 56th," she continued.

Mick blushed. "Yeah. Yes, that's me. How do you—"

She waved the question away. "We know most of the people who 'practice magic.' Several of us have heard of you."

He let it lie but wondered if the "we" and "us" referred to other witches.

"All that to say, we need your help sending me back."

Mags nodded. "I understand. Since you're here, though, why not stay?"

Rashik shook his head and said simply, "Can't."

"Why not?"

"Whatever he did to bring me here wasn't a sanctioned summon, and I'm not even supposed to be able to travel. I'm a truant wraith. The longer I stay without permission, the worse I'll get."

"Well, that's no good." She tapped her lip. "Now, to send you back, we need to know exactly how you got here. Mick," she turned her stern gaze to him, "can you tell me exactly what you did to summon him here?"

He related the story, starting with the rocks and the home-made Grace—which she actually laughed aloud at—and then the Ouija board. She listened intently at this point and when he was finished, she nodded.

"Right. So you set this all up, accidentally created a sum-moning circle—"

"*I* didn't do anything."

"—and said some mumbo jumbo incantation?"

Sigh. "Yes."

"What was the incantation?"

"It was something in Latin, something I saw a long time ago and, I don't know, felt like it fit at the time. It was '*Libera nos quidam malo.*'"

The room was silent. Then Mags burst into laughter, which any other time might have been a beautiful sound. Rashik sat on the couch next to Mick staring at him in shocked disbelief.

"I don't... I don't know what it means." He glanced ner-vously between them, feeling very exposed.

When Mags stopped laughing, she wiped her eyes and said, "It's a play on part of a Catholic decree. In English the translation of the decree is roughly 'Deliver us from evil,' but what *you* said was—" she couldn't finish and instead began cackling even louder.

Mick turned to Rashik. "What did I say?"

"You know you should have told me this back at the shop. Would have saved me some embarrassment."

"Sorry" was all he could manage.

"Roughly translated," continued Rashik, "instead of 'Deliver us *from* evil,' it means 'Deliver us *some* evil.' Roughly."

Mick, who hadn't thought any of this was funny up until now, couldn't help but join Mags in the laughter.

"It's not funny," said Rashik, who crossed his arms over his belly and began to pout.

"So you're telling me that instead of summoning some big bad nasty demon, I asked for just a tiny dose of evil? And whatever fills summoning orders found you to be just '*some*' evil?"

Mick's stomach and face were hurting from laughing so hard. Mags, now seeming much friendlier to Mick, slapped her thigh with each breath.

"You're both assholes," said the demon, taking another drink of his tea.

After several minutes, Mags and Mitch had calmed and were able to discuss the situation without sudden laughter interrupting them.

"What we'll need to do is bind you to an item that will return you to the Plane that you were drawn from."

"Sounds easy. What do you need?"

"Well, first we need an item from your Plane. Last we spoke, you were on the Ver'shak Plane. Is that where you still reside?"

Rashik shook his head. "No, I moved out of there when Urmek moved in."

Mags rolled her eyes. "Gross."

"Now, I'm in the Dep'osadi Plane. Some others went with me when one of the Big Guys disappeared, so it was free real estate."

"Dep'osadi. Okay. I don't think I have anything from there. If you'd still been in the Ver'shak Plane, I have a relic tied to there. Can we just send you back there?"

Rashik shook his head. "Nope. My essence isn't tied there anymore. That would be like trying to use a moonrock to connect you to Mars. Just ain't gonna happen."

Mags nodded. Mick remained silent. This was a little out of his league. His mind was still reeling with the fact that he'd actually been playing with powers far beyond his imaginings. In fact, he felt as if he'd been playing next to a giant cliff without knowing it was there. Or dancing around a bear trap. He shuddered when he imagined the terror of accidentally summoning something far worse than little Rashik.

"I wish there was more I could do. I can try to connect with my circle of friends and see what we can come up with. In the meantime, I'd say you'd have better luck going back to this man's shop and looking for a way to return home."

Mick looked at Rashik who nodded, disheartened.

"Thanks, Mags," he said and hopped off the couch. "The tea was perfect, as usual."

Mick stood and held out his hand. "Yeah, thank you. Sorry to barge in on you like this."

She waved him away and leaned in to kiss his cheek. "Never a problem. My door is always open. Figuratively speaking, of course."

CHAPTER 6

Mick and his demon companion stood outside of Mags' house under the yellow streetlamps. Night had fallen in the city, but that didn't mean it was dark. They made their way back to the shop, passing by Arjesh's shop. Mick spied the Indian man sitting alone at one of his booths. When they made eye contact, the deli owner waved him in.

"You mind?"

The demon shrugged and followed Mick into the empty deli.

Mick sighed as he settled into the booth opposite Arjesh and moved over to make room for Rashik. Arjesh looked at him quizzically and then Mick remembered that his friend couldn't see the little demon.

Arjesh looked a little paler than usual, drawn. "You okay, buddy?"

His friend shrugged and took a deep breath. "Desmond came by today."

Mick sat up. "Oh shit. What happened?"

Desmond was the man who owned the block on which Mick's shop and Arjesh's deli sat. Technically speaking, the man owned far more than that, but had allowed the rental of the shop—and the subsequent division of it—by Mick and Arjesh without much of an issue. The one caveat that Desmond had given them in the single-page contract, is that he—Desmond—had final say on when they had to move out. "I'll give you plenty of notice, but don't be surprised if I turn up one day and tell you to hit the road," he'd said in his stereotypical movie-like New York accent.

From the time they signed the papers, there was very little interaction with what they believed was a real estate mogul. Of course, there were whispered ties to the mob or some other conglomerate, but the price was a steal and the location was pretty great. Mick didn't hesitate to sign his name.

Arjesh shrugged again, then said, "Not much. Just said that he liked the place. Said it was a shame it wouldn't be around much longer."

"Ah Christ," said Mick before catching himself and glancing at Rashik, who'd made a gurgling sound in his throat. "Sorry," he said to the demon.

Arjesh stared at Mick and the place where Rashik sat, but said nothing.

"So that's it, then? He gave you the boot?"

"Seems like it. Didn't give me any more information than 'Don't get too comfortable,' before he and his hulking goon left." The man sniffed. "And he smelled bad. Not like body odor, but definitely gross. I can still smell him."

Mick sniffed his armpits and the air, but didn't smell anything. "Sorry. But damn it, man. I can't believe that."

"Neither can I. After years of *very* good business, they decide to just come in here and flush it all away. Jesus, man."

Rashik gagged again, and Mick tried his best not to glance in his direction.

"Do you think I'm next?"

In the back of his mind, he'd always feared the day would come. But he didn't think it would be this soon. Nearly eight years is plenty of time to become profitable, yet Arjesh had done it in only a few months of being open. If anyone was at risk of getting evicted, it was Mick. His shop barely broke even.

"I'm sorry, Arjesh."

"Yeah. Fuck me, right?"

They sat in silence for a few minutes before Arjesh broke the silence.

"You know what really gets me, though? That big guy that follows Desmond around. His bodyguard or whatever. The guy's pretty new, I think. But he acts like he's more than just the muscle."

"What do you mean?"

"I watched Desmond pull up in his black Escalade." Arjesh pointed out the front glass windows that lined the street. "The bodyguard wasn't even in the front seat. He was in the back. *With Desmond.*"

Mick shrugged. "That's not all that weird, right?"

Arjesh shook his head. "Not from what I understand. And a man like Desmond?" He blew a raspberry. "That guy thinks he's Jesus Christ himself."

Rashik vomited across the table, tea-colored bile splashed across the cleaned surface and sprayed Arjesh.

Mick was too stunned to speak.

Rashik looked sheepishly at Mick and shrugged. "Oops" was all he managed.

"What's that smell?"

Mick looked at Arjesh, who had vomit across both of his folded arms and flecks of it on his cheeks. It took considerable self-control for Mick to avoid vomiting, too.

"Do you want me to let him see me?"

Mick shot a glance at Rashik. "What?"

"Who the fuck are you talking to, Mick? You're making me nervous. You cracked?"

Mick ignored his friend. "It's up to you."

Rashik shrugged. "Sure. But he'll probably lose his shit."

"Do you think he can help us?"

"A deli owner? You think he secretly runs an occult shop in the kitchen and can help me get home?"

Mick frowned. "No. But maybe he knows someone?" He didn't mean for it to be a question, but it came out that way.

Rashik shrugged and looked at Arjesh.

Nothing changed in Mick's eyes, but when Arjesh suddenly jumped and tried to leap backward out of the booth, Mick assumed Rashik had made himself visible.

Arjesh's eyes were wide—wider than Mick had ever seen them. The deli owner yelped in terror and scrambled out of the booth, looking from the little green creature next to Mick and the puddle of spreading vomit on the table. It took a couple of seconds for Arjesh to see his vomit-speckled arms.

"That's the smell," said Mick, pointing to his arms.

"What the fuck is *that*!" Arjesh said, pointing at Rashik. Tiny chunks of vomit sailed through the air and landed with tiny wet *splats* on the table.

"I'm Rashik. This moron accidentally summoned me this afternoon."

"And he's a demon," Mick added levelly.

"A... a what?"

"Demon," Rashik answered.

"Jesus—"

"Don't!" Mick yelled as Rashik doubled over and gagged. "He doesn't really like that name."

"Oh my god. Are you kidding me? What the hell, Mick?"

Mick tried to look like he was ashamed, but it didn't work. "I didn't *mean* to. It just sort of ... happened."

"What's it doing here?"

"Nothing. We're just trying to figure out how to get it home so it doesn't die."

"When you say 'home' you mean, like, Hell?" Arjesh squeaked.

Rashik stood on the booth seat, palms placating. "That's a misconception. Not *all* of us come from Hell, okay? There are several different planes. Do I know some demons from Hell, sure. I mean, who doesn't? But I'm not one of them."

Arjesh made to sit down, but when his eyes found the vomit on his arms and the bit of it now dripping off the table, he grabbed a nearby bucket of water and a rag to clean it up.

The next several minutes were filled with Mick and Rashik answering as many rapid-fire questions from Arjesh as they could. To be fair, it wasn't very many, as Mick didn't know the first thing about demons and Arjesh didn't know the right questions to ask.

"This is insane. You know that, Mick?"

"I know. Trust me, if I wanted to summon something, it wouldn't have been a three-foot green child from Hell."

Rashik rolled his eyes, but didn't respond.

Mick continued, "What are we gonna do about Desmond?"

"I don't know, Mick. I'm going to assume he's coming for you tomorrow. For all I know, he could have stopped by, but since you were out, he couldn't break the news to you."

Mick nodded, uncomfortable knowing that his number might be up. "Listen. Let's talk tomorrow about it. It's getting late. I'm tired, I know you're tired, and we'll probably be able to solve this problem better in the morning."

"Which problem you talking about?" Arjesh nodded toward Rashik and then looked around his deli.

"Yeah. I don't know. Both. Maybe neither. But tomorrow. And maybe by then, Desmond will have come by and I'll be on the hook, too."

"Alright. Yeah." Arjesh sounded tired. "I'll see you tomorrow then. Just come over here, and I'll make us some omelets."

"Sounds good."

"Nice to meet you, little demon."

"Yeah, nice to meet you too, I guess." Rashik nodded to the man and then walked to the deli entrance.

"Tomorrow," said Mick, meeting Arjesh's eyes.

"Tomorrow," replied his friend.

Mick and Rashik returned to the shop next door and spent the next hour tidying up as much as they could. Rashik admitted to looking through several boxes while Mick had been unconscious, but he didn't find anything useful.

"I could have told you that. Most of it is junk. Or party props."

"You're a real dumbass, you know that?" said Rashik.

"Yeah, that lesson is really being pounded into me today."

When they could walk through the shop without tripping over the multitude of flipped boxes and metal objects, Mick told Rashik he was going to bed.

"That's fine. I'll sleep in the Summoning Room. Smells like home."

Mick turned to go in the final room that remained locked— his bedroom—but turned back to Rashik.

"Hey, about that. Could Arjesh smell you? Earlier, I mean."

"Yeah, probably. I mean, he smelled my puke, right?"

Mick thought for a moment. "Yeah, but he mentioned Desmond's bodyguard smelled, too."

Rashik shrugged. "Maybe your friend is just one of those sensitive humans."

"Maybe," thought Mick, unconvinced but uncertain as to why.

"I'll see you in the morning."

"Yeah," said Rashik before moving the beads out of his way and disappearing into the room.

Mick's sleep was full of nightmares. A mix of Desmond turning into a devil transitioned into Arjesh making a sandwich out of Mick and feeding him to a horned duck. He didn't sleep well, and when his alarm went off at seven, his head throbbed with a deep ache over his right eye.

He was just pouring his coffee when a pounding at the door made him spill hot liquid all over his hand.

"Goddammit," he said. Then he shouted, "Just a minute, coming."

He made his way to the front of the store, peeking into the séance room where he saw Rashik bundled into a corner.

He pulled the curtain aside and his heart leapt into his throat.

On the other side of the bulletproof glass stood an enormously fat man in a business suit that strained at every seam. He had a cigar clenched between his teeth, and his lips sneered at Mick when he saw the curtains move. Desmond Westrench waved his pudgy sausage hand while his bodyguard stood at the man's shoulder, towering over him by more than a foot.

Mick took a deep breath and unlocked the door.

CHAPTER 7

The man that stepped through the door wasn't just pudgy. "Pudgy" would be a fleshy bulge rolling over his belt that indicated he just couldn't turn down an extra slice of Aunt Becky's chocolate pie. "Pudgy" would be an extra "X" on his t-shirt size. Desmond Westrench's stomach protruded so far in front of his belt that it looked as if he were smuggling Santa's sack of toys beneath his shirt. The fat around his neck resembled an inflated pool ring and made his shoulders transition straight into his head. His hands reminded Mick of a latex glove filled with air. Small, nubby fingers protruded from a club of meaty flesh where a palm would be.

The man was immensely overweight: a testament to his appetite and his ability to sate it.

The second man to enter was enormous. But where Desmond Westrench flaunted his status and wealth by over-indulging in everything, his new bodyguard towered over his boss the way a sturdy oak tree towers over a pot-bellied pig. The man was massive, and Mick had to stop himself from swallowing in fear as the bodyguard ducked beneath the door-frame to enter the tiny shop.

"Mr. Westrench," Mick said with what felt like noxious glee. "What brings you by today?"

Desmond's beady little eyes could barely be seen beneath rolls of fat that functioned as eyebrows. They wandered around the shop beneath his Appalachian mountain eyebrows. The cigar that was clenched between yellow teeth was nearly black with moisture. Mick had to repress a gag as the man's tongue rolled over the wrapped tobacco like an octopus probing for purchase.

"I just figured I'd stop by for a chat, Little Mickey." Mick hated that nickname, but Desmond had said it from the moment they met. Desmond's thick New York accent could have been pulled straight from The Godfather. "As I'm sure you've no doubt heard, the deli owner next door will need to pack his things in the near future."

Mick only nodded.

"I'm also sure you've begun to question the status of this little shop, as well."

Again, Mick nodded.

"Unfortunately, the owners of this block, the very same who rented it to you for pennies on the dollar, will need to—" he wiggled his pudgy meat stick fingers in the air and turned his bulk toward the giant behind him. "What's the word for that, Barry?"

The man in black behind him opened his hands that had been folded across his chest and shrugged. The square jaw looked very much like it could bite Mick in half. When he opened his mouth to speak, there was a perfect line of stark white teeth against very red gums. His voice was a gravelly bass that resonated in Mick's chest.

"Recant, perhaps. Or even retract would work, boss."

The boss tried to snap, but the fingers couldn't touch. "That's the one."

He turned back to Mick.

"The company needs to retract its offer of tenancy."

Mick tried to smile, but his face wouldn't move. He licked his lips and blinked a few times and shrugged.

"No problem," he managed to squeak out.

"I know this isn't necessarily the news you were hoping to hear, Little Mickey. But unfortunately, I'm merely the messenger."

The fuck you are, he thought.

"The good news is," Desmond's sweaty hand reached over to land on Mick's shoulder. Even though they were the same height, the boss' arms barely reached the short distance between them, "that you have a week to clear out. Should be plenty of time to move all this..." he left the sentence unfinished but gestured vaguely around the shop entryway.

"That's great. Thank you."

Their business concluded—well, the message delivered—Desmond turned to leave.

"What if I'm not able to get everything out by then?"

Desmond paused and the big man—Barry—centered his dark gaze on Mick. This time, Mick did swallow.

Mr. Westrench pulled the cigar from his clenched teeth and used it to point at Mick. "You'd better pray to Jesus fucking Christ that you can."

Mick, having been through Rashik's violent response to the name multiple times, still cringed slightly at its mention. He heard a retching sound from the séance room.

Desmond nodded at Mick as if to say "You understand me, dipshit?" but Barry stood up straighter and stared down the hallway where the noise had come from. When Desmond turned to leave, he had to stare up at the colossal man.

"What the fuck, Barry? Move, let's get out of this shit heap."

Barry didn't respond immediately to Desmond but stared back at Mick, seeming to stare right through him and into the wall behind which Rashik's stomach was emptying its contents onto the séance room's carpet.

Then the bodyguard took a long, deep breath through his nose. The giant's nostrils flared with it, and then he smiled at Mick. It wasn't a good smile, it was an "I know what you're hiding," smile, and Mick was immediately afraid. So afraid, in fact, that he had to grip the counter to prevent his knees from buckling.

"You listening to me you big dumb idiot? What's wrong with you? Move it." Desmond was used to being obeyed immediately.

"Yes sir, Boss," Barry said before opening the door and ducking once more beneath the frame to hold the door for Desmond.

They didn't look back after leaving, but through the curtain, he saw Desmond take out a handkerchief and clean his hands off. They moved back toward the black Escalade that had parked outside, and Mick watched several of Desmond's attempts to lift his bulk into the back seat. Finally, Barry stood close enough that Desmond could push him hip-to-hip into the car, which bounced with the sudden surplus of additional weight.

It would have been funny, but Mick was in no mood for laughing. In fact, he felt as if a timer had begun. Not for his shop, but for him. And when it finally reached zero, he'd be dead.

CHAPTER 8

As soon as the Escalade pulled away from the curb and merged into the traffic heading down West 56th, Mick let out the massive breath he'd been holding and hustled back to the séance room.

"Rashik!" he shouted as he rounded the corner and ducked through the beads covering the door.

"I'm fine," said the little demon from the corner. He stood over a puddle of red bile that was already soaking into the carpet. "Sorry, Mick. Couldn't help it. I tried, but with what he said, and the time passing on this Plane..."

"It's okay. But we've got a problem."

"Yeah I know, I feel like shit."

"No, something worse. Come out here, to the front."

Mick led the way and Rashik followed, his feet making a *flap flap flap* sound even on the carpet of the store.

When they reached the front desk, Mick turned and saw Rashik frozen mid-step in the hallway, not quite in the front entryway.

"Shit," he said.

"Shit," echoed Mick.

"This is bad."

Mick stared wide-eyed at Rashik. "I have no idea what is even happening, but even *I* know that. But how bad exactly?"

"Very," he replied.

"He heard you, you know."

"Who, the fat man? Desmond?"

Mick shook his head. "No. The other one. The *huge* one. When you barfed back there, he looked in the direction, then back at me. Then he smiled like he wanted to eat me."

"He probably does," said Rashik off-handedly.

"He *what?!*"

Rashik shrugged. "If it's who I think it is, and based on the smell in here I'm positive it is, then yeah, he likes to eat humans. Now the smell in the deli makes sense."

"Oh Je—well, you know."

"Yeah, thanks."

"So who is he?"

Rashik rubbed his nose as if the smell of whoever—or whatever—was here was making him sneeze. "You know how last night when we talked with Mags she asked me which Plane I came from?"

Mick nodded. "Sure, you made up a bunch of words and pretended they were real places."

Rashik mimed laughter then frowned. "Ha ha. I'm serious. I moved from the Ver'shak Plane to the Depo'sadi Plane. I moved there because a certain Big Bad disappeared. Most of us thought he'd moved on or been banished to the Nether Realm."

"But he hadn't."

Rashik shook his head. "To our misfortune."

"So that's him?" Mick pointed out the front door. "That's the 'Big Bad' that disappeared?"

"Yep."

"What's his name?"

"He goes by a few names in other realms. Here, he goes by 'Barry' apparently."

"What's his real name?"

Rashik shuddered a little bit then sighed. "He's best known by his royal name. Barzumel."

"And he's real bad."

"Real bad. Like I said, he likes to eat humans."

Mick rubbed his jaw. "Makes sense that he'd come to an all-you-can-eat buffet, then."

"Yeah, I guess so. But what I don't get is why he's latched himself on to this Desmond guy. As far as I can tell, the big fatty doesn't have any powers or authority over poly-planar beings."

Mick stared dumbly at Rashik. "Come again?"

"Poly-planar beings. Entities that can cross different realms without actually being summoned or invited. Realmwalkers, Planestriders, Traveling Salesmen."

Mick had to laugh at the last. "That's not real."

Rashik nodded vehemently. "Oh, yes it is. How do you think we get extra-planar items. How do you think Barzumel gets humans without coming up here?"

That stopped Mick's laughter. "I see your point. So this Barzumel, he's a... a Realmwalker?"

"Most of the royalty are. He's the great grandson of some creature or another that people have forgotten. He's powerful, like the others that rule the Planes."

"And now he's here. What's that mean for us."

"Well, it means that he can easily kill me; I'm no match for a Demon Prince. And you're just someone pretending to be powerful, so you're obviously no match for him either."

"Thanks," said Mick sourly.

"Just being honest."

They stood in silence for several minutes.

"Why can't I just leave? I mean, he gave me a week to pack up. I'm not happy about it, but doesn't it make sense that I could just up and go and then be done with it? This Barzumel has no beef with me. Maybe he does with you, but as soon as we send you back it won't matter anymore, right?"

"I wish that was true. The Demon Princes take their rule very seriously. If it was just you, then leaving might actually be an option. The problem is that now he knows you've meddled with the other Planes. Maybe not exactly *how* you've meddled, but meddled nonetheless. As a Demon Prince, he's duty-bound to stop it and correct it. And he gets a sick amount of pleasure from this kind of thing."

"And by 'correct it' you mean..." Mick trailed off.

Rashik drew a black-clawed finger across his neck.

Mick nodded. "Great."

The front door squealed open, making them both jump. For a moment, Mick expected to see Barry-Barzumel duck through the door with a hungry grin splitting his face in two.

Instead, Arjesh closed the door behind him and jumped only a little when he saw Rashik.

"I saw Desmond leave a few minutes ago and figured I'd give him time to get out of the neighborhood before coming over. How'd it go?"

Mick sighed. "Same news for me. I have a week to get out of here."

"Damn," said his friend.

"That's not even the worst of it."

"Oh shit, did he mention me?"

"No. Yes. But that's not important."

"Thanks a lot, you bastard."

"Shut up for a minute, Arjesh. The problem isn't Desmond. It's his bodyguard."

"The muscle? What's he got to do with this."

Rashik piped in, now. "He's not a human. He's a Demon. A bad one."

Arjesh paled a little.

"A Demon *Prince*, to be exact."

Arjesh paled more.

"Who likes to eat humans."

"Oh my god," said Arjesh whose skin had paled almost to blue.

Mick snapped and looked at Rashik, then said, "Why don't we go back to Mags?"

"Who is Mags?" Arjesh said shakily.

Mick ignored her. "She's got to know how to help, right? Surely some witch lady who already knows you also knows about the Demon Princes. She can help, right?"

Rashik looked doubtful. "I don't know, Mick."

"*Princes?*" Arjesh said in a high-pitched squeak, "as in more than one?"

Again, they ignored him.

"Come on, we don't have any other options."

"Yeah. Yeah, I guess it couldn't hurt," said the demon.

Mick clapped. "Excellent. Let's go."

"Will you fuckers please tell me who Mags is?"

"She's a doctor, buddy," said Mick as he ushered Arjesh out the door. Then he turned and locked his shop behind him.

"A doctor is going to save us from a Demon Prince?" he asked, but the other two were already walking down the sidewalk. Arjesh hurried to catch up. "Will one of you answer me?"

CHAPTER 9

When they knocked on Mags' door, they incorrectly assumed she'd be home. After the fifth knock without an answer, Mick slapped his forehead. "Oh my god, she's not here. She's working at her real job."

Rashik blinked. "Real job? What does that even mean?"

Arjesh shrugged at them. "I wondered why we were looking for her at home. It's like ten in the morning, people are at work."

"She's at the hospital. Or clinic. Or wherever she works. Where does she work?"

Rashik looked around. "I'm not even from around here. How am I supposed to know?"

"Nevermind. I'll look it up."

Mick took his phone from his pocket and, after a quick search, found the address of her place of work.

"Thank god for the internet. But she's not close. It'll take us an hour to get there."

"That's perfect. She can take her lunch break with us," Arjesh piped in.

"That... Actually, that is pretty smart. Let's get going."

Mick hailed a taxi while the other two waited patiently. They piled into the car, letting Rashik sit in the front passenger seat. After his first two questions were ignored, the taxi driver went silent. Mick noticed several instances when the man unconsciously leaned away from Rashik in the passenger seat, but didn't mention it.

Arjesh and Mick talked quietly in the backseat about some kind of plan. Rashik interjected with his own input, and the human duo behind the driver only got a few looks of curiosity. But weird in New York was the standard, so the trio wasn't worried.

"Keep the change," said Mick as he paid the man in cash then shut the car door before the driver could respond.

They walked calmly up the steps and through the front doors of the unassuming gray building. The receptionist at the front was a pretty brunette with glasses who made eye contact with the two men immediately, watching them make their way across the lobby.

"Can I help you?" she said suspiciously.

"Hi, we're here to see Mags—uh Maggie."

"Dr. Margaret Claremont?"

Mick glanced at Rashik who laughed and nodded. "Her 'real name' gets me every time. "

"Yes," Mick said to the receptionist.

"Do you have an appointment?"

"Uh, no?"

She folded her hands with a kind of haughty pleasure. "I'm sorry, Dr. Claremont is busy at the moment."

"I really need you to get her for us. It's an emergency."

"Are you family?"

This one doesn't miss a beat, Mick thought with frustration.

"We're actually from her neighborhood and her house burned down."

Arjesh had spoken from behind Mick and Rashik who both turned slowly to stare in disbelief.

"Oh my god," said the receptionist, stunned.

She then picked up the phone and spoke quietly into it. After a short exchange of words, she put the phone back in its cradle and said, "She'll be out shortly."

The trio stayed at the counter and waited.

The waiting room was almost full. And as Mick glanced around, he began to feel uneasy. Several pairs of eyes stared back, and they all belonged to women. In fact, as he tried to look unconcerned, his concern actually grew. He and Arjesh were the only men in the room. There were perhaps twenty women, many of them glancing at the suspicious pair of men leaning on the front counter.

Mick spoke out of the side of his mouth. "Am I missing something here or are we the only men in the room?"

Arjesh, who didn't have a surreptitious bone in his body, glanced around.

"Looks like it. But that would make sense. This is a women's clinic."

"How do you know that?"

Arjesh pointed at large silver words on the wall behind the receptionist.

Montefiore Women's Center

"Oh."

Arjesh stared at Mick. "You literally looked it up."

"I was focused on the address, not the name of the place. That's all I gave the taxi driver, too." He said weakly.

Almost on cue, a woman walked through a door into the waiting room with a panicked look on her face. When she saw the two men standing with a child-sized demon, her expression turned to exasperation.

She approached them, and Mick thought she looked rather furious. "What the fuck are you doing here? Did my house really burn down? And who is this?" She stared at Arjesh.

Mick folded his hands in front of him. "I'm sorry, Mags, we had to talk with you. No, your house is fine, but it is still an emergency. And this is Arjesh; he owns the deli next to my place on West 56th. But again, this is an emergency!"

"Of course, it is. Pleasure, Arjesh. Now out with it."

The laughing woman from the previous evening was gone, replaced by this doctor who no doubt ran a tight ship.

It was Rashik who spoke up, somewhat hesitantly. "It's Barzumel. He's here."

Mags blinked, then threw up her hands and paced several steps away. She turned so quickly on her heel that the two human men and single demon retreated a step back.

When she spoke, it was in a hissing whisper. "Okay. Okay. Come with me."

She led them through a door that led down a quiet hallway, and she motioned them into a room to their left, all four of them stepping in, uncomfortably close. "Rashik, you look terrible. How do you feel?"

The little demon shrugged, and now that Mick looked at him, he did look drawn.

"Okay. Well, hopefully we'll figure it out soon enough. And if Barzumel is here, then it's not just Rashik that's in trouble. He's here for something. If the Demon Princes are known for anything, it's always planning and scheming."

Mick interjected. "Yeah, but he's some lackey for a minor gang boss, Desmond Westrench."

Mags nodded, eyes darting back and forth as if she were putting pieces together in her mind. "That makes sense.

Barzumel hasn't ever been one to reveal his hand until he's sure that he'll win. But how do you know it's him?"

"Rashik said he was the one that left whatever Plane he was on. When Desmond and Barzumel—who goes by 'Barry' now—came to the shop to evict me, Rashik smelled him. Turns out he was just vacationing on Earth."

She looked at Rashik, who nodded.

"Damn. Does he know you're here?"

"Unfortunately, he does. Desmond cursed, and I blew chunks. The human gang man didn't respond, but Barry did."

"So what are they doing? Barzumel wouldn't tether himself to a human for any reason except to further his own goals. What's this Desmond up to? You said he's evicting you?"

"Both of us," Arjesh piped up.

"Why?"

Mick and Arjesh shrugged. "We don't know. It's not like he told us anything beyond 'get out asap.' After that they left."

Mags drummed her fingertips on her bottom lip, thinking. "Your shop, you said it's on West 56th?"

"Yeah, and 11th."

"That's close to the Hudson. I know it, but I can't remember why. Some of my friends may know."

"Friends? Or *friends*?" Rashik emphasized the second word suspiciously.

"Yes, my *friend* friends. Other witches. They may know. I'll have to contact them immediately and have a meeting at my house tonight. Can you all make it?"

The three exchanged looks and then nodded. Mick said, "Yeah, I think so."

"Well if we can figure out why Desmond is evicting you, then we can figure out why Barzumel is tagging along with

Desmond. Once we figure that out, we can then understand what Barzumel wants and maybe stop him from getting it."

"Or..." said Rashik.

"Or we can help him get it, as long as it doesn't interfere with our own world's rules."

Mick nodded. "Yeah that makes no sense to me whatsoever. We'll just see you at your house tonight. Six?"

Mags nodded and swept out of the room, hospital coat flaring behind her.

Arjesh stared at Mick. "I have no idea what ninety percent of those words meant."

"I'll explain it all on the way. Let's go."

"Can we get some lunch, I haven't eaten in like, 30 hours." Rashik rubbed his greenish belly.

"I can make us some lunch at the deli. Make it our 'Last Supper.'"

Mick nodded, and they hailed a cab to take them back to lower Manhattan. On the way, Mick and Rashik relayed to him their situation. Arjesh nodded at all the right places, but by the time they paid the cabbie and stepped through his deli doors, he looked even more confused than when they'd left Mags back at the women's clinic.

"So this Barzumel is a super powerful Demon Prince, and he wants to rule Earth?"

"More or less. And since he and Desmond are working together, we have to assume that whatever Desmond is doing lines up with his goal of world domination."

"Maybe we could just ask Desmond what he intends to do with the building after we move out?"

Rashik and Mick looked at each other. "I'm not sure that Desmond would tell us. Especially with Barry standing there.

I doubt he'd feel the need to explain it to someone as low on the totem pole as us."

"Yeah, that makes sense."

Arjesh spent the next half hour making several cold cut sandwiches and a pitcher of iced tea. They ate quietly, each of them thinking of some plan that would get them out of this mess. By the time crumbs peppered the table, they'd come up with exactly nothing.

Rashik looked a little better after eating something, but he still appeared to be pale. But Mick only had the last 24 hours to go on.

"Rashik, explain this Realmwalking thing to me. You said that some demons can do it. Can humans?"

"Eh, I doubt it. There have been rumors of it, but I've never seen a human Realmwalker. Mostly because humans don't last long when it comes to traversing the Planes where demons live."

"Are there only bad Planes? Like, there aren't any good ones?"

"Oh, there are good ones. Ernan is a really nice place. It's full of angelic beings that walk around naked all day. I mean, it gets pretty hot there."

"That sounds pretty great, actually," Mick said with a smile.

"It is. It's not like the nude beaches on Earth where everyone romanticizes the idea of a bunch of naked pretty people only to arrive and see the only people comfortable being naked in public are those that shouldn't be."

"Hey, don't body shame." Arjesh prickled a little and pointed a finger at Rashik.

"Oh, you're saying that you like to see old wrinkly sand-bags up top and wrinkly sandbags below?"

Arjesh screwed his face up. "That's not what I'm saying at all. You know what, nevermind. I'm not going to explain it to a resident of Hell."

"Anyway," Mick said emphatically enough to stop their bickering, "so no humans can do it. But Demon Princes can. What about regular demons? Like you or something."

"I'm flattered that you think I'm a 'regular demon.' Truth is that I'm a level *below* 'regular.' I'm a Lesser Demon, an imp actually. And no, imps can't Realmwalk. Some 'regular demons' can that have the abilities to learn, but like humans, not all of us can learn that skill. Takes a certain disposition. And all Princes can, yes. They just choose one Plane and sort of stick to it."

"And in order to cross between them, you have to what, attune to that realm?"

"It's far more complicated, but yeah, something like that. It's an attunement of sorts. Barzumel can travel between realms easily. It's annoying, actually, and he's really good at it. I'm here because you yanked my ass out of my realm somehow. So I didn't really Realmwalk, I was brought here."

Arjesh, who had been wiping the table off and pouring himself another glass of tea, said, "Why can't Barzumel just take you back? You said he isn't happy you're here. Maybe he could just send you home? You know, ground you for a millennia or two."

Rashik sighed deeply, his bony green shoulders rising and falling. "That's the thing. Barzumel, as the Demon Prince that has no doubt laid claim to this Plane, gets a say in who comes and who goes. What's happened with Mick and I is an anomaly. We broke his rule. Somehow, I don't know how, but we did. He sees that as an affront to his rule. It's like we're showing everyone that he can't maintain control here."

"We're saying that if a nobody could do it, a somebody could, but even easier," Mick continued.

"Exactly. And if he lets us live, then he's inviting others to do it. And he won't like that."

"Wait, you said 'lets us live.' You mean he's actually got it out for me? Like, he wasn't yanking my chain?"

Rashik nodded slowly. "He'll either find out or he already knows that you're the one who brought me here. Demon Princes have a kind of sixth sense about interplanar travel. Like a flight board in one of your airports. He knows I'm here with you, probably because whatever entity messed with the Ouija board told him. The simplest explanation is usually the right one."

"Well that sucks." Mick pushed his empty plate away from him, and Arjesh scooped it up to wash it while Mick and Rashik sat quietly. When he'd placed it back in a stack behind the counter, he sat back in the booth and asked Rashik a question.

"What's so bad about Barzumel, by the way. Other than the fact that he's a Demon Prince, human-eater, and therefore probably really bad by nature."

"Oh yeah, he's really bad. You know The Holocaust?"

"He did that?"

Rashik nodded a kind-of-yes-kind-of-no shake of his head. "He was Hitler's SS leader. All Barzumel had to do was tell Hitler what to do. That wannabe art boy was deranged enough to believe it all."

"My god," said Mick breathlessly.

Arjesh only shook his head in disbelief.

"All that to say, we have to find out why Barzumel is here."

"Wait, one more thing," said Arjesh.

"What?"

"The Holocaust was like, forever ago. You're saying Barzumel has been here that long? But you just got here, he just started working with Desmond. How does that timeline level out?"

"Time is different in every Plane. An hour in Depo'sadi might be a decade here, or vice versa. And then in Ernan it might be less than a second. I don't know why, but it is what it is."

"But if you're getting sick, and you've only been here a day, why isn't Barzumel getting sick?"

"Realmwalkers are different. They don't get sick like lesser demons when visiting other Planes. Like I said earlier, I didn't Realmwalk, and I didn't have permission to leave. I'm under a Truancy Curse." Rashik tried to glare at Mick, but a coughing fit ruined it.

They resumed their silent thinking. Mick pulled the pendant from beneath his shirt and began rubbing his finger across its surface. It was an old habit, one he'd tried to break a thousand times without success.

"Why do you do that?" Rashik asked, staring at Mick. "Do that with that medallion?"

Mick looked down at the pendant pinched between his thumb and forefinger, then shrugged. "Old habit."

"Yeah, but what is it?"

"It's just a necklace," he said, self-consciously tucking it back under his shirt.

"No, what *is it*," Rashik repeated.

Mick sighed, realizing that the little demon wasn't going to relent.

"It was a gift from my dad, before he left my mom. It's the classic story of a deadbeat dad going out for cigarettes and never coming back. Left me and my mom high and dry. He was a loser. I'm sure he died somewhere. Hopefully in a ditch," he finished bitterly.

Neither the demon nor the deli owner pushed further, sensing that it was a sensitive topic for Mick.

"I know it's not even close to six yet, but do you guys wanna go next door and tidy up? If we get out of this, it would be nice to be packed up and ready to go so that if Barzumel doesn't kill me, Desmond doesn't get the chance to, either."

"Sure, I'll help," said Arjesh.

"Yeah, fine," Rashik replied a little sourly before hopping down from the booth.

CHAPTER 10

The trio spent the next two hours tidying up the curio shop while Mick directed them. They put a plethora of unused items in boxes and stacked them in the room Rashik had ravaged. By the time they needed to go meet Mags, Mick couldn't tell that anything had even happened.

"Thanks for the help."

Arjesh nodded as he put a small metal disc back on its stack on a shelf. Rashik was waddling down the hallway with the stack of books that had been a hazard for months. Mick took them and lined them up neatly on the front book shelf, then dusted off his hands.

"There. I think that'll do for now. It'll be a helluva lot easier to pack up now that the process is started. You guys ready to go meet Mags?"

Rashik said, "Yeah," and Arjesh nodded.

Mick followed them through the door and locked it behind him. Their walk to Mags' place was comfortable. The weather was warm but not hot and surprising all of them, the foot traffic seemed lighter today.

She must have seen them coming because as soon as they approached the steps, the door swung open and Mags, still in her work clothes, was standing in the entryway waving them in. "Come on," she said breathlessly.

They entered and were surprised to find five other women there.

"Sit down, sit down," she told them. The couches were taken by the women, but Mags had pulled in some wooden chairs from the kitchen and placed them in the gaps between couches and chairs.

"Everyone, this is Mick and Arjesh."

The short introduction was enough that the women nodded at the two men as they sat. Altogether they made the semblance of a circle, with everyone facing inward. A pitcher of cold tea stood untouched on the table in the middle next to the same number of cups as now-present guests.

Mick stared around the room. With the five additional women and now the three of them, a total of eight beings sat in Mags' living room. Their host looked at each of them in turn before speaking.

"We have a very serious problem to discuss this evening. A Demon Prince has begun to make a move to exert control over this Plane. Not only that, but as far as we know, he lives here, in New York City." The five women gasped and looked around at each other.

"How can you know this," said a pale woman with her silver hair falling in a braid down her back.

"And which one is here?" asked another portly woman with an orange shawl draped across her broad shoulders.

"This man, Mick Jameson, accidentally summoned a lesser demon to this Plane."

Mick then became the object of pursed lips and withering glares.

"Though it was accidental, it also became an opportunity. The demon he summoned is one that several of us have had dealings with. Rashik the Lesser is here with us as well."

He revealed himself then, and to Mick's surprise, none of the women jumped.

"Surprise," he said unenthusiastically.

They merely looked at him, then directed their attention back to Mags.

"Unfortunately, Mick summoned him improperly, and Rashik is under a Truancy Curse. He's dying, and quickly. We need to get him home. On a somewhat related note, however, there is something else. Through a series of events, we've discovered that the Demon Prince in New York is none other than Barzumel, and he has been assisting a local crime boss in acquiring real estate on West 56th, where Mick's shop and Arjesh's deli now stand."

"Barzumel?" said a young woman. Her dark skin contrasted beautifully with the yellow blouse she wore. Her hair was braided intricately, each with several beads at the ends that clicked together as she turned her head to face the others in the circle. "What purpose could Barzumel have on this Plane right now? And why should we get involved?"

Several of the women nodded and murmured their agreement.

Mags waited for a breath before continuing. "Ali, our involvement does not extend beyond one simple task. Rashik must be returned to his Plane before Barzumel can capture him. Or worse."

"I'm not sure what that has to do with us." A third young woman with a round face turned to Rashik. "I'm sorry, but your well-being doesn't supersede my own." Despite her words, her tone held no apology.

"Gail!" said Mags in surprise.

"What? Rashik, as far as demons go, is fine. If he perishes, of course that would be sad. But unfortunately Rashik has no effect on my daily life. If I get involved and Barzumel finds out, that could affect my daily life much more than the death of a lesser demon."

Again, several women nodded their agreement. The woman in the yellow blouse spoke up again. "Perhaps not, Gail, but our bond requires us to aid others, whether they're from this Plane or not."

"I seriously doubt the bond would *actually* impose its will on us in this instance." The woman who spoke was middle-aged, perhaps the same age as Mags. But where Mags held a fierce countenance, this woman was downright scary.

"Yannica," said Mags confidently, "it's not my place or yours to question the bond. We obey it, simple as that. If Rashik is in need of assistance, then we must heed the call and assist. Even if Rashik isn't in need of assistance, these two humans are. Arjesh and Mick will certainly be destroyed when Barzumel finally gets what he wants, or to get them out of the way so he can.

"What this means for us, though, is that we need to discover first and foremost what Barzumel is after. Realistically, what the man he's working for wants. What's his name?"

"Desmond Westrench," said Mick quietly.

"Right." Mags addressed the rest of the gathering. "This Desmond Westrench has been buying up land in Lower Manhattan for some time, but is now beginning to evict his tenants and we need to know why. Do any of you have any idea what value this area holds?"

The women in the room thought for a moment while Mick and Arjesh exchanged shrugs.

After several minutes of silence, the fifth woman spoke. She was old, older than Mags. Her hair was white and thin and her face was wrinkled to the point that it was hard to find an inch of smooth skin. Her voice was firm, however, and while it cracked in several places, it was confident, and her words were certain.

"A couple of decades ago, maybe less, a new business moved into Lower Manhattan. It didn't stay long, like most of them, but I believe that this business did it on purpose. They moved into the area, stayed for half a year, maybe more, then moved out."

Mags sat up a little straighter. "Elena, do you know why? Or what this company was for?"

"Rumor has it that they were researching alternative energy sources. Now I don't know if that's a front or not, of course. But their goal was to research the area. At the time, I was sleeping with a man in the energy sector. One night after a particularly sweaty sexscapade—"

Mick groaned, and Rashik chuckled, but it turned into a phlegmy cough.

"—he got drunk and told me about the time he dug into them a little. I forget the name, of course, memory isn't what it used to be. But what I do remember is that their interest in New York City didn't move any further north than West 58th. Their base of operations was a small run-down building on 11th, but they never moved east of 9th Avenue.

"While curious, my contact said they'd visit buildings and businesses in those 15 blocks, run some tests, and then move on."

"I'm not sure what bearing that has on the current situation, Elena, however intriguing it might be."

"I'm not done, dear," said Elena with a smile that somehow told Mags to politely shut up before continuing. "You see, I've always felt that Lower Manhattan was special. Most people do, you know. I think if you take a moment to think about it, you'll remember that when we're in that area of Lower Manhattan, things feel ... different."

"I was on the shores of the Hudson just west of 11th when I was able to complete my first Binding. It was the woman in a yellow blouse, Ali."

Mags nodded at her. "Yes, I remember that, Ali."

"And I was in Balsley Park when I first summoned Helnak."

Mags nodded again. "Yes, Gail, you're right." She turned to Elena. "Elena what are you saying? That there's something in Lower Manhattan that both an energy company and a Demon Prince would want?"

"This energy company was researching something called 'Ley Lines.' We all know those have been a bit of a buzz word for some time. What I'm proposing is that perhaps they're real and we've just never felt the need to find them. If two Ley Lines intersect in Lower Manhattan, more specifically on the corner of West 56th and 11th, then perhaps the reason this Desmond wants the property is because Barzumel wants it. If Barzumel can utilize Ley Lines—I'm not sure how, mind, I'm not part of the Crimson Council—then it would fit that he'd want access to that site."

The room was silent for a several heartbeats. Each of the women—Mick realized they were powerful—looked at the others or down at their hands, thinking.

Arjesh stared around the room and then quietly asked the group, "What is a Ley Line?"

Mick feared that the question—one he had himself but dared not ask—would upset the group. Instead, Rashik barked a laugh, and Mags chuckled a little.

"I'm sorry. For many of us, these words are part of almost every day language. A Ley Line is believed to be a pathway, or a stream of energy. As Elena said, they're a bit of an urban legend. People believe they are a natural part of the world and cover the planet in straight lines, more or less. They can go east and west or north and south. When one of the east-west lines crosses a north-south line, that's what we call an Intersect. Most of these Intersects are merely places where crops grow better or where birds plummet randomly from the skies—"

"Or where ships and planes mysteriously disappear," interjected one of the women.

"Yes, that too. Humans—most humans, at least—can't detect them. They might feel a subtle warmth in their body or perhaps a general feeling of happiness around the Intersects. But for the most part, they're completely oblivious. Many times, cities are built on the sites of these Intersects. Humans don't know they're doing it, but they may say things like 'It just seems right' or 'I like it here,' that kind of thing."

"New York is supposedly built upon an Intersect," said Ali.

"Yes, 'supposedly.' As is London. Chicago, Las Vegas, Rome—all built upon these supposed energy sites. It's rumored that Atlantis and Babylon had been, as well. But that's even more ridiculous."

Arjesh nodded when they were done with the explanation, then said, "So you don't believe they're real. Or didn't?"

Mags and several other women glanced at one another. "Well, that's the question isn't it?" said Mags. "We don't know if they exist at all. The problem is that if they don't, then Barzumel is here for another reason. If they *do* exist, then we can assume that he's trying to utilize that site as a kind of funnel to fuel his own agenda."

"Which is, of course, something we cannot allow," Elena said abruptly, her long silver hair swayed as she stood a little shakily. "I'm afraid we don't have the luxury of waiting. We must assume that Barzumel the Demon Prince is here to hijack a source of power that humans don't know even exists. If he's allowed to do this, he'll become nearly unstoppable on this Plane. If a Demon Prince wants it, then it must be bad."

"Isn't there some other great and powerful being that can stop him? What about the other Demon Princes?" Mick figured that at least *someone* would also want him stopped.

Rashik laughed outright. "You really are an idiot. No offense."

"Go on," Mick said with chagrin.

Rashik stood on his chair, making him eye-level with most of the others. He drew himself up as much as he could, and Mick noticed the effort it took. "The other Demon Princes don't care about Barzumel or what he does. They sure as shit don't care about humans. Oh yeah, maybe they like that they can visit here or something. But there are a thousand different places they could visit. In their minds, Barzumel can have this Plane. They have others. If Barzumel destroys this Plane, it doesn't hurt them. They're too focused on their own plans of advancing through the Crimson Council to give a rat's ass for humanity."

Then the little demon sat back down, a blue blush creeping up his cheeks. "And don't get me wrong, I don't really care about humanity, either. But I'd miss this Plane. And some of the people. There isn't anyone to help," he finished.

Arjesh and Mick glanced at each other over the demon's head. Arjesh pointed to himself and then to Mick, and Mick shrugged.

"Rashik is right." Mags stood to address the group. "There is no one else. We must be the ones to stop the Demon Prince. If we assume that Barzumel is going to use the Intersect to gain power, then we just prevent that. We must perform a binding on the Demon Prince."

"To do that, Mags, we'd need a relic from his Plane. As far as I know, Depo'sadi has very few relics, if any at all." It was Gail who had spoken.

"Yeah," piped in Yannica, "I know for a fact that we have no relics from that Plane. And in our Second Circles there are none. Even if we could contact them tonight, I doubt we could contact *their* Second Circles in time to stop him. If he's asking Mick and Arjesh to move out, then his next move is imminent."

"You three," snapped Elena, still standing and leaning on a cane, "do you have *anything* at your shop that could be used. I know you're a fake, but even a broken clock is right twice a day, as they say."

Mick looked at Rashik. "I don't think so. We just finished cleaning and organizing quite a bit of it. If there was something, I'm sure we'd have run across it. Or Rashik would have."

"No, everything there is meant to disguise that this guy's a fake. A very good fake, but no. Nothing there."

"Go back and check again," she said in motherly tones. "I don't want to be too heavy, but there might be a lot of lives at stake."

"Oh good, just like in a superhero movie. 'Save the whole world, normal guy.' Love that."

Mick's mood was growing foul. He never asked for this. All he wanted was to make enough money to not have the mob breathing down his neck. Maybe move to the beach one day. Maybe someday marry a pretty girl. Turns out, that instead, he'd need to accidentally summon a demon and then fight a worse one to save all of humanity.

"My fucking luck," he muttered only loud enough for his own ears. Then to the others. "Yeah, okay. We'll look again tonight, and what, let you know tomorrow?"

Mags approached and held out her hand. "Give me your phone. You can text me or call me tonight, and I'll let the others know. We may need to talk more."

She typed her number in and saved it then handed back the phone.

"Keep us posted." She was stern-faced, but her eyes held worry, and that scared Mick more than facing down Barzumel. "We'll make some preparations here."

CHAPTER 11

The three left Mags' house in a state of frustration. It didn't feel like they'd made any progress and unfortunately, they were running out of time. The air outside smelled thick and smoky, making them cough several times as they turned toward home.

They walked in silence until they crossed the street onto West 56th. In the light of the city, it hadn't been noticeable. But now that they were nearer, the flashing blue and red lights reflected off the sweating pavement and store windows. The smell of smoke was thicker here and as they stared, a black billowing pillar rolled into the sky above their building.

"Is that...?" Mick said, stunned.

"That's..." said Arjesh, also stunned.

"*Shit,*" said all three as they broke into a run.

The line of firemen and police officers stopped them from getting more than a hundred feet from their shops.

"But those are *our* stores!" said Arjesh pointing at the burning buildings behind the man.

"I'm sorry, pal, I can't let you two in. Too dangerous."

"What? There are—" three of them, Mick meant to say, but stopped when Arjesh grabbed just above his elbow.

"No," said Arjesh and pointing to Rashik.

The officer looked where Arjesh was pointing, but with the two men stopped, his attention was drawn to other pedestrians advancing on the line of wooden rails.

"Let *him* go take a look."

Arjesh asked Rashik if he would, and Rashik shrugged once before limping down the sidewalk, unseen, toward the engulfed building.

Mick took the pendant from under his shirt and began to run his finger along its worn surface. All of his things were in that shop. What if there was a relic that they'd missed? What if there was something there that could have been used to stop Barzumel, but it was all burned to melted slag, now?

Arjesh patted his friend on the back and Mick, realizing his friend had also lost his shop, did the same with a tight-lipped smile.

They watched the direction Rashik had gone for several minutes without seeing or hearing anything. But without warning, a section of the building collapsed, sending orange sparks and flames to join the billowing cloud of smoke rising toward the stars. The crowd that had gathered gasped and shouted, but it looked, from this distance, like the buildings were empty of service workers.

An inhuman screech sounded from that direction, however, and a string of curse words.

"That's Rashik," said Arjesh, a note of fear in his voice.

Just before Mick could confirm, the little green demon appeared from behind a fire truck. He was half-running, half-lumbering across the pavement, no doubt as fast as he could. His feet made a wet slapping sound as he fled the scene, glancing behind him and grinning.

"Are you okay, Rashik? What happ—"

But he wasn't grinning. He was panting, and his face was a mask of pure panic as bile leaked from the sides of his mouth. He swallowed hard and pointed back in the direction he'd come. "Grom!"

"What..." said Mick, staring where he pointed.

Then two dog-like forms burst from between the fire trucks. They looked like dogs only in that they were running on all fours—wait all six of their legs. Their backs were covered in armored plates that glowed like embers in a dying fire. Smoke and sparks spewed forth from their mouths as they panted and heaved with each rushing gallop of their gait. Mick saw a flash of silvery teeth lining their mouths. They sped forward, and Mick ran the quick calculation that they'd be upon them in less than ten seconds.

The three turned and ran. There weren't many places to go, but the nearest alley might provide a fire escape or a dumpster to climb upon.

Mick's heart sank when he turned into the alley, breath already coming in ragged gasps, to find it completely empty of cover or help. They ran for only a few more seconds before the pattering sounds of the Grom began echoing off the narrow alley walls around them.

Then they turned, all three, to face their attackers.

The Grom were stalking down the alley, six legs slowing as they neared their frantic prey. Strong muscles rippled beneath the wan light from the street. In the dimness of the alley, their eyes glowed a subterranean orange and to Mick, their mouths were twisted into vicious grins.

"What do we do?" questioned Arjesh, a note of panic turning his voice into more of an exhalation of breath than a sentence.

"Rashik?" asked Mick, just as panicked.

The little demon was quickly searching the area, his breath going in and out of his lungs in frantic, heavy gasps.

"Rashik!" yelled Mick a little harsher than he'd intended, but he figured the demon would forgive him if they made it out of their current predicament.

"I'm trying!" yelped Rashik. "There's nothing, though. There's no way out. There's nothing we can do!"

"What?"

The Grom were only a dozen yards from them, and their prey huddled together like trapped gazelle. The Grom's growls, which seemed to come from the depths of Hell, rattled in their throats with guttural anticipation. The air smelled like sulfur, and the smoke that streamed from between the Grom's teeth was roiled and coiled around the creatures in black and putrid tendrils.

The larger of the two stepped forward and, in one swift motion, stood on its hind legs in a very human manner. The other followed a split-second later.

"What the fuck!" screamed Arjesh in surprised terror.

"We're dead," said Rashik in a matter of fact tone.

The Grom held their hands up and claws that resembled a dinosaur's, black and razor sharp, suddenly extended from each of their four toes... fingers?

Mick, knowing his death was imminent, turned his face away and closed his eyes. He imagined their claws ripping through his flesh, tearing him to shreds and either devouring him while he was still alive or leaving him to bleed out and watch while his friends suffered the same fate.

His shoe scraped against something, and he peeked at what it was. A small wooden rod that was splintered at both ends rolled an inch away from the toe of his shoe.

Knowing he had little choice, he bent to pick it up. It was such a quick motion that when he lunged down, the pendant beneath his shirt swung free and tapped him on the nose before falling back over his shirt.

Mick brandished the ridiculous excuse for a weapon, eyes wide with terror, and with a shaky voice, said, "Leave us alone!"

The leading Grom actually did grin, it's mouth splitting its face in two and showing dozens of razor teeth. Both the creatures were only feet from the three huddled beings. It reached slowly, almost carefully out and placed a hand on the wooden weapon, then pushed it casually aside.

Then Mick knew he was dead.

Only, as soon as the rod was down, the Grom's eyes focused on Mick's chest. It's expression changed from ravenous anticipation to surprise and, then just as quickly, to fear. The Grom dropped its hands to its side and then dropped back to all six feet. It lowered its head to the ground and remained that way for several seconds.

The other Grom looked confused but did the same, bowing its head toward the three and remaining still.

"Rashik," Mick whispered out of the side of his mouth, "what is happening?"

Rashik had hidden himself behind both Arjesh's trembling knees and Mick's barely more solid legs. The demon peeked out, and when he saw the Grom bowing close to the ground, he stepped out from behind the men.

The sound that came from Rashik, then, was a language of some kind, but impossible for Mick to understand. It was a mix of guttural barks, hisses, and syllables not meant for human ears. The Grom responded in the same throaty language. This continued for several seconds before the two would-be assassins scampered—and that's exactly what Mick believed they were doing—away. *Almost as if they'd been scolded*, thought Mick.

After the patter of their galloping steps faded from around the mouth of the alley, Arjesh and Mick collapsed against each other on the sticky ground. They both pretended like they weren't wiping tears of relief from their eyes, but then started laughing when they realized there was no hiding it.

Rashik, meanwhile, stood with his arms crossed and glaring at the two men.

No, actually, he was scowling directly at Mick with a look of unhinged disappointment etched across his hellish features.

"When were you going to tell me?" the little demon asked. He sounded very much like a father who found out his son had been skipping seventh period to smoke pot behind the gym.

"Tell you what?"

Rashik scoffed and pointed to Mick's chest. "About *that*."

Mick looked down and lifted the pendant he'd worn since his father left him.

"My necklace? It's just some stupid thing my dad gave me, I told you that."

"No, that's not just some stupid necklace."

"Rashik, yes it is." Mick became insistent despite Rashik's argumentative tone. "My dad put it around my neck the night he left my mom and me. He never came back, but I kept it. I don't know why, I just did."

"Again, that's not some stupid necklace," he repeated. "You may not know what it is, but they sure as shit did!" He pointed toward the mouth of the alley.

"The Grom? What... I don't understand."

"The Grom were sent here by Barzumel to kill us. Obviously. Unless you're as stupid as other humans, you already guessed that."

"Well, yeah, that seemed pretty obvious from the way they drooled when they looked at us."

"And yet we're still here. Which means what?"

Mick felt like he was being cross-examined, and he tried to look at Arjesh for help, but his friend ignored it. "I don't know, Rashik. They changed their minds?"

Rashik growled in frustration and spit a gob of phlegm to the scummy asphalt. "No, Mick. Grom don't *change their minds*. They have one purpose, and that's to serve the Prince to which they are bound. *Those* Grom are bound to Barzumel. They *must* do his bidding. If they fail, they die."

"So they're going to die? Good. Two less Grom might be a good thing."

"No. No no no." He waggled his hands back and forth as if warding off stupidity. "You don't understand. Grom *must* enact their master's will. They are *bound* to it. They have no choice in the matter."

"But... but they didn't kill us, so either they actually do have some kind of choice or there's something that supersedes their Prince's will." Arjesh piped in from the ground.

"Well, maybe you two aren't as dumb as the rest of these meat bags. Or he isn't at least," Rashik said nodding at Arjesh. He laid the sarcasm on thicker than necessary, in Mick's opinion.

"Okay, so they *have to obey*, unless what?"

"Unless they are given an order that goes against the Crimson Council."

"Okay," Mick said, standing up and dusting himself off. "Okay. Wait. I've heard this Crimson Council thing too much, and I don't know what the hell you're talking about."

Shaking his head and clenching his fists, Rashik responded through clenched teeth. "We don't have time to get into it. Suffice it to say, they're the ones that control the Demon Princes."

Mick's eyebrows rose in surprise. "Checks and balances even in Hell. Interesting."

"Anyway, to summarize, Grom have to obey the Prince to which they're bound unless it goes against the will of the Crimson Council."

"And since we're still alive, they found out that the Crimson Council wants us alive?"

"No," Rashik said pointedly, "they want *you* alive."

"That makes no sense. How do they even know about me? What do they even have to do with me? I've never even heard of them!"

"You said your dad gave you that necklace?"

Arjesh snapped his fingers. "Your dad is on the Crimson Council."

"That's impossible."

"Ole RJ is right, Mick." Rashik was smiling, now, a smile of disbelief.

"But he was just a regular guy."

"I seriously doubt that. Maybe to *you* he was. That necklace you wear, that little pendant you play with when you're nervous, that's a relic from Sheol."

"What's Sheol?"

"It's the Plane *above* every other ruled by the Demon Princes."

"So?"

Rashik's face went slack, and he looked at Arjesh. "Is he really your friend or you getting paid by someone?"

Arjesh grinned then said to Mick, "If Sheol is above the other Planes, then that little coin trumps every other lower Plane. That means that if someone, say Barzumel, tells a few Grom to come kill you, they can't. The Crimson Council has given you immunity from any harm the Demon Princes could inflict upon you."

Mick looked at Arjesh as if he'd grown another head. "You got all of that from this stupid little imp's half-assed explanation of netherworld politics?"

His Indian friend shrugged, "It's easy when you listen."

Mick was silent for a moment then shook his head and asked, "So my dad is a demon?"

"Probably," Rashik said, "maybe. In the end, it doesn't matter. He's on the Crimson Council. That means that for us, we have a small bit of immunity to help stop Barzumel."

"But how can we be ready? Do we like ... call them or something?"

"If your dad gave you that, then he already knows what you're mixed up in. He may come to our aid."

"Oh sure, the guy who left when I was eight will come back when he's needed? That makes a ton of sense."

"Trust me. Just like the Princes are bound, so are the Council. Have you ever taken that relic off?"

"Maybe a few times, but never longer than a shower or shave, probably."

"Then it's attuned to you and, therefore, so is the Council." Rashik was getting tired, Mick could tell in the way his voice was beginning to falter.

Mick blanched. "They've been watching me?"

"Probably."

"But like ... they've been watching *everything*?"

Rashik grinned slyly at Mick. "You mean when you were rubbing one out in the darkness at thirteen? Yeah, they saw that."

"Jesus Christ!" Mick yelled without thinking.

Rashik, who'd been laughing, doubled over. Green bile spewed from his mouth, but he was still laughing, which made Mick and Arjesh join in.

When the little demon was done, they looked at each other.

"What now?" asked Mick.

"Welp," said Rashik, who mimed hiking up non-existent britches, "Now that we have a little more firepower on our side, we confront Barzumel. And maybe I go home. Finally." Then the demon sauntered toward the street.

"This won't end well, you know," said Mick catching up, Arjesh not far behind.

"It never does for someone. Let's hope that someone is Barzumel."

CHAPTER 12

The three friends stood at the barricades the police had erected to keep people out. The smoke still billowed, but there was less activity and the firemen walking around seemed to be in no hurry. The danger was gone, or near enough.

Mick called Mags on his phone and told her to meet them at the shop. She was confused at first, but eventually agreed. Mick felt a second wind rise within him.

"She'll be right over," he said after hanging up.

"Does she know our building's burned down?" Arjesh asked.

Mick nodded once. "She and the other four are on their way. She said not to worry about it; she'll find us."

That seemed to answer Arjesh's concern, and the three went back to thinking.

"Barzumel will no doubt want to see his handywork." Rashik was keeping a keen eye on the activity around the husk of the shop. "He'll be there. The rest of those humans need to get out of the area, though. I'd hate for this confrontation to have a large amount of collateral damage."

"But a little is okay?"

"It's the whole human race, remember?"

"For a demon, you're fairly altruistic."

"Meh," he said unenthused, "not all of us are assholes. But I'm not the morality police by any means."

Mick nodded and was silent for a moment. "So my dad was part of the Crimson Council. Does that make me..."

"Half-demon? Maybe." Rashik was staring at the fire trucks. "It's amazing you humans spend so much time, energy, and money trying to put out fires. On my Plane, most demons can simply command them to start and stop at will."

Mick and Arjesh followed his gaze. "Yeah that would solve a lot of problems for humans. But seriously, what am I, then?"

"Half-demon, full human, half-nargrat? Who cares? You like your life? You want it to continue? Then it doesn't matter. All that matters is we stop Barzumel."

"What about you, though? Don't you want to go back?"

"Sure. Sure I do. We'll find a way back. Relics from Depo are hard to find, but not impossible. And I'd be surprised if Mags' plan to use ole Barzy in lieu of a relic doesn't work. She's way smarter than both of you. No offense, Arjesh."

The ex-deli owner leaned on the barricade and shrugged it off. "None taken, friend."

"How are we supposed to get close enough to use Barzumel like a relic?"

"Yeah I don't know. Honestly, that's a tricky part. I'm hoping that Mags and her circle of friends have a strategy about that."

With a multitude of questions rolling through Mick's head, he sat and watched as the firetrucks left one by one. Eventually, only two remained, and those two had stopped spraying water on the collapsed building he'd called home.

After another half hour, both trucks had gone, and only the Fire Marshall and a few extra firemen remained. The billowing smoke had been reduced to a few black wispy streams. Except for the fluorescent streetlights a few dozen yards in either direction of the rubble, it was as dark as it would get in the city.

Mick tried to imagine what it would be like to meet the Crimson Council, if what Rashik said was true. And had his father actually been watching him all this time? All the times that he was in trouble or needed help, his father had seen and just, what, let him suffer?

"You know, if what you say is true, my dad is a bastard."

"Most of the Council are," said Rashik, nonplussed.

"He's watched me struggle through life, and he could have done something, but just ... didn't?"

"Sounds about right, yeah."

"Nice," Mick said with a scoff.

"Don't feel bad, friend," interjected Arjesh with a smile. "My father left when I was five to join a Catholic convent. He left my mother and her six children. I was the second oldest and helpless as two of my siblings died from hunger. My mother died of drug overdose when I was twelve. I was lucky to get out when I was fourteen."

"Arjesh, god, I'm so sorry, I had no idea."

His friend shrugged. "I know what bastards fathers can be."

"Yeah," said Rashik, "My dad ate my mom. Not in a sexual way, either. Well—" he stopped himself and looked skyward. "Maybe it was, now that I think about it."

"Thanks, Arjesh. And you, too, I guess," he said cocking his head at Rashik while mouthing "What the fuck" to Arjesh.

They laughed and then nodded at one another in understanding, and Mick's spirits were raised a little. But when Rashik said, "I need to sit down," Mick's concern came back for his new little friend.

"Mick! Arjesh!" A woman's voice reached the trio at the barricade, and they looked around curiously. Mags was waving at them frantically, as if they'd have a problem picking out her and the four other women trailing behind her on the empty sidewalk.

Mick waved back and waited for the group of women to close the distance.

When they reached the two men and a demon somewhat out of breath, they looked between the three and back to the smoldering building behind them.

"What happened?" asked Mags in shock.

"Barzumel is what happened," answered Rashik.

"Damn him to the Ninth Circle!" she said bitterly.

"Eh, that's nothing."

"Rashik you look terrible. Gods above and below, what can we do to help?"

He coughed, shrugged, and his red-rimmed eyes blinked heavily. "Send me back."

Her expression turned from outrage at Barzumel's arson, to concern for Rashik, and then finally to curiosity, but it was Arjesh who answered.

"Apparently, Barzumel—or his minions at least—can't touch us. Well... Mick, at least."

"Can't ... Mick ... why?"

Mick tried not be dramatic, but he pulled the pendant from beneath his shirt and held it as far as the cord would allow from his neck. "Because of this."

Mags stepped closer and, in a very characteristic move, snatched the pair of glasses that hung around her neck and placed them firmly on her nose before inspecting it.

"I don't understand. What is this?"

"That," said Rashik, making up for the lack of drama from Mick, "is a relic."

"From where," piped in Gail from behind Mags' shoulder.

Rashik looked at Gail, Mags, and the rest of the women before answering. "From Sheol."

Five women gasped, and Arjesh barked a laugh. Mick couldn't help but smile, though he knew he contributed little to their success apart from providing an absentee father.

"But how?" asked Elena, the old woman who peered at the curious coin over Mags' other shoulder.

"This might be the best part," said Rashik, doubling down on the dramatic flair.

"Confound it all, you meager demon, answer the question!" Yannica spoke this time, if Mick's memory served.

"Fine fine. It's from his dad. Mick's dad gave that to him before giving this Plane the slip!"

"Your father?" Then to Rashik, she asked, "Is he attuned?"

"It would be safe to test it, but I don't think we have the time. He hasn't taken it off for more than a few minutes in the past few decades. I think we're safe to assume he's attuned to it."

"This is excellent news!" Mags smiled back at her coterie and they clapped their hands together primly. "This means that Barzumel is bound to obey the will of the Council! He can't do anything to you, not without severe consequences."

Rashik held up a finger. "That's all true. And for pretty much any other demon, I'd say we're in the clear. But with Barzumel, he can't do anything to us without severe consequences *if the Council finds out*. You don't know the Barzumel that I know. Yeah, on this Plane he's a little more self-controlled. But something this important, potentially something that would allow him to rule this Plane uncontested? He'd raze the entire city if it meant ensuring his victory. Yeah Mick might die, and sure the Council may eventually find out, but then again, they may not."

"Wait, I thought you said earlier that they were watching me with this thing?"

Rashik looked between Mick and Arjesh, "He really is that dumb, isn't he?"

Arjesh shrugged, but Mick grew much more concerned.

"It's not like they're watching your life through that little coin, Mick. They can hone in on your location, watch from afar if they're on this Plane, but that means they have to *be* here. I doubt your dad, let alone the Council, came to visit more than maybe a few times to make sure you're still alive.

"Even though we can invoke the Council with this relic, they don't have to answer. And if we confront Barzumel, and they don't..." the little demon ran a claw across his throat.

"Ah, okay. So the relief I felt after the Grom retreated was just you being nice."

"You were attacked by Grom?" Several of the women asked some variation of that at the same time that Rashik answered, "Not exactly, I've been thinking about it since we learned about Mick and trying to figure out what's what."

"So we might be screwed or we might be gods. Perfect." Mick wanted off this roller coaster.

"Are we not even going to address the fact that Mick might in fact be a Princeling?" Ali was looking between the other members of their gathered party.

"Princeling?" asked Mick, not liking the sound of it.

Rashik answered. "We aren't going to address that right now." He turned to Mick. "If your dad is on the Crimson Council, then his full-demon children are Demon Princes. Half-Bloods are considered Princelings. Subtle but important distinction."

"Oh, okay perfect," he said again.

The next few minutes consisted of the witches teaching a binding incantation to Mick and trying to instruct him on its use. Mick was terrible at it, and any hope he'd had at using Barzumel to send Rashik back and bind the demon to his own will was lost after several failed attempts to even repeat the words the women used.

"Remember, Mick, Rashik and Barzumel must be touching for it to work. Barzumel's will can be bound and then used as the anchor with which to send Rashik home."

"Okay, got it." But he didn't get it.

"Sisters, gather. Let's give Mick and Rashik the bulk of protection we've contrived. Arjesh, we assume you'll stay mostly out of it."

The Indian deli owner nodded. The five women encircled Mick and Rashik and for the next ten minutes, spoke strange words and made odd motions with their hands. Occasionally, they moved in unison around the man and demon. There were several instances when Mick's skin began to itch, or he felt as if someone had tossed cold water across the nape of his neck.

Mags sighed heavily and arched her back. "That will have to do. We've got something more important to address."

She pointed over the wooden barricades to where a black Escalade had just pulled up to the smoldering ruin. The Fire Marshall walked calmly up to the vehicle, and from Mick's perspective, he exchanged words with a person in the backseat. *Desmond, no doubt,* he thought.

The group watched silently as several minutes passed, the Fire Marshal talking and laughing until eventually he barked so loudly that Mick could hear him across the distance. Then the man got into his truck with the remaining firemen and left the scene.

A Barry-dressed Barzumel stepped out from behind the steering wheel and opened up the back door. Desmond got out and began surveying the damage. There was no sign of the Grom, but Mick figured they'd been banished back to their Plane.

Or something.

He didn't know how this worked.

"I think it's time we end this," said Rashik without his usual confidence.

"Yeah. I don't think we'll get a better chance than this."

"Let me help you," said Mags as she and two other women helped lift him off the ground. He felt a strange tingle on the back of his neck and sneezed twice. "That's the best we can do. Best of luck, Mick. We'll stay back here, but if we can help, we will. And Rashik, it was good to see you. Come back soon."

Mick nodded, and Rashik actually kissed her hand before ducking under the wooden rails of the barricade. The men tried to help the women over, but they waved them away scornfully while Rashik paced impatiently, though he looked subdued and sickly. Mick knew that the second Desmond or Barzumel saw them, the clock on their lives would start.

They were able to make it all the way to Desmond's Escalade in a hunched kind of walk before deciding to break their silence. Barzumel and Desmond had gone inside the front door to Mick's shop, despite most of the ceiling missing.

"Try to stay out of danger, Arjesh," said Mick.

Arjesh nodded, his jaw set firmly, and Mick was surprised at how determined his friend looked.

Hoping his friend would avoid harm, Mick yelled to get the Demon Prince's attention, it took several seconds before he and "the boss" appeared around what looked like a charred bookcase.

"Well, well, well, as I live and breathe," said Desmond, accepting a steadying hand from Barzumel as he stepped over the rubble-strewn threshold, careful to avoid sullying the white suit he wore.

"You told us to move out. we were going to do that. Why did you burn our stuff to the ground?" Mick was more furious than he expected to be.

Desmond chuckled as he picked his way across charred rubble. "The insurance on this building was actually pretty good. When I found out that I could collect if it accidentally burned down, my hands were tied. Besides, a week wasn't fast enough. Barry here gave me the idea for the fire, and if you boys happened to get caught in the blaze, two birds and all that."

Barzumel wasn't even looking at Mick. The Demon Prince was staring directly at Rashik, who was trying to smile confidently, but it looked much more like a plea for mercy.

"You have any idea what Barry is? You have any idea who you've been working with?"

But instead of answering, Desmond snapped his fingers.

Mick didn't even see it happen. One second, Barzumel was standing next to Desmond and the next he was a foot in front of Mick, elbow cocked with his melon-sized fist speeding toward Mick's surprised face.

CHAPTER 13

A crack sounded across the empty street, and the sound of shattering glass sounded in Mick's head. There was a flash of light, and Mick was thrown back a dozen feet. He landed on the ground and rolled. But despite that, he didn't feel any pain. After several seconds of blinking and stretching his jaw to get the ringing out of his head, he stood and lumbered toward the group.

"We invoke Sheol! We invoke Sheol, you bastard," Rashik was yelling hoarsely at Barzumel while Arjesh and Desmond argued something.

Barry—Barzumel—looked very unconcerned.

"Hey," shouted Mick, still shaking off some of the punch. Apparently, Mags' protection had done something after all.

"Seems like you've got special friends, little human." Barzumel boomed, then grinned viciously at Mick.

"We do," said Arjesh, but Barzumel ignored him.

"Seems your little sidekick here believes that you're under the protection of the Council. I don't think that's very likely. And by the looks of him, I don't think he'll last long enough for it to matter."

"This might change your mind," said Mick.

He reached beneath his shirt and pulled out the pendant. It was dull and didn't shimmer in the fluorescent street lights, but the markings on it had to be obvious to Barzumel.

Desmond reacted a little by shrugging and looking at Barry for explanation. Barzumel's lack of a reaction was much more telling than any scoff or laugh would have been. For the moment, the Demon Prince was uncertain. Mick took his chance.

"Desmond, you've always been a piece of shit. I'm assuming you know 'Barry' isn't really a human."

The fat crime boss shrugged. "I wouldn't care if he was a mermaid with legs as long as he does what he's told."

Rashik turned to Barzumel. "And you're gonna take that? You've eaten people for less."

Barzumel didn't reply, but instead licked his lips with a grotesquely oversized purple tongue.

Rashik continued, "So you're working for this schlup so, what, you can get access to the Ley Lines? So you can have more power on this Plane and enslave everyone here? Or eat them?"

Desmond laughed, the fat around his neck jiggling with each chuckle. "Barry. Will you finish these guys off already? We've got work to do."

But Barzumel didn't move. Instead, he looked between Mick and his Pendant, then Rashik and Arjesh.

"Seriously, come on. I want this rubble bulldozed out so we can start building as soon as next week. We've got big plans for your spot, boys, and Barry here is gonna make sure I get what's mine."

Desmond had spoken while walking back to the Escalade. Mick was reluctant to admit it, but he was impressed with the man's assumption of safety. The crime boss knew he was dealing with someone stronger than himself, something otherworldy, but didn't care.

Desmond turned, disbelief plain on his face when Barzumel didn't respond.

"Hey, meat head! Did you hear me?"

"It's no longer in my best interest to be partnered with you." Barzumel was eyeing Mick's pendant.

Desmond's laugh echoed in the empty street. It held no humor. "Ha! You think this is a partnership? You think you can just quit anytime you want? I *own* you, Barry. You do what I say, when I say it. Now get rid of them, then get in the goddamn car."

Mick wondered later, that if Desmond knew those were to be his last words, if he'd have said something else.

Barzumel growled and then flexed. Mick's eyes must have been playing tricks on him because the air around the large creature also *bent* inward. The fabric of Barry's suit ripped, and it seemed like the skin beneath did, too. A tearing sound rent the air and in an instant, the large human where Barry had been was replaced by a twelve-foot gray-skinned reptilian monstrosity with horns.

"Oh my god," whispered Arjesh who retreated several yards.

Rashik and Mick followed their friend's lead and stared in horror as Barzumel's true form pounced on Desmond, who despite being a monstrosity in his own right, looked positively puny compared to the giant horned reptile demon.

Desmond didn't even have a chance to scream. Barzumel's gaping mouth split his head in two—wider even than the Grom—closed around the fat man's head, and bit it clean off with a *crunch*. There was a wet sloppy sound, and the fat body collapsed to the ground in a fleshy heap. Barzumel crunched on the skull loudly, swallowed, and turned back to the trio.

"That's better," he crooned after licking blood spatters from his snout.

Barzumel's gray tail lashed back and forth. The Demon Prince's head resembled a short-snouted alligator. Two large horns curled back from the beast's head, but protruded from beneath black bone plates that ran the length of his spine.

"You can't claim us, Barzumel," said Rashik with confidence, "We've invoked Sheol. You risk their ire if you even attempt to harm us."

"The Crimson Council hasn't traveled to this Plane in almost thirty years. I hate to break it to you boys, but they don't give a shit for you. Or this place. Why do you think I'm here? I can do what I want without any consequence. The Council doesn't care about some backwater Plane on the edge of existence. A Plane where its inhabitants are as smart as the dumbest vermin in Sheol."

"He's talking about us?" asked Arjesh.

"You don't believe that, or you would have killed us by now," Rashik replied.

"I will admit," he said, licking more of Desmond's blood from his pale lips, "your little reveal did catch me off guard. I came here expecting to find two charred and twisted bodies. When I didn't, I assumed you'd both taken what little you wanted and skipped town. To see you return with such confidence almost makes me want to spare you."

"We'll give you one chance, Barzumel, to leave this Plane. You can't have the Ley Lines here or anywhere else. This Plane belongs to humanity. You can't have it."

The gray hulk's mouth opened up to the sky, and it roared with laughter. A purplish-green tongue protruded with each guffaw, and it made Mick want to vomit.

When Barzumel was done with the theatrics—it seemed demons had a thing for that—he fixed his blazing gaze on Mick.

"This Plane is mine. The power here is mine. And there's nothing you can do to stop me."

"Well, we're going to try" is what Mick had intended to say.

Instead, Barzumel lunged and shoved him out of the way. The giant demon's hand wrapped easily around Rashik's whole body and began to squeeze. The little demon's eyes bulged, and a viscous fluid began leaking out the sides of his mouth. Mick expected to see his friend pop into a burst of slimy liquid.

Mick began muttering the words of the binding, trying to remember each syllable that Mags and the other women had taught him. But he kept stumbling over them and having to start over.

"Wow, this is just sad," said Arjesh quietly from Mick's shoulder.

"Do something!" Mick screamed at him.

Arjesh sighed and opened his palm toward the two demons. Instantly, Barzumel rippled and then froze. The giant demon's fingers uncurled from around Rashik, and the small green demon fell to the ground, limp. Mick believed he was dead.

Barzumel stared at Arjesh, who had somehow grown in stature. Where before Arjesh was unassuming in both word and build, he seemed broader now. His mouth was set into a self-assured smirk, and he showed no signs of fear of the Demon Prince Barzumel.

"Seems I was mistaken," growled Barzumel. "The Crimson Council *has* been watching."

"For some time," replied Arjesh.

"What?" managed Mick in disbelief.

But there wasn't time for explanation. Barzumel lunged at Arjesh, who dodged quickly out of the way in a splash of color.

Mick took the opportunity and dashed to Rashik's body. He didn't want to touch it, knowing any injuries might be made worse.

"Rashik! Rashik wake up, are you okay?"

The demon's eyes fluttered, but he didn't respond. The noise of Barzumel chasing Arjesh around the street was growing louder.

Mick turned to see the hulking reptilian form of the Demon Prince leap into the air to land on the pavement where Arjesh stood. But Mick's friend disappeared and reappeared a dozen steps away.

Barzumel roared with frustration, caught Mick looking his way, and grinned wickedly.

"Mick, run!" yelled Arjesh from beside the Escalade.

But Mick's mind was reeling with what was unfolding and his body refused to obey.

Barzumel leapt at him and landed only a few steps away. Arjesh appeared for an instance and began to do ... something ... to Barzumel, but the giant demon batted Arjesh away, who hadn't expected the backhand to land so quickly.

The giant demon bent and grasped Mick painfully by the forearms. The demon's palms were rough and prickly, and his iron grip was impossible to escape.

Barzumel bent low, his gaping razor maw inches from Mick's. "I'll enjoy this even more because boiling demonic royal blood takes that much longer, and it tastes ... divine."

The demon's hands began to glow a hideous red. Pain lanced into Mick's forearms, and he thrashed wildly. He tried to find Arjesh, but his friend was a crumpled heap behind Barzumel. Mick tried to call out, tried to call for help. Maybe

Mags and the other witches would be able to do something, but instead, he could only scream.

His body was heating up, the blood in his veins was searing its way through his skin, and his mind was becoming a toxic mix of thoughts and prayers. The medallion sizzled against his chest, and in spite of all the pain that coursed through his body, the smell of his own skin melting was the worst.

The pendant sank deeper into the skin of his chest glowing an angry red, absorbing much of the heat that Barzumel poured into his frail human body. Mick prayed for death. Prayed for it to end.

Perhaps it had only been a minute, perhaps mere moments, Mick couldn't tell.

When Barzumel suddenly released him, Mick collapsed to the ground, panting beside Rashik's still form.

Arjesh was bleeding from a wound in the side of his head, but he'd done some kind of magic to stop Barzumel, at least momentarily. Barzumel shook his head, the scales and plates across his back shuffling with a clatter.

"You can't stop me, you know." The demon growled at Arjesh.

"I actually think that I can," he replied with a smirk.

Mick heard all of this, but his gaze was focused elsewhere. He stared down at the cement and couldn't be certain of what he saw. It was either a hallucination brought on by a boiling brain or something else entirely.

A long pillar of blue light glowed beneath the concrete. Well, not beneath really, it was almost transposed against it, but deep and incredibly long. Another, running perpendicular to the first, intersected almost beneath his feet. The blue lines pulsed with a kind of rhythmic heartbeat, something that he mistook for the heartbeat in his own chest. Only, after listening for several seconds, he realized it wasn't his heartbeat that was thumping.

He reached up with a shaky hand and touched the raw and bleeding place where the Relic of Sheol had been burned into his chest. It sizzled at his touch and he winced. But it thrummed in time with the blue cords that his eyes could now see.

The Ley Lines, he thought. He was seeing the Ley Lines. And somehow, the Relic had, what, attuned itself to him deeper? Had given him this otherworldly sight? Imbued him with some kind of magical sight?

He glanced up, tears leaking from his eyes and steaming on the sides of his singed face.

Arjesh was fighting Barzumel, but even now, Mick could tell that he wasn't going to defeat the giant demon. Barzumel was too strong, too practiced in delivering killing blows, and Arjesh was just a deli owner who could use magic.

Shakily, Mick tried to stand, stumbled, then regained his balance. He limped toward Barzumel and tried to shout out his name. Only a raspy gust of air came out. The moisture in his throat and mouth was gone, and no amount of swallowing was going to help.

Barzumel reached for Arjesh, who dodged out of the way but appeared suddenly when the demon's tail whipped forward unexpectedly. Arjesh's body went flying through the air, straight into Barzumel's outstretched hand like a baseball player catching a fly ball.

"Your turn, Sheolite." The big demon wrapped his other hand around the one that gripped Arjesh and began to squeeze. Mick tried to run, but the second he took a step, he was next to the battling duo.

Surprised, Mick hastily reached out and grasped Barzumel's wrist. Mick could wrap both his hands around the demon's wrist, and the fingers still wouldn't touch, but he gripped it hard enough to get the demon's attention.

"Stop it," said Mick hoarsely.

And then he did something, something he didn't know he could do. Much like the manner in which he'd summoned Rashik, he simply pretended to know what he was doing. In that moment, strange as it was, a distant memory floated up from his subconscious, something his father had said to him. *"Even if you don't know how to do something or don't know what something means, if you do that thing or say that word with confidence, people will believe you. Because people are stupid, and they'll believe anything."*

This wasn't a person that Mick was trying to convince, but he did believe that his father had been right about one thing—pretending can be just as powerful as the real thing.

Mick felt the pulsing relic in his chest, and he *pulled* from the power beneath his feet, the power that pulsed along great threads within the Earth. He drew it up from beneath and funneled it into Barzumel. He didn't know how, but he was pretending to, and it seemed to be working.

"What the—" said the giant demon, glancing down at Mick's hand and back to the human's now glowing blue eyes.

"Sheol commands it," intoned Mick. The power that suffused his hands was pouring into Barzumel. Mick didn't know how, but he was channeling it.

"Get off of me!" Barzumel roared, releasing Arjesh and trying to yank his arm from Mick's puny grasp.

Instead of throwing Mick off his arm, however, the gray Demon Prince's wrist and hand remained where they were in Mick's grasp while the rest of Barzumel backpedaled several yards from the momentum. The malefic demon stopped, stared at the stump spewing black liquid in a single stringy gout, then began to howl.

Mick was pretending to be floating in front of Barzumel, holding the demon's throat.

And then he was.

Power coursed through Mick's body, power that pulsed in time with the medallion on his chest and the Ley Lines that powered an entire planet.

Barzumel's roar choked off into a squelching squeak as Mick crushed the demon's windpipe.

"I don't believe you have any more power here. In fact, I believe I'll take yours for my own."

And with that, Mick believed he was siphoning the power from Barzumel.

And then he was.

The Demon Prince shrank, reminding Mick very much of the pitiful brown creatures in a mermaid movie he'd seen decades before after they were cursed by a sea witch.

But before taking *all* of Barzumel's power, he pulled Rashik's body from the pavement and held it in a glowing aura between himself and the diminished Prince.

He could sense some kind of tether to a very distant place. It was a feeling of terminal presence rather than a tangible thing. He shifted his focus toward the pendant burned into his chest and felt a similar tether to a different place, Sheol, he assumed. Barzumel had something similar, and it converged distantly with Rashik's.

Mick focused on that distant place, a glowing angry ember full of *movement* and presence. He recited the words Mags told him to say, speaking them clearly and in perfect sequence. Rashik rose briefly through the air, and in a blink, he was gone.

"Thanks for visiting this Plane." Mick said, boring his blue-fire gaze into Barzumel's eyes, which bled profusely. The Prince pleaded soundlessly for mercy, which Mick ignored. "I believe your visa's been revoked." Mick tore the head of the Demon Prince Barzumel from its shoulders and tossed it carelessly aside.

Mick settled his feet back to the ground and stared at the bleeding mess that was what remained of the Demon Prince of Depo'sadi.

Arjesh limped up to Mick, holding his side. His friend's eyes were nearly swollen shut and several of his teeth were missing.

"Wow. You look like shit."

"All thanks to you, asshole," said Arjesh with a gap-toothed and bloody smile.

The sounds of people running toward them made Mick and Arjesh turn. Mags and her group of witches were staring slack-jawed at the two men.

"What was that?"

"Who are you?"

"What did you...?"

"Where's Rashik?"

All the questions poured from the women and were directed at both men. Mick held up his hands, which smoked with subtle gray tendrils.

"I don't know what that was. Barzumel tried to burn me, my medallion burned into my chest and it, I don't know, connected me to the Ley Lines? That's my best guess."

"That's a very succinct explanation for someone who fakes the arcane arts," said Mags with disbelief.

"Yeah, well, it's the best I got. And I don't think I'm done pretending."

"And you?" she said at Arjesh.

He bowed, "My name *actually* is Arjesh. I'm a member of the Crimson Council. Well, assistant *to* the Crimson Council. I was tasked with watching over Mick for his father."

The women exchanged looks and *oohs* and *aahs* before returning their questions to Mick. It was Elena who spoke first. "So you really are royalty, it seems. And you can do quite a bit with that little medallion, there."

"It would appear so. Though to be perfectly honest, I don't know what it all means."

"I'm sure there will be time to find out, Mick," said Ali with a smile. She had a beautiful smile, and he wished he would be able to see it more.

"Unfortunately, there isn't much time." Arjesh's bleeding had stopped, and he was standing a little straighter. *The magic of poly-planar beings*, he guessed.

"What do you mean?" asked Mick.

"The Crimson Council is on its way to meet you."

Mick tried not to, but gasped anyway. "They're on their way *here*?"

"No, they're already here."

Mick didn't know what he expected, but when a strange red oval with smoking and sparking borders appeared near Barzumel's crumpled body, he said, "Isn't that a little too on the nose?"

When three black horses—with flames instead of mane and tail—stepped through and onto the pavement, burning horseshoe prints into the asphalt, he said, "Oh come on."

The riders on the backs of those horses wore a mixture of red, white, black, and gray suits, most with gold buttons down each side of their torsos. Two were incredibly handsome men, and two were incredibly beautiful women. That is, if Mick could get past the fact that each of them had a pair of horns protruding from perfectly styled hair and grins that showed just the very white tips of very sharp canines.

"I feel like I'm in some teenager movie," he said with a sigh.

CHAPTER 14

The four riders approached Mick, who didn't back away when he heard the retreating shuffles of the others.

"Hello, Mick," said one of the women. She had pale red skin and was strangely attractive.

"Hello demon-lady. I don't think we've met."

She laughed, a lilting chuckle that seemed more for his benefit than hers. "Oh, you're funny. And handsome. Just like your father. I'm Nivara."

The other female-demon stepped her horse forward. The asphalt hissed as the horseshoes of her mount burned infernal patterns into it. "Mick, my name is Halek."

One of the male-demons introduced himself quickly. "I'm Itaro."

"And I'm Tevin," said the other just as quickly.

"Lovely to meet all of you. Really great. One question. Um, what the fuck do you want?"

All four of the demons looked at one another and laughed.

"He's just like his father," said Halek to Itaro.

"Hopefully an improvement," Nivara remarked to the others.

"We're here, Mick, to escort you to Sheol, where the Crimson Council can help you. It seems you've already learned to harness part of your Gift, but we'll be able to hone your abilities better within the Ashen Crescent."

"Abilities? Ashen Crescent?"

"Well sure. The pendant, having been attuned to you all these years, helped you tap into the Ley Lines of Earth. We can teach you how to access those powers on Planes *without* Ley Lines."

Mick gaped.

"I... I..." stuttered Mags.

"That's right, Mick. You're a Realmwalker, now. You can move freely throughout the Planes, with a license, of course—"

"Which we'll give the Princeling without an exam, obviously," said Nivara.

"Obviously," Mick said to himself and not quite believing it.

"What do you say? Ready to go?"

"Like, now?" He looked at his friends. "What about them?"

Itaro waved the question away like it didn't matter. "They don't matter."

"They absolutely—" he began, but Tevin interrupted, shooting a withering glance at Itaro.

"They *do* matter, of course they do. We'll send up some Grubbins to help clean up the mess."

"Um. Okay?" He offered the last as a question, but the four demons only nodded.

Mick turned to his friends. "Uh, I guess I'll see you guys around? I don't know, I'm kind of stunned right now."

Mags hugged him, and the other women did, too. "We'll be here when you get back. Congratulations on your promotion."

"I don't know what that means," he said with a shrug and a smile.

"Arjesh?"

The Indian man-turned-bodyguard stepped up to the portal and said, "I'm coming. It'll be nice to go back home for a bit."

"For a bit?" Mick said, stopping at the crackling red door to another world.

"Well sure," said Arjesh. "Your home is here. You'll return here a lot, but have access to travel anywhere. Come on, we'll get it all laid out to us soon."

Mick nodded at the Crimson Council members who returned his nod before stepping back through the portal they'd opened. Only Nivara glanced at the withered, headless form of Barzumel, shaking her head in disappointed amusement.

Mick took a deep breath, waved at the witches who'd helped him and his two friends, and stepped through.

No time like the present, he thought briefly before all thought went spinning wildly.

CHAPTER 15

Mick spent several weeks on the Sheol Plane with Arjesh and the four Council Members. They rotated in and out, teaching him how to tap the power that he'd inherited from his demon father, but everyone refused to talk to him about his lineage.

When those in charge of his tutelage decided he'd learned enough to avoid killing random beings or himself, they agreed to allow him to return to Earth. He'd practiced Realmwalking enough that he'd gotten it down pretty quickly. In fact, it was very much like what he'd always done, pretended.

"When you get to Earth, you need to know that time passes faster there."

"How much faster," he asked Itaro.

"We've spent five weeks in the Ashen Crescent since your Awakening. On Earth, it's been about five months."

"Well, that's a significant difference."

"It is. But rest assured, Arjesh has traveled back and forth many times to check on your friends. They're all thriving."

"That's good. That's good. And Rashik?"

Itaro rolled his eyes. "I don't know why you insist on fraternizing with such a ridiculous creature, but yes, he will be traveling with you. It's all been arranged."

"Excellent. Thank you for your teaching, Itaro."

"It's been my pleasure to teach you, Princeling."

"I guess I'll see you around?"

"Probably not."

Itaro disappeared in a wisp of smoke and ash. "Great," muttered Mick. Itaro had been the most strict of his instructors. The male demon always wore a red suit, tailored perfectly. His black wavy hair was a prick of jealousy to Mick's wavy-but-unruly hair. And the demon's horns somehow always looked ... *styled* was the best description Mick had. Tough teacher, but probably the one who made him progress the fastest.

He approached the stone circle used for Realmwalking and imagined the intersection of West 56th and 11th. He pictured his and Arjesh's shops, pictured the crosswalk and the chips in the concrete curb, sun shining on his face and the chatter of New York City in the background of it all.

Then he stepped through innumerable Planes of existence, through time and space and being.

The bright light of afternoon sun blasted his eyeballs, and he bent double in the sudden pain. "Jesus Christ!" he exclaimed loudly.

A *gurk* sound next to him made him jump back. When his eyes adjusted after blinking rapidly for several seconds, Rashik stood before him.

"Well how about that," Mick said, eyeing the demon up and down.

"Whaddya think?"

The endless stream of commuters passed easily around the two beings, most of them unaware they were even avoiding Rashik's invisible form.

"Greater looks good on you!"

Rashik the Lesser had been promoted—in the way the Crimson Council does—to Rashik the Greater. He was large now, larger than Mick. His green, vomit-colored skin had been replaced with a deep volcanic red. Two horns curled down beside his cheeks.

"Borrow that from our old friend Barry?" Mick asked, indicating the stone plates on his spine as they began to walk down the street.

"It's a good look," replied the demon defensively. "Besides, it makes me harder to crush. I didn't like that. Hopefully, you don't get me into a situation like that again."

"Yeah, let's hope. Anything new with you?"

They were passing Arjesh's old shop, which, after being rebuilt, had been replaced with a dog grooming service.

"Other than this? Nope. You?"

Mick's old shop was next, and he stared at the building that replaced it, a collectible card game shop. *Fitting,* thought Mick.

"Other than becoming one of the most powerful Realmwalkers in a few millennia? Nah."

"Wow. Millennia?" asked Rashik, feigning being impressed. "How lucky am I?"

"Very, let me tell you, pal."

They exchanged small talk, with Mick relating some of his training and Rashik the events that followed his banishment back to Depo'sadi. They made their way the few blocks toward Mags' house, where Arjesh told them she'd be waiting for their return.

She was sitting on the steps to her home and waved as they approached. "Hey there, strangers," she said affectionately. "Rashik, you handsome devil."

To Mick's surprise, the hulking demon blushed, the skin on his cheeks burning like molten lava for a moment. "Stop it," he said quietly.

"And you, Mick, let me look at you."

"You guys can call me that, but that's not what the Council wants me to be."

The Witch-Doctor ignored his comment and walked around the man who had come to her as something of an idiot.

"The shoulder pads are a little much, don't you think?"

The Crimson Council had insisted that he update his wardrobe. He didn't *want* to, but when four nearly all-powerful demons insist, there's not much room to argue.

"You should have seen what they suggested. A war helm with spikes, gauntlets made of living lava, and a cuirass made from a falling star. It was something else. We settled on a couple of spikes on the shoulders. That way I could pass as an emo kid who never grew out of the phase."

"It's not just a phase, dad," said Rashik with a chuckle.

"Well, come in for some tea. Please." Mags led them inside and they spent the afternoon talking. Elena had died shortly after their encounter with Barzumel, but they'd replaced her in the circle with a young woman named Leah.

"You'll probably meet her soon," said Mags cleaning up the empty pitchers and glasses. "You might even like her. I'm sure she'd be impressed with a Realmwalker."

"Playing matchmaker, now, are we?" he asked with a good-natured shake of his head.

But Mags' response was cut off by a knock at the door.

"You expecting visitors?" Rashik flexed his massive muscles as Mick prepared to draw upon the Ley Lines. Something that was remarkably easier now that he was in same Plane where they existed.

"No, but we have had ... visitors ... since you left."

"Visitors?" the two asked in response, but Mags was already at the door and peeking through the curtains that covered the long windows to either side of the front door. She looked back at Mick with pursed lips and opened the door a crack.

Mick strained his ears to listen, but they were speaking in low tones, and he could only pick out a word here and there.

Eventually, Mags opened the door and a handsome man of about thirty stepped through. The sunglasses he'd placed on the top of his head reminded Mick of a pair of bug eyes, but the smile the man wore was warm.

"Mick, this is Malcolm. He's been looking for you since ... well, since you left."

"You know this guy, Mags?" he asked, ignoring Malcolm for the moment.

"I do—", she began.

"We could definitely take him," said Rashik, who hadn't yet revealed himself to this unknown quantity.

"And that won't be necessary, Rashik," Mags finished.

Malcolm approached and held out a hand for Mick to shake. "How do you do. I'm Malcolm Casey, and I'd just like to speak with you for short time."

Malcolm's accent was British, but beyond that, he wasn't well-versed enough to place *where* in Britain.

"Uh, sure. Can we sit?"

"Of course, of course," said the man, and Mags joined them in the living room.

"Well, what can I help you with, Malcolm?"

The Brit licked his lips and looked from Mick to Mags nervously. "I'm not exactly sure how to say this, so I'm going to come right out with it."

"Ah, an honest man. How unfortunate," joked Mick, and Malcolm chuckled.

"We've heard rumors that something happened here several months ago. Something that can't be explained. I'd like to ask you to tell me exactly what happened. I understand you were involved directly."

"I don't think you'll believe me if I tell you what happened." Mick tried to laugh it off, but Malcolm wasn't smiling.

"Try me," he said with gravity.

Mick shifted on the couch uncomfortably. He looked at Mags, who nodded, and then he told Malcolm his story. There were only a few points where the man asked for clarification, but other than that, he listened the entire time. At one point, Rashik revealed himself, and other than a slight jump, he only said "remarkable," before continuing to listen to Mick's story.

Rashik sipped on a glass of the tea that Mags brought for them all to share, holding the glass primly in his gargantuan hand. When Mags brought cucumber sandwiches, he daintily picked them up between his clawed thumb and forefinger and munched contentedly. Mick and Malcolm were too involved in the story to be bothered to eat or drink.

"And so now I'm back, more or less fully trained by a group of demon rulers in a different Plane of existence."

Malcolm sat up, excitement clear on his face. "I have someone I'd like you to meet, Mick. If you'd be willing. Your … companion? I'm sorry, I'm not sure how to reference you, can come of course."

"Friend will do," said Rashik around a mouthful of sandwich.

"Great, your friend can come, too."

"Where to?"

"We'd be flying to Chicago to meet several others who would be *very* interested in your story."

Mick's hackles rose at this. "You keep saying 'we,' and I have no frame of reference. I'm assuming that this 'we' is some circus or something?"

Malcolm burst into laughter. He calmed after several great gasping breaths, then burst into laughter again.

"I don't know what I said to be so funny," said Mick, looking between Rashik and Mags, who both shrugged.

"No, no it's not that. It's ironic that you'd call *us* the circus when our goal is to get rid of the circus!"

"Not a fan of clowns, I take it?"

"No, Mick. The circus that runs the country. The circus that masquerades as every government on the planet."

"Oh." Mick realized this was much more serious than a chat.

"We are a group of people who are sick of the way the world has worked for hundreds of years. The rich get richer, the poor get poorer, then the poor get blamed by the rich when their profits shrink to an amount that could run a small city for a year. The NP have found strength in something new, Mick. For the first time in history, there's something that we can use to change the world."

"I don't disagree with you. But what's the... the NP, I think you said?"

"Right. The 'NP' is short for Neo-Pagans. We're a... a group of people who are trying to enact change for *everyone*, not just for the ones who can afford it. In fact, we want to enact change for the underdogs—that is, the everyman."

"So these Neo-Pagans are Anarchists."

Malcolm shrugged. "If that helps you understand it better, sure. We like to consider ourselves agents of change."

"And Chicago is special because...?"

"That's where our leader is. And he's asked me to bring you back to meet him."

The ex-charlatan-turned-demi-god looked at Mags who nodded and said, "Might as well check it out."

Rashik nodded in agreement. "Yeah, I don't have anything going on."

With a deep breath, Mick said, "Well, I think my schedule is clear. How long until we leave?"

"I've got a plane prepped right now. It'll take a few hours to fly there, but we can be there by tonight."

"Uh, okay. I guess if I need anything I can just hop around to grab it."

Malcolm chuckled; Mick could tell that Malcolm didn't quite get it.

"Well, Mags, thanks for the tea. I'll keep you posted. Raincheck on that date with Leah, yeah?"

She walked them to the door and hugged both Rashik and Mick. "You both be safe, you hear me?"

"Yes, ma'am," they said in tandem.

Mick and Rashik followed Malcolm down the steps and Mags watched them drive off in an unmarked black Cadillac SUV.

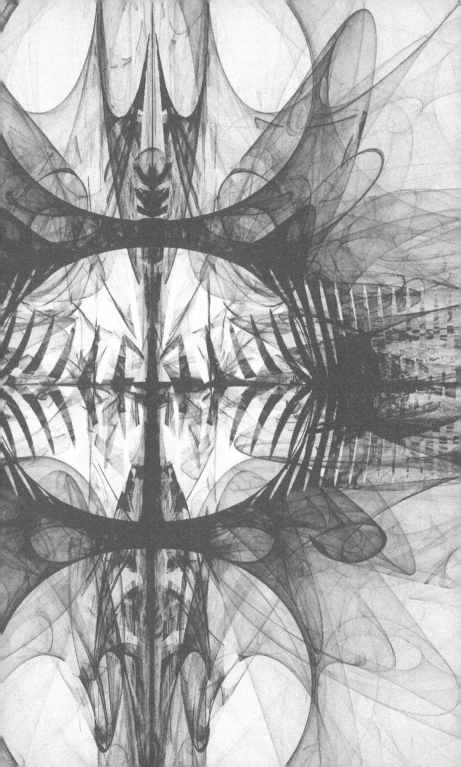

EPILOGUE

The elevator didn't play any music as it hummed up several dozen floors. Mick and Rashik stood shoulder-to-shoulder with Malcolm watching the numbers slowly increase above the door. They were the only ones on the elevator, and the silence hung uncomfortably around them.

At floor fifty, the elevator slowed and *dinged*. Then the doors slid open to reveal a penthouse-like room that provided a breathtaking view of the city through the windows that lined the entire suite.

It was crowded in the room despite its size. Several dozen men and women dressed in all different styles faced away from the elevator, but they turned when the three stepped out. Those in attendance moved to the side slowly, staring and beginning to whisper as Mick nodded at them. Rashik and Mick followed Malcolm as they made their way to the front of the room.

Rashik decided on the elevator that it would be best to let others see him. Malcolm had asked if that would be okay, as word of Mick's companion—friend—had reached the NP's ears. Mick was surprised to see the lack of fear and surprise on the onlookers faces.

At last, the crowd of people thinned enough to reveal four people. There were two men to the side, a woman on the other side, and a tall young man with blond hair standing between them, back to the crowd.

Malcolm indicated that Mick and Rashik should stand over to the side where the other two men were. It almost had the feeling of a wedding, where he was now one of the groomsmen waiting for the bride to enter. Malcolm went to stand beside the woman.

The blond man was staring down at something while the woman to his side spoke quietly to him and pointed at things on a table before them. The man was young but tall. He had a commanding presence and didn't turn when Mick took his place. From his perspective, he seemed normal, but the way everyone in the room continued facing his direction quietly told Mick there was more to him than his appearance.

Mick looked at the man next to him. He appeared to be of Latin descent and while there was an air of power about him, he appeared very normal and was dressed in a black cassock.

"Hey, how ya doin'?" whispered Mick.

The man, who at first didn't think Mick was talking to him, started and shook Mick's outstretched hand. "Estoy bien, how are you?"

"Never better. What's your name?"

"I'm called Hosanek." The man's smile was genuine and his tone was gentle.

"Weird name, but nice to meet you. This is my friend Rashik."

Hosanek smiled up at the demon and grinned. "Amazing to meet you, my friend."

Mick looked around Hosanek at the dark-haired and haggard man on the other side. "What about you, bud? What's your name?"

The man turned and stared at Mick with a gaze that could only be described a thousand-yard stare. His eyes were unfocused and a silvery liquid orb floated above his shoulder.

"Woah. You good?" Mick remarked.

"I'm The Mandible King," the gaunt man replied, calmly but his voice was hoarse and came out in two octaves.

"Uh, nice to meet you, sir?"

"What about you, señor," asked Hosanek, eyes shining with camaraderie.

"My name used to be—" Mick began before he was cut off.

"No—" said the blond man suddenly. Mick hadn't seen him turn toward the trio making whispered introductions, and as Mick gazed around, he gulped. Every eye in the room was looking at him.

"Not your human name. We're not interested in that. What's your *real* name?"

Mick swallowed again. Whoever this guy was, he was very obviously in charge here.

"My name is Nazerak; it means Scorched Mist." He felt very self-conscious with such a ridiculous title, but here, he believed it would be accepted without question.

"Nazerak." The blond man nodded in approval.

Then he held out his hand for Mick to shake it and looked deep into Mick's eyes. Mick felt sweat bead on his brow and was very aware that he hadn't washed his hands after going to the bathroom on the plane.

The crowd around them all knelt and raised their hands in what could only be worship, but Mick's eyes were glued to the man's in front of him.

With a voice that seemed to weigh a thousand years, the blonde man said, "Welcome to the Neo-Pagans.

"You can call me Keller."

THE END

BOOK CLUB
DISCUSSION QUESTIONS

1. Many times, when a new perspective is offered, our immediate reaction is to balk at it. What is the innate fear humanity fears with change?

2. Some people find solace in the quiet of solitude while others find it in the energy others bring around them. Why do many living things require community in order to thrive?

3. How does trauma impact a person's outlook on life, family, relationships, etc.? And why is it so difficult for humans to move past it?

4. What role does faith play in society as a whole? How is it a positive influence? How is it a negative influence?

5. How do cultures identify and work through the difficulty of the teenage "immunity complex"? What does this phase teach and what value does it bring as teens move into adulthood?

6. Many religions require self-inspection to achieve enlightenment. What is it about religion that can make self-inspection so difficult?

7. For polytheistic cultures, what value do multiple gods bring to the daily ritual of life? In what way is this reflected in modern societies?
8. What is it about the unseen that intrigues humans?
9. What stories or evidence do you have of the unseen? If you're willing to share the story, do so with your group.
10. Morality is rarely black and white. Within this final short story, what morality did you see that you didn't expect. What areas in your life could you look for morality more readily?

BIO:

Ty Carlson is a sci-fi writer who delights in the unseen strangeness and wonder of "what if." Growing up in the Ozarks of Arkansas gave him and his three siblings plenty of room to play knights and dragons or jungle explorers, igniting his imagination early on. Ty started writing at a very young age and his passion has only grown over time. He loved to read so much that he once was grounded from reading, a fact that his brothers tease him about to this day. He hopes readers discover new ways to see the world through the perspectives offered in the stories he tells.

Some of Ty's favorite reads include the classics from Fitzgerald to Tolkien to Card, and he has fallen in love with a multitude of worlds. When he's not writing, he's playing with his kids or enjoying some time in a video game. On the rare occasion, when his wife and he can get a few minutes to themselves, they enjoy listening to the sounds of the world waking up while enjoying a cup of coffee—with cream of course. His Debut book is "The Bench," which marks his first steps as a Sci-Fi author like so many he's admired (and been grounded from)!

SciFi

DISCOVER MORE AT
4HORSEMENPUBLICATIONS.COM

Milton Keynes UK
Ingram Content Group UK Ltd.
UKHW010638150124
436059UK00004B/342